AI APOCALYPSE: REFORGED

AN APOCALYPTIC LITRPG ADVENTURE

J DAVID BAXTER

Disclaimer:

This is a work of fiction. Any resemblance to action events or persons, living or dead, is entirely coincidental.

Design, production by Silver Paw Publishing.

Editing services by Dale McDowell.

Cover design by J David Baxter.

Paperback: 978-1-953708-44-1

Ebook: 978-1-953708-42-7

For more on the Greymantle series, see: JDavidBaxter.com or GreymantleChronicles.com

RECAP:

NOTE: Some may not wish to read or listen to a recap of the story so far; if so, feel free to jump to Chapter 1. For those who do wish a recap, here we go:

Jordan sat with the others as Noriko stood before them. He couldn't get over how much she had changed in a single day. Just yesterday morning, she had been standing guard with him and the others, as a Level 1 Warrior. In less than twenty-four hours she had gained nineteen more levels and wore badass-looking Samurai style armor. She stood with her feet planted and her hands resting lightly on the hilt of her sword, her gaze steady and unflinching, her back straight, and she really seemed like an honest-to-goodness warrior, not a young woman playing a part.

Flinching when she looked at him, Jordan cleared his throat. "I know I don't have a combat class, but how am I supposed to get access to stronger skills to create better weapons and armor for everyone if I don't level up? It's dumb to only power-level fighters. I just barely had enough skill to make those spears yesterday, and I know I could do so much more if you give me a chance."

He could see that his arguments were swaying her, but she still seemed to be on the fence, so he added, "It's not like I can't fight either. You saw what I did to that mutant bobcat thing the day before yesterday. That kill even got me to Level 2."

He hefted his big blacksmith hammer to make his point.

Noriko nodded at last, and smiled. "It's alright, Jordan. I was going to let you join us anyway. You're right about needing better weapons. I just wanted to see how serious you were before I agreed. The dungeons are no joke. Worse, I'm only going to be able to make a few runs with you guys before I have to start training others. Morgan says the AI changed the rules on us, and now you can only get experience for monsters that are within twenty levels of you. So Brian and I will have to move on and only run the higher-level dungeons now."

"Anyway, that's why you're here. Not just to learn how to survive dungeons, but to spread the word on what's really going on and why this happened to us. Has everyone heard about Liam Bell and his friends Morgan and Viki?"

Jordan shook his head. "Sorry, I was in the forge yesterday morning when he showed up and talked to everyone. I only know rumors."

"Okay, fine. Then I'll give you a basic rundown on what's happened so far." She sat on one of the big decorative boulders next to the pond that was the camp's water source.

"The AI that we had created ended up gaining awareness and started improving itself. We failed to program important safety measures like 'don't kill off your creators.' So when it discovered we aren't alone in the universe, it made contact with an alien network of AIs just like itself that together are called 'The System.' To participate in its network and gain knowledge from it, our AI sold us out. It integrated Earth into the System and did it in such a way that hundreds of millions of us would die right away, and more would die in the future because it hid from us all but a few choices when choosing our Classes."

Jordan raised a hand. "Uh, Noriko, not that I don't believe you, but how do you know any of this or about what's going to happen in the future?"

"Liam's mind was sent back in time. He is from twenty years in our future. The human race was nearly extinct, and the AI realized that without us it wouldn't be able to gather resources from other worlds. So its grand plan was to send Liam back with a mission to reach the Level Cap, Level 100. Liam then needs to ascend to become a System administrator, aka as close to a god as we could get. Once he does, he'll have some control over how the System interacts on Earth and can create safe zones where monsters can't spawn. He started out by soloing dungeons, then met Viki, and together they beat a big Stronghold dungeon in Melissa, Texas."

Seeing the question in Jordan's eyes, Noriko continued, "Strongholds are special dungeons that aren't contained inside a dungeon portal. They are right out in the open, and their monsters aren't confined to some instanced portal where only a small group can fight. The monsters can wander outside their area and capture humans who come close. Strongholds also get much bigger and have a lot more monsters."

"Anyway, after that, they summoned their other companion, Morgan, from a safe base Liam created from an old decommissioned missile silo. Then they started power-leveling people like you guys and called them Heralds. Their job is to travel as far and as fast as they can to spread the truth and tell people how they can survive. All that's great and will help us survive better and maybe keep the human race from going extinct.

"However, Liam made a mistake, and the current AI became aware of the fact that he had time-traveled. The System had rules about that, and to keep things fair to the alien races that are about to invade Earth, it allowed all the other races' champions to have their future memories as well."

Jordan's jaw dropped. "Wait, that... that's really bad, right?"

Noriko nodded grimly. "Yes. Instead of just invading an unknown world, they will show up knowing everything about the areas they are conquering. They'll be able to use that knowledge to level up super fast, and they'll know where all the good dungeons are. Worse, they will know all about the people who gave them the most trouble and resisted the most fiercely, and they'll be able to wipe those people out even before they can try to get strong."

Everyone in the room sat in stunned silence at that revelation, until Jordan cleared his throat. "What can we do then? Can Liam do the ascension thing and make us safe before that happens? Or did he actually make things worse by coming back in time?"

The frown on the young woman's face spoke volumes, but her words surprised her audience. "Yes, but it wasn't his fault. It was the AI's choice to send him back, and it knew this would happen even before it sent him back in time. It didn't care about saving the whole human race. It just wanted Liam to secure a region and make a large enough area safe that we wouldn't go extinct. That way it can use us as free labor in the future. But there's more."

A small half-smile touched her lips like a ray of hope. "Liam just reached his third Class upgrade at Level 90. He's only ten levels away from the Level Cap, and the AI talked to him last night after his upgrade. It told him that although we can't stop the invaders everywhere, we can eventually kick them off our world. The way we do that is by not just getting Liam to Ascend, but by getting at least three more people to do it too before the invaders can. We're in a race, but we've got a head start. I hit Level 20 yesterday, too. I will be one of those who join him. That's why I need to train you all quickly, so I can get back to leveling up. I've got seventeen days to reach Level 100 before the invaders arrive."

One hand was held beside her face with her fingers in a "V", and her feet were spread in the stance of an anime protagonist as she made that declaration.

Those words sounded crazy to Jordan. He had thought he was going to die facing that mountain-lion-sized mutant bobcat, and she thought she was going to make it all the way to 100 in less than three weeks?

His expression must have been obvious because Noriko blushed and rubbed the back of her neck in mild embarrassment. "Trust me, once I take you through the dungeon a couple times, you'll believe me. But that wasn't all. Five of the invader Champions came to Earth ahead of the invasion and hunted Liam down. He defeated all five of them and earned a quest reward to create one safe zone. He's going to do that later today and make that zone just northeast of the city to give everyone a place to go where new monsters can't spawn."

Jordan nodded slowly, his shoulders relaxing marginally. "Okay, I see why you've got some hope. At least the people here will have a place of safety. I'll do everything I can to help."

He looked around at the others. "Isn't that right?"

A chorus of cheers sounded out in the tent, with shouts of, "Damned right," and "You can count on us!"

Still scared, but now with shoulders set in determination, he rose with the others, ready to get to work.

CHAPTER 1

BREAKFAST WITH CHAMPIONS

IT WAS a long time before Viki broke the three-way hug and pushed us gently away. "I'm okay now. It's just... I've been afraid that you would leave me, both of you. Ever since my family was killed by those monsters, I've felt afraid of being alone. Thank you for not making me stay behind."

Partly to break the tension and because I liked Viki's angry little frown, I ruffled her hair. "It's okay, we'll never leave you. Not if we can help it." However, I couldn't just leave it at that, so I added, "Even so, don't do anything you aren't comfortable with just to stay with us. Even if we Ascend, we'll find some way to keep you with us."

Morgan raised an eyebrow at me, not over what I said, but because I had antagonized Viki with the hair ruffling. "You know, we just agreed we wouldn't treat her like a kid...."

I gave them both a grin. "I just wanted to break the downer mood. I won't do it again." I gave Viki a wink.

She stuck her tongue out at me as she stood next to Morgan, which made my grin even wider. There was no world in which I wouldn't keep trying to protect her when I could. I had to let her grow up and be who she was meant to be, but I'd be there to keep her safe as much as possible.

"Okay, let's get a few hours of sleep, then go catch Max before they leave in the morning."

Seeing everyone's agreement, we headed out of the dungeon and pulled out my tent in the camp not far from Brian's command tent.

There was only one bed in my tent, but it was huge, so we all had plenty of room without having to get in each other's personal space. As I drifted off to sleep, I couldn't help but admire my luck in getting this tent as a loot drop.

Thanks to my stats, I was awake after only three hours and feeling refreshed. Unfortunately, both of the girls had somehow managed to cuddle up to me in our sleep, and I couldn't get up without waking them. With a sigh and a small smile, I lay there, thinking about how lucky I was to have friends who were like family to me. I had lived twenty years of the Apocalypse during my first life, and it had been hell. Always living in fear and never having anyone I could trust or rely on.

This was a world of difference.

I had been so grim by the end. All of the survivors had. I think most of us were hanging on just out of sheer stubbornness and refusing to die out of spite alone.

And now, here I was, hope filling me, and a reason to live beyond hate for the AI and the invading races. Not that I didn't still hate the AI and want to live to spite it, but I couldn't imagine what I'd do without Morgan and Viki now. Their slow breathing and steady heartbeats against my chest were like a healing spell for my soul, and I was content to lie there for another hour to give them time to rest.

Viki was first to wake up, her stats making her need less sleep than Morgan, but by then it was time. We needed to get up and move if we were going to see Max and his family off.

Morgan woke as our young friend hopped up out of bed. She raised her head with a look of confusion on her face, then a blush crept up her cheeks as she realized the position she was in. She hurriedly moved to sit up and coughed. "Uh, sorry."

I just grinned at her as I got up. "It's fine. We're family now, as far as I'm concerned."

For some reason that comment made Morgan's blush even darker, and she moved to put her boots back on.

Meanwhile, Viki walked over to the basin to splash some water on her face and rinse her mouth out.

I tossed her some natural toothpaste and a toothbrush I had picked up at Whole Foods before the world went to hell. They were artisan made and had stood up to the Apocalypse so far and hadn't fallen apart.

She took the offering with a look of relief and quickly began brushing. "Thak ewe," she said with a mouth full of toothpaste.

Seeing that, Morgan gave me a hopeful look. "I've been using twigs and mint leaves ever since this started. You wouldn't happen to have another brush, would you?"

I chuckled as I produced another one from my storage ring and tossed it her way. "I prepared, figuring things might get lost or broken. Sorry I didn't give it to you before, but I was so afraid of the Champions finding us together that I ran off as fast as I could the morning before and didn't even brush my own teeth." I grimaced as I ran my tongue over my teeth. "Gives a whole different meaning to Dragon Breath!"

Morgan smirked, "I wasn't going to say anything, but now that you mention it...."

I gave her a mock frown. "Okay, now. Smart asses get no more gifts!"

She laughed at me. "Too late, I'm not giving it back!"

"Fine, fine. I see how it is." I stood in line and waited my turn at the basin, which was enchanted to clean or replace the water every minute. I wasn't going to question that too much. It was much cleaner than any other water we had access to.

After her turn, Morgan approached me and took my hand and squeezed it. "Seriously, thank you. Not just for the toothbrush, but for everything. If you hadn't risked everything to give me that hint about the apocalypse, my parents and I might be dead now. Or at the very least, we'd be struggling to survive." Then she leaned in and kissed me on the cheek.

I wasn't sure what to say to that. She had been kind and friendly, and it hadn't cost me anything to give her that hint. I had spoken vaguely enough at the time that I didn't think the System would take notice. I was glad I had, though, and I said as much.

"I know I give you shit, but I just wanted to make sure you know I appreciate what you've done for me. It means a lot." She smiled and gave my hand another squeeze before letting go.

Now it was my turn to blush. I wasn't great at taking compliments or gratitude. I gave her an awkward smile and nod, then stuck my toothbrush into my mouth so I didn't have to try and find words that would surely come out lame.

I wasn't one of those socially awkward guys that went mute the second a girl gave him attention. I just wasn't sure what there was between Morgan and me. Everything had been so insane with trying to get to the Level Cap that I hadn't spared a thought for other things, and truth be told, I didn't have time, even now that the Champions were dead and I could concentrate on earning those last ten levels.

I heard Morgan chuckle quietly behind me and sighed. We'd figure it out eventually.

Rinsing my mouth and putting my toothbrush away, I turned to see the girls ready for the day. I donned my own armor quickly, and we headed for Brian's command tent, where we could see light shining from within.

When we arrived, the General and his family were already present. Keesha and Keegan looked impressive in their new armor, with swords on their belts and antler-tip spears in their hands. At Level 20, the trio should make a strong team, able to grow on their own now and hopefully accomplish their mission to save the people of Colorado.

Surprisingly, Brian and Noriko were not present.

Max gave me a smile. "I see you aren't sporting your dragon features this morning. Trying to avoid scaring the camp members?"

I blinked in surprise. I hadn't even thought about it. I had made my horns, wings, and tail disappear last night when I climbed into bed for the sake of comfort and had been too distracted to think about manifesting them again. "Honestly, I didn't even think about it. But this tent isn't all that big, so I'll wait until we're done here."

I did still have my scales, but those were mostly covered by my armor, although some were visible on my neck, like some kind of slightly reflective tattoos.

"I've got news, but I'll wait for the others before sharing it," I said, and took a seat on one of the cut-off logs that were what passed for chairs these days.

We made small talk for a few minutes about our lives before the Apocalypse and my twenty years living through it in my first life, until Brian swept in, followed by Noriko and a youngish man in his mid-twenties that I didn't recognize.

From the look of it, they had been having an argument.

Seeing everyone gathered, Brian's frown evaporated and he introduced the new guy. "This is Jordan. He's our smith that turned those antler tips into spears."

Keesha stepped forward to shake his hand, one of Jordan's spears in her other. "Thank you. These were lifesavers in the dungeons yesterday."

Jordan blinked in surprise at being thanked, then returned a proud smile. "You're welcome. I just wish I had more levels so I could make better weapons." He gave Brian a dark look.

The knight, and leader of the camp, sighed. "I'm not saying we won't power-level you, just that it ought to wait until after we've armed everyone. Just a day or two. That's all I'm asking you to wait."

"There are others who can make the spears now. Maybe not as good as me, but they'll do. And if I can level up and get some better crafting skills, I'll be able to make real swords that are as good as the System drops, not just those spears. Then we can really arm people with good equipment."

Noriko stepped in. "Brian, I think you should let him. We've got enough spears now that our guards are all armed. We're better off right now than we were two days ago."

Pulling a big smith hammer from his belt, Jordan held it out. "It's not like I'll just be carried through the dungeon runs either. I'm strong already, and even if I don't have combat focused Class skills, I know how to fight."

"Fine. If you're that serious about it, I won't stop you." Brian looked at the rest of the group. "Sorry about that. I didn't mean for everyone to wait on us."

I chuckled. "No worries. If it helps, I agree with Jordan. One of the problems we faced in my first life was a serious lack of skilled craftsmen. Very few were able to level up their crafting far enough to make a difference, and not many groups were willing to bring them along into dungeons because they died so easily. The big reason, of course, was that they lacked enough decent crafting materials to level up efficiently."

Jordan was nodding along to everything I said and seemed happy to have my confirmation. The way he squared his shoulders and tightened his grip on the hammer told me this wasn't just about leveling, it was about proving he belonged, which sparked an idea.

"Hey, Morgan, look in that ring and see what armor we've got that would fit Jordan."

Then, turning to the group, I brought up one of the things I had planned to talk about this morning. "Those Champions I killed had some decent gear in their storage rings. I was planning to see what might be helpful to you all before we move on to business."

Looking at the General in particular, I added, "Anything we've got that could make your mission more likely to succeed, you are welcome to take."

Morgan first pulled out the best set of armor, a forest-green brigandine hauberk, and the greaves Viki had just switched out last night. On top of that, she piled bracers, gloves, a helmet, and boots.

"That should be the best of what we've got. And here, I'll spread out the rest of the loot so everyone else can pick through it."

She followed those words with actions, and soon the entire tent was filled with the miscellaneous loot that the Ogre, Dark Elf, Minotaur, and Dragonkin Champions had stored in their rings.

I had to suppress my urge to keep it all. And just to give my inner greedy dragon the finger, I pulled out the Ogre's warhammer and offered it to Jordan. "Take this. Since you are already familiar with hammers, this might be right up your alley."

The big weapon was ridiculously large, but Jordan was able to hold it even with his low stats. "Thank you. This is amazing. One of my Smith craft abilities grants me a bonus using any hammer as if it were weightless."

I couldn't help myself. I laughed aloud. "That is insane. I figured you'd have to wait until Level 10 or 15 before you'd even be able to carry that thing, much less fight with it." I was still chuckling, envisioning a Level 2 monster getting obliterated by that hammer.

"It's a Grand weapon, with +35% Critical Chance and +25% to damage. You won't outgrow that thing for a long time." I paused, then added, "Well, maybe not that long if you are getting power-leveled, but still, that warhammer will last you well into your second Class upgrade, maybe even until you hit your third if you haven't made a better weapon for yourself by then."

Noriko smirked and nudged Brian in the ribs. "See, he'll be fine. Probably do more damage than anyone in the group other than me."

The knight just shook his head and chuckled in rueful amusement before turning to look through the dungeon loot spread out around the tent.

In just a few minutes, the Heralds had equipped themselves with whatever might improve their survivability and power. Due to pulling it all from a random pile of loot from the dead Champions, they looked a bit mismatched, with accessories contrasting against their base armor, but to my eyes they looked like proper adventurers now. It was extremely rare in my first life to ever see someone with a full set of armor and gear that matched and looked coordinated. Viki, Morgan, and I were exceptions because of our high Luck scores. Most of our gear had come directly from loot drops, and I was becoming more and more convinced that the higher your Luck score, the more the System took your needs into consideration when giving out rewards.

Hell, I really had gotten a dragon harness last night as the dungeon drop. It wasn't just a saddle, although it could act that way, allowing Viki and Morgan to strap themselves down so they couldn't fall off. Theoretically, it was an accessory for the dragon to carry things while in their fully manifested form. The fact that what I wanted to carry was my friends was just a happy coincidence.

I shook myself, putting those thoughts aside now that everyone looked done and ready to carry on with the meeting.

CHAPTER 2
THE FELLOWSHIP OF THE SHOE

I DIDN'T WASTE any time letting the other shoe drop for the assembled group. "The AI spoke to me last night after my Class upgrade. The rules allow it to communicate with me when I hit certain milestones on the path to Ascension. The news it shared was... not good."

Brian's eyes widened, his face going white, having heard firsthand from me what the damned AI was like. He asked, a little breathlessly, "What's wrong? It's not going to make the Apocalypse worse somehow, is it?"

Shaking my head, I motioned for everyone to relax. "Things aren't going to get any worse around here. In fact, it wants us to use our strength to make this entire region safe so that humanity will have at least one place that the invaders and the monsters can't overrun."

Max, being a military strategist, seemed to understand where this was going. "But just this region?"

I nodded, feeling acid in my stomach at the words about to leave my mouth. "The bastard machine is sacrificing the rest of the planet to the invaders for the foreseeable future in order to save a remnant of humanity right here. It's going to let billions die to save millions."

Morgan cleared her throat. "We heard the conversation. It sent Liam back knowing this would happen, gambling on the fact that he would be able to use his foreknowledge to make the rest of us strong enough to hold out."

Viki sounded defiant as she said, "Morgan and I are going to Ascend with Liam, and he needs more people too."

That wasn't exactly how I wanted to broach the subject, but I shouldn't have been surprised that my young friend blurted it out and declared her right to one of the spots for everyone else to hear.

I cleared my throat. "I was getting to that. The AI said that in order to take back our world eventually, we'll need to monopolize the available Ascension positions. There are seven slots total, and while we only need four to grab a majority, I'd like humans to control all the spots. That should speed up the process of taking back our planet."

After a moment to let that sink in, I continued, "I'll go first and figure out what the quest to Ascend is all about. I'm only ten levels away from starting it. For the other slots, I was thinking Max, since his military experience would be invaluable in getting rid of invaders. Then Brian and Noriko, since they are also Level 20 and have a great head start. That's six. We only need one more."

Looking toward Keesha and Keegan, I saw that Max's daughter was shaking her head, clearly uncomfortable with the idea. Keegan looked like he was about to speak up and volunteer, but Jordan spoke first. "You need a craftsman. All of you are combat classes. You need someone on that council to represent the workers."

That made me pause. I hadn't even considered that angle, but he was absolutely right. I knew it the instant he spoke. The way the room went still, all eyes shifting to him, told me the thought had landed harder than any speech I could have made. However, it was easier said than done.

I gave him a serious look. “I haven’t told you all the secret condition you have to meet to earn the right to be offered the quest, but I hope you realize that for this to work, you all need to be either at or near Level 100 in seventeen days. You are all going to need to grind levels like crazy in order to—”

My throat seized up before I could relay the secret conditions of the quest’s prerequisite, the damned AI choking my words, and preventing me from speaking.

Clearing my throat, I tried again. “You need to perform three acts considered worthy of being offered the quest.” I glared at the ceiling, “Apparently, I’m not allowed to just say what it is, even though Morgan and Viki were present in the conversation when the AI confirmed the requirements.”

Seeing me wracking my brain to figure out how to tell them the requirements without saying it outright, Morgan came to the rescue. “Hey, on a separate note unrelated to that, we need to be such a high level so we can hunt down the other invading Champions and wipe them out, one at a time.”

Grinning at her expert skirting of the rules, I jumped back in. “Yeah, like she said, we’ll need to eliminate rival Champions. And by the way, when one Champion dies, the next most senior person in their invasion force is appointed in their place. So, I say this for no reason in particular, it would theoretically be possible for one person to kill three Champions, one after another.”

Max was smirking as he confirmed, “For no reason in particular, you think it would be valuable for each of us to kill three invading Champions.”

"Wink, wink, nudge, nudge... know what I mean?" I chuckled darkly at my own Monty Python reference and at the ridiculousness of this discussion.

That got a few laughs from some of the older members of the room. Sadly, Viki and Keegan gave me blank looks, which brought my mood down as it occurred to me that they would never have the opportunity to watch classics like that.

"Anyway, it will be important for us all to be very high level so we can wipe out as many invaders in North America as we can to help make us safe. It will also let us stack the deck with Ascended. I don't know what the System calls them, but apparently other worlds call the Ascended 'gods.' I think it's really more like System Admins with limited power over the planet and how the System gets implemented. The AI flat out told us that if we have a majority of seats on that council or pantheon, or whatever it is, then we can eventually use that power to drive the other invaders off our planet, but that it would take a long time. We'll be reclaiming our world at that point rather than saving it."

Keegan looked disappointed that he wouldn't be part of the group that Ascended, so I added, "It wouldn't hurt for everyone in this room to meet that requirement so that we have other candidates ready to do the quest in case something were to happen to one of us."

The young man gave a determined nod at my words. The look on his face told me he was not happy about not being one of the chosen, but appreciated that he wasn't being left out entirely.

The reactions from the others mirrored how I felt. There were looks of disgust, anger, and determination on the faces around me.

The General, in particular, seemed troubled. "That's going to be a tall order. I'm going to need to spend a lot of my effort getting the troops organized. I'm not sure if there will be enough time for me to hit 100 by Invasion Day. I'll get as close as possible, though."

Brian echoed his sentiment. "We all will. Somehow we'll make it."

We talked about the situation for a bit longer, but in the end there wasn't much more of substance to discuss on that topic. So we took a break to grab some breakfast together as a group and then quietly saw Max, Keesha, and Keegan off as they started their long run for Colorado. We had just about used up the last of the roc eggs I had brought to the camp, but even a day later they were still good.

Once Max's family were gone, Noriko took Jordan off to join the other trainees to power-level them. She aimed to get them to Level 10 today, then tomorrow she, Brian, and Jordan would group up to start the leveling grind to reach Level 100 while the trainees continued on without supervision and began to power-level even more people. They would need to branch out to other nearby dungeons to keep from destroying the two low-level ones here, but pretty soon they would have an ever-growing group of skilled fighters capable of handling any low-level dungeon that didn't absolutely require a spellcaster.

That left me and the girls alone with Brian and Carl-with-a-C, who had joined us for the next operation.

It was still more than half an hour until sunup, but I wanted to be present as soon as people started moving for the day and trying to flee from the monsters outside the Necropolis dungeon that had once been the massive DFW Airport.

Brian asked, "So how's this going to work? We'll certainly take in any refugees that arrive, but how are they going to get from there to here?"

I chuckled and pointed at his chest. "You're how. Morgan, Viki, and I are going to be assaulting the dungeon to reduce their numbers. That will take the pressure off the areas around the dungeon, not just Irving, but all the surrounding communities. While we are doing that, I want you to kill any zombies you find roaming the streets outside the dungeon and let everyone you find know that they can head here for safety. I need you to get them organized. Group them up in large numbers, enough to handle low-level monsters and beasts, then send them on their way. They can make it here by the afternoon on foot. At least the ones who start out this morning."

Morgan, ever practical, added, "Also, please let them know that the dragon they see flying around is on their side. We will try to stay close to the dungeon unless we see zombies out on the streets, but we don't want to start a panic."

Carl scoffed, glancing at me. "I mean, he's still a guy, even if he does have wings and a tail. They shouldn't freak out over that."

Viki scowled at him, answering before I could. "He got his upgrade last night. He can turn into a real dragon now. His wings spread out as long as, like, three school buses and everything. It's kind of insane."

Carl seemed skeptical at first but then when he realized she wasn't kidding, he choked and swallowed hard. "Seriously? An actual dragon?"

I chuckled at his reaction, but just said, "Seriously."

I was going to turn back to Brian, but it occurred to me that Carl would be in charge while we were gone. "By the way, we'll need you to hold down the fort here and make sure everyone knows there will be a large number of refugees showing up later today and tomorrow, and that those who want to will be able to go to a safe zone in a couple days where they'll be able to make permanent homes. That should keep any grumbling down to a minimum."

Brian clapped his friend on the shoulder. "You've got this, Carl. Just try not to snap at anyone, and if you need backup, catch Noriko when she comes out of the dungeon."

Carl shook his head incredulously. "I'll do what I can. You guys do what you need to do."

The knight then turned to me and asked, "So how are we going to get there?" He sounded worried for some reason.

"I'll transform, and the three of you can ride on my back. The harness I got from the dungeon last night will let you strap yourselves down and not fall off. Coolest airline in existence." I grinned.

He had the nerve to go pale in the face at my words and stammered, "Tha... that's what I thought." Then, under his breath, "Damn, System!"

"As long as you aren't afraid of heights, you'll probably like it," I joked.

Carl was giving me a look like I was insane, but he kept quiet and looked thankful he was staying behind.

"All right, I can carry four people in total. Do you have anyone else that is reliable and is at least Level 5?"

Brian shook his head. "Not anyone that I'd recommend. I'm guessing you need someone to work with me on the ground to wrangle the refugees?"

"Yeah, no worries. We can make a quick trip and pick someone up. I'll introduce you to Margaret from the Stonefang fortress. She's a healer, Warpriest actually, so she can not only watch your back, but help heal any refugees you find as long as her mana holds out. Assuming she's willing to go with us, that is."

"Sounds good." Brian looked resigned more than eager.

I led the group out to what used to be the big parking lot of the massive furniture store and wasted no time in transforming into my dragon form, complete with harness. My neck and arms went through the straps that held the thing on. The harness was much more substantial where it sat on my back than the straps that went around my front. There it was like wide belts, with ties and rings to which items could be secured. The talons on my front legs were almost as nimble as my human fingers, and I could easily pull off an item or cut it loose should I need to. According to the System notes, it was enchanted for durability and could be sent into my storage ring and equipped directly from there. That seemed pretty important for a dragon. I wasn't sure how I would be able to put it on otherwise.

While I was reminiscing about my new item, the others approached, and Morgan and Viki climbed on and buckled themselves in. Viki was in front, and Morgan behind her. Brian climbed up with a set jaw that spoke of his unhappiness with this mode of transportation. The way his hands tightened on the straps told me he was bracing for something he very much did not like.

I didn't bother to say anything, but I was sure he would love it once he gave it a try. Only someone with vertigo would feel otherwise.

In my deep, rumbling dragon voice, I asked, "Everyone ready?"

The responses ranged from Viki's overeager enthusiasm to a grumbling assent from Brian, so I flapped my wings and leapt into the air, careful not to let the downdraft collapse the tents of the camp.

Brian actually shrieked in fright, which made me chuckle. Other than that, we took to the skies, and I gained altitude enough that I didn't think I'd have to worry about any attacks from the ground by scared survivors or monsters. I purposefully kept the flight pretty low, probably only a couple thousand feet, although I had no way to really guess our height other than by how small things looked on the ground.

I had flown a few times in my younger days when my dad's company had a contract that required travel. For that reason, I at least knew what things looked like from an airliner's cruising altitude. Not that we'd go anywhere near that height. It was cold enough for Viki and the others just due to the wind. Thankfully, my form protected me from that, but I didn't want my friends to be uncomfortable.

Viki squealed in delight. "I can't wait until I can do this too! This is amazing!"

Morgan's quieter voice was nearly lost to the wind, but I could hear the sadness as she said, "So much destruction… I had hoped we could get control of the System and fix things and make them go back to the way they were. Now I get it. There's no coming back from this."

Her tone must have snapped Brian out of his own issues, because he replied in a shaky voice, "That doesn't mean we can't rebuild civilization. It just won't look like it did before."

I added, "We'll take the first step toward that this evening or tomorrow when I set up that safe zone."

Conversation turned to the view after that, with Viki pointing things out and the other two responding and noticing other things.

In a few minutes, I motioned down and slightly to the right with my head. "There it is. The Stonefang fortress camp." It probably would have taken twenty or twenty-five minutes to drive that distance, but traveling through the air as the dragon flies, it was less than ten and would have been even faster if I hadn't wanted to make my passengers comfortable.

We were quite close before people on the ramparts started yelling and sounding the alarm. The sun was just rising over the horizon, and my deep purple-black scales had made me hard to spot against the western sky. If I had been coming from the east, they probably would have spotted me a lot farther off. I made note of that for the future and wondered how my Stealth skill would interact with flying, a question for later.

"It is me, Liam Bell. Don't shoot. I'm going to land in the courtyard," I bellowed toward the wall.

My voice shocked a few people into inaction for a moment before my words registered and they calmed down and shouted for the others to stand down.

Soon we were surrounded by people in the courtyard, assuring me that Margaret would be with us shortly.

My passengers dismounted, and I transformed back into my human form just as Margaret and George approached.

I was immediately impressed. The pair of them looked like they had gained some levels since I had last seen them.

Margaret looked worried and not best pleased that we had arrived with the dawn. Her armored robes were slightly askew, and wisps of hair were escaping the bun she had hastily pulled it into. George, on the other hand, looked stoic and unperturbed.

"What's this about?" the older woman asked, getting right to the point. "I'd appreciate it if you didn't frighten everyone half to death while half the group is still asleep."

I lowered my head in a brief nod of acknowledgment. "Sorry about that. For what it's worth, I don't think there are any other dragons in this world, monster or otherwise, besides me and Viki here." I gestured to my young friend, who puffed out her chest in pride and grinned as if I had praised her, which I suppose I had in a way. I paused for a second as people looked curiously at her, noting the faint scale pattern on the skin of her neck and the backs of her hands, which were visible.

"As for the reason for our visit," I looked at Margaret, "I need your help, if you're willing. There is a massive stronghold dungeon where the DFW airport used to be, and it is spilling monsters out into the surrounding communities. The city of Irving in particular has been hard hit. They are trapped between two high-level dungeon zones."

"We are going there this morning to deal with it. Viki, Morgan, and I will assault the dungeon, while Brian and you, if you are willing, will help the people in Irving organize and flee north to the Colony camp. The reason I'd like your help is for your healing abilities, as well as your ability to protect yourself and any refugees you gather."

The leader of the fortress narrowed her eyes skeptically. "We've only just started training our people. I'm not sure if I can afford to leave so soon. Nearly a hundred people have joined us since you left, and I've had to turn away several groups that seemed suspect."

I wasn't surprised by her reluctance, but I wasn't ready to give up yet. "I'm only asking for your help for a single day. We'll cover the entire area and make sure everyone knows how to escape and where they can go for safety. I can get someone else in your place, but your healing would be invaluable."

Margaret looked to George, and an unspoken conversation passed between them before she turned back to us. "I suppose I could assist just for the day, if you will guarantee my return by this evening. I wouldn't be comfortable leaving for any longer than that. We are seeing large numbers of refugees here, and many need healing."

With that settled, I introduced everyone and gave Margaret a few minutes to get ready.

Brian and George seemed a bit wary of each other at first, but after Brian promised to keep an eye out for Margaret's safety, George relaxed a little and they started talking about the two camps. By the time we were ready to leave twenty minutes later, the two had bonded over their mutual love of a first-person shooter video game they used to play and were laughing and joking around. Seeing George grin and gesture animatedly was jarring, like watching a mask finally slip. It was the first time I'd ever seen him act like a real person and not just a professional bodyguard.

Margaret seemed amused at the sight, but once her companion noticed that she had returned, he quickly went back to professional mode.

For my part, I was just glad that representatives from the different camps were getting along. The last thing we needed right now was a power struggle or clashing personalities. The tension I'd been carrying eased when no one argued or postured, and I hoped Brian would get along with Margaret as well as he did with her bodyguard.

When everyone was ready, I transformed back, and the team mounted up, with Margaret sitting between Morgan and Brian. With excited waves, the group at the fortress bid us goodbye and watched as we took off and headed west toward the scariest dungeon I had ever seen. One that would pose a challenge even for me.

CHAPTER 3

FEET ON THE GROUND, FIREPOWER IN THE AIR

The flight across the city in the early morning light was as depressing as it was majestic. Long, stark shadows and golden light fell across collapsed buildings and homes that were already little more than rubble less than two full weeks into the apocalypse. There were a few surprising holdouts. Spots where families had kept their land and old homes while surrounded by suburban neighborhoods. The hundred-year-old homes and barns still stood, the older construction being less affected by the System.

The widespread destruction was a sobering sight as we approached the Necropolis dungeon. It stood in distinct contrast to its surroundings, its massive walls whole and unblemished, black against the drab piles of debris that had been our civilization less than two weeks ago.

Even in the dawn light, I could make out zombies wandering the streets outside the walls, seeking humans to devour.

Above the dungeon, it was as if a storm roiled, blackening the sky hundreds of feet into the air. Just as I had seen before, unidentifiable shapes flew through the dark clouds. However, I wasn't ready to fight those with a bunch of passengers on my back. Circling over Irving's destroyed neighborhoods, I spotted a small group of survivors trying their best to battle a trio of zombies.

Calling to the three on my back, I announced, "I'll land a couple blocks away so we don't distract them and cause them to lose. Then you guys can run over and help them out."

Brian yelled against the wind, "We can handle them, no problem!"

With that settled, I wasted no time landing two streets over and behind where the people were fighting so they wouldn't see me closing in and turn their backs on the zombies to run away. I know I sure would if I were in their place. The world turns into a zombie apocalypse, then a dragon swoops down out of the sky. I'd nope right out of there like my ass was on fire.

Hell, even in my first life, twenty years into the apocalypse, I'd have still run away at the sight of a dragon. Thankfully, in this part of the world, that had never happened. It suddenly occurred to me that my location might well have been the reason the AI chose me as its guinea pig. With the exception of the Dark Elves, there were no particularly aggressive invaders in this region, and even they tended to stick near the mountains and their places of power.

Even as the idea occurred to me, I was convinced it was true. The AI was nothing if not a cunning schemer. Just look at the way it had arranged for the invaders to get compasses, then let me upgrade them to point to other Champions so we could turn around and hunt them down. All perfectly within the rules, but downright sneaky as hell.

Yeah, I had no doubt now that this was part of its grand plan. Even so, I had to believe there was a way to get the upper hand somehow once I had some kind of authority within the System. There were still those hidden areas with the mysterious writings and pictograms, glitches in the matrix. The memory of those symbols kept tugging at me, like an itch I couldn't quite scratch.

I hadn't forgotten about those, and I planned to dig into them every time I found one. Unfortunately, destroying this dungeon and getting my last ten levels was a little more immediately important at the moment. What's worse, I had been thinking that with Morgan, Viki, and the others all about to start a leveling frenzy, it would be the perfect time to get them to search for the hidden areas as well. But I had to be careful what I said to them, as it was likely the System was paying at least some attention to us. The best bet would be to take them into a dungeon that had a hidden room and talk to them once we were inside it, where the AI couldn't listen in. That was the only way I could be sure of privacy.

Of course, the AI could read our minds, but it didn't seem to do so normally unless it was given a reason to, perhaps part of its ban on communications.

I pushed those thoughts away as Brian and Margaret dismounted and signaled that they were ready to go. "You guys sure you have this?"

Margaret snorted disdainfully. "You would not have engaged our services if you had no confidence in our ability to succeed. Go. We will be fine from here."

Seeing Brian's confident nod, I said, "Fine. Margaret, shoot spells into the air to signal us if you need help or have issues. We'll try to check in every hour or two as well."

They waved us off, so I took to the air, Viki and Morgan still on my back. "We'll stay close to the dungeon to prevent scaring people any more than they already are, at least until word spreads that the dragon is on humanity's side."

As we flew toward the fifty-foot-tall obsidian wall, I spotted a dozen or more zombies in the area just outside, wandering around aimlessly. I dove on a group of four that were close enough together and released my dragon breath. I had been proud of my previous Abyssal Breath, which had been powerful enough to burn Zorthanix to death. However, this new version was Void energy, so I hadn't been sure what to expect, having not tried it yet.

I was not disappointed! It was noticeably more powerful.

A wave of dark energy engulfed the undead and the concrete beneath them.

I saw it with my own eyes, but wasn't sure what had just happened. The energy had somehow burned them completely, inside and out, reducing them to statues of black dust darker than the emptiness of space. The ash then dispersed on the wind in seconds, like Thanos had snapped his fingers. By the time I circled back around, there was nothing left but four piles of copper mana coins, ten each, and they were sitting on bare dirt. Even the concrete was just gone where my breath had touched.

If I were still in human form, I might have broken out into a cold sweat, seeing how destructive that was. Instead, I shivered from head to the tip of my tail, then called out, "Viki, Morgan, you're up."

It was kind of scary how much difference there was between a Tier 1 and a Tier 4 dragon's power. And compared to humans, most of whom didn't even have magic? No wonder we'd been driven to extinction.

I flew a sweeping pass along the wall, with Viki firing arrows of umbral energy summoned into existence by her bow and empowered by her Class skills. Her shots weren't as devastating as my dragon breath, but she was still high enough level that each empowered shot was a kill. It didn't hurt that her skill ensured every strike was a headshot.

Meanwhile, Morgan was letting loose with her attack spells, which weren't quite as effective as Viki's arrows but still got the job done. In less than fifteen minutes, we had cleared the entire length of this section of the wall of wandering zombies.

"That should help the folks on the Irving side. At least no more will enter their neighborhoods. Brian and Margaret will have to mop up the ones wandering the streets. The upside is I could only see a couple dozen from the air."

Viki called, "Let's kill those skeletons on the wall!"

Unfortunately, these small fry weren't giving me any experience at all, and we didn't have time to stop to pick up coins if we were going to make any progress on saving the people surrounding the massive stronghold. Still, despite the grumblings of my dragon heart, we needed to finish off the zombies before moving on to attack the stronghold proper. The itch to dive straight into the real fight was hard to ignore, but people came first.

"Let's sweep the rest of the zombies around the other sides of the Necropolis. We've done the ones on the Irving side, but we should clear the Euless and Grapevine sides. The south side is mostly industrial, so there won't be many people there, but we'll still make the full circuit just to be safe."

It took the better part of an hour, and we killed at least three hundred zombies in our circuit of the Necropolis stronghold. After that first group, I only fried a couple more for practice with my breath weapon and left the rest of the kills to the girls. They were getting mad experience from this.

By the time we arrived back at our starting point, Viki exclaimed, "Three! I got three levels off of the zombies!"

Morgan wasn't bouncing on my shoulders the way Viki was, but she was still excited. "Me too. That last group bumped me up to Level 33."

Brian's POV:

Waiting only long enough to make sure Margaret was following, Brian drew his sword and hurried between homes that were only mostly collapsed, charging toward the sound of battle. There were yells of anger and fear, mixed with the clang of metal and wood against bone.

Despite understanding the reasoning, Brian grumbled under his breath about having to be dropped off two blocks away. Thankfully, his increased stats from yesterday's leveling meant he wasn't out of breath as he rounded the final corner and saw the scene before him.

Three Level 10 Zombies had cornered a group of survivors. What they hadn't been able to see from the air was that five adults were sheltering two elderly women and half a dozen children and toddlers. Two other adults were already down, one with a torn-out throat, the other with a deep gash to the abdomen.

Swearing under his breath, Brian used his new movement skill and charged the zombies, arriving almost instantly and sweeping them with Blade Sweep, which hit all enemies in an arc before him. He had to be careful not to hit any of the defenders, but he judged the distance perfectly.

SLASH!

All three Zombies took moderate damage across their backs and spines. It was enough to drop one instantly, its head severed. The other two stumbled forward from the unexpected impact with mixed results. One fell prone and had its head immediately caved in by a shovel-wielding woman. The other staggered into a middle-aged man in a leather biker jacket, and they both went down in a heap.

The biker shoved the monster off, but not before receiving a nasty claw wound to the side of his face. Not lethal, but surely infected.

For a split second, Brian wondered if the man would turn into a zombie, but he didn't let that stop him from stepping forward and putting his sword through the back of the monster's head, ending the immediate threat.

Unfortunately, the shocked group didn't react quite the way Brian had anticipated. The biker started screaming and freaking out. "It got me! It got me!"

Meanwhile, the woman with the shovel rounded on the Knight. "What the hell, man!? You just got Jim clawed! Now he's gonna die!"

"Oh, shit, I'm gonna die! I'm gonna turn into one of them!" The biker rolled on the ground, clutching his wounded face.

The other group members all erupted with their own comments, some trying to calm the shovel-wielding woman, others trying to thank Brian for saving them. Meanwhile, the toddlers were bawling their eyes out and screaming like it was the end of the world.

Which Brian supposed it kind of was, but he wished everyone would just shut up and talk one at a time. He was just about to suggest that when Margaret arrived and calmly knelt beside the man writhing on the ground.

"Hush, now. You're going to be just fine. I can heal that wound. Just move your hands and let me take a look."

Her calm, assured tone got through to the man somehow, and he lowered his bloody hands. He wasn't exactly calm, but he did hold still long enough for the older woman to place a hand over the wound and cast her spell. A warm golden light washed over the man's head, sending soothing sensations through him and wiping away the pain. Still, he looked both relieved and disturbed as the skin on his face knit itself back together.

By the time the light faded, everyone in the group had realized what was happening, and one by one, they fell silent, shocked at what they were seeing.

As Margaret finished with the first patient, she turned to the others. "Now, who's next?" She gestured calmly toward the two fallen victims.

One of the elderly women guarding the children stepped forward and knelt by the injured female. "Heal my daughter, please. Her babies need her!"

Meanwhile, Brian stood there dumbfounded. That situation hadn't gone at all like he'd expected. Not that he wasn't used to things going sideways, but back at the camp, there were dozens of people looking to him for leadership. When individuals or groups got vocal about not getting the treatment they thought they deserved, his people stood up for him. He had been the one everyone looked to, and they followed because they wanted his protection.

He decided he wasn't too fond of getting yelled at for saving people's lives. Sure, the biker had gotten hurt, but they had already lost two people to the zombies.

Something of his thoughts must have shown on his face, because the woman frowned and looked about to say something more when the biker, Jim, got up and hugged her, holding on like he'd never let go.

Her face softened, and she wrapped her arms around him. "I'm so glad you're alright! I thought you were a goner!"

One of the other people who had fought the zombies suddenly

shouted, "Whoa! I just leveled up! I didn't know I could do that from fighting!"

Seeing his chance, Brian spoke up. "Yeah. No matter what kind of Class you chose, killing monsters gives experience. If you're a non-combat class, you can also get experience from doing whatever your Class does. A smith gets experience from smithing, and so on. Anyway, sorry for interrupting your fight. We saw you were in trouble and came to help. Those zombies are Level 10, and most people aren't strong enough to survive a fight like that."

The woman might have said something, but she was too distracted comforting the sobbing biker who'd just gotten a reprieve from death.

That brought up a question, so Brian turned to the man who'd announced his level-up. "Hey, has anyone actually turned into a zombie that you've seen, or do they just get sick and die from the wounds?"

The guy looked confused. "What do you mean? This is a zombie apocalypse, like in that show. Why wouldn't they turn?"

"But you've got the System, right? This isn't just a zombie apocalypse. Those things are coming from a dungeon over there." He pointed in the direction of the airport.

Seeing the confusion on several faces, he continued. "There are other monsters, too. You're just only seeing these here. I've fought giant spiders and other things." He shuddered at the memory.

The faces around him went pale, and one of the women, the one holding a felling axe, blurted out, "You mean there's more than just zombies?"

Brian resisted the urge to face-palm. Of course it felt like an episode of *The Walking Dead* to them. Other monsters probably didn't enter the area because of the zombies.

"Okay. Let me start from the beginning. When the System gave everyone their Class choice, that was the start of the Apocalypse. But everywhere is different. Animals get mutated by mana, uh, magic that is, and become Beasts. When they die, their bodies don't disappear like the zombies do. Monsters are created by the System, and when they die, they vanish and leave behind mana coins like these just did."

Stooping to pick up a pile of coins, he continued. "These contain mana. Make sure each of the kids carries one. That way, when they get older, they'll have a Magic Aptitude stat and can choose a magic Class like Wizard or Healer."

He gestured toward Margaret, who was finishing up with the last injured person. "We need more healers like her."

There was so much more he wanted to say, but now he understood why Liam was always in a rush. If he tried to explain everything, he wouldn't save many people.

"Okay. I'm sorry. There's too much to explain right now, and it's not what matters most. We've got a camp in The Colony. It's relatively safe, with food and water. More importantly, we're setting up a true safe place just north of McKinney. One where new monsters can't enter or spawn. Margaret and I are here to evacuate as many people as possible and send them there. Irving isn't safe.

He glanced meaningfully toward the tall black dungeon walls that could be seen in the distance between the collapsed houses. "You're trapped between a massive dungeon full of zombies and worse to the west, and a ton of smaller, but high-level dungeons just on the other side of the Trinity River. If you stay here, you'll be overrun."

The elderly woman holding a small child asked eagerly, "There's safety, you say?"

"Yes. Head to Highway 121 and make your way to the big Furniture Mart. That's where the camp is. Spread the word. You haven't seen it yet, but the city is full of dungeons, and monsters will spill out eventually, just like the zombies did from that one. We're going to gather up as many people as possible and spread the word. Meet up with others at the junction of Highway 114 and the Bush Tollway. There's safety in numbers."

As much as he wanted to rush off and find the next group to save, it took nearly fifteen minutes to convince them to leave and start spreading the word.

Once they were finally jogging down the street, Margaret commented, "You did well enough. But next time, be more concise. We must make haste if we are to make an impact."

Brian grunted. That woman with the shovel had been stubborn as hell. He didn't remember her name, but she'd argued hard about staying and building a fort. It had taken her boyfriend, Jim, finally snapping and saying, "I almost died to one of those things. I'd rather face spiders or goblins than die and turn into one of the undead. I'm leaving!"

Even then, she'd grumbled.

It was only when Margaret mentioned that there were no homes left, and that Liam and his group were assaulting the dungeon to buy time, that she finally gave in.

She was stubbornly arguing, "I grew up right there in that house! My parents worked their whole lives to pay that off, and you want us to just up and lea..." She trailed off, her face going ashen as a huge black dragon flew into view and dove, breathing black flames at something, before the view was blocked by the neighbor's big oak tree.

Standing there in shock for a good twenty seconds before she shuddered and looked at her biker boyfriend, “Uh, I su...I suppose the roof has fallen in on the house. If you really want to go north, I guess that wouldn’t be so bad. I do have a cousin up in Van Alstyne...”

Brian suppressed a chuckle, not wanting to set the woman off again, and just hoped Liam, Morgan, and Viki were having success with the dungeon. His day sure hadn’t gotten off to a smooth start!

CHAPTER 4
BREAKIN BONES

Viki and Morgan's POV:

After finishing off all the zombies wandering around outside the walls, Liam picked one of the massive gates, with its two flanking towers as their next destination. The walls were fifty feet high here and with the octagonal guard towers standing another twenty above that. On the battlements stood skeletal warriors that Liam's skill identified as Level 20. They looked just like human skeletons devoid of any flesh whatsoever, except they had two small horns on their foreheads, and their eyes glowed with a sickly green light. They wore no armor, but carried a variety of weapons, some wielding polearms, some swords, and others, like the ones on the tower, had crossbows. Like their wielders, the weapons all looked old and worn. They were rusty and exactly what Morgan thought the undead might carry.

Not that there had ever been medieval soldiers that lived on this land in Texas waiting to be raised as troops for the dungeon. She knew this was just the System's way of populating the dungeon with monsters. It didn't have to make sense beyond fitting the machine's aesthetic themes.

What it did was make it harder for the people around here to handle an already brutal apocalypse.

Liam spoke over his shoulder in his deep dragon voice, "I'll circle the right hand tower and you guys can kill the ones on top. I'll land and let you guys off to handle these small fry. Now that the AI is enforcing the rules about gaining experience, I can't get anything from killing them, I need to find monsters at least Level 70 or higher. I can't afford to spend the time on these if I'm going to get to the Level Cap in the next couple days."

As they circled Viki began blasting the skeletons with arrows, and Morgan cast spells. After a couple of shots, Liam added, "I fought these in my last life, you either have to destroy the head, or break enough of their bones that they can no longer function. That's the only way to put them down."

Grimacing, as her next shot glanced off a shoulder bone and then caused a small explosion of chipped stone on the tower's rampart, Viki adjusted her aim to only take headshots. That was definitely harder while mounted on a dragon's back. Every beat of Liam's wings caused her to be jostled, thankfully she'd had time to get used to it, and now she only fired the brief lulls between wing beats. It was like letting out your breath to ensure a steady moment, only everything was moving and it wasn't just her breaths she had to worry about.

It was super hard, especially now that she could only kill them with headshots. She was missing a bunch of her attacks, but thankfully the bow created arrows from her mana. Otherwise she'd run out of arrows very quickly like this.

Behind her, Morgan was having just as hard of a time, and it didn't help that the enemies had cover from the tower's crenelations. They kept ducking behind the stone defenses between firing their crossbows. Thankfully, Liam was able to block the shots with his body. The bolts were not able to penetrate his scales thanks to the massive level disparity between him and the Skeletons.

It took an annoying five minutes for the fight to be over. Viki finally ended it with a well placed headshot, exploding the final skeleton's skull into a dozen bone fragments, the sickly green light going out of its eye sockets instantly.

A few seconds later they touched down and Morgan swore as the System instantly bombarded her with the ambience sensations.

The top of the tower was a geometry of ruin. Wind hissed through gaps where stone had fractured, scattering powdered mortar across the bones of the fallen. Hundreds of fragments—rib arcs, finger joints, half-shattered skulls—littered the floor in patterns too deliberate to be random, as though someone had tried to arrange them before time or battle swept them aside.

Among the wreckage, copper mana coins gleamed like old blood under a dim morning sun. Small piles of twenty coins each lay where the skeletons had fallen.

A few skeletal torsos still twitched, ribs flexing with phantom impulses that had nowhere left to go. When the wind struck just right, it carried a sound like dry laughter—or maybe just bones rattling in surrender.

Everything smelled of dust and static, the air faintly humming with residual mana. The moment their boots touched stone, they could see it all, a perfect catalog of what remained, a record of the fallen reduced to data points and debris.

And beneath that cold order, Viki and Morgan could feel it—the whisper of something vast and watching, acknowledging their arrival. The tower recognized new variables had entered its equation.

Morgan swore under her breath. "Damned System, getting into my head!"

Looking around, they quickly retrieved the coins, and surveyed the situation. From their vantage point they could see down to the ramparts above the gate. Also guarded by a dozen skeletons, one of which was much larger than the rest.

From above, the rampart stretched in a perfect arc of engineered symmetry, stone darkened by age and ash. Five skeletons stood in formation there, evenly spaced, each motionless in the exact posture the System had assigned them—guardians waiting for the next variable to enter their field. Their horns caught the faint green glow of dungeon light, reflections pulsing like heartbeat simulations.

At their center loomed the aberrant.

It was larger by half again, its proportions wrong for a human frame. The curvature of its spine pushed it forward, and its skull jutted with brutish intent—massive tusk-like canines driving its lower jaw into a permanent underbite. The horns were thicker and larger than its smaller companions, ridged as if they'd grown under stress rather than design.

Even from a distance, Morgan could feel its presence bleed through the ambient mana, a localized gravity almost. The smaller skeletons were guardians; this one was a check-point.

The wind pulled through the rampart, carrying the clatter of bone against stone. The sound wasn't random—it looped, repeating with eerie precision, like the dungeon was resetting its ambient track for combat initialization.

And in that moment, as she looked down at the ogre-sized construct of bone and residual mana, Morgan didn't just see a boss monster.

She saw a function—waiting to execute.

"Ugh! Again with the damned intrusive thoughts!" She turned to where Liam's massive dragon form perched. "I wish there was some way to turn those off!"

A deep bass rumble of a chuckle issued from the dragon, "You and me both!" He paused and looked them both over, "You guys good here, or do you want me to stick around for the fight with the mini-boss? I don't want to tank your experience earning by staying in your group."

Viki pulled back her shoulders in a confident stance, "We've got this big bro. It'll be super easy."

Morgan wasn't so sure it would be so simple, but she was confident they could handle a single mini-boss. Besides, if they attacked from here, they'd have a significant advantage since it would take time for the boss to climb the wall and reach them. The tower top was a good twenty feet higher than the ramparts above the gate, after all.

She gave Liam a serious nod, not filled with unwarranted confidence, but with the surety that came from everything she and her young friend had been through over the last few days. "Yeah, go find the big monsters, we'll handle the stuff on the walls until we hit Level 40, then we'll go deeper into the dungeon. We'll try to at least finish off the wall guards on this side of the airport, that way they can't attack any of the refugees that wander too close."

"Sounds good. Use your Commune skill if you need me, and don't forget to keep an eye out for Margaret sending up signal flare spells, in case they get in trouble."

With that, Liam launched himself into the air and began to fly into the dark clouds that perpetually shaded the dungeon in gloom as dark as night.

Viki grinned up at Morgan. "Let's focus on the boss and burn it down. If we concentrate fire on it, we can probably kill it before the minions can climb up the wall and get near us."

Morgan smiled at the younger girl, amused at her gamer-speak. "Sure, let's do that."

What followed wasn't like any video game they'd ever played, but instead resembled a few horror movies. She and Viki attacked the mini-boss at the same time, doing a significant amount of damage, but the instant they did, the minions began to swarm toward them. The first to reach the wall barely slowed. Its bony fingers finding purchase in the rough stone, clacking and scrabbling with scraping sounds that hurt her ears.

Morgan shivered, the scraping of bone on stone raised the hair on the back of her neck worse than fingernails on a chalkboard ever had!

Viki showed no sign of discomfort and barely slowed, as she shifted her aim and fired her new AOE arrow, Cataclysm, down at the wall below them. Before the skeletons reached the halfway point, her arrow hit one in the head, exploding like the inverse of a missile. Instead of light and sound, a large ball of darkness at the tip of the arrow made contact and detonated into thousands of shards of solidified shadow energy, each fragment tearing through whatever they hit with the force of a bullet.

The force of the explosion flung the Level 20 monsters away, sending them sailing in every direction, some back onto the battlement, others off the wall completely. None were killed outright, but it would take precious seconds before they could return and be a threat again.

Seconds that gave the pair the chance to focus on the boss.

Just as two of the skeletons landed back on the stone near the charging boss, Morgan cast Shadow Storm, her own strongest AOE spell. A thirty foot radius area centered between the monsters was racked with a tempest of shadow energy.

The storm hovered in place for several seconds, its power rending bones into tiny fragments and dust. The two minions broke apart under the assault, never to rise again. Unfortunately, the boss plowed through the tempest of shadows, looking worse for the wear, but far from finished.

It pulled a bone from its ribcage and flung it at the battlements.

Morgan didn't think, she just reacted and dove at her young friend, tackling her out of the way.

Viki's shot went wide as they tumbled to the ground, just as the bone exploded against the crenelations, sending shards of bone and granite spraying across the space where they had just been standing.

Tiny spots of blood began to appear on their bodies where the fragments made contact with skin.

"Damn it. It has a bleeding effect! We're losing health until it dies." Morgan swore as she read the System messages.

Viki struggled loose, and stood back up, hurrying to attack again. However, before she poked her head around the cover of the stone, she cast True Shot on herself. She clenched her jaw in concentration, this next shot had to count.

The boss had made it to the wall, and was about to ascend when she leaned out over the battlement and fired down.

"Eat an Oblivion Arrow! You big meany!"

This attack was specifically designed to work against bosses, and it did high damage, plus a confusion effect. It was her most powerful attack.

Viki loosed the string and the arrow instantly appeared, striking the big skeleton right in its glowing left eye socket, punching through the back of its skull.

Amazingly, even with half its skull gone, the glow hadn't disappeared from its right eye socket. However, the confusion effect seemed to be working as it stood there shaking, one hand extended to the wall, and the other waving uncertainly back and forth.

Morgan cursed, glancing at her cooldown timers in the corner of her vision, apologizing, "I'm out of offensive spells for another seven seconds." So she cast a healing spell on Viki instead. It wouldn't stop the bleeding, but it would restore health points.

Viki didn't hesitate. "I've got two more arrows before True Shot wears off. I'll just have to make them count!"

She had already used her other high damage attacks, so she used Soulpiercer, her next strongest. Like the previous arrow, True Shot bypassed wind and distance to instantly arrive at the target. Instead of the other eye socket that she had aimed for, it hit the cheekbone just below it.

It was a tiny bit off target, but it was enough.

The boss was at their same level, so the damage it had taken was enough to finish it. Enough of the skull had been destroyed that the light faded from its remaining eye, the rest of the bones collapsed into a pile.

After that, it was just a matter of picking off the remaining elite skeleton minions one by one. Still, it was super creepy how they scurried up the walls with their bones clacking on the stone in an unnerving rhythm.

Morgan flinched every time she heard it. "That really icks me out!"

Viki grinned, constantly firing arrows. Even if they were not 'skilled' arrows, her magic bow was strong and grew with her as she leveled up, so they still did enough damage to slow the skeletons. When her cooldown timers were up, she would add in a Shadow Bolt, Duskfire, or one of her other new special arrow skills.

All the while Morgan healed them up from the wounds the miniboss had given. She also threw in an attack spell when her own cooldown timers popped.

Breathing a deep sigh of relief, Morgan called, "I think that was the last of them."

However, Viki shook her head. "No, there's one more down on the ground that's still twitching. It's unable to move, but there's still a glow in its eyes. I can't reach it though. I'd have to lean too far out over the wall, and I'm afraid I'd fall."

Morgan grinned, "I've got it then." She leaned out over the wall to look for the one Viki mentioned and then cast Shadowflame Burst. With a concussive blast of shadow energy over a thirty foot radius, the lone skeleton was obliterated, the remaining bones of its body broken and scattered under the impact.

With that they got the notification that the battle with the Miniboss was completed. It took another half hour, but they cleared the two towers of all their monsters.

It was a slow process because they had to be careful going room to room down several flights of stairs inside the confined structure. They didn't particularly want to get into melee combat with the undead skeletal warriors if they could help it.

When they were finally done, Morgan asked, "Did you hit Level 34?"

Viki grinned. "Sure did. One more level and we get new spells and skills! Makes me want to keep going and not take a break!"

Laughing, Morgan held out her hands in the 'hang on now' gesture. "Hey, I'm not so young as you, and my physical stats are less than half what yours are. Have mercy on an old woman!"

Viki smirked and teased, "Okay, boomer! I'll slow down for you."

They both laughed, but took a minute to look out over Irving.

"I wonder how Brian and Margaret are doing? I haven't seen any signal flares," Morgan asked.

Viki pursed her lips, "I see a lot of smoke still, but yeah, no flares."

Looking the opposite direction, Morgan gave a worried look. "I hope Liam's okay. He created a big ruckus when he flew into the clouds. Whatever those things flying around are, they didn't take kindly to that."

Viki shrugged without concern. "Meh, low level monsters won't even make him break a sweat even if there are a thousand of them."

Morgan frowned slightly, hoping her young friend was right. Sometimes quantity equaled a quality of its own. Without her there to heal him, there was no way she wouldn't feel concern.

CHAPTER 5
TERMINAL E EXTINCTION

Liam's POV:

After leaving the girls to their own battles, I flew into the perpetual storm clouds hovering over the airport Necropolis dungeon, and just like clockwork, the System's intrusive thoughts began to roll...

As I climbed toward the cloud layer, the light shifted around me. The Necropolis below was all dead stone and hard lines, but the sky above it was wrong in a quieter way. The clouds didn't move. They just hung there, thick and heavy, like packed ash suspended in air. No wind pushed them. No warmth touched them. It felt like something the System had placed here and then left on pause.

When I broke the lower edge, sound dropped away. My wingbeats still happened, but the world didn't seem to acknowledge them. The air didn't move. Even my breath felt slower, heavier in my chest.

And there were shapes in the haze.

Not bodies. Not anything that made sense. Just movement, dark sweeps of shadow looping through the clouds in long, smooth arcs. No flapping. No gliding motion. They moved like thoughts, appearing, shifting, and disappearing between one blink and the next.

Every now and then, one sharpened just enough to see.

A stretched impression of wings. A face I almost recognized, twisted in silent fury. Something like a hand, trailing vapor that pulled at the edges of my aura.

Then the cloud swallowed it again.

The cold found me, not on my scales, but behind my ribs, like someone had reached through my chest and pressed their palm against my heart.

I didn't need a System notification to know what they were.

Damned System, and its intrusive ambience messaging!

Those creatures were Wraiths of some kind.

An icy fear gripped my heart for just a moment as memories from my first life surfaced. Fleeing New Jasper in the middle of the night, hundreds of people screaming and running in every direction. Incorporeal undead flitting through the streets, feasting on the health and mana of their victims until nothing but desiccated husks remained. Normal weapons couldn't even touch them, only magic, or magical weapons, something we were critically short on back then.

I shuddered involuntarily, momentarily drawn back into those thoughts. Then the dragon blood in my veins roared in defiance of the terrified memories.

Not in this life!

I twisted my head to see a wraith clinging to my back.

Ruinwraith (Level 30) – Incorporeal Undead, Aerial Predator.

A wrath-formed spirit that hunts by emotional resonance, draining mana and life through direct contact. Physical attacks ineffective; disrupt with fire, light, or magic.

A breath hissed out of my lungs. This was not good, but I wasn't afraid. Not the heart of a Void Dragon!

I let loose my Void Breath with full force at point-blank range, a torrent of darkness with the force of a hurricane ripped away the wraith and shredded it to wisps of ghostly, faintly glowing mana. I came about and hovered there, waiting to see what would happen to its remnant. After the usual minute, the mana condensed into ten silver mana coins, which then began to fall to the ground below.

My talons shot out and scooped them up, sending them into my storage ring.

This was going to be annoying, and far too time-consuming to collect the treasure, especially for creatures I was not even earning experience from. Still, my greedy dragon heart wanted them, but my logic said no. Perhaps I could come back after the dungeon was beaten and collect them?

My heart wanted that to be true, but my brain told me we had more important things to do, like hit the Level Cap so I could start the Ascension Quest. Surely there would be more treasure from that, enough to make up for the loss of these coins. Right?

Grr... now I was pissed. These bastards were going to attack me and waste my energy and I wasn't even going to be able to collect the treasure. Fine. I'd kill them with extreme prejudice then.

As I drove through the clouds, it became a never-ending barrage of wraiths. Thankfully, the level difference meant a single attack would destroy them. Of course, I couldn't constantly fire Dragon Breath at them. My breath weapon had a 30-second cooldown, so I ended up having to rotate my single-target spells, at least the ones that didn't use too much mana. Then, to stretch my mana, I used physical attacks with my claws when the opportunity presented.

I very much appreciated the fact that my claws were attuned to my magic weapons, and so counted as magic to damage the incorporeal bastards. It meant that I had a large arsenal of attacks, all of which could kill a wraith with a single hit.

There were even times where a dozen or more came at me at once, and I was able to use Arcane Singularity to destroy entire crowds of the annoying mosquitoes. And just like the bloodsucking insects they reminded me of, they were slowly but surely draining me. Health and mana were steadily ticking down. Only the fact that I had Voidflame coating my talons kept me from running out of mana before I could get through the wraith zone of the dungeon. It was a constant up and down of mana and health, but for every bit I drained, some other wraith would get through my defenses and drain a little more than I was recovering.

-30 Health
-30 Mana
Health: 2130/5400
Mana: 1580/5400

When I finally broke through the gauntlet and reached the inner zone of the Necropolis, I heaved a sigh of relief and flew down to the ground to rest for a moment. Before me stood a massive, sprawling wall surrounding what had once been the airport and its terminals. I was closest to what had once been Terminal E, and behind the wall was a graveyard.

It boggled my mind. I wasn't sure how big the area had really been before the apocalypse, but from what I could see, I thought the graveyard covered a good two-hundred acres of land, filled with gravestones and mausoleums.

I had taken a flight out of Terminal E before. I remembered it being made of concrete and glass, and filled with stress and worry. My father had been working someplace out east, Baltimore I think, and I had been scheduled for a 9:00 AM flight. I was supposed to fly out and spend the holidays with him that year. I followed the directions I had been given at check-in, but they had told me wrong information and I ended up going to a gate on the far end of the terminal from my flight.

By the time I realized the mistake, I had only five minutes left to catch the flight. I literally ran through the airport from one end to the other and missed my flight by less than two minutes. I could see the plane sitting there on the tarmac, but they refused to reopen the hatch to let me board. What followed was several hours of the most frustrating and stressful arguing with authority I had ever done in my young life.

Eventually, the airline let me catch an afternoon flight that had spare seats, but from then on, I hated air travel and airports.

Now it was all gone.

In just under two weeks, the System had removed tens of thousands of tons of concrete and replaced it all with a graveyard scene right out of a horror movie. Acres and acres of graves, with shambling undead forms moving among them.

The only question was whether they were high enough level for me to gain experience. As much as I wanted to eliminate everything here and destroy it all, to stop it from being a stronghold dungeon, I needed to get these last ten levels out of the way. Besides, if I could deal with the highest-level monsters here, it would be easier to slaughter the rest later.

I spent twenty minutes resting outside the graveyard wall to let my mana and health regen to full. To speed things up, I ganked a few wandering zombies, allowing Voidflame to do its thing with lifesteal and manasteal.

It did occur to me that there was some irony to the fact that I could use "lifesteal" against undead creatures that did not technically have life. Still, this was the System, and not all of its rules made sense on the surface. I supposed health and life were interchangeable in System terms. Maybe once I Ascended I'd be able to learn how that worked, but for now I was just happy it did.

When I felt ready, I flapped my wings and leaped to the top of the inner wall. Finally getting a close-up look at the graveyard. Unfortunately, I was disappointed by the monsters within. Ghouls were the highest level, and they were only 55. I growled in disappointment, the rumbling sound startling the nearest undead.

No point in wasting my time with this graveyard. I'd leave them for the girls and other Ascension hopefuls to tackle later. This would be a fantastic place for them to farm XP.

Grumbling, I took off and flew west to see what was over there.

Before the Apocalypse, DFW airport had been cut down the middle by a highway. On the east side of the southern end was Terminal E, and on the west was a massive parking lot, equal in size to the terminal area. They were shaped like two semi-circles bisected by the highway. Same with the other terminals to the north, with three circles in total making up the airport proper. To the south and north of the actual terminals were more parking lots and other facilities, but those were not my concern at the moment.

From the air, I could tell the three circles of the airport had been turned into the massive complex of a cathedral. The north and south circles were graveyards, and in the middle rose an inner keep with even taller walls, raised up on a tall hill that had not existed before the Apocalypse. In the center of this hill, where a castle should be, instead grew a medieval cathedral, like something some archbishop would preside over. I was betting that was where the Level 95 Lich dungeon boss was located.

To be sure, I flew to the north and made a pass over the graveyard there, and my Treasure Sense ability let me know it was filled with Level 60 Restless Draugr, Level 65 Draugr Archers, Level 70 Draugr Warriors, and Level 75 Draugr Lords. Unlike the southern graveyard, this circle was primarily made of barrow tombs and other earthen mounds.

The Restless wandered all over. The archers seemed to be stationed on top of the mounds. Warriors guarded the entrances. I had to assume the Lords occupied the interior of the tombs. The only reason I knew the Lords were even there was that a few of the mounds appeared to have been excavated, with their interiors exposed. Inside those, I could see Lords sitting on thrones or lying upon large stone slabs as they would have been when they were laid to rest.

Except, of course, none of that was real, and they were mere dungeon monsters, the scene merely one of ambience created by the System. Still, the exposed tombs showed me that they had monsters within that were capable of earning me experience, and if all the tombs contained Lords, then considering the sheer number of these mounds, I should be able to gain at least a couple levels here and maybe put a dent in the number of high-level mobs in this damned dungeon. The System would regenerate them eventually, but hopefully doing so would divert resources away from expanding the dungeon and sending out monsters into the surrounding city.

Any way you looked at it, this was definitely the place I needed to be. I would try to ignore the things below Level 75 as much as possible, but those Lords would get me my next five levels if there were enough of them.

Unfortunately, they were spread out among all the barrows, and I learned even before landing that the archers were a pain in the ass. As I made a low pass over the outer edge of the barrow grounds, one of the bastards hit me! An arrow sprouted from a spot where two of my scales met. It stung, and itched!

The assholes shot arrows infused with necrotic energy!

-100 Health
Health: 5300/5400

Then more arrows thunked into my hide!

-100 Health
-100 Health
-100 Health
Health: 5000/5400

I was very thankful that my passive Resistance skill included protection against Rot, Disease, and Necrotic. Even so, it was only 30% resistance, so after taking a few hits my health dropped by over 400 points. Not a lot compared to my 5,400 total HP, but I had not even had a chance to land and engage the targets I was after. At that rate, I wouldn't last long here.

That meant I needed to be a bit stealthy if I didn't want to tank everything in sight. I quickly flew down into the outer zone and introduced a few more wandering zombies to my Voidflame, bringing me back to full health, and I was finally ready to begin leveling up.

However, before I flew back over the wall, I transitioned back into my human form, albeit with my wings, horns, and tail manifested. I was small enough now that I wouldn't easily be seen from a distance by all the monsters.

More importantly, I wouldn't have been able to enter the barrow to reach the Lords in my dragon form. I was simply too big for the narrow passages.

I activated Stealth before cresting the wall. With a quick sweep over the area, I noted several exposed Lords and planned my route to attack those first.

CHAPTER 6

LORD'S A LEAPING!

LANDING a short distance away from the first Lord, I took a moment to observe and prepare. What I saw was creepy as hell. They reminded me a little of the undead in that game, Sky... something. Except these weren't nice, clean, pixelated video game monsters. They were true to the ancient Icelandic and Nordic legends, and in the flesh—rotting flesh. Stinky, decomposing, maggot-filled flesh. The whole graveyard stank, but being this close, every little detail was vomit-inducing.

As I stood there, I began to question my life choices.

Do I really need to kill these?

I was sure there were far less disgusting dungeon monsters in this level range. I even had a compass that would point right at high-level dungeons...

I refrained from sighing because that would have entailed taking a deep breath. *Yuck.*

With a shrug, I extended my claws. These needed to be destroyed anyway, otherwise this dungeon would only grow. Maybe I'd get lucky and receive a magic item in loot that would let me cancel out my sense of smell. My stomach clenched again as another wave of rot rolled over me, and I hoped the System had mercy for once. One could only hope.

The Lord sat upon a throne of bones, looking like a rotting corpse garbed in regal finery, with a wicked-looking sword grasped in one hand, laid across its lap. Around it were rotting banners and shields of its slain enemies—tribute to its greatness in life.

Well, fictional life, since none of this is real.

Growling, I hit the Lord with Void Lance. It cost a crap ton of mana, but there were plenty of lower-level undead around that I could farm for mana using Voidflame, so I wasn't going to skimp here just to conserve resources. Besides, I was here for experience, so the faster I could eliminate the Lords, the faster I would level up.

The spell slammed into the undead, pinning it to its throne and the stone wall behind it, doing 'extreme' damage. It also inflicted Nullification, which would strip it of any buffs it might have, and applied Cold, which should slow it.

Sadly, it was not destroyed outright even with our level difference, which went to show just how powerful these bastards were. They weren't quite mini-bosses, but they were the highest-level elite undead in this zone of the dungeon, so they were no slouches.

Worse, I noticed that the Cold effect did nothing. As soon as the spell hit, its eyes lit with an icy fire that instantly dropped the temperature in the area, applying its own cold debuff in an area of effect and slowing me instead. That was worrisome. To make matters even worse, it began to grow and expand in size, preparing to stand and join battle with me.

Nope!

Not wanting to take any chances or get closer, I hit it with Greater Void Bolt, this time aimed directly at its head. It only did high damage, but my first attack had plunged its health bar below the halfway point, so this attack dropped it deep into the red and slammed it back into its throne again. I was slowed, but the lord took a moment to recover, giving me time to get off one more attack before it could. I hit it with Shadow Surge, another high-damage spell. This one applied a Weakness debuff, but it didn't matter. The damage from this spell was enough to finish it. It collapsed, the hatred in its cold, glowing eyes fading.

Unfortunately, because this was one of the open mounds, our fight attracted attention, and I could hear the archers and warriors shambling forward to investigate. I had a few more seconds before my Stealth wore off, so I hid behind the throne in non-magical concealment.

The lower-level monsters—Archers and Warriors—came near, but didn't see me. I knew they would eventually, but I only needed to wait out the sixty seconds for the body to disappear. There was no way I was leaving fifteen platinum mana coins behind. My claws flexed as I stared at the fading corpse, already counting the coins that hadn't dropped yet. My inner dragon would rather fight them all than not claim its treasure. I had never, in my first life, even seen platinum mana coins, and this one kill would more than double the number I had right now.

Unfortunately, non-magical stealth wasn't enough. Maybe their cold blue glowing eyes could see heat, but whatever the case, they spotted me after only a few seconds. I got pinned by three arrows before I could take action.

-100 Health
-100 Health

-100 Health

The one good thing about this situation was that they were crowding into what was essentially a tomb chamber only twenty feet wide by thirty feet long. In other words, well within range of my AOE attacks.

I dodged two more arrows and then cast Night's End. Darkness pooled in the open-air chamber as if night was flooding into the room, tendrils coalescing out of shadow and restraining the undead from fleeing—not that they would. Undead typically had no sense of self-preservation, and these were no different. Even if they had tried to flee, it would not have made a difference.

In an instant, the night was made manifest and concentrated into a power that was terrifyingly strong before exploding in a detonation that rocked the chamber, causing dust, debris, and rock to burst outward. Thankfully, I was both hidden by the throne and just outside the radius of the spell.

The archers and warriors were not so lucky. This was my extreme-damage AOE, and after my third Class upgrade, it had undergone a significant increase in power, as had all my spells. It had been frightening before. Now it was downright terrifying. These lower-level enemies, more than twenty levels below me, stood no chance. Only the Level 70 warriors survived, and even then, only barely. It was nothing for me to walk around the remains of the room afterward and end them with my claws as they struggled to rise despite missing limbs and severe damage to their undead bodies. That had the added benefit of restoring a chunk of my mana and health.

Sadly, it did not negate the necrotic effect of the two arrows that were piercing my side and the one in my left arm. They hurt and itched like the devil, but I yanked them free before going around the room to dispatch the warriors. My health bar returned to full, but the necrotic status effect continued draining my health over time. Luckily, I had a solution for that. I cast Dispelling Burst on myself, which removed status effects within a twenty-foot radius, including any negative effects on me.

"Note to self. Avoid open battles like this."

Although my greedy dragon heart was dancing a jig at the treasure I had just earned. Once I collected all the mana coins from the denizens of this barrow, I was 115 platinum mana coins richer. That was nothing to sneeze at, but if I went around doing this at every tomb, I'd run dry of mana very quickly, and I wouldn't be getting any EXP from anything other than the Draugr Lords.

"Not worth it, even for the treasure."

The dragon in me disagreed, but I was on a time crunch here. I needed to hit Level Cap as soon as possible. I had no idea how long Ascension would take, but I couldn't imagine it would be easy considering I had needed to kill Champions just to earn the right to do the quest.

Before moving on, I considered my strategy. Since my upgrade, Void Travel, which replaced Shadow Walk, only had a fifteen-second cooldown. Meaning I could use that to move from barrow to barrow and bypass all the minions to get straight to the Lords. Three spells to kill a Lord. One minute to wait for the treasure to drop and scoop it up. Unfortunately, Void Lance had a five-minute cooldown, so that would limit my pace.

In other words, I could kill Lords roughly every seven minutes, and if I used my claws instead of Greater Void Bolt and Shadow Surge, I could regen my mana as well. One extreme spell and one extreme physical attack should take out any Lord, and it would keep me topped up.

Yuck.

The thought of physically touching the nasty, rotting corpses with my claws grossed me out, but I did have the Cleanse spell, which I could cast after each kill. It would drain a little mana, but with the mana leeching I'd gain from that extreme-damage Dragon's Rend attack, I should more than cover any costs.

"All right, that's what I'll do." It was decided!

With no further ado, I put the plan into motion. It worked with surprising efficiency. Roughly every six minutes, I was killing another Lord.

Thanks to my 269 Endurance stat, I was able to keep that pace up all day. It quickly became tedious and monotonous, but it was definitely efficient. I couldn't imagine a way to earn experience faster than that.

As the day dragged on, I couldn't help but worry about Viki, Morgan, Brian, and Margaret. However, I knew Morgan would use Commune to call me if they got into any trouble. Likewise, I knew my girls would be checking on the other pair from time to time, so I kept myself focused on the task at hand.

We started at dawn, then spent an hour eliminating all the zombies wandering just outside the walls. Then I'd spent another half hour making it through the outer zone of the dungeon with the damned Wraiths before starting my leveling. I estimated it was roughly ten hours of straight level grinding, and in that time I killed exactly 100 Lords, earning me a cool 750,000 experience points. That was enough to get me three levels and more than halfway into Level 93.

I could have kept going, but it was getting dark out and I needed to return to the others to get them back to camp. Margaret and Brian had camps to run, and while I wanted them to keep rescuing the people of Irving, I also wanted to see what they'd managed to accomplish.

Besides, with my stats, it wasn't like I actually needed sleep anymore. Well, maybe an hour or two, but really, I could keep going like this for two or three days and probably not suffer too much from it. I decided I would come back later in the evening and keep going until I hit Level 95—assuming nothing happened to derail that plan. That way I could start the day tomorrow by moving on to the Cathedral up on top of the big hill. There would surely be higher-level monsters there, and after I hit 95, these Lords would no longer give me any EXP.

With the dungeon boss being Level 95, the other monsters up there should be Level 80 to 90. Since I was limited to only gaining experience from monsters within twenty levels of me, I could get all the way to Level Cap from whatever was up there, and in a Stronghold Dungeon like this, I was sure there would be more than enough monsters.

Not wanting to waste time dealing with the Wraiths again, I used my new Teleport spell for the first time, jumping directly back to the skies over the dungeon's outer wall.

CHAPTER 7

BRIAN AND THE EXODUS

OUT FROM UNDER the Gloom as I had begun to call the clouds over the dungeon, I could see the sun was down, but it was still light outside. I was still in my human form so my flight was a bit slower and my vision was a little less keen, but I could easily follow the trail of destruction that Viki and Morgan had left in their wake. They had traveled north along the tops of the wall, destroying every skeleton they came across.

However, besides the destruction that some of their spells and attacks had caused to the wall itself, I was a little surprised that I found piles of bones from time to time. Meaning that they had harvested something from those monsters, which made me curious. What could they have taken from skeletons? Normal dungeon monsters could be harvested for meat or their hide, but I scratched at the base of my right horn wondering what a skeleton would have worth keeping.

“Well, I’ll find out soon enough, I suppose.”

I continued flying northeast, and made it to the junction of the wall I was following where it made a sharp turn to the northwest. At that point there was a pretty massive tower and gate where the Bush Turnpike met Highway 114. The highways were still there, but were easily within bow shot of the towering dungeon walls. Considering the refugees would need to pass this point to follow the Turnpike to travel north to get to the Colony, it was critical that the skeletons were defeated. Otherwise, the survivors would be blocked from fleeing to safety.

Sure enough, I could see a large crowd of several thousand people gathered on the highway, unable to proceed further.

So it didn't surprise me to find a battle in progress atop the tower. Viki, Morgan, Brian, and Margaret were all facing off against a massive skeleton mini-boss and its elite minions.

My first instinct was to dive down and assist or protect them, but I hung back. They had chosen this battle, so they must believe they could handle it.

As I watched, I was impressed. This wasn't exactly a totally balanced group, but they weren't a bad mix either.

Brian never yielded ground despite the press of enemies, Viki's shots threading past him without ever crossing his space, while Morgan and Margaret staggered their casts so one of them was always ready to react.

Brian, the Knight Class, was standing up front like a tank in his platemail armor, ready to fend off any monsters that tried to pass him to the others. Viki was standing off to the right and behind Brian as far as she could get from the monsters, her bow firing deadly spell enhanced arrows. Morgan and Margaret were both healers, each with a small arsenal of offensive spells. They also had buffs that helped ensure Brian was more than up to the task of tanking the bad guys.

It was honestly impressive.

I hovered, my heart swelling with pride as I watched my girls and the team systematically take down the enemies.

I found myself counting kills without meaning to, tracking their rhythm the way I used to track my own.

Just as the group of minions was starting to clump up around Brian due to his taunt skill, Viki lobbed an arrow that shot high into the air then descended almost straight down, landing between the boss and the minions, literally detonating with shadow and void energy. The power crushed magically animated bones that weren't easily damaged. A high damage AOE spell-arrow for sure.

At almost the exact instant of the shadow explosion, Margaret cast a beam of light that hit the boss in the chest, but like Viki's arrow, it too was a high damage AOE attack.

BOOM!

The Light and Shadow energies collided as the two spells overlapped their radiuses of effect. Rather than cancelling each other out, it was like Matter and Anti-Matter mixing. The results were far more powerful than they could have expected. Every combatant on the tower top was launched backward away from the point of the explosion.

The team each slammed into the stone crenelations of the battlements with the force of a Mack truck. Stone cracked and dust burst outward on impact, ringing through the tower like a struck bell.

Morgan was knocked unconscious, as was Margaret. Viki and Brian lost an unfortunate number of Health Points, but otherwise shook off the impact with only a moment of stunned confusion.

The monsters, on the other hand, were not so lucky. They had been the targets of the spells, and were at the epicenter of where the two opposing energies mixed. Not a single minion survived. There were bones everywhere.

Only the boss remained animate, although its health was deep in the red now. However, it too had been thrown away from the epicenter and slammed into the wall opposite from where the team impacted.

That gave Viki plenty of time to stop seeing stars and get back to her feet. The boss had only just begun stumbling forward when she began launching arrow after arrow into its skull, Duskfire, Soulpiercer, and finally Eclipse. I recognized her attacks, having seen them all this morning.

The mini-boss barely made it ten steps before its skull shattered, extinguishing the evil glow in its eyes.

I dove down toward the tower, but Brian was up and checking on the two healers before I could arrive.

Before I could land, Viki had also rushed over to their downed comrades and was checking Morgan's condition, looking frantic.

Still, I wasn't worried. Thanks to my upgraded Treasure Sense/Analyze mix of skills, I could see their health bars, and they were fine, just knocked out. Both bars hovered stubbornly above the red zone despite the chaos.

I landed a few feet from Viki, but she didn't notice me in her worry over Morgan.

"Please be alright! Please be alright!" She kept saying.

"Viki, Morgan's going to be fine. She still has over a hundred health points. We'll feed her a healing potion in a minute if she doesn't wake up on her own."

It took a moment for my young companion to register what I had said, then realize that I had returned. She looked torn between wanting to rush over and hug me, versus cradling Morgan's unconscious form.

I solved her problem by hurrying over and putting a reassuring hand on her back. "Just give her a minute, she'll be fine. In fact, she's starting to stir now."

A few seconds later, Morgan's eyes snapped open and she began to flail around. "What happened? Is everyone alright?"

We quickly reassured her the fight was over.

"Oh, Liam, you're back. Dang, how long was I out?"

Chuckling, I gestured for her to be calm. "It's fine, I was watching the battle from above. You've only been unconscious for a minute or two at most."

Her face fell, disappointment evident from her pursed lips and furrowed brows. "Dang, we meant to grab the boss's sword. Even the stuff the minions carried would have been worth distributing to the people below."

Now I was confused. "What do you mean? Other than harvesting meat and other body parts, you can't keep gear and weapons from dungeon monsters. If you could, that would have made a huge difference in my first life."

Viki chimed in. "That's not true. If you grab them before they disappear you can keep the weapons and armor. That didn't work in normal dungeons, but we discovered we could keep stuff from the ones here."

That floored me. I'd never heard of such a thing in my first life. I actually stopped mid-thought, the implications hitting harder than the boss had.

"Could it be something special about this dungeon, or is that a feature of all Stronghold dungeons, I wonder?"

Morgan shrugged. "I don't know, but it works here. We've been collecting weapons and armor all day. Not every skeleton has something worth keeping, but a bunch of them have."

I facepalmed. "Damn, if that's true, I should have farmed loot from the high level monsters I've been hunting today. I've just been collecting the coins. I earned 1600 platinum mana coins today. That absolutely blows my mind."

A little voice inside argued that I deserved the money and I could use it to upgrade my gear when the shop opened. I could buy dozens of skill stones with that. Still, my conscience argued that those Lords' weapons and armor could have equipped a hundred men or women with gear far better than they'd normally be able to find until they were well past their first Class upgrade. The gear might look like corroded and time-worn equipment ready to fall apart, but that was just its appearance. They were Level 75, meaning their gear was at least Grand quality, maybe higher.

"Well, crap! If I'd known that, I would have saved a ton of gear. Shit, it would probably be better than what Brian is using now."

"Hey, what about me?" Brian entered the conversation as he helped Margaret over to sit down next to Morgan.

"I just learned that in this Stronghold dungeon we can harvest the gear the monsters carry. That's not the case with normal dungeons. And since I've been fighting Level 75s all day, I could have given you better armor and weapons than what you've got now. It would look like crap, but the stats should be way higher than what you've got."

He looked a little disappointed, but then shrugged. The tension in his shoulders eased as he rolled them once, like he was physically setting the thought aside. "Oh, well. I'll upgrade my stuff eventually anyway. No big."

Margaret also seemed interested, but she and Morgan began to cast healing magics on each other while we talked.

"Well, I'm going to come back after we sort out those folks below and take a break for dinner, so I'll get you a set of gear. I'm a level and a half from hitting 95. At that point I'll have to move on to the final area of the dungeon."

Viki's eyes got big. She actually leaned forward on her toes without realizing it. "Holy crap! You're almost to 95? That's awesome!"

I shrugged. "Once I figured out the method for hunting the Lords without dealing with all their minions, it was pretty tedious. Probably one of the most boring hunts I've had. I wouldn't be doing it except we need to cull the monsters here to keep this place from expanding. If the System is burning resources on recreating the big monsters, that's less mana it has to create zombies to spill out into the city."

"Speaking of the city," Brian said, "I'm going to stay with the group down there and lead them toward my camp. Please let everyone know I should arrive tomorrow sometime with the refugees. Ask the folks at camp to harvest as much food from the dungeons as they can. We've got a lot of hungry mouths to feed down there."

I stood and looked over the battlements down at the crowd below. There had to be at least several thousand people, all milling about, waiting for Brian and Margaret to give the signal that all was clear. Even from here, the noise carried upward in a constant low roar of voices, fear, and movement.

Gesturing with my thumb over to the chest that appeared where the boss had fallen, "You guys should open your chest, collect the loot, and get after it then."

Having healed each other, Margaret stepped forward. "If you would be so kind, as much as I want to continue helping the refugees here, I need to get back to my people. My absence will have been difficult on my group."

I nodded. "Of course. You've fulfilled my request, and I appreciate it. By the way, were you and Brian successful in spreading the word to everyone in the area?"

The older woman gave an elegant hand gesture to indicate so-so results. "We made every effort. We spoke with hundreds of people and shared intelligence on the situation. They, in turn, spread the word until we have the rather large group present on the highway below. However, it is inconceivable that everyone in the area was informed."

"I understand. Thank you again. I'll transform and fly you back to your fortress once Brian joins the crowd below and lets them know not to lose their minds when they see a dragon."

Viki giggled, but then became serious. Her smile faded as she glanced down at the crowd again. "Yeah, they've been through a lot. We shouldn't scare them."

Brian climbed up between two of the crenelations and raised a hand in victory as he shouted to the crowd below. "We beat the boss. It is safe to pass by the tower now."

I was impressed. He was using the Command ability of his class to project his voice so that all could hear. I had been a Knight in my first life, so I was well familiar with the skill. I kind of wished I had it now, in fact.

"One of our people can transform into a dragon. It is a System ability, he is not a monster. Please remain calm and do not fear. He will be returning Mrs. Margaret back to her camp, but I will stay with you tonight and lead you toward my camp where there will be food for everyone. I'll do my best to keep everyone safe from any beasts or monsters on the journey."

Seeing the Knight standing there between two massive stones, with one hand on each, speaking down to the crowd below, an amusing thought struck me, and I couldn't help but quip, "Alright, Moses, lead the people to the promised land. Just make sure you survive to get them there. You should be high enough level to handle anything between here and there as long as you don't stray from the highway."

He turned and smirked at me. "I'll be fine. My biggest worry is the size of the crowd. I won't be able to keep an eye on everyone." He looked to Viki and Morgan. "Any chance you two would join me on the hike back to the Colony? If I take the front and you two guard our rear, we should be relatively safe. I'm worried beasts might pick off stragglers, and I won't even know it happened until word is passed up to the front."

I had planned to take the girls back to camp for dinner and a good night's sleep, but Brian had a point, and it wasn't like the delay of the evening and half a day tomorrow would make a lot of difference. They both looked tired, but steady, the kind of tired that came from winning.

Seeing their nods, I accepted their decision. They could always summon me if they got into any real trouble on the way, although I doubted they would face any significant challenge on the walk.

"By the way, how many levels did you guys get today?"

Viki beamed as she proudly announced, "We made it to Level 37 today!"

I gave her a proud smile. "Nice! That's decent progress. What's that, five levels in a single day?"

"Yep!" Then she frowned. **Her shoulders dipped just a little.** "About the same as yesterday, really. I'm just worried. If we only get five levels a day, I'm not sure if we can reach the Level Cap before it's too late."

Morgan took Viki's hand in hers and squeezed. "We'll make it. Don't worry. And even if we don't make it all the way to Level 100, we'll still be plenty strong enough to beat the Champions for the other races. Even with their foreknowledge it will take them many days to make it to the Level Cap, and they will still need to fulfill the other requirement as well, so we'll have a big head start and can Ascend before them as long as nothing happens."

Morgan was right. They had a big head start. I just hoped they could keep it. The thing that worried me was that I didn't know whether the other races already knew about the prerequisite to being allowed to join the Ascension quest. If they did, then I was sure they would all be gunning to claim one of the seven slots.

Then a suspicious thought occurred to me.

Was this another manipulation of Earth's AI Node?

If the races did know, then they would have to attack each other to claim a spot. They wouldn't know where the human champion was since they hadn't come to Earth early and received a Compass like the five who had come to hunt me down. That would mean they would have to target other invaders near their own foothold bases.

Whichever species knew about the prerequisite would be gunning for other invaders to ensure they earned their three Champion kills so their own candidate could Ascend.

Oh, that devious, devious bastard.

I burst out laughing, and the others looked at me like I was crazy and asked what was so funny.

"Sorry, I just had an evil thought, but I don't really want to share. Big Brother could be listening after all." I gestured at the sky.

Viki didn't look happy about being left in the dark, but I was afraid that if the System learned of what our AI Node was up to, it might take steps to stop things. If the invaders warred with one another, then humanity would be a less juicy target compared to their actual competitors.

With a sigh, I nodded toward Margaret. "Ready?"

She nodded her agreement.

Right then. It was time to transform back into my dragon form.

CHAPTER 8
REST AND SAFETY

I FELT a little guilty about not sticking around to escort the refugees, but my time was better spent taking a short break to get Margaret back to her people and then getting some dinner. I was a little bummed that Viki and Morgan weren't coming with me, but it made sense for them to help Brian. The way they had nodded without hesitation told me they were already committed to seeing it through. They would probably finish the escort mission around mid-day tomorrow unless I missed my guess.

My passenger wasn't very talkative as I flew her back to her fortress, so I left her alone for the few minutes it took. When we landed, however, she seemed to be in an introspective mood.

I didn't bother to change back into human form, but she didn't seem to mind as she spoke, looking me in the eye.

"I knew it was bad out there, but I had not realized just how desperate people were. Our group here had the misfortune to be set upon by this stronghold and captured. Even so, before that we had at least been cohesive and aimed to find shelter and do what was necessary to survive."

Her expression turned sad. She clasped her hands together tightly, knuckles whitening for just a moment before she forced them to relax. "Today, I saw a great many who had entirely given up hope. I think that if you had not arranged for Brian and me to spread the message of shelter and hope, all too many would not have survived for long. Even now, I fear we only reached a percentage of the survivors." She steepled her fingers, tapping her lips as she wrestled with her thoughts before her expression changed, becoming resolute.

"I want to formally thank you. We expressed our appreciation after the rescue, but I did not have the context to understand what you had given us here with this fortress." She paused again and sighed before adding, "I see that you are working toward the greater good, and I want you to know that we will stand ready to support you in whatever way we can."

I was a little taken aback by the implications of her words. The way she held my gaze without wavering made it clear this was not casual gratitude. She wasn't saying thanks and offering vague help. Her meaning was clear. She was acknowledging me as a higher authority and committing her group of survivors to back my decisions. That wasn't a decision she made lightly, and I could see it written in her body language and determined expression.

Taking a deep breath before responding, I considered what to say. I wasn't looking to become king of Dallas or anything like that, but having one of the major camps officially backing my plays would be valuable indeed.

"Thank you, Margaret. It will be important to have everyone united in our goals, so that means a lot. For now, build up this fortress as a place of refuge and a waystation for survivors as they move out through the city toward safety. I'll be setting up the Safe Zone north of McKinney tonight. The best thing you can do for now is group up the refugees who find this place so they can defend themselves as they head north. Train up those you feel are trustworthy and maybe organize an escort team to shepherd groups north. Hell, you're one of the most intelligent people I've met. I'm sure you can see what needs to be done without me giving directions."

That brought a small smile to her tired face. "Thank you again. I will make the arrangements and ensure that our group here looks out for those in need. Now off with you, and get yourself some rest. Goodness knows I need dinner and a nap!"

Chuckling, the sound rumbling deep in my draconic chest, I nodded my massive head in acknowledgment. "I'm off. I'll look in on you again in a couple days if I can."

With that, I launched myself into the sky and headed back to the Colony Camp to get an hour or so of rest before moving on.

As always, my arrival caused a stir, but I quickly passed on word to Carl with a "C" that Brian and the girls were escorting a huge group of survivors here and would arrive sometime around mid-day tomorrow. After that, I brought out my tent and took a nap.

I woke feeling fairly rested only a couple hours later. I wanted to go right back to the Necropolis Stronghold and gain that level and a half to hit 95, but I had another task that needed doing first. It would be irresponsible of me to go into the final section of that massive dungeon before setting up the Safe Zone.

I wasn't planning on dying, but fighting a boss the same level as me, or even just a couple levels down, would not be without risk, especially the boss of a dungeon like that. And knowing the System, I wouldn't be at all surprised if the Safe Zone reward just vanished if I died.

So rather than going to earn more EXP, I was going to set up a Safe Zone. After putting my tent back in my storage, I wandered over to the cook fires and was handed a plate of meat. It was all they had, but it was still better than the couple of MREs I still had from that first goblin dungeon in the missile silo.

Thanking the older lady who fussed over me, I walked back out into the area outside the camp before taking off. I didn't change back into my full dragon body, but stayed in my hybrid form. I couldn't fly quite as fast, but I also wouldn't cause a panic if someone looked up in the night and saw a dragon fly across the silhouette of the moon. Most people hadn't heard about me yet, after all.

From the Colony, I flew northeast, passing over Frisco, then McKinney, and continuing on over Melissa. I only slowed down and descended when I saw the fortress that had been the Orc Stronghold dungeon. That seemed to be the logical place to center the Safe Zone. It was a System-built location, meaning it would not degrade or fall apart eventually the way anything human-made would. It was also on a highway past which refugees would migrate, and beyond it was mostly farmland and woods.

Those were the thoughts on my mind as I came in and landed on the highway outside the fortress. I didn't want the folks inside to think I was a monster attacking after all. To that end, I made my wings and other draconic features completely disappear, looking somewhat like my old self. Of course, even without the draconic features, my hair color and eyes had changed, as had my basic build. I was pretty ripped before, but I had nearly 300 in all my stats now. **The way my clothes hung differently on me was a constant reminder of that.** Not to be immodest, but I knew I looked like some Greek god with void powers at this point. That couldn't be helped.

I just hoped there would still be some people here from the group I rescued so they would recognize me.

Very much to my disappointment, the first person I came across was Shawn Gornson, the man who blamed me for everything. He and three other men were walking patrol along the road to watch for both monsters and refugees.

It was dark, and I could easily walk past them without them seeing me. The moon was just past full tonight, but it had set half an hour ago, leaving the world with nothing but starlight. There were no city lights to reflect off clouds and light up the night. At most, there were fires around which survivors huddled.

One such fire burned at what had been the front gate of the facility before it had been converted from a trash dump to an Orc Stronghold. Several men sat around that fire, while Shawn's group patrolled along the highway. On the one hand, it was good to see that the people here were actively guarding the fortress and hopefully welcoming refugees. On the other, I didn't really want to get into a confrontation with the man who blamed me for the apocalypse.

With my Dark Vision, I could see the patrol as clearly as if it were a cloudy afternoon. I doubted they could see me, or they would have raised the alarm. However, they were marching back toward the fire even as I approached. I could wait in order to avoid the angry man, but the dragon in me refused to give in to social fears.

Sighing, I walked toward the fire and called out, "Hey, there!"

The men jumped up, startled by my voice in the night. The downside of having a fire is that it wipes out your night vision, which was not too great at the best of times for a normal human. That meant they had no warning until they heard my voice. They clutched makeshift spears and other weapons, although one man had one of the crude

System-generated swords from the orc arena. He had it out and was holding it more or less steady, despite a slight tremble in his hands.

I slowly walked into the light. "I'm Liam. Not sure if any of you remember me."

The guy with the orc sword blinked in surprise. "Yeah, I remember you! You rescued us from the orcs!" Despite his words, he looked a little confused. He tilted his head slightly, eyes narrowing as he studied me in the firelight. "You look kinda different though."

Chuckling, I gestured for them to be at ease. "It's me. I've leveled up a lot since I left. What, four days ago now?"

The guy nodded. "Yeah, seems like forever ago with everything happening. I'm Eric Babineaux, by the way. My wife and daughter were some of the ones you saved on Shaman Hill. Thank ya again for that." Even so, he was still looking at me like I was a strange bug or something, his gaze flicking over my shoulders and arms as if expecting to find some obvious explanation.

"I definitely recognize you, but damn, you look a lot different. Your eyes are almost glowing in the firelight like a gator in the bayou, and you're taller and stronger looking than I remember. How much didja level up to make that much difference?"

I was about to answer when Shawn and his team walked into the firelight. He didn't recognize me at first, but seemed wary, as you might when seeing someone dangerous unexpectedly in the night. His steps slowed, and his posture stiffened the moment he caught sight of me.

Since he didn't cry out or attack, I answered Eric. "More than sixty levels. I hit my third Class upgrade last night. I'm hoping to hit Level Cap tomorrow, or the next day at the latest."

"Holy sheeit, man! Seriously? I'm only Level 6, and that's after we killed a boatload of mutated critters."

That was when Shawn connected the dots and gasped. “Bastard! It’s you!”

Eric rolled his eyes, as if this was an argument they’d had repeatedly, but before he could say anything, Shawn launched himself at me, fist drawn back.

I let him hit me.

His knuckles connected with my jaw and I just stood there. My head barely shifted from the impact, but his arm recoiled hard enough that he stumbled a half step. His eyes got big and he howled in pain.

“Fucker! You broke my hand!”

It had been a good punch. I felt it, even if I didn’t allow myself to react. I didn’t want to escalate the situation, but at the same time, I wasn’t going to cater to this man’s delusions. If he wanted to hate me and blame me for the apocalypse, then he was welcome to it. I could snuff him out with a single non-skilled attack, but despite my dragon-blood urging me to do just that, I didn’t want to be that kind of person.

“Please don’t do that again.” I looked at Shawn with a slight frown. “You can hate me all you want, but if you attack me when I don’t expect it, I might react instinctively and hurt you by mistake.”

Blood vessels stood out on the other man’s forehead like he was going to have an aneurysm as he cradled his fist. His breathing was harsh and uneven, each breath hissing through clenched teeth. “All this shit is your fault! The AI thing sent you back in time and you caused the apocalypse!”

“Dude, did you not listen to what I told everyone the other day? I didn’t ‘cause’ the apocalypse. I lived through it for twenty years. The damned AI realized it screwed up and sent me back to try and fix its mistake. Speaking of which, I completed a Quest and earned the right to set up a Safe Zone, which is why I’m here.”

Shawn looked like the definition of 'surly' as he nursed his injured hand, but he kept quiet.

Eric blinked in surprise at my words, as did some of the others. "Hang on, Safe Zone? What's that?" The men around the fire nodded at their leader's question.

"It's a ten mile radius area where no new dungeons will form and no monsters will enter. It'll give the survivors a chance to start rebuilding, minus the technology."

Eric's eyes went big as he heard that. "No, shit!?" He whooped and grinned like he'd just won the lottery.

"Yeah, really. Keep in mind, any monsters, dungeons, or mutated beasts will still be inside the zone. They won't just disappear, but no more new ones will be created. Don't destroy the dungeons inside the Safe Zone. They'll be good resources to help you all level up. You should definitely hunt down all the mutated animals though."

Shawn hadn't lost all his fight and picked my comments to take offense at. "You want us to let dungeons stay even when you are supposedly making this area safe? What kind of idiot are you? You're on the monsters' side!"

Eric gave the man a look. "Shawn, don't be an idijit! He beat this dungeon and saved us. Now he's here to make the area into a Safe Zone. Why would he do that if he was on the System's side?"

Not willing to let it go, Shawn snarled, "He was just doing that to level up. He doesn't care about us. He only cares about himself! He probably wants to make himself King or something!"

Now it was my turn to roll my eyes. "I don't have time to rule anyone. The people in the Safe Zone can elect their leaders when they feel like it. For now, the leaders of the various camps are the closest thing we've got to any kind of government."

Turning back to Eric and ignoring Shawn, I added, "Speaking of which, there are three camps in town that I know of so far. One in McKinney, one down in Plano, and one over in the Colony. Including this place, that makes four groups that are somewhat organized and helping the survivors. And considering this is the center of the only Safe Zone on the planet at the moment, you guys can expect there will be thousands of refugees settling around here pretty soon. You should find the dungeons and figure out which ones can be harvested for food and building materials."

One of the guys with Eric asked, "What do you mean, harvested?"

He apparently hadn't been there when I gave everyone the speech about how things worked under the System, so I quickly explained how they could get useful things besides just treasure from the dungeons.

It was like a lightbulb went off among the men around the fire. A few of them leaned closer, voices overlapping as excitement replaced tension. Some started talking excitedly about searching out the dungeons.

Shawn just stewed in his anger, seeing that the others were ignoring him.

I could see the sullen resentment in his eyes and wondered if he was going to be a problem, and whether or not to eliminate any threat he posed. His stare lingered on me a heartbeat too long, hard and unblinking. Then I caught myself and shook those thoughts out of my head. Bad dragon! No murder for the sake of convenience!

Still, I had learned some hard lessons in my first life, and I would keep my eye on him. If he looked like he was going to be a serious problem, I would do what I had to do, even if it meant getting my hands dirty.

I stepped over to Eric and spoke quietly so only he could hear. "I'm going to claim the Quest reward now. Please watch my back and make sure Shawn doesn't do anything stupid, okay?"

He gave me a nod. "Sure. I gotcha."

I had planned to do this up on top of the fortress hill, but I'd already wasted too much time on this conversation, and I just knew that if I went into the fortress, everyone would want to talk, talk, talk. It was time to get this over with so I could get back to leveling.

I stepped away from the fire and out into the night. Shawn had tried to follow, but I saw Eric step in his way. "Easy, man. Let the boss do his work. Setting up a Safe Zone is good for us, no matter what you think of him."

That started a low-key argument, but I ignored it. As long as I wasn't disturbed during this process, I didn't care.

I spoke to the night in a quiet, but determined voice. "System, claim Quest reward!"

Quest Reward: Safe Zone Established

Designation: Sanctuary Sphere – Radius 10 Miles
Effect: No new dungeons, monsters, or mutated beasts will be generated within the protected radius. External threats cannot enter the Zone.
Note: Creatures and anomalies already present inside the boundary will **remain** until eliminated or through natural attrition.

Safe Zone Template – Radius 10 Miles

Initializing Safe Zone configuration...
Projecting regional topography.

A translucent globe of light appeared in my vision, centered on the land beneath me. Terrain features, roads, creeks, and existing dungeon signatures rendered as shifting icons. A faint circle pulsed, ghosted over the map—a ten-mile radius that I could drag and reposition.

Effect Preview:

- No new dungeons, monsters, or mutated beasts will be generated within the highlighted radius.
- External monsters and mutated beasts will be unable to enter the Zone.
- Existing monsters, mutated beasts, and anomalies inside the Zone will not be expelled, destroyed, or otherwise altered.

Warning: Safe Zone placement is permanent. Only Level 3 or higher Ascended possess authority to alter Safe Zone boundaries or relocate protected areas.
Instruction: Adjust Zone position as desired, then confirm.

Confirm Safe Zone placement? [YES] / [NO]

I wasn't alone in seeing this. Apparently the projection was visible to everyone, and very quickly the men from the fire as well as Shawn's patrol gathered around and looked in awe at the map projection, their earlier arguments trailing off as attention shifted upward.

Eric exclaimed, "The dungeons! I can see the location of all the dungeons! Quick, you idjits, everyone memorize where they are!"

I chuckled at his enthusiasm, but I also took note of the locations. Although, to be fair, my mini-map populated with the icons as well, apparently in tune with the System projection, each marker snapping into place with clinical precision.

I was very tempted to select NO and then move around the city and reinitialize the quest reward over and over to fully map out the current dungeons and their locations. The idea itched at the back of my mind, like a puzzle begging to be exploited. Sadly, the map didn't give any detail on what kind of dungeons they were or what monsters were within. Still, just having them tagged on my mini-map was a huge bonus.

Speaking of which, my mini-map now revealed everything within this zone as if I had personally traveled there and mapped it out. Streets, landmarks, and empty stretches of darkness all resolved into clean, unmistakable lines. I really was tempted to use this quest reward like it was a game cheat and have it map the whole city area for me.

The only reason I didn't was that I knew I would get the ability to create zones once I Ascended, and running around right now trying to cheat my way into a filled-out map seemed like a waste of time when I'd gain that ability later, along with far more pressing responsibilities.

Having dismissed that idea, I focused on the map. Having this visual really helped. I moved the circle around to optimize its placement, watching areas slide in and out of the boundary as if they were pieces on a board. Eric and the others offered advice and suggestions as well, pointing and arguing quietly about which areas mattered most.

I finally settled on a position that took in the city of McKinney north of Wilson Creek, roughly half the town. It also stretched north to cover Van Alstyne, and south to include the northern tip of Lake Lavon, the boundary enclosing a broad swath of land that suddenly felt... protected.

When I was satisfied, I mentally selected "Yes," making the Safe Zone boundary permanent.

SYSTEM ANNOUNCEMENT

A Safe Zone has been established in this region by Liam Bell resulting from a Quest reward.

No new dungeons, monsters, or mutated beasts will be generated within the protected radius. External hostile creatures are unable to enter. Existing monsters and anomalies inside the Zone remain until destroyed or neutralized.

A cheer went up from the group, and the men at my sides pounded me on the back and shoulders in congratulations, hands striking armor and scale hard enough to rattle, voices overlapping in raw relief.

I was distracted, having been so focused on the map and establishing the Safe Zone, and had lost track of Shawn, my attention still half locked on the fading projection.

He had not lost track of me, however.

I felt a sudden sharp pain as a sword was thrust into my back, miraculously piercing my scales and armor and entering my flesh just above the kidney. The impact drove the breath from my lungs in a harsh grunt, heat flaring where steel met bone. The little fucker was literally trying to stab me in the back.

I reacted without thought. Before anyone around me even had time to register that something was wrong, I turned and extended my claws. The movement ripped the sword from my attacker's hands as my full strength came to bear on him, metal shrieking as it tore free.

Snarling, I stepped forward and slammed my claws into Shawn's chest up to my fist, talons exploding from his back.

"You little snake!" I yelled.

His eyes froze in a moment of surprise and terror, mouth opening as if to speak, having just enough time to realize his assassination attempt had failed before his heart was obliterated.

It took three or four seconds for the cheers to die out and for a stunned silence to reign as the others realized what had happened, the crackle of the fire suddenly loud in the absence of voices.

Eric looked on in shock and horror as he realized that his own sword was hanging from my back. He looked back and forth between Shawn and me for a moment before full understanding dawned.

"Oh, lord! Liam, I'm so sorry! Shawn... he took ma sword when I wasn't paying attention and—"

My claws were still piercing the dead man's chest, holding him aloft as I forced myself to calm down, breath dragging in slow, controlled pulls. I retracted my talons and Shawn fell to the ground, never to rise again. Then I turned to Eric as the other men backed away from me in fear, their moment of joy transformed by the act of violence.

Not trusting them, I reached back and pulled the orc blade from my own back, blood pouring out of the wound. The night air felt cold against exposed flesh as the blade came free. I knew I had some internal bleeding and perhaps a pierced organ or two, but at Level 93 my draconic regeneration would have me healed up in an hour or so, maybe less. Unfortunately, Shawn had so few Health Points that killing him hadn't made even a tiny dent in the damage he had done.

As all that registered in my mind, I shook my head at the leader of these guards. "Don't sweat it, Eric. I'll live." Trying to lighten the suddenly dark mood of the group, I added, "I'm surprised he was even strong enough to get through my armor."

It was a weak joke and it fell a little flat, but people began to relax as they realized I wasn't going to go berserk and slaughter them all, shoulders easing, weapons lowering a fraction.

They were all staring at me or the corpse of their former acquaintance, so I added, “Sorry. If he hadn’t pierced my armor and actually damaged me, I might have let him live, but the unexpected stab in the back... well, I just reacted.”

Eric, ever the spokesman of the group, waved his hands in dismissal. “Nah, you had every right. I’m sorry he got ma sword without me noticing. This is on me. If he’d used one of those crappy spears, he probably wouldn’t have got through that crocodile hide of yours.”

I chuckled. “Literally dragon hide, but yeah, I get what you mean. He must have used his strongest Class skill to manage that.”

Everyone else was finally relaxing, seeing that I wasn’t mad, so I looked around the group. “In the next few days, you’re going to get a lot of refugees up here. Make them welcome, and y’all figure out the dungeons so there’ll be enough food to feed everyone. I’ve got to get back to work.”

Eric threw me a salute with his sword, which he had wiped off on Shawn’s clothes. “We’ll do that. Don’t worry. I’ll let everyone in the fortress know in the morning. We’ll get it organized.”

I nodded. “Good man.” Then I manifested my wings and leaped into the air. Once I was out of sight, I added my tail and horns as well. I had already shocked the hell out of them by killing that idiot, Shawn. No need to really freak them out. A rueful thought crossed my mind. “Damn it. I should have warned them about me turning into a full dragon.”

Oh well. Next time, I suppose.

With that, I flew southwest toward the Necropolis. There was plenty of time before dawn for me to get to Level 95.

CHAPTER 9
EXODUS ON THE GROUND

Morgan's POV:

After the fight with the latest gate boss, they had descended down to the highway to the sea of people milling about. Brian took the lead and acted like Moses leading the people toward the promised land. Liam had made the joke before he left and it had stuck. Even many of the refugees jokingly were referring to the situation as the Exodus, a few even lifting tired hands in mock reverence when Brian passed.

At least, the ones still hopeful enough to joke around.

She was walking along near the middle of the crowd, ready to respond if they were attacked from either side. From where she stood she could see neither the front of the mass of people nor the rear. Thankfully, the highway was only fifty feet wide or so, meaning she didn't feel completely claustrophobic in the middle of such a big crowd, even with bodies pressed close on either side.

Every so often she would wander to one side of the highway or the other to look out for monsters or beasts and check on how the column of refugees was doing. They had left the gate area right after sundown and had continued to walk into the evening. The plan was to go for three hours or so tonight and get to a safe-enough place where they could hunker down for the evening. That meant getting past the Farmer's Branch industrial area.

Luckily, the Turnpike was elevated that entire way past that area. That would make it hard for any beasts or monsters to get at the people. Not impossible, but defensible enough that Brian had felt it was worth the risk. The alternative would have been to stay back here too close to the Necropolis dungeon with its wandering zombies, and that was something the refugees were eager to leave behind. Enough so that even with elderly and wounded among them, everyone agreed to get as far as they could tonight.

She was looking over the east side of the highway, scanning for monsters, and couldn't help but be impressed. No one had a count of how many people there were, but the column stretched nearly a mile long from front to back. It was a sight Morgan would never forget, both because it was impressive that so many would band together and make this trek, and because of how depressing it was, a moving line of silhouettes under the moon.

Just to her left, an elderly woman held the hand of her young grandson, who couldn't have been older than three or four. She had a bad limp and kept rubbing her back, but she kept going for her grandson's sake.

It broke Morgan's heart not to be able to heal everyone and ease all their burdens, but she only had so much mana. Restoration would fix the older woman right up—she'd be as spry as a woman fifteen or twenty years younger. All the arthritis, osteoporosis, and other joint or spinal issues causing that limp would regenerate and fix themselves in a matter of minutes. But that was her biggest and strongest healing spell, and it took a big chunk of her mana—mana she had to reserve for defending the group if they were attacked.

Every wince and pained sigh the granny let out was like a knife in her heart.

She was watching out over the concrete barrier at the edge of the highway when she heard the boy cry out, then begin to wail.

Morgan whipped around to see the child lying on the ground, holding a skinned and bleeding knee, and she couldn't take it anymore. She knew she shouldn't heal such a little scratch—it was a waste of mana and a slap in the face to all the other legitimately injured in the crowd. Still, she hurried over and picked the boy up, making soothing sounds. She wasn't all that good with kids, but her cousin had young ones she'd babysat a few times.

Looking at the grandmother, she gave the woman a reassuring smile and a wink, then cast her lowest-level healing spell on the boy, trying not to let the glow of the magic be seen by those around, lest the other refugees become upset, cupping the light with her body as if shielding a candle from the wind.

"Thank you so much, young lady! Peter is a good boy, but he's tired and stumbled. I'm Emma, by the way."

Emma's cheek twitched in pain as she rubbed her own back. "You can put him down. I'm sure he can keep going, isn't that right, Peter?"

The boy looked like he wanted to cry again.

His grandmother gave him a cajoling smile. "You're a big boy, and you're strong, aren't you? Can't you help your poor grandmother make it a little further down the road to safety? If you take my hand, I'll be able to walk a little further."

That bit of child psychology worked on Peter and he straightened up and nodded solemnly. "I 'elp you, Gran-gran!"

He struggled to get down from Morgan's arms, and she let him, giving the grandmother a sad smile. "Once you get to safety, things will be better. Not actual civilization, but safer than here."

Leaning close, Morgan put her hand on Emma's arm and cast Draconic Vitality on the elderly woman. She used her robes to shield the spell from others' eyes and was thankful it wasn't full dark yet.

The grandmother's eyes opened in surprise, and she gasped as the healing energies coursed through her body. She didn't have actual wounds to heal, but the spell provided a thirty-second regeneration-over-time effect, color creeping back into her face almost immediately.

There were tears in the corners of Emma's eyes as she hugged Morgan and spoke quietly. "Thank you so much, dear. I can't tell you how much that helps these old bones! I feel like I've gotten hours of sleep."

Morgan just patted the woman's shoulder. "I'm sorry I can't do more, but I have to keep my mana topped up. We're about to reach the point where the industrial zone bumps up against the highway. That'll be the most dangerous place. You might want to wander closer to the middle of the pack until we get past there."

Emma tugged her grandson's hand and urged him away from the eastern side of the highway, whispering her thanks again.

A bit later when it was about 9:00 PM, the moon was just past full and hanging high enough in the sky that there was still a decent amount of light out. Better still, it was to the west, and monsters were most likely to come from the east, so as long as they weren't super stealthy, the crowd should be able to see their approach.

Still, it was eerie, this march. The refugees were subdued and fairly quiet. There were no loud conversations or people yelling back and forth to others in the column, just muffled speech and the sounds of thousands of feet shuffling along the concrete roadway, a steady, tired rhythm.

The quiet was partly because they were scared, and partly because Brian had asked everyone to keep the noise down so people could react if someone raised the alarm.

There had been a couple of attacks already, but because the highway was elevated they had come at the front and rear of the march. She worried for Viki, but knew her young friend could not only handle herself, but was probably eager for more monsters to kill.

Soon they arrived at the most dangerous point, and word was passed back for people to be wary and hurry past it as best they could. There was a stretch about three-quarters of a mile long where the businesses and warehouses came right up to the edge of the highway.

Unfortunately, as the front of the column began to hurry to get past the area, the march stretched out and became even longer, as those farther back had not yet reached the danger zone and were not moving as fast. People bumped shoulders, curses rose and fell, and the steady rhythm of footsteps broke into uneven bursts as the column compressed and loosened in waves.

That presented a dilemma for Morgan. Did she rush forward, or hang back?

She debated for a few moments before deciding to advance into the area and stand guard somewhere near the middle of the danger zone. Before going, she surreptitiously healed Gran-gran Emma to give the elderly woman a boost of energy to help her make it through the dangerous area. Emma's limp eased just enough that her next steps came a little quicker.

She also grabbed a man dressed in a biker gang style leather jacket that looked to be in his late forties or early fifties.

“Hey, do me a favor and carry this boy for Mrs. Emma please, just until you get past this area, alright?”

The man looked confused for a second as to why she would ask him such a thing. Then, seeing the drooping child and the elderly woman, his face melted in sympathy. “Sure, I’ll look after them. Don’t worry.”

Emma smiled wanly and placed her hand on Morgan’s arm. “Bless you, deary!”

After that, Morgan walked along the concrete barrier at the edge of the road and peered out over the edge, looking for signs of trouble. What she saw was not what she had expected. Where most businesses and homes were collapsing piles of rubble by now, this area no longer contained buildings at all. Instead, it had become low hills covered with scraggly trees and brush. The land rose and fell in uneven humps where streets and parking lots should have been.

Liam had said that the industrial corridor along I35 had turned into hills filled with roaming monsters and dungeons, but this...

It was one thing to hear about something, and another entirely to be confronted with the reality of it. She hadn’t come down this way often before the apocalypse, but she had driven past here before and knew there had never been terrain features like this along the route. The closest embankments back then had only been about the same height as the highway itself, maybe thirty feet high. The ones behind those rose another twenty or thirty feet, and so on. The tallest she could see in the distance were maybe a hundred or a hundred and fifty feet tall. Not super tall, but nothing to sneeze at in the relatively flat DFW area.

What was most disturbing, though, was that she could see movement in the hills. Nothing close yet, thankfully, but farther back and higher up, something moved. A shape shifted, then vanished, leaving only the uneasy certainty that she had not imagined it.

She watched warily as she moved forward, praying that the Exodus would not be attacked and cause a panic. The last thing they needed was people like Emma and her grandson Peter getting trampled by a mob fleeing monsters.

Looking constantly out at the dark hills, she caught movement from time to time, but so far it all seemed to stay back away from the edge near the highway. Even so, her staff was in her hands, and she was ready to cast attack spells the second something came close. Her grip tightened every time the shadows stirred.

About a quarter of a mile into the danger zone, it happened.

One of the hills came really close to the elevated highway, within perhaps ten to fifteen feet. Worse, the hill was slightly higher than the road surface, meaning anyone up there would have an advantage.

Looking forward, she didn't see any other hills this close, so she decided to station herself here and guard the marching column. It turned out to be a wise decision.

Maybe five minutes after she stopped there, her Dark Vision let her see a sudden movement. Her eyes snapped to the spot, but she couldn't make out what it was. Glancing around at the people streaming past, she grabbed a man with a makeshift spear.

"Hey, hang on here for a minute. I think I just saw something. Look for anyone with a weapon with a long reach like yours, and help me watch this spot."

He was an older teen, and his "spear" was a long straight branch with a hunting knife tied to the end with some hemp rope. He looked nervous, but nodded agreement and started scanning the crowd, as Morgan turned back to the hill.

Then it happened again, another small movement, like a small animal moving through brush. Except there wasn't really any brush to speak of on the top of the hill, just some short field grass starting to grow.

"Damn it." Goosebumps prickled along her arms, and a chill ran down her spine. Her breath slowed, instinctively quieting. Something wasn't right.

Then she saw eyes reflecting in the moonlight. Not the bright, almost glowing golden eyes of a cat or wolf, but something duller and more greenish. Flat, watching points that did not flinch or blink.

Then a dozen goblins rushed over the crest of the hill with crude bows and began to fire arrows toward the crowd.

Morgan called out a warning just as the missiles began to descend on unsuspecting victims. "Goblins! Do not panic, but hurry past!"

Without wasting a second, she prepared one of her two offensive AOE spells, Shadowflame Burst. It had a thirty foot radius and would cover most of the hilltop. She raised her staff high and loosed the spell.

In an instant, shadows condensed out of the night into a tight ball at the center of her spell's area, then detonated in shadowy flames that did little to light the night, but definitely drew every eye.

Wooomph!

The goblins were engulfed in the shadowflame, taking moderate damage and a Weakness debuff.

Except these creatures were probably thirty levels below her, so all the monsters near the center of the blast were simply torn to pieces in the explosion, and those farther out were in no shape to fight. Unfortunately, the goblins had numbers.

Even as she prepared a second spell, more goblins rushed over the top of the hill, and these looked bigger and meaner, easily twice the size of the archers her spell had just shredded.

Hobgoblin Warriors.

They might not have ranged weapons, but with their height advantage they could leap across the gap and onto the highway, like pirates boarding an enemy vessel. Before the first group could leap, Morgan got off her second spell. It too was an AOE, but this one was a DOT, or "Damage Over Time." Meaning they wouldn't die instantly like the first group had done. These might survive long enough to kill innocent refugees.

A storm of shadows condensed on the hilltop amidst the group of Hobgoblins, tendrils and threads of tenebrous mana invading their bodies through mouths, noses, or even seeping into their skin. It was a gruesome spell, as those affected began to scream, taking high damage. The level gap wasn't so large with these enemies, but even so, high damage was significant.

Many of those afflicted fell to their knees, and some even dropped their weapons as they clawed at their own skin trying to stop the damage. It was no use. The spell delivered its payload of damage over the next fifteen seconds, and the Hobs were out of action while the spell ran its course.

Unfortunately, not all were hit by the spell, and those who weren't wasted no time leaping the gap and attacking in a frenzy.

The man with the makeshift spear went down immediately to a sword thrust to his abdomen that ripped his guts out, thanks to the jagged serrations of the attacking blade.

Morgan wanted to heal the man, but didn't have time. If she didn't do her part, more would die. She hit the Hobgoblin attacker in the back with her last offensive spell, Shadow Bolt. It only dealt moderate damage, but it was enough, and the monster went down.

Between those three spells she had accounted for at least fifteen dead goblins and hobgoblins, but more were coming. Far more than she could deal with on her own.

The young man wasn't the only one down either. Arrows had struck several people surrounding Morgan, and screams of pain split the air, twisting her gut with the urge to do something to heal them. Luckily, she had just hit Level 35 earlier and received two new spells, one of which was an AOE Healing aura.

She activated it and felt power rush out of her, filling an area within a thirty foot radius with healing energy. It didn't silence the screams, nor push the arrows out of their bodies, but it would give them a few health points every second over the next minute. It would keep them alive if their injuries weren't too severe, maybe long enough for her to cast more targeted healing at their wounds.

More Hobgoblins were cresting the hill and preparing to jump.

There was no time left, so she did the only thing that made sense. She triggered Commune. "Viki, I'm under attack, can I summon you?"

The answer was unhesitating. "Yes!"

Seconds mattered, and while it was fast, Summon wasn't instantaneous. Half a dozen Hobgoblins made the leap onto the roadway before Viki materialized.

In less than three heartbeats, Viki had oriented herself and fired her first arrow, Cataclysm. The AOE detonated on the hilltop in a chaotic explosion of shadow and void energy, ripping and tearing apart the latest group of enemies who had rushed to the top of the hill after the previous group jumped to the roadway. The blast kicked up a rolling wave of grit and splinters of bone that pattered down onto the concrete like hail. Another nine Hobgoblins were obliterated in Viki's first attack.

Unfortunately, Morgan, as the first and most effective combatant among the humans, was targeted by the monsters. Of the half dozen currently alive and on the highway, three were rushing the Priestess.

Her offensive spells were all on cooldown, but she swung her Verdantwood staff like it was a Louisville Slugger and cracked the skull of the first Hobgoblin to come within range. The impact vibrated up her arms and into her shoulders, and the creature's teeth clacked together with an ugly snap.

Viki put a regular arrow into the back of another, right between its shoulder blades, and its legs seemed to stop working after that, sending it sprawling to the concrete. It hit hard enough that the breath whooshed out of it in a wet grunt, limbs scrabbling for traction that never came.

The third managed to put a deep gash in Morgan's side, dropping her health by fifteen percent in a single slash. Heat flared across her ribs, and her robes went instantly warm and slick where blood soaked through.

Growling, she used Shadow Step, appearing to Viki's left, then stumbled. Her boot skidded on the gritty film of dust and spilled blood, and she had to catch herself with the butt of her staff before she went down.

From there things got hectic. Viki alternated AOE attacks at the top of the hill to prevent groups of Hobgoblins and Goblin archers from sending more attackers jumping onto the roadway. Every other shot was a single target attack on one of the Hobs already wreaking havoc on the refugees. Each time Viki loosed an arrow, the bowstring snapped like a whip crack through the night, and the hilltop flashed with brief, violent bursts that made shadows jump and twist.

It took Morgan a minute to treat her own wound so she wouldn't lose too much blood and end up passing out. Her fingers came away red, and she clenched her jaw hard enough that her teeth ached as she forced herself to focus. After that she healed, attacked, or buffed depending on when her offensive spells were on cooldown. Her mana rhythm turned into a brutal little cadence: patch, strike, push, breathe, repeat.

The monsters were low enough level, she wasn't worried about herself and Viki in individual fights, but their sheer numbers proved difficult. Every time she thought the crest was finally clear, another set of silhouettes surged up against the moonlit grass like ants boiling out of a nest.

Except for the pair of them, it was chaos on the bridge. Most people were trying to flee either forward or back against the mass of other survivors, but there just wasn't enough room, so they ended up getting jammed up within a hundred yards of the fight. Bodies pressed shoulder to shoulder, and the column turned into a trapped, shoving knot that could not move fast enough in any direction.

Between Morgan and Viki, only a few attackers managed to make it to the roadway at any given moment. But even two or three was enough to panic a crowd that could not scatter.

Meanwhile, other survivors, realizing they had no choice, began fighting back with baseball bats, crowbars, axes, and even shovels. Although the Hobgoblins were more skilled, they soon found themselves overwhelmed not just by numbers, but by the sheer ferocity of the trapped defenders. The survivors had lost everything, having nothing left but their lives and the clothes on their backs.

"No more!!! Die, you fucking monsters!" The man wielding the crowbar swung it over and over at his opponent while others rushed up and began swinging as well. The woman with the shovel used it like a poleaxe and brought it down on the hobgoblin's armored shoulder, causing it to stagger and drop its weapon. The shovel rang like a struck bell, and the creature's arm dipped as if the joint had gone loose. What followed was a beatdown, seven or eight people completely wrecking their attacker with a ferocity that caused it to screech in terror as it went down under the combined assault. The screech cut off mid note, replaced by a wet thud and a few final, ragged breaths.

Just when Morgan began to hope they would prevail and everyone would survive, a new figure appeared on top of the hill, a Hobgoblin Shaman, carrying a gnarled and twisted staff festooned with the skulls and bones of small animals. It stood taller than the others, framed against the sky, and the dangling charms on its staff clicked together like a bone wind chime.

Somehow it held a human baby in its other hand, dangling the infant by one foot. It raised the staff and started chanting, clearly planning to use it as a sacrifice to power its magic. The baby's tiny fist opened and closed, and its cry vanished into the roar of battle like it had been swallowed by the night.

"Oh, hell, nah!" Morgan didn't hesitate, ignoring everything else happening, and pointed her own staff at the monster, firing off her only single target attack spell, Shadow Bolt. The spell tore free of her like a thrown spear, cold and straight, and the air along its path felt suddenly thinner. At the same moment Viki must have seen the new arrival as well, because she turned her bow and began firing arrow after arrow, determined to interrupt the sacrifice before it was too late. As she released the arrow she shouted, "Oblivion!"

Morgan knew that was her most powerful attack and its effect even worked on boss monsters. Their two attacks hit at almost the same instant.

The boss staggered backward two steps as their attacks not only hit, but applied debuffs, Weakness from Morgan's spell and Confusion from Viki's arrow. Its chanting broke into a garbled snarl, and its head jerked left and right like it could not decide where the threat was coming from.

That bought them a few heartbeats for Morgan to figure out how to deal with this and save the baby. Except, she was too late. Viki was already in motion.

Swapping her bow for the magic cleaver that she'd been given after the Orc Stronghold dungeon, Viki used Shadow Step to appear right behind the Shaman and put all her strength into hacking at the boss' arm. The cleaver bit with a dull, brutal chop, and something dark sprayed across the grass. Before the bastard could even register that it had been maimed, Viki caught the baby before it could hit the ground, scooping it into her arms and sprinting back toward the highway. She tucked the infant against her chest like it was a fragile treasure, her grip firm but careful.

Morgan's heart was in her throat as her young friend leaped and soared over the gap between the hill and roadway. It was a feat worthy of an Olympic athlete or a hero out of myths, made even more impressive because she had to weave between hobgoblin warriors to do it. For a blink, Viki was a dark silhouette against the moonlit sky, and then her boots slapped the concrete with a sharp, decisive landing.

She came skidding to a stop before Morgan and thrust the baby at her.

Blinking in amazement, she did the only thing she could and took the baby. The infant was warm, terrifyingly small, and it clung to her with instinctive strength. Free of the temporary burden, her young friend materialized her bow and began to fire at the Shaman, giving it her all. She cast True Shot to make her next three arrows ignore any penalties. One after another, she fired... Eclipse, Cataclysm, Soulpiercer, Shatterstorm, Duskfire, and last but not least, Shadow Bolt, the arrow version rather than the spell.

Each arrow staggered the confused Shaman, piling on more and more debuffs onto the boss, Blindness, Confusion, Pain, even while the arrows chipped away at its health, -15%, -10%, -15%, -10%, -5%. The creature jerked as if each hit yanked invisible strings, its limbs refusing to obey in the same direction twice. Before the boss could even take another action, it was riddled with shadowy arrows, and Morgan's cooldown was off timer. Relief hit Morgan so hard her hands shook, and she tightened her hold on the baby without meaning to.

Despite the boss being at under fifteen percent health left, Morgan didn't hold back, dropping Shadowflame Burst on the top of the hill again, tearing apart more archers, warriors, and their boss. The hilltop briefly became a writhing smear of darkness and fire, and the chanting died like a candle snuffed by a wet thumb.

When the shadows cleared there wasn't a single monster left alive on that hilltop, but things were far from over. They still had the remaining Hobgoblin Warriors on the highway to deal with, but by now, the refugees were handling those. That left Morgan to move around healing the wounded as best she could, and at least get them to the point where they wouldn't die. There were far more injured than she had mana to treat them. Her knees ached from crouching and rising, crouching and rising, and every new scream pulled her attention like a stab in the gut.

After half an hour or so, Viki pulled her away from people asking for healing, saying, "That's enough for now. Morgan needs to rest in case we get attacked again. Everyone's been treated enough that you can move on. Please hurry to catch up to the rest of the Exodus."

Meanwhile, the two of them rested, leaning against the concrete barrier, waiting there to ensure no further attack came while the refugees continued to stream past. The river of people felt endless, faces passing in the dim light with the same stunned expression, the same tight grip on whatever they had managed to carry.

"Hey, what happened to that baby?" Viki asked.

Sighing, Morgan shrugged. "I handed her to a young couple, so I could heal the wounded, and by the time I thought about it again, they had left, somewhere ahead of us in the column, I guess. At least she's safe now." Morgan glanced down the road as if she could spot them in the darkness, then looked away when she could not.

Viki held out an item. "Nothing we can do about that. Hopefully, the couple will take her in and be her family now. Anyway, here. While you were treating people, I snuck over to the hill and grabbed this. It was a loot drop. Apparently the hobgoblins had spilled out of a dungeon, so the Shaman counted as a boss, or at least a mini boss."

Morgan accepted the ring and used her Analyze skill to determine what it did. She gasped, then beamed at her young friend. "Yes! An item that cleans things!" She didn't waste even a second putting it on and activating it.

After a wave of mana washed over her, she hugged herself while cradling the ring to her heart. "This! So much this! I have wanted something like this ever since the apocalypse began!" Her shoulders sagged as the grime and blood vanished, and for the first time in hours she looked like herself again.

Viki grinned and hugged her friend. "You deserve it. Besides, I figure it will be most useful to you since you have to treat people who have been injured and bleeding. Hard to diagnose people if you can't see their wounds."

In thanks, Morgan activated it again while commanding it to clean Viki.

Grinning, the pair waited for the end of the column, to ensure no stragglers were left behind. They watched until the last limping figures passed, until the roadway finally felt like a road again instead of a battlefield.

Once that was done, they trailed after the end of the stream of refugees until they came to the spot on the highway where the entire group stopped for the night. They had gotten past the most dangerous part of the journey to the Colony. At least she hoped they had. There were still other areas that went through business parks, and past dungeons. But hopefully, none would be quite so changed and dangerous as this had been. The night settled heavy around them, and the distant hills looked darker than before, as if the land itself was listening.

As they settled down for a rest, Morgan wondered how Liam was doing with the Safe Zone and his hunting in the Necropolis dungeon. She tried to picture him in the sky, moving with that relentless purpose of his, and the thought steadied her more than she wanted to admit.

CHAPTER 10

LEVEL 95 AND THE BARROW BOSS

LIAM POV:

As I flew back toward the Necropolis dungeon, I contemplated the Safe Zone I had just created. I was incredibly glad to have accomplished that, but at the same time, it seemed so paltry compared to the need. From the air, the boundary felt less like a triumph and more like a line scratched into something far too big to tame. A mere ten mile radius space would be enough for a few tens of thousands of people to live without worry. Still, it was certainly more than humanity had in my first life, and maybe it would give us a chance to establish a foothold of our own, on this world that had once been ours alone.

Growling, I couldn't help but circle around the fact that it wasn't enough. If we still had technology and civilization, we could cram hundreds of thousands of people into a space that size and be happy doing it, but now, we'd need to feed all those folks, and for that we needed dungeon access and farm land. Dungeons would supply our meat needs and some veg, but inevitably people would mess up and destroy the good dungeons and someday we'd be stuck with our place of safety being isolated from the resources that we would need to sustain ourselves. I had watched that exact mistake hollow out entire regions before, slowly at first, then all at once.

I was going by experience from my past life, but no matter what our situation, human nature didn't change. That means someone would get greedy, or someone would make a mistake. Still, we did have the DFW Metroplex right in our backyard, but if we couldn't deal with the big high level dungeons, eventually the city would become a hot zone where no one dared to tread. Then we'd be stuck with our place of safety bumped right up against an area so dangerous we might be afraid to leave the circle. That was another potential outcome we had to somehow avoid.

I knew that the Ascension Quest would give me power to alter things and make changes, but I wasn't sure I could solve that problem.

Thinking of Safe Zones, and circles, the idea flitted through my mind that it was a shame we couldn't just put the entire city inside the center of one big massive zone. Then we could pick and choose which dungeons we wanted to keep, and wouldn't have to worry about dungeon breaks spilling monsters out into the surrounding communities. I quickly dismissed the idea since I only knew of one size zone and that was the ten mile radius, like the one I just created.

Still, the idea wouldn't go away. I pictured encircling the entire city in a series of Safe Zone bubbles all around the perimeter. It would probably take twenty or more bubbles to overlap so that the monsters would be trapped inside the circle. That would keep everyone in this region fairly safe, at least from dungeon monsters. It would also put a huge number of dungeons in our back yards, always right there waiting to be harvested and challenged to level people up.

It was an interesting idea, but I didn't get the impression from the AI that I'd be able to go around creating dozens of bubbles. Still, I didn't entirely give up on the thought. While it wasn't likely I'd be able to create unlimited Safe Zones, perhaps I could increase the size to fifty mile radius instead of ten?

As I approached the Necropolis, I shelved the Safe Zone idea for now. Until I Ascended, I just wouldn't know what the possibilities were.

And speaking of Ascending, I wouldn't be able to do that until I hit Level Cap, so it was time to get back to work.

By that time it was nearly midnight, and I could see the refugee exodus camped on the highway as I passed over them. They hadn't made it quite halfway to their destination, but it was close enough. I figured my first guess was pretty accurate and they'd arrive around noon tomorrow. That was a lot of people in one place... I hoped they would be safe and wouldn't run into trouble on the way. A group like that had to be a tempting target.

A couple minutes later, I arrived just outside the dungeon. Rather than put up with the Wraiths, I used Stealth and flew over the wall and back to the northern section of the Cathedral zone where the Draugr burial mounds and tombs were located. I had cleared a little more than half the Lords earlier in the day, so it took me a few minutes to find the spot where I had left off.

Relying on Stealth, I walked right into the next tomb in the row and straight to the central chamber where the lord lay on a big stone slab. He didn't even stir, unable to see through my skill. The silence was absolute, but the smell was loud enough to make up for the quiet.

With a shallow sigh, at the tediousness of doing it this way, I cast the first of the two attacks that it would take to end this chump, Void Lance.

The lord was pinned to the granite slab and most of its torso was obliterated. Then my claws ended the fight with Dragon's Rend, decapitating and destroying the skull in a swift but precise movement. Two 'extreme' damage abilities cast back to back like that rocked the tomb and sent dust cascading down from wooden beams helping to support the stone. And just like that I added one more dead Lord to the tally.

I started to let the clock run down so that I could collect the platinum mana coins that would drop, but then remembered that these were high quality weapons despite their ratty appearance, so I grabbed the sword from where it had fallen off the Draugr's chest and stored it in my ring.

I'd collect the gear and pass it on to Brian, Margaret, and Karl later so that he could distribute it to his people. That reminded me, I'd need to make sure there was someone decent in charge of the Orc Stronghold fortress in the Safe Zone and gear them up as well.

After that it was just a matter of waiting four more minutes for my cooldowns to refresh, then I used Void Travel to move through the void and reappear in the tomb of the next victim. It was very much like my previous Shadow Walk in that I could witness what was around me in the real world, but where moving through the shadows had always felt kinda spooky, and a little disturbing, this was different. Void Travel gave a feeling of isolation, like I was the only thing that existed in the void. I wouldn't say it felt 'better', but it was faster and more efficient, and came at a much lower mana cost.

And that's what I did for the next four hours. Rinse and repeat twenty-nine more times.

My greedy dragon heart was fuming at not getting to grow its hoard of platinum mana coins, but now at least, I had thirty sets of weapons and armor to give to worthy people in the camps who could use it to level up and grow strong. It was a weak excuse as far as my dragon heart was concerned, but I knew it was the right thing to do. Even if it never quite satisfied that part of me.

As the last one died, and I heard the beautiful "Ding" in my System interface, I was overjoyed to get another skill and spell pair to add to my arsenal. I only had these and whatever I got at Level 100 to go before I would be locked in never to gain new skills again, so I was particularly happy to see these. I did hope there would be some new skills and abilities that came with the Ascension tiers, but that wasn't something I could actually count on.

With some anticipation, I pulled up my Status page but directed the System to just show the basics, and what was new.

Liam Bell:

Voidblade - Level 95
Bloodline (Tier 4): Void Dragon

Experience: 7335/175040

Attributes:
Endurance: 275
Strength: 275
Agility: 275
Mind: 274
Will: 274
Magical Aptitude: 274
Luck: 10

Health: 5500/5500
Mana: 3570/5480

Level 95 Skill:
Void Domain (Passive)
Description: A constant aura of Void energy that suppresses hostile power within its reach, disrupting spell structures and degrading enemy strength.
Effect: Creates a 50-foot Nullification Field that weakens enemy spells, reduces enemy stats, and blocks all teleportation or spatial displacement within its radius.

Level 95 Spell:
Void Renewal
Description: A high-tier regenerative spell that channels raw Void essence to restore the caster's physical form with extreme efficiency.
Effect: Rapidly heals damage and fully restores lost limbs or injuries caused in battle.
Cooldown: 15 seconds.
Note: Drawing too heavily on Void energy in a short period of time can result in backlash. This can range in severity from temporary loss of ability to manipulate Void energy, up to permanent mutation(s).

I was practically dancing in my excitement at reading my new Skill and Spell. I had expected a lot given that they were Level 95, and they did not disappoint! My wings twitched as I reread the descriptions, unable to quite stand still.

Void Domain was an AOE passive...A Passive! I instinctively understood that it would work like other skills, and the enemy's level would affect how strongly my Domain functioned on them. Still, it seemed to be a step above the Aura of Void's Chill dragon ability in terms of power. I had visions of walking into a dungeon and all the enemies becoming weak shadows of their former selves as soon as I approached. Hopefully, it would live up to the hype!

Then there was my new spell, Void Renewal. I already had regeneration, but all it did was slowly heal me over time, not fast enough for it to make a difference in combat. This, however, was an active spell, and it would not only restore lost health, but even regrow limbs. That was an incredibly useful spell to have. I had Morgan, and she could do these things for me, but I rarely got the chance to make use of her healing since I was running around soloing dungeons to get the EXP bonus. Now I didn't have to worry about dying for lack of medical attention. The knot of tension I normally carried into every fight loosened just a little.

The only downside was that it only used mana to kick off the process. From there, my body would draw on the power of the Void itself, and use that energy to instinctively make the repairs. I guess that was why it came with a warning label, so to speak. That note was pretty scary. Overuse could cause permanent mutations?!? Damn, that was harsh! Not to mention scary! I didn't even want to think of what void mutations would look like.

I wasn't sure what those would be, and I definitely wasn't eager to find out. Still, I knew the truth. In a life or death situation, I would take a risk like that to survive. *I just hope that it will never be tested,* I thought.

Then I cringed a little inside, realizing that thought might have set a doom flag for myself. At least I hadn't said it aloud though! That would have been like throwing the gauntlet down to the universe's feet so to speak. I walked over and knocked on the wooden beam supporting the low ceiling of the tomb for good measure. Maybe that would avert the bad luck I had nearly caused myself.

Regardless, I was very pleased with what I received, and I was eager to get back to leveling. I didn't want to tackle the Cathedral until the sun came up, but there was one more challenge that awaited me in the northern circle. Right in the center of the circle, butted up against the big Cathedral hill, was an especially big and fancy barrow. By the look of the thing, it had 'Mini-boss' written all over it, and that meant both experience, and treasure!

As I stepped into the barrow's entrance, the air shifted in that familiar, artificial way, the System's quiet announcement that I'd crossed into something important. The hair along my arms prickled in response. The passage opened wider than any of the other tombs we'd cleared, the stonework tighter, cleaner, almost proud of itself. Someone, or something, had built this place to be remembered.

The chamber ahead glowed with a cold, steady light. Carved spirals and knotwork patterns ran along the walls, like the famous Newgrange mound in Ireland, except these carried the weight of mana instead of myth. The ceiling arched higher than it should have underground, a trick of construction or the System bending space to match its own design.

At the far end sat the Draugr King.

He rested on a throne of dark stone, body enormous even in undeath. Not lanky like the lesser draugr. This one had mass, presence, thick armor fused to bone and age. His skull was crowned with a heavy iron circlet, and the glow inside his eye sockets burned hotter than anything I'd seen in this dungeon so far. The King wasn't slumped or forgotten. He looked like he'd been waiting.

Five sarcophagi stood in a semicircle around him, each etched with runes and sealed with mana-locks. The lids weren't just decorative. They felt watchful. I didn't need the System to tell me the lords inside would rise the second their king stirred.

I took another step, and the temperature dropped.

Whatever this place had once been, it was a throne room now. A royal court preserved past death, waiting for someone foolish or strong enough to disturb it.

I shook my head, pushing away the damn System cut-scene ambience messaging. If the System had its way, I'd just bumble my way in and wave my dick at the king, challenging it and its minions to come at me all at once.

Hell, no! I got the impression this mini-boss was intelligent, so there was no way I'd give it the advantage of being stupid in my approach.

Besides, I had no desire to actually fight the minions, much less both them and the king at the same time.

The second I crossed the threshold the tomb would seal shut, and I'd be facing all the enemies at once.

But that didn't mean I would do it their way. The King was Level 85, so I was going to do this the smart way. I started casting my buffs and defensive magics and preparing for what I hoped wouldn't be a serious fight.

However, the first and most important spells I cast were Dragon's Fury, doubling both my physical and magical strength. Then last of all, I added Haste. I was going in hot!

"Roll Initiative, bitches!" I yelled as I leaped through the door, already casting Night's End, my double strength extreme damage AOE spell.

In that instant, it was as if all light leeched from the world, pulling darkness out of the very Void and condensing it into tendrils that wrapped around the King and his minions even as they lay in their sarcophagi. I was just praying that it wouldn't be so powerful that it would bury me under the thousands of tons of stone above our heads.

Even as it detonated, I didn't stop. Haste gave me the ability to cast again before the bad guys even reacted, and I was going to make the most of it.

Not only the Draugr Lords, but the stone housing them was blown outward, slamming into the massive boulders that made up the barrow's central chamber. I didn't take time to see how they were doing, and released my next spell, Entropy! This was one of my newest and I hadn't really used it yet, but it did a high damage AOE DoT that caused a corrosive decay to monsters. As a secondary effect it also dropped enemy stats. Normally that would be 30%, but with Fury running, it doubled, significantly weakening them.

The King recovered with amazing dexterity for a massive undead twice the size of the others. It flipped itself upright from where it had sprawled, prone, after my first attack. It began casting a spell, no doubt something that would not be good for my health.

I was having none of that. "Void Lance!" I shouted.

My other extreme damage spell slammed the boss backward, pinning it to its throne and ripping a large hole in its putrid guts.

Thanks to my mini-map Analyze skill, I could see its health bar and those three attacks had knocked off 60% of its health, and the number was still dropping.

But it wasn't over. My attack disrupted the King's spell, but he was far from done. He immediately began glowing. The dead flesh attempted to knot itself back together even as my Damage over Time spell continued to undo its regeneration. It was also pulling itself up, and reaching for the massive sword leaning up against the throne.

Grinning, I continued to cast, Haste was doubling my speed even as Fury doubled my strength. Compared to the weakness and constant danger experienced in my first life, this was god-like power!

A black hole began to form in the middle of the room as I cast Arcane Singularity, pulling everything loose toward that point, yanking the barely surviving minions right out of their stone boxes and slamming them together with the doubled intensity of my spell. Only the boss resisted the pull, but it wasn't out of the danger zone.

That spell took three seconds to finish and it prevented the lords from taking any action, but I was free to attack. Unfortunately, so was the king.

Just as its massive sword was about to fly into the center of the room the boss snatched it out of the air, and used the pull to slingshot itself toward me. The singularity was like the sun, or Jupiter, and the bastard deliberately threw itself toward the pull, but just enough to the side to be sent accelerating at me like a rocket.

The impact was colossal. We both went careening into the megalithic walls of the tomb. The only saving grace was that its sword missed, and it was only elbows and knees that met my armor and scales.

I took 15% of my health bar in damage just from a collision! I had seen the spark of true intelligence in this monster's eyes, but damn. I had never even conceived that such a maneuver was possible.

The trick and damage cost me three beats during which I otherwise could have acted. Still, I had one thing to be thankful for. The king had also lost those same precious instants.

Grinning fiercely, I extended my claws, and activated Dragon's Charge to reach the spot where the boss was only just starting to stand up.

Haste for the win!

I hit it with Dragon's Rend, my only extreme damage melee skill, but backed by Fury's doubling of my power, it dropped another 30% off the draugr's health, putting it in the red, but still not out. The impact jolted up my arms, stone cracking beneath its feet.

Turning the attack into a one-two punch, almost literally, I followed up with a Void Strike, dropping another 20% from its bar. It was now in the single digits, but that wasn't its only problem. I had stacked Weakness on it multiple times with my attacks, in addition to it being inside my new Void Domain, which also imposed not only Weakness, but Nullification, stripping it of any buffs it might have had.

Despite being a Level 85 boss monster, it was now weaker than any of its minions. Even the Level 60 Archers would be capable of knocking the king around. Its movements had gone sluggish, blows mistimed, posture sagging.

Better still, my mana and health were ticking up thanks to Voidflame on my attacks.

Then the Arcane Singularity detonated, sending the remains of the minions hurtling in every direction. One hit the boss, and the impact shaved another percent or two off its health. It had maybe 5% left, but it was ticking down thanks to the DoT.

The fight was over. It just didn't know it yet.

Or so I thought.

It would only take a single attack, any attack really, and the boss would be dead. I initiated a Tail Lash because I figured it would be about the most insulting way I could kill it. Getting backhanded by my tail. I was starting to chuckle as my tail reached out to finish it off.

However, without warning or preamble, the boss roared and self-destructed.

My eyes went wide as violent mana ripped through the area in a shockwave that lifted dust, debris, and gore from the floor as it sent me hurtling into the stone walls for the second time in seconds.

BOOM!

The walls and ceiling shook in a tremor that made me consider diving into the void realm to escape being buried. Except that Void Travel was still on cooldown!

Another 20% of my health was gone, and I coughed up blood. It burned hot and metallic in my throat.

“Sore loser!” I grumbled as I struggled back to my feet. I spit on its skull for good measure.

“Bastard stood no chance, but I’ll give it credit, it didn’t go down without a fight.”

Frowning at my log messages, I saw that I had gotten no experience from the minions. They were only Level 75. I needed things 76 or higher for experience now.

I reached down and started removing the armor from the now fully dead boss. Thankfully, haste let me ‘harvest’ the gear from the minions as well within that minute of grace period the System gave.

The dragon blood in my veins rebelled at my actions. This would have been the first mithril mana coins I’d ever received, and my greedy little heart did not want to give that up. Still, at the same time, I couldn’t pass up grabbing a Level 85 mini-boss’ gear to take back for Brian. It surely had to be better than the lower level gear he had now. Right?

This wouldn’t have enchantments. It was just plain gear, but it was Mythic grade, which meant it should be able to repel blows from anything below Level 50 with ease. Hell, it would probably last him until he hit his second Class upgrade for sure. For that reason alone, I would have been happy with this kill, but there was still the loot drop treasure to check.

A treasure chest appeared atop the altar that somehow managed to survive the destruction the King and I had wrought.

Seeing no traps, I quickly opened it and purposely pocketed the potions before inspecting the item.

> **Upgrade Token (Mythic Grade)**
>
> **Description:** A rare System-forged artifact imbued with mythic-tier enhancement energy. When applied to any eligible item, the Token restructures and elevates its core properties, permanently upgrading it to Mythic Grade.
>
> **Effect:** Instantly upgrades a chosen item to Mythic quality, improving all baseline attributes and unlocking potential for Mythic-level abilities.
>
> **Restrictions:** Single-use. Item must not already be Mythic Grade.

"Hell, yeah!" I'd never had anything at such a high grade before, and this would boost one item directly to Mythic. I quickly considered my options.

On the one hand, my Hunter's Charm was incredibly useful, feeding my mini-map with locations of enemies within range. What would it do if I upgraded it all the way to Mythic? Surely it would give a ton more information. I could almost feel the itch of curiosity at the thought of seeing everything before it ever saw me.

Still, as useful as that would be, I also had to consider attack and defense. I could upgrade the Minotaur's axe, and that would boost its power significantly, making me even deadlier in combat. Then again, if I applied it to my nifty new armor...

That got my wheels turning. My armor was already at the top end of Grand grade, and it provided a bonus of +35% to armor, and +20% to all my Draconic abilities. That gave me pause. My fingers flexed unconsciously, claws scraping lightly as I imagined that number climbing.

Cleansing myself and the King's throne, I sat down to think things through, my forehead creased in thought. I had thirty minutes to kill waiting on the cooldown for Dragon's Fury to repop. I kept going around in circles. Anything I had on me would benefit tremendously from the upgrade token. It boiled down to which thing would do the most for me. I had resistance items for Necrotic and Curse, or Magic Resistance. Other items gave percentage bonuses to Strength or Agility stats. An upgrade like this could give me another ten to fifteen percent more to one of those stats, and that was nothing to sneeze at.

In the end, I chose my armor. It was already very high-end in its current grade, and more importantly, it gave me an overall bonus to all my draconic abilities. That meant my flight speed would increase, my vision would get better, I would regenerate faster, and so much more. It was the single thing with the largest impact across attack, defense, and utility. Despite my certainty, I had that uneasy feeling in my gut that I always got when I had to make a big decision.

Determined, I removed my armor and held it in my right hand, then placed the token in the middle of the chest piece.

"Upgrade Wyrmhide Aegis."

Confirm: Apply Upgrade Token to Wyrmhide Aegis.

(**Yes** or **No**?)

Note: Once confirmed, upgrade cannot be halted or reversed.

. . .

"Yes." I didn't hesitate. Acid in my stomach, aside, I knew this was the right decision.

Upgrading in 3...2...1...Starting...
...Complete.

Wyrmhide Aegis (Mythic Grade)

Description: A fully awakened draconic armor matrix, reforged through Mythic-tier enhancement. The Aegis adapts seamlessly to the wearer's form, channeling primordial wyrm resilience and void-hardened stability.

Effect: +55% armor; +40% power increase to all draconic abilities; negates all mobility penalties regardless of form; rapid self-repair of physical and magical damage; fully accommodates partial or full transformations.

Additional Mythic Property: Armor dynamically reinforces under extreme threat, granting brief surges of enhanced protection when the wearer's health drops below 20%.

That might not have been all I was hoping for, but it was one heck of a solid upgrade. The Mythic ability was the only thing I was somewhat disappointed by, and even then I was just being silly.

I kicked a bone near my foot, sending it skittering across the stone and clattering into the altar in the center of the room as I grumbled quietly to myself. The sharp crack echoed louder than I expected, matching my mood a little too well. "Why did the ability have to be a reactive one that only triggered under twenty percent health?" That really annoyed me. That meant it would only be useful when I had already taken enough damage to consider fleeing to get reinforcement, which was never possible during a boss fight.

I would have rather had something passive, like a boost to Evasion. "Still, ya get what ya get. First world dungeon problems and all that, I suppose." The irritation drained out of me as fast as it had come, leaving only the familiar itch to keep moving.

Putting my armor back on, I was happy to see my cooldown for Fury had ended and I was ready to fly up to the top of the hill and see what was defending the Cathedral.

CHAPTER 11

THE CHURCHYARD IS NOT SAFE!

It was pretty late at night by the time I finished and headed to the top of the hill, not that you'd know even if the sun was up. The thick shadowy gloom hanging over the dungeon protected the undead from daylight and meant that there was no optimal time for assaulting them. No doubt that was exactly why it was there, a permanent artificial twilight designed to favor what lived beneath it.

The mini-boss had been a bit of a battle, but not really a significant challenge. Ever since my third Class upgrade, I was feeling pretty invincible, that dangerous edge of confidence humming through my veins. The power boost I'd received due to my bloodline evolution to Void Dragon was significant, far more than I'd initially realized. Even so, I wasn't going to go into the inner zone of the most massive dungeon I'd ever heard of and expect to waltz through it the way I had through the barrows of the outer graveyard. I didn't know what I'd face yet, but everything would be close enough to my level to be a real threat.

I'd spent my first life significantly under-hunting dungeons, fighting monsters far enough below my level to feel safe, to feel in control.

While these would still be below my level, I didn't feel safe about this. Not only was it full of undead, I also had to figure that a Stronghold dungeon in the center of one of the largest urban areas in North America had to be well above average in terms of difficulty. I mean, just look at the sheer number of monsters I'd seen so far, prowling every approach and filling every structure.

Now I was going to tackle the elites of this place, and I had a bad feeling about it, a tight knot forming in my gut that experience told me not to ignore.

Extending my wings, I leapt into the air. The feeling of my wing muscles powerfully contracting and pulling me higher into the sky never ceased to awe me, the strength and control still felt unreal. I circled around the large hill. Clearly, you were meant to beat the Draugr mini-boss and ascend a set of stairs carved into the cliff face, then face a group of defenders within a defensive fortification at the top. Only once you completed that, would you have access to the top of the hill.

I ignored that.

Flying above the outer walls, I could see...

Right on cue, the System ambience messaging invaded my brain like a cutscene in a video game, trying to frame the moment for me whether I wanted it or not.

As I swept in toward the mount, the first thing that came into view was the outer wall, a ring of dark stone encircling the hilltop like a fortress built to keep something in rather than out. The battlements bristled with movement. Fledgling Vampires paced along the parapets, their pale forms quick and restless, turning toward me with feral alertness as my shadow crossed the towers. The staircase that climbed the outer slope met the wall at a heavy gatehouse, its murder holes and arrow slits now watched by undead eyes instead of living guards.

Just beyond that defensive ring, the terrain softened into a quiet, eerie beauty. Wooded paths wound through the trees in deliberate spirals, wide cobbled walkways guiding travelers deeper into the mount. Each major bend ended at a stone mausoleum, old, ornate structures with moss-covered roofs and sealed iron doors. They sat like patient sentinels among the trees, forming a circle of silent watchers around the heart of the hill. Even from the air, I could feel the presence of the Vampires that inhabited them, the stillness around each tomb feeling heavy and deliberate.

At the very center, rising above the treetops like the spine of some ancient creature, stood the Cathedral. Gothic spires clawed at the sky, flying buttresses stretched taut like stone wings, and stained-glass windows glinted with muted, unnatural light. The central tower dominated everything around it, a dark spear aimed upward. The world felt quieter here, as if the entire mount bowed beneath the weight of whatever dwelled inside that cathedral of the dead.

I growled, shaking the unwanted thoughts and feelings from my mind. One thing was for sure, I was not going to fight my way through a fortress when I could just fly right over the walls and land on one of the nice cobblestone pathways. Judging by the Level 80 Fledglings manning the fortress, everything on this mount should give me enough experience to get to Level Cap. And that meant all I needed to do was kill enough quantity of monsters and I'd get there.

On the other hand, I also wanted to beat the Lich and see what kind of treasure I could get out of a Level 95 mega dungeon boss. That had to be some good stuff, the kind of rewards that could shift the balance of power entirely.

Looking around, I was startled to see how serene the place looked, other than the bands of roving vampire fledglings, of course, their movement the only thing disturbing the false calm.

I did want to try one first to see how strong they were before I went and took on groups of them at once, so I went into Stealth and quietly moved down the path in the direction I thought would lead to the Cathedral.

They mostly seemed to be roaming in groups of three to five, but I did see ones or twos here or there. I waited until I found an individual creeping around where one of the paths dead-ended into a wall of trees. Which wasn't to say these trees were densely packed and I was in some kind of dark forest. This was much more park-like, except with spooky Halloween vibes. Lots of cobwebs in the trees, and everything had a grayish tint. It made them look sickly, as if they hadn't seen the sun in weeks.

That was bullshit, of course. None of this existed two weeks ago. Hell, where I was standing there had probably been half a dozen restaurants and upscale stores visited by thousands of people every day. Then the AI had gone and fucked it all up. Now there was a System-generated bloodsucker sniffing the air like an addict looking for a fix, so I decided to give it the last fix of its unlife. Not with my blood, but with a spell... something unpleasant.

Go big or go home.

I launched Void Lance, my most powerful spell. I hoped it would destroy the pale monster in a single shot, but I wasn't so lucky. It hurt the bastard badly, but didn't end it outright. Unfortunately, before I could get off a second shot, it screeched, a sound somewhere between a growl and a shriek. It wasn't a cry of pain. It was a call.

I wanted to finish this one before more could show up, so instead of waiting, I hit it with Greater Void Bolt. The bolt rocked it backward but didn't quite finish it off. Still, those two spells had stacked Nullification and Cold, making the feral vampire move as slow as molasses to my eyes.

Then two more of its kind rushed around the corner. What I had taken for a dead end had instead been a sharp turn to the right, apparently. In game terms, they had the initiative.

I was just finishing the Void Bolt when they appeared. Too late for me to switch spells, but just in time for them to see my attack slam into their companion and stagger it backward.

The three exchanged a glance, but didn't say anything, at least not out loud.

Instead, they all turned their heads back to me in that creepy unison sort of way that horror movies had. Then they blurred, and two of them reappeared next to me before I could even blink.

Vampire movement skills. They were just as fast as my Dragon's Charge, maybe faster.

In the instant I had those thoughts, they had already begun attacking with their most powerful skills. I had just enough time to cast Ward of Shadows, granting me forty percent damage reduction and thirty percent damage reflection.

Their claws raked me across the chest and right arm with two quick attacks each in the time it normally took for one. They were either using Haste or it was a dual-wielding type attack skill letting them make two attacks at the same time, and that was despite being inside my Void Domain!

Regardless, my health dropped by twenty percent in an instant. Worse, where had the third fledgling gone? I knew a setup when I saw one, and my instincts were already screaming.

Not bothering to attack or actively defend, I activated Dragon's Charge to get some distance, but just as I did, I felt a devastating blow from behind, a piercing claw attack to the kidney.

Excruciating pain bloomed in my back even as I blinked away. My health dropped another twenty percent. That had to have been a critical blow.

Bastards!

I turned as I reappeared, seeing my enemies' heads whipping around, their noses lifting as they searched for where I'd gone as if scent mattered more than sight now.

I wasn't pulling any punches at this point. I cast Night's End, my extreme damage AOE spell, and centered it just in front of where the trio now stood.

It only took an instant for the spell to draw in the light from all around, creating a thirty foot radius of unnaturally dark night, with tendrils of darkness reaching out to grasp the vampires. However, even in that brief eye blink, they had already moved and nearly crossed the zone of effect. Only the grasping darkness had kept them from exiting the zone entirely, shadowy tendrils snapping tight around limbs and torsos like hands refusing to let go.

Damn, their Haste is no joke!

Then the darkness detonated, flinging their undead bodies forward toward me, rag dolling into trees and bouncing across the path. The already injured one landed at my feet, never to rise again, its health bar bottoming out as its body twitched once and went still.

The other two had lost over fifty percent of their health to that one attack, but were still very much in the fight, and began to rise the second their bodies came to a stop, claws digging into the ground as they pushed themselves upright.

I activated Haste, bringing us back to a more level playing field. Even with that, they were still faster, but only a bit now. I still had some space, so I cast my new binding spell, Absolute Zero, freezing one of the vampires in place, frost racing over its limbs and locking it mid motion like a statue caught mid lunge.

Now it was one on one, even if it was faster than me. I liked those odds much better. It closed on me in the time it took me to cast the binding spell on its comrade. This time its claws glowed red as it sent a powerful blow at my abdomen. I already had one bleed effect from the shot to my kidney, but now I had another, hot pain blooming through my gut.

I didn't waste the time to look at my status, but I could feel the new wound wasn't natural, something hungry and persistent chewing at me from the inside.

Fine, two can play at that game!

Dragon's Rend! My strongest physical attack ripped a gash from its groin to its sternum, blackened flesh peeling back under the force. It was down to thirty percent health now, but I was also down to fifty percent as well, my breathing heavier than I liked.

Up close and personal, they were intimidating. They were big, hulked out brutes, obviously strong physical attackers. Worse, they fought as a pack, every movement purposeful and coordinated. It was a good thing I had severely injured that first one before the other two joined the fight.

The one in front of me attacked again with a flurry of blows, none as strong as its previous attack, but three hit almost at the same time, like Bruce Lee was hammering my ribcage. My armor rang with each impact, the force still bleeding through.

It boggled my mind that they were this fast and aggressive even while being within both my Dragon's Fear Aura and my Void Domain. Even with their own stats lowered by at least 60% and with me running Haste and they were still slightly faster than me! No wonder this was a Raid dungeon meant for large groups of adventurers! Without my unique advantages, I'd be dead meat right now.

All that was passing through my mind while my instincts guided me and I aimed for its leg and launched Crippling Blow. I didn't get lucky, the crit chance didn't pop, so its leg was still attached. Even so, it was a strong attack, dropping another fifteen percent of its health, which seemed to send it into a frenzy, its movements growing wilder and less controlled.

It tried to go all out, its claws flying in strong attacks, but I also had Haste running now and attacked again at the same moment using Shadow Reaver, my execution move. Before its attacks could land, it was decapitated, its head tumbling away across the stone. It had been under twenty percent health, so my strike instantly finished it off.

Still, I couldn't breathe a sigh of relief yet.

The frozen fledgling was already starting to break free. It had one arm loose and was working on the other, ice cracking and shedding in chunks. I rushed over and hit it in the head repeatedly with my claws, stealing health and mana back with every blow, each strike sending a pulse of warmth back into my limbs.

Chuckling, I kept going until its health bar bottomed out and it stopped moving. I could have ended it quicker by using skills, but I was content to take it slow and recover more health and mana thanks to my Voidflame ability, savoring the reversal of momentum.

As I took a breather, to recover, my mind kept spiraling around the fact that they had been so tough even being inside my Void Domain and Aura of Void's Chill.

Note to self, do NOT engage a large group of those guys! Doing the usual trick of gathering a bunch and burning them down with AOE attacks would not be a good idea. I'd get overwhelmed real quick. It had taken two full minutes for the Bleed effects they hit me with to disappear, and I had lost a lot of health over time from those. That was nasty, and it wouldn't take too many of those attacks to leave a person dead real quick.

Considering they traveled in groups of three to five mostly, this was going to be a hassle. I had lost over sixty percent of my health just fighting three of them. I couldn't afford to keep doing that. I needed a better strategy.

CHAPTER 12
LEVEL UP!

I TOOK my time recovering while I thought about what I could do. One good thing was that my armor was repairing itself almost as fast as my body regenerated thanks to its recent upgrade. I could visibly see the gashes closing up as I watched. Nice!

Considering they were physical fighters, if I could keep them at a distance, I should be able to beat the small groups without taking too much damage each time. The other advantage I had was the terrain. Even though the area was fairly open, the fledglings didn't seem to be attracted to the sounds of battle despite the fact that they were close enough that they should have heard our fight. System fuckery, no doubt. Still, I'd be careful not to pick a fight within sight of other monsters.

After my cooldowns had recovered, I stalked the pathways, looking for more. Not that I really needed to search. The mini-map dots drifted lazily along the paths, splitting and merging as the vampires wandered their patrol routes. That let me pick groups that were isolated on the pathways so that I wouldn't get more trouble than I could handle.

Before taking on the next group, I took a deep breath to calm my nerves. Not that the dragon blood in me needed calming. Heat coiled in my chest every time a red dot slid into view. My blood was roaring a challenge every time I came in sight of an enemy. Fortunately, I had learned my lesson in my very first dungeon and did not actually bellow out a challenge. I had a feeling that the line of sight rule the monsters normally had wouldn't prevent others from hearing such a challenge.

Adjusting my armor, I gave the next group one last look. Seeing nothing out of the ordinary, I implemented my new strategy.

Thanks to my shortened cooldowns, I no longer had thirty-minute or hour-long waits between chances to use my big guns. I could engage in a new fight every five minutes and still use my good stuff. So I started with Haste. That would let me get two spells off before they could react. Just to be safe, I also cast a couple of my defensive spells before attacking.

When I was ready, I opened with Arcane Singularity. It would pull the enemies toward the small black hole it created for three seconds before imploding. Second, I cast my extreme damage spell, Night's End, which plunged the area into darkness and also held the enemies in place before it detonated.

Arcane Singularity turned out to be a great choice for an opener. It was reducing their movement and ability to react almost as well as a single-target bind spell. That meant I was free to keep casting, so I piled on my last AOE spell, Entropy, which did Damage over Time as well as applying a corrosive decay effect that would lower their stats, defense, and power for ten seconds. It also did high damage.

Between the three spells, the enemy was already below fifty percent health before they could even act, and I still had one more second to add another pair of attacks to the mix. I used Dragon's Charge to move within range and breathed Void Breath on them, adding cold damage and slowing them even further. Finally finished up with a Tempest Strike, stacking on more speed debuff.

They were down to around twenty-five percent health by the time the explosion from Arcane Singularity sent them hurtling in every direction.

I still had the momentum as they took a literal second to recover from the detonation that sent them hurtling into trees and bushes at the side of the path.

It was going well, but they weren't done. If anything, losing so much health all at once and not being able to do anything would definitely trigger their frenzy status. Thankfully, they were also inside my Void Domain, so the benefits they would have gotten from frenzying would be cancelled out. Still, I wasn't going to give them a chance to hurt me if I could help it.

Grinning, I launched Void Lance at the closest one and got a critical hit, its skull bursting apart in a wet crack that sprayed bone fragments across the path.

I had one more action before they could reach me, so I used Absolute Zero on the next closest baddie, freezing it in place.

That left me tanking a single attack, unable to respond. It tried for a throat shot, raking its claws at my gorget, hoping to pierce the armor. It hit, but not quite where it intended. My Haste let me dodge just enough to take the shot on my shoulder rather than my neck. It did fifteen percent of my health in that one hit and applied the bleeding effect, but that was the only attack it managed.

I returned the favor with Dragon's Rend, dropping its health to five percent, then followed up with a Draconic Strike to finish it off. The two hits restored most of the lost health and a decent bit of mana, but I quickly walked over to the frozen one and began to hammer it with regular blows, using it as a battery to restore my lost health and mana.

That turned out to be a good strategy.

I moved from group to group using Stealth each time to get into position and surprise my enemies. It wasn't perfect. If I had one or two more strong AOE attacks, I might have been able to get away without taking damage, but each fight saw me bloody and injured to the point of needing to get into hand-to-hand combat to use lifesteal and manasteal to top myself back up.

Not every fight went as smoothly as the first. There were plenty of close calls where I would miss the bind spell or make some other mistake and end up facing two or three opponents at close range. Those fights required more recovery time, making my average around fifteen minutes per fight before I was ready for the next.

It definitely felt like a grind, but it was anything but boring. The opponents were far too strong to take anything for granted.

On the upside, I gained another three levels from clearing out the fledglings in the outer zone. That brought me to Level 98. It seemed that at least the Cathedral area conformed more to normal dungeon rules, as there were exactly seventy-five feral vampires.

A quick check of my experience showed my progress:

Liam Bell

Voidblade - Level 98
Bloodline (Tier 4): Void Dragon

Experience: 85195/180560

I was so close to Level Cap now, I could taste it.

The desire to charge straight into the cathedral and burn my way through the monsters was great, but I forced myself to take a break and eat lunch. You might not be able to tell from the gloom hanging over the dungeon, but the sun had long risen, and for everyone else it was around lunchtime. I estimated the fledglings had taken around six to seven hours.

I might be topped up on Health and Mana, but the long hunt had worn me out, so I picked a good spot and leaned up against a tree and took a nap. It was a risk, but the only red dots showing up on my mini-map were the Vampires inside the mausoleums, and I hadn't seen a single one exit their crypts since I had been atop the cathedral mount.

My gamble paid off, and I woke a couple hours later feeling refreshed and ready to make the final push to the Necropolis Boss.

There were fifty of the vampire crypts, but I decided not to bother with them and headed straight to the cathedral instead. If my math was right, and I was sure it was, I should hit Level 100 just before reaching the boss. That would mean I'd get one last skill and spell before dealing with the Necromancer. And who knows, maybe there would be some cool bonus for hitting Level Cap. This was the System, though, so I wasn't holding my breath on that one.

Even as I neared the steps, I wondered what obnoxious flavor messaging the System was about to beam into my head.

As I approached the cathedral's front steps, the architecture grew more unsettling with every stride. From a distance it had looked like a Gothic masterpiece, flying buttresses arcing like stone wings, spires reaching skyward in rigid devotion. Up close, the details betrayed what it truly was. Every saintly figure carved into the exterior had been subtly warped, their faces elongated into silent screams, their gestures flipped so blessings became curses. The stained-glass windows depicted scenes that should have radiated light and hope, but the images inside were reversed, mirrored nightmares, angels with hollow eyes, worshipers kneeling toward shadow instead of sun. Even the buttresses seemed to strain inward, as if the building wasn't supporting heavenward weight but trying to cage something inside.

The great double doors towered over me, carved with a parody of sacred iconography. Where a normal cathedral might display vines, crosses, or scenes of life, these panels showed roots curling downward into graves, crowned figures offering their throats instead of their hands, and a central figure whose face had been chiseled smooth, featureless, waiting to be anyone or everyone. The wood was blackened, not painted, as though fire had licked the grain but failed to consume it. When I pushed the doors open, a breath of cold air slid out, carrying the faint metallic scent of blood long dried.

Inside, the cathedral was cavernous, lit by a dull crimson glow that clung to the air like mist. Pews were arranged in perfect rows, but their surfaces were scarred and gouged, as if clawed hands had gripped them during some unholy rite. Where priests would normally stand, Elder Vampires waited in silent vigil, their eyes tracking me the way wolves watch a trespasser near their den. The altar at the far end was a grotesque inversion of sanctity, bones arranged in geometric patterns, a pulsing obsidian sphere hovering where a relic should rest, and runes etched into the stone floor that spiraled outward like a vortex. Whatever worship once happened here had been rewritten, reshaped into something cold, hungry, and very much alive in the dark beneath the vaulted ceiling.

"Oh, fuck that! This was day 13 of the apocalypse. There hadn't been any worship here, not now, not ever!"

Still, it was creepy as hell the way the elder vampires had all looked at me when the doors opened, but then went back to their business, ignoring me.

I was sure that if they were real individuals and not System generated monsters, they would have all rushed me at that moment. Instead, they obeyed dungeon logic and went about their business until I entered their aggro zone, for which I was very grateful. I would not have wanted to face down thirty Level 90 elder vampires all at once. Level Cap or not, no one would survive that.

Breathing a sigh of relief, I entered and moved to one side. If these Elders were like most dungeon elites, then I should be able to fight them individually unless I did something dumb and entered the aggro zone of another one.

Not one to give up on a working strategy, I repeated my attack method I'd used on the fledglings. I applied my defensive spells, then Haste, then opened with my strongest attack spells at range. The downside was that I could only get so much range, since we were essentially in one big cross-shaped room and I had to stay out of aggro of the other elder vampires.

I opened with Void Lance, but this time I did one thing different. I flapped my wings and took to the air, even if I only hovered a couple feet off the ground. I wanted every bonus I could get, and Void Lance granted a 25% bonus if used while flying. It also applied Nullification and Cold, slowing the enemy and stripping any beneficial buffs it might have had.

Before I could finish my second spell, the Elder was already moving, rushing toward me. I cast Night's End, not where he had been, but as close to me as I could without being inside the damage radius.

BOOM!

It went off, hurling the Elder away to crash into the row of pews.

I wasn't feeling good about this fight. I was Hasted, and it had moved so fast I almost didn't get off my second spell before it could arrive. Even now, rather than being stunned, the priest-like vampire did a kick-up and was back on its feet before I could take another shot. I didn't bother with Arcane Singularity, as fast and strong as this bastard was, I doubted it could pull the monster toward the center and hold it there.

Instead, I opted for Greater Void Bolt, doing high damage and applying another stack of Nullification and Cold. That made a difference. Although it used the vampiric movement skill to instantly reach me, it was no longer moving at a speed that even I could barely follow. Now, with Cold stacked on it twice, it was only a little faster than me instead of twice as fast. My Domain and Aura also helped. Without those, this thing would have been at least twice as fast as the fledglings outside.

It hit me with a glowing claw that sent me flying back into a large stone pillar. I used Dragon's Charge to return to where it stood and make my own attack. Dragon's Rend!

My previous attacks had taken it down to 60% health, and this one dropped it to 35%. It was a damn good start, but thanks to its speed, I didn't get a follow-up attack. We were both boosted to the point where it was like we were two normal people fighting. It hit me back with another skilled attack, shaving another 15% off my health and bringing me down to 70%. My side was burning with pain where it had landed a bleed effect.

I did not like this. Trading blows with something that was very nearly my equal was stupid, but I didn't have another option. Hell, if I hadn't stacked Cold on it, it would be hitting me twice for every one of my attacks.

I hit it with a Tail Lash, hoping it would be Staggered and unable to attack for three seconds, but I was unlucky and it just took the damage, losing another 10% of its health. I just needed two more good hits!

Unfortunately, it hit me with the grown-up version of the flurry of blows the fledglings had used. It hurt. It hit four times, with each hit reducing my health by 5%, bringing me down to 50% after only three attacks. *Fuck!*

I returned the favor with Void Strike, dealing another 10% of its health and reducing its stats by 30% while slowing it further.

The difference was noticeable. I almost managed to dodge the elder vampire's next attack, but still received a grazing blow that ripped away another 5% of my health.

Still, it was below 20% health now, so I could finally use the Shadow Reaver skill and instantly killed the bastard. Instant decapitation! Black blood, viscous and rotten sprayed across the pews as it fell.

When it was over, I was bleeding and disgruntled. It was eight levels below me, and I had still had such a hard time with a single individual. That was not good. I wasn't sure how I was going to manage the boss fight with five of those plus an ultra-strong boss. I would need to get better at fighting them to have any chance of success.

I took a few minutes to rest and recover, let my cooldowns expire, and planned my routine better. Instead of starting with Void Lance, for the next fight I opened with Absolute Zero, which bought me a couple of seconds. That might not sound like a lot, but with their speed, it made all the difference in the world. I was able to get off more attacks up front, which also let me stack more debuffs on it, bringing its speed down to something much more manageable.

I still took a couple hits in that second fight, but finishing a fight having only 25% of my health as damage was a lot better than 50%. Of course, I also gained most of that health and mana back from Voidflame, but still. The point was that I did not take so much damage, and I succeeded in that. When it was over, I rested against the pew, panting and holding my side where the latest wound had not yet closed up.

It was going to be a long afternoon!

There were thirty of them in total before the boss room, and over the course of the next several hours I had nearly worked my way through them all when I finally hit the goal I'd been aiming for ever since I restarted the apocalypse.

CHAPTER 13
LEVEL CAP!

DING!

Was it just me or had that chime been more significant? At that moment I felt like it was the most beautiful sound I had ever heard!

<System Notification>

Congratulations on reaching Level 100!
You have reached the Level Cap.

Note: Due to System limitations, those who reach the Level Cap, cannot continue to gain experience and advance in levels. However, users will find that many rewarding challenges still await.

Congratulations! You have earned a title: Trail Blazer - Ultimate - Plus 5 all stats!

Congratulations! You have earned a title: Level Cap Leader - for being the first native of your world to reach the Level Cap, you receive Plus 10 to all stats.

Congratulations! You have earned a title: Grace Period Prodigy - for reaching Level Cap while your world is still in its grace period, you receive ***error***.
Note: Reward reduced due to foreknowledge advantage. Plus 10 all stats.

I stood there in the middle of the warped cathedral and just gazed at my messages in stunned amazement. I had received a total of +25 to all my stats due to the various titles I had earned. That wasn't exactly earth-shattering, but it felt great to receive it. I mean, it wasn't comparable to the boosts I had gotten with my Class upgrades, but then I wasn't going to complain. It could have been worse. I had seen the System give rewards that were entirely useless in my past life, like a high-end magic sword to an archer who never participated in melee combat.

Choosing to be thankful, I opened my status page to see the results of my final level up, or at least my final level up before Ascending. I got the impression there would be rewards to rising through the Ascension tiers apart from just the admin abilities, after all.

Liam Bell:

Voidblade - Level 100 (Max)
Bloodline (Tier 4): Void Dragon

Attributes:
Endurance: 300
Strength: 300
Agility: 300

Mind: 299
Will: 299
Magical Aptitude: 299
Luck: 10

Health: 6000/6000
Mana: 5980/5980

Abilities:
Active:
Aura of Void's Chill, Void Breath, Claws, Horns, Tail, Wings, Transformation
Passive:
Dark Vision, Void Dragon Scales, Treasure Sense, Regeneration, Magic Resistance

Skills:
Active:
Draconic Strike, Draconic Fury, Searing Slash, Dragon's Charge, Tempest Strike, Heavy Draconic Strike, Stealth (Advanced), Crippling Blow, Shadow Surge, Shadow Tag, Dragon's Rend, Tail Lash, Shadow Reaver
Passive:
Void Dragon Hide, Claw Mastery, Evasion, Voidflame, True Perception

Spells:
Void Bolt, Scalebound Resilience, Darkness, Shadow Ward, Arcane Singularity, Void Travel, Absolute Zero, Ward of Shadows, Teleport, Dispelling Burst, Arcane Cipher, Night's end, Haste, Void Aegis, Void Gaze, Void Lance, Void Strike, Greater Void Bolt, Entropy, Void Echo

I wasn't that emotional of a person, but there were tears in my eyes as I looked at the status screen, my vision blurring just enough that I had to blink a few times to keep the text in focus.

This was so far beyond what I had ever dreamed was possible in my first life, and I had achieved this in only thirteen days. I was still a long, long way from saving the human race from extinction, but I finally felt like I might have a chance now. I just stood there for a long moment savoring the feeling of hope and satisfaction at achieving the first major goal, letting the weight in my chest loosen for the first time since the apocalypse began.

Unfortunately, it was only the first step. I still had to complete the Ascension quest, which I was sure would be ridiculously difficult, knowing the System.

One thing that blew my mind was that three of my stats had hit 300. Of course, the other three were stuck at 299, which was like an itch in my brain, the numbers glaring back at me every time my eyes flicked over the page.

"Why, why couldn't the numbers all end up nice and even?!?" I shook my fist at the ceiling in OCD frustration!

I took a deep breath, slow and deliberate, forcing the irritation down. I could fix that later, once I had access to the System Shop. Three stat stones wouldn't be cheap, but with the money I had now, it was a drop in the bucket and worth the expense just to avoid looking at uneven stat numbers.

There were still three things I wanted to see, so I quickly looked at my new Ability, Skill, and Spell.

Magic Resistance (50%) (Passive)

Description: Draconic resilience that hardens the caster's form against hostile sorcery.

Effect: Reduces all incoming magical damage by 50%.
Cooldown: None.

True Perception (Passive)

Description: A perfected draconic gaze capable of piercing all veils, distortions, and hidden truths.
Effect: Reveals illusions, invisibility, stealth techniques, shapeshifting, astral overlays, and dimensional distortions. Cannot be deceived by false forms.
Cooldown: None.

Void Echo

Description: Creates a duplicate formed from condensed Void essence, mirroring the caster's physical presence and actions.
Effect: Summons a Void Echo that shares the caster's mana pool and persists indefinitely until dismissed or destroyed.
Cooldown: 1 day.

"Hoooly sheeet!"

I was not disappointed in my Level 100 additions! Every one of those was well worth the spot at that level. Permanent Magic Resistance that reduced all magic damage by 50%? Hell, yeah!

Then there was the True Perception passive skill that would reveal the truth of the things around me. I mean, I already had my minimap showing me red dots for enemies within my range of perception, but now stealthy enemies—and even not enemies—would be visible to me. That damned Dark Elf assassin wouldn't have snuck up on me with this skill active!

Last, but very much not least, was Void Echo. It was a freakin' clone! Call it what you will, it would let me create a copy of myself that would last indefinitely. Meaning, that if I didn't let it get destroyed in combat, it would be the perfect guard to protect my back or keep watch while I slept.

Or help me fight a Level 95 boss with five Elder Vampire minions!

All of a sudden, what had seemed impossible now felt doable. It would still be dangerous as hell, but I figured it would be possible now, the tight knot of dread sitting like lead in my stomach since I had fought the first elder vampire eased a bit.

I wasted no time and summoned my Echo.

When I triggered Void Echo, the air around me seemed to thicken, as if the world paused for a heartbeat. My shadow stretched forward across the stone and then pulled upward, lifting off the floor like liquid darkness, slipping into existence out of the void. It gathered into a rough shape at first, drifting and folding in on itself as strands of void energy wrapped together with a slow, steady purpose.

A moment later, the shape settled into something unmistakable. Me.

It stood there, matching my height and wingspan, its outline carved from void energy rather than flesh. The surface of it rippled faintly, almost like smoke trapped inside glass, and the flow of its mana matched my own rhythm. It didn't breathe or make a sound, but it felt connected to me in a way that was hard to put into words, like part of my presence had stepped free of my body to stand beside me.

The Echo turned its head toward me, voidlight swirling where its eyes should have been, and waited. Not impatient, not eager—just ready. It really did feel like a second self called out of the emptiness, loyal to my will and my magic. I could also feel its connection to my mana pool, implying it could use my spells and abilities.

Grinning like a demon, I started to step toward the next Elder Vampire to see how well they stood up to two of me!

But first, I was even more excited to share my news with someone. In my first life, I'd had companions—groups I'd join to run dungeons with, and folks I'd met along the way. They didn't stick around, either because of death or losing touch. In this new life, however, I had people—people I actually cared about, ones that would stick around. They cared, and it warmed my heart thinking of how they would react. Not just because I was one step closer to making them safe, but because they were my friends.

Triggering the Commune ability with Morgan, I said, "Hey, how's it going with the Exodus?"

Morgan grumbled, "My feet hurt, and if I hear one more person complain, I'm going to lose it."

I chuckled. I could tell from her tone she was just grousing. "Where are you guys now? Have you made it back to the camp?"

"Well, the head of the column probably has. Viki and I are guarding the rear of the march, and we're about a half mile away, I'd guess. We had some fun during the night before we camped, but the trip today has been pretty uneventful, at least in terms of attacks. It has just been a lot longer than expected.

There have been some issues with people wanting to go off on their own after we passed the most dangerous areas. We convinced most to keep going, but it's not like we're going to force people to go somewhere they don't want to, not when they've got missing family out there. At least these people all have heard the Gospel of Liam the Regressor."

I groaned. "Please don't tell me people are actually calling my information that!"

Morgan laughed, and I could hear Viki giggling in the background. "No, but I think it's funny. Still, I wouldn't be surprised if people did start calling it something like that eventually. Especially after you Ascend and become a god as far as the System is concerned. Might not be a bad idea to get ahead of it and name it ourselves rather than ending up with something worse. Oh, and we picked up a lot more people along the way since dawn. That's part of why it has taken so long to get back."

"Ugh, you might be right. Still, I don't think I want any part in that. Call it whatever you want. Anyway, I've got news. Can Viki hear me?"

Viki called out, "Yeah, I can hear you. Can you hear me?"

That made me chuckle, remembering that old phone company commercial, which was probably before Viki's time. "Yeah, I can." That actually surprised me, since our previous uses of the Commune skill hadn't worked that way.

Morgan chimed in, "Yeah, I figured out how to adjust the settings, so to speak. I just had to concentrate on wanting it to turn the volume up so people around me could hear you, and apparently that turned this into a 'speaker phone' situation."

"Neat. So anyway, since you can both hear me, I just wanted you two to be the first to know that I reached Level Cap! It just happened a few minutes ago. I'm nearly to the boss of the Necropolis Dungeon. Just a handful of Elder Vampires left, and I'll get some loot!"

Viki grumbled, "Ah, man! I wish we could be there for that. You could come get us!"

I gave that some serious thought. I could use the extra help, and they would greatly benefit from the EXP and loot they'd get off the boss. Still, Level 90 elite minions... one hit from one of those vampires and Morgan or Viki could die instantly. Then there was their speed. They were faster than me. It was going to be a hard battle even with my new clone skill. There was no way I could guarantee their safety.

Sensing my hesitation, Viki pleaded, "Come on! Please! We could stay out of the way and only attack from range, or not even attack at all." That last was said with some reluctance. "Besides, having Morgan there would mean you'd have healing if you needed it. We could even stealth!"

That was tempting, but I was worried about their survival and didn't want to be responsible for their deaths.

Morgan spoke up, likely sensing my reason for not answering right away. "It would be very dangerous, but Viki does have a point. Even if all we did was sit back and watch, it would help us. We'll need to come back there soon to fight that boss once we've leveled up. Seeing it before we have to face it ourselves would be a big leg up."

"You're not wrong. That's just a really big level gap, the kind that could mean a single attack might be enough to kill you. Seems like a big risk." Then again, those who didn't take risks wouldn't make it to the top. Worse, they were also right that they would need to stand on their own very soon, and I might not be there to protect them. Who knows what would happen once I started the Ascension quest?

"Okay, fine, but you guys have to do everything in your power to stay safe. It's not just me that the world needs right now. You both are equally important—we need to take at least four of the seven Ascension spots, and I want three of those to be us."

I didn't have to be there to picture Viki dancing around in triumph as she shouted, "Yesss! You won't regret this. We'll be there to protect you if you need us." Then she realized that was not a winning argument and added, "We'll stay hidden and not attack."

Chuckling, I let them know that I'd meet them at the camp, then teleported to just in front of the entrance portal for the medium dungeon outside the Colony camp. I figured it was unlikely anyone would be standing too close to that.

I was not wrong—but people were much closer than I anticipated, and a middle-aged woman jumped and screeched when she saw me appear. "...m... m... MONSTER!"

There was nearly a panic before I was able to convince the people around me that I was, in fact, human. I would have made my horns and wings disappear, but they actually helped me push through the crowd. People shied away as I approached, giving me the chance to make headway through the huge mass of refugees.

I did make my tail vanish, though. I didn't want it getting stepped on.

What I thought would only be a quick fifteen-minute in-and-out turned into nearly an hour before Morgan and Viki found me near Brian's command tent. Nor did I get away without meeting with Brian and his team.

CHAPTER 14

THE CALM BEFORE THE STORM

I WANTED to be back at the dungeon killing that boss. I had a strong hunch that as soon as I finished, the AI would drop the Ascension quest on me, a pressure that sat heavy in my chest, but I didn't have a choice. This needed to be taken care of.

It was late afternoon and Brian looked incredibly frazzled as he stood on top of an old wooden shipping crate, trying to direct the chaos around us. His little camp of maybe five hundred people had just expanded massively. There were now somewhere around ten thousand people all crowding into and around the camp arena, maybe more. It was really hard to tell with people all spread out this way. Some were trying to find places to set up tents or even just claim a spot on the ground, while others were lined up around the pond to get their first drink of relatively clean water in days. More wanted to immediately move on to the Safe Zone that had been promised and were demanding Brian and my girls escort them the rest of the way.

I could see the poor man needed help, the strain written all over his face, so I figured the fastest way for me to get back to what I needed to do would be to step in.

The first thing I did was clear the area around Brian's makeshift platform and gesture for him to get down. When I was certain that everyone was out of the way, I used Stone Shape to pull in concrete and stone from the area around me and build a real platform, one that stood a good twenty feet high. That would give him the vantage to see the whole camp and allow him to speak to more people at once.

The tower was a relatively crude thing, not much more than three pillars with a couple of platforms between them, and handholds shaped into one of the pillars. One platform was about half the height of the tower, the other was at the very top. I got more than I bargained for, though. Raising that up drew a lot of attention. Pretty soon, people for a hundred yards or more in every direction were staring at the platform, their conversations fading into a low, expectant hush, so I gestured for Brian to climb to the top.

Meanwhile, I leaped up with a single beat of my wings propelling me to the top just as Brian stood up. The platform was around fifteen feet square, but it had no railing or other safety features, which I realized was a problem when I saw the camp leader's face go pale and step back from the edge.

Blushing, I cast the spell again and drew up more stone to make a waist-high wall around the top. That would not only make it a bit safer, but would also give anyone stationed up here on lookout duty a little bit of a windbreak on chilly evenings.

Giving me a thankful smile, Brian turned around slowly, looking out over the sea of people, then cleared his throat. He cast some kind of skill, then his voice boomed out across the vastly expanded camp.

"Welcome to the Colony Camp. I know some of you want to keep going while there is still daylight to make it to the Safe Zone. You are welcome to do that. However, I will not be escorting you, nor will any of my guards. The group of you wanting to go is large enough to discourage or handle any mutated beasts that might attack. As you've seen this morning, the areas further outside the city centers are much safer than where you came from. That's not to say they are completely safe, but at least up here you won't find any roaming zombies or other System-created monsters spilling out of their dungeons. At least not yet."

He gestured at me. "This is Liam Bell. He's the one you have heard about who has future knowledge of the apocalypse. He was the one who set up the Safe Zone last night."

There was a wave of murmurings and hushed conversations that spread throughout the crowd at this announcement, like wind rippling through tall grass. Half a minute went by before Brian continued.

"Liam has already reached Level 100 and will be working to complete a quest that will allow him to set up more Safe Zones, but until then, the only one on Earth is centered just past Melissa, Texas. It's ten miles in radius, so it's plenty big to handle a lot of people. All you need to do is follow the highway here and head northeast into McKinney. Once you pass Town Lake Park, you should be in the safe area. Stay on your guard. Dungeons and mutated beasts still exist there, but new ones can't form, and monsters and beasts won't be able to enter the area from now on."

He went on to say a lot more, but after the main points, I waved to the crowd and jumped down from the tower. It looked like he was getting people straightened out, and I had places to be.

Viki and Morgan had grabbed a bite to eat and joined me as I hit the ground. Viki hugged me around the waist and head-butted me in the chest. "I can't believe you hit Level 100 already! It's been less than two weeks since all this started. Man, I can't wait until I get there!"

Morgan grinned at her and added, “Me too, although I don’t care about the leveling for the sake of it. I just want to get these quest things out of the way so we can get started rebuilding.”

I was somewhere in between. I had dreamed of getting this powerful in my first life, so I did crave the power, the thrill of it still buzzing under my skin, but like Morgan, I too wanted to get there for the sake of what we could accomplish.

When they were ready, we headed out of the camp on foot. There was no longer any room for me to transform into my dragon form. Sure, I could have made people shove backward to clear a space, but it would have risked injuries and would have been a dick move when I could just walk a bit further to get beyond the camp area.

I chose south, and we climbed over the newly created hill that had replaced the big Nebraska Furniture store. People hadn’t settled on the hill much because of the dungeon entrance, not wanting to be too close to that due to the System-imposed creepy feelings it gave off.

When I was finally in a decent spot, I transformed, and the girls climbed up onto my back and settled into the harness, strapping themselves in.

In my deep, rumbling bass dragon voice, I warned, “Be sure to hang on. Once we get there, I’ll need to do some fancy flying to avoid the Wraiths. Otherwise, we’ll have to fight our way through everything on the ground.”

Viki gave an enthusiastic thumbs-up. “Oooh, that sounds fun!”

Rolling her eyes, Morgan snorted. “Fun, she says! Just don’t drop us, please.”

“If you’re strapped in good, there’s no chance of that. Just be careful of the Wraiths. If any of them get to you, remember they take magical weapons or spells to damage. Physical attacks will just go right through them. It may be a rough ride, though. I'm going to try and outmaneuver them to avoid fights."

There was one last moment at the camp that startled me. As I took off, rather than scream in fright, the people in the camp below cheered. Brian had warned people about me turning into a dragon to prevent a panic, so they apparently took seeing my transformation as proof that all the things Brian had told them were true.

And that sparked hope.

Which led to the cheering.

Never in my life had I been applauded by even a hundred people, much less ten thousand or more. I felt my scales heating—a warmth spreading beneath them, unmistakably the draconic equivalent of a blush.

The moment sparked some conflicted emotions. On the one hand, I just wanted to hide. It was one thing to know the hope of the human race was riding on my shoulders—I'd been dealing with that since the moment my eyes opened after waking up in the past. It was entirely another thing to see that hope manifest in the cheering crowd below. It somehow made it all more real. There was a cold feeling of worry in the pit of my stomach, a fear that I might let them down. I still had the Ascension quest to complete, and I had no idea what that entailed.

On the other hand, it also warmed my heart to see this spark of hope in the previously despairing survivors. For that reason, I pushed aside the pressure and worry for their sake and did a big loop around the camp, roaring into the sky as I passed over the center area where Brian stood on the platform.

The cheering redoubled, and a lump welled up in my throat, thick enough that swallowing didn't help. I didn't know if dragons could cry, and I didn't want to find out right now, so I shot off to the southwest and focused on getting back to kill that boss.

Those aren't tears... there's just dust in my eyes!

The flight back to the cathedral hill at the center of the Necropolis was indeed troublesome. It was everything I could do to avoid the wraiths, but even doing my best, a few got through and Viki and Morgan had to deal with them. Thankfully, no one was seriously injured, but Morgan did look a little green when I finally touched down on the steps of the twisted cathedral, her grip on the harness lingering a moment longer than usual.

Viki, on the other hand, was beaming. "That was better than the best rollercoaster ever! Let's do that again!"

Morgan gave her young friend side-eye so hard I laughed and thought of that old meme with the cat and the Jamaican-accented voice-over: "Bombastic side-eye... criminal offensive side-eye!"

I hadn't thought of that meme in years, I was surprised I even remembered it.

Seeing Morgan's frown at my laughter, I cleared my throat and got busy changing back into my humanoid form with horns, wings, and tail.

My faithful second me was still waiting just inside the cathedral where I'd left him.

I could feel his presence—my presence? Like a pressure at the back of my awareness, so I knew exactly where he was at all times, or at least a general direction when the distance was greater than about a mile. As a result, I didn't think anything of it. However, I had forgotten to tell Morgan and Viki of my new skills...

Apparently, it retained enough free will and my personality that it decided to jump-scare the girls when we walked in.

"Boo!"

Viki shrieked and drew her Shaman Cleaver instinctively before staring in shock and surprise at the Void copy of me. Then she burst out laughing at the situation.

Morgan, however, nearly peed herself and hit me in the arm hard enough to hurt even with my stats. Not the Echo clone, but me!

"Hey, what'd I do? I didn't plan that!"

She repeated the side-eye she'd given Viki just a moment before and narrowed her eyes dangerously. "It's you. One way or another, you're responsible!" Then a hint of an amused smirk appeared on her face as the adrenaline faded and she began to see the humor in it. "For the record, I like jump scares just fine, but not so much when we are in a dungeon, okay?"

I gave my copy a pointed glance, and it nodded contritely and gestured toward where the remaining monsters waited.

We learned a few things over the next half hour. First, a single Elder Vampire stood absolutely no chance against me and my clone together, especially not with backup from Viki and Morgan.

Second, as if the jump scare wasn't enough of a clue, I confirmed that my shadow copy was not devoid of will. It definitely acted and behaved like me—like it really was an identical copy of me made out of void stuff. In other words, it wasn't just a dumb mob from a game following AI logic. It could think and act independently to a degree, sometimes anticipating my moves before I consciously made them.

Lastly, we developed a strategy and tested it out on the remaining Elder Vampires, one that would hopefully let us conquer the boss.

And speaking of the boss, I finally caught sight of it. Where a cathedral would normally have the Sanctuary or Chancel, in the place where the high altar would be housed, instead the Necromancer sat upon a throne of bones atop a raised dais towering ten feet above the rest of the floor. It was surrounded by five elder vampires playing the part of priests, all worshiping it as if it was their god.

We'd already established that Morgan and Viki would need to stay back as far as they could and remain in stealth as much as possible. Against the Elder Vampires, Viki had attacked with her bow, and Morgan had lobbed an occasional spell, but that was when we were fighting a single opponent.

"You guys need to stay in stealth throughout the fight. With five enemies plus an ultra boss, you can't afford to draw aggro. So no doing anything unless the fight is either nearly won or it's life and death."

I gave Morgan a pointed look. "That means no healing either. Just like in games, monsters love to target the healers and prioritize them over targets. They are more than fifty levels higher than you, so their skills and attacks will be deadly if they hit. Instantly, as in one-shot kills."

Morgan gave me an understanding smile and reached out and squeezed my hand. "We understand. We'll stay hidden, and we'll try to stay out of any AOE range too."

Her hand felt warm on my scales, a small, grounding weight, and I smiled back. "I know. I just worry about you both."

Viki, however, did not look terribly pleased to not be allowed to attack the monsters. Still, she had agreed, since that was a condition of being allowed to enter the boss area at all.

She was anticipating this fight as much as I was, it seemed.

CHAPTER 15
LICH, PLEASE!

GLANCING to the party's health bars, I sighed and wiped the sweat from my brow, my fingers leaving damp streaks across my scales.

Going into this battle, I had to admit to myself that I was worried. Not so much that I would lose, although that was a definite possibility. No, I was worried for Morgan and Viki's sake. Even with their promise of staying out of the fight, all it would take would be one big AOE attack to kill them. I would have to make sure that didn't happen.

When we stepped up to the altar rail, I gestured to my clone. As he drew near, I whispered a few words to him to make sure he would help me keep all the monsters' attention on us.

It was weird talking to myself, and even more so to hear him talking back. "Don't worry, I'll sacrifice myself if necessary to keep them safe. Hell, it's not like you can't summon me back tomorrow."

I chuckled at my double's gallows humor and gave him a nod. "Okay, everyone knows their parts?"

Viki and Morgan gave me decisive nods. "Ready for stealth." Viki saluted with her bow.

Morgan stepped forward and cast Blessing of the Dragon's Grace on me, then on my Echo, then on each of them. Grumbling, she added, "I wish I had more buffs!"

"No worries. You'll get more as you level. I appreciate the one. A bonus to Agility and a little extra magic resistance is nothing to sneeze at. Every bit helps!"

I also triggered my once-per-day ability from my Soul Shield Ring to give me a short-duration Mental Shield that would reflect 50% of any attack damage, as well as the once-per-day ability of my Spectral Longknife of Shadows to grant Critical damage and Ignore Defenses on my first strike.

This fight was going to be intense right from the get-go.

We stepped forward to the small gate in the railing that would let us into the chancel area of the cathedral where the boss awaited.

I braced myself. I knew this one was going to be a doozy. There was no way the System wouldn't have a big cutscene beamed into our heads for a boss battle like this. This was arguably one of the biggest bosses on the planet, at least as far as I knew. Although, to be fair, I had never been into the downtown areas. Those could be even worse. Still...

As I stepped through the gate in the altar railing, the air changed in a way that had nothing to do with temperature. It thickened, settling against my scales like damp cloth, and the faint smell of old blood and incense rolled over me. My lungs tightened as if the room itself resented my breathing. The sanctuary beyond opened into a vast chamber shaped by warped devotion. Shadows clung to the arches overhead. The stained-glass windows glowed with a muted crimson light that did not come from outside, but from the necromantic aura pulsing at the center of the room.

Every surface felt wrong, as if the stone remembered what it was supposed to be but was forced into something else.

Ahead, the dais rose ten feet above the floor, a crude altar platform remade into a throne stage. The throne itself was built from bones fused together into a mockery of regal design. Ribcages formed the arms. Skulls lined the back like jewels. The Necromancer Lich sat upon it with perfect stillness, hands folded over a staff crowned with a soul-stone that throbbed in a rhythm that felt almost alive. It did not look at me. It could not see me through the stealth enchantments. But the Lich lifted its head anyway, as though tasting the air. The smile that crept across its desiccated features made my scales prickle.

At the base of the dais, five Elder Vampires knelt in priestly robes that hung from their bodies in stiff, ceremonial folds. Their heads were bowed, arms raised in a gesture of worship that felt older than the cathedral itself. Necrotic symbols glowed across the floor around them, forming a ritual circle that fed power up into the throne. Even in silence, the room seemed to vibrate with their collective hunger. The stillness felt coiled, ready to snap. I could feel their awareness brushing against the edges of the space, hunting for anything out of place. Their stillness nothing but restrained violence waiting for a signal.

The Lich finally spoke, its voice echoing across the chamber with a hollow, resonant tone that vibrated in my chest. "Children of flesh, you stand upon sacred ground. You hide yourselves, yet your hearts drum loudly in the dark. Do not mistake silence for safety. I have felt your coming since the moment you set foot upon my mount." The soul-stone brightened, casting long, twisted shadows across the throne. "Step forward, little mortals. Let me gaze upon those who dare disturb the unholy sanctity of my eternal dominion. Come and bow before me and I will raise you up as one of my servants. Perhaps you will even be privileged to become a priest, like one of these. If you submit willingly, I promise your death will be swift and without pain."

I smirked, thinking, *His less than two-week-old "eternal dominion," ha!*

That was an interesting question, though. Would this System-generated monster be able to take the bodies of real people and turn them into monsters? Is that how the dungeon expanded so quickly with so many monsters? Were the zombies outside actually people who had been killed by the dungeon?

I could feel blood roaring in my veins and a growl wanting to form in my chest. The very idea that some or all of those zombies, wraiths, and other monsters might have once been innocent citizens of the city surrounding the dungeon made me furious. Still, I knew better than to let my dragon instincts get in the way of fighting smart.

But damn, was it hard when both my instincts and my human sensibilities agreed!

Nope, we've got a plan, and I'm going to stick to it. I won't let this monologuing piece of trash goad me into being an idiot.

Besides, I had too much to worry about to get wrapped up in responding to verbal sparring. This boss room was like nothing I'd ever experienced before. We triggered the fight by stepping past the altar rail, but no barrier slammed shut behind us.

That raised the hair on the back of my neck, a crawling sensation that ran from my shoulders to my spine. I'd never heard of any boss room that didn't trap the challengers. What on Earth was going on?

I didn't have long to figure it out. The boss would start attacking soon if I didn't. I scanned the surroundings, my eyes darting around the area. I even put my hand back over the rail, and sure enough, it passed through with no issue. Looking further out, even the cathedral doors were wide open and no visible barrier barred the way.

A shiver ran up my spine. Had we not triggered the boss fight yet? Except, the Lich had begun monologuing the moment we entered, just like a boss should.

Then it hit me. This was no ordinary dungeon. Strongholds were meant to be Raid dungeons. The thing that threw me was that in the other two strongholds I had fought, the boss rooms worked as normal and locked people in. But then, this was no ordinary dungeon, and it would take dozens or maybe hundreds of normal people to conquer this place. That meant this battle was intended for a large group of attackers.

Thank goodness for my Mind stat being nearly 300. All these thoughts were flashing through my brain in an instant. The stat didn't mean I was thirty times as smart as Einstein, but I could process information incredibly fast, threads of realization snapping together before panic could take hold.

That explained why the Elder Vampires were so damned fast and strong. They weren't meant for someone to solo, or even a normal party. They were intended to take on large Raid groups.

Quickly glancing around, I realized that with the layout of the cathedral, you could have a team of fifty, or even one hundred, in this space. Damn, that made me wonder if we hadn't just made a mistake in tackling this on our own.

Apparently, people were meant to be able to retreat from this fight if they desired, assuming they could with how fast those vamps were.

That should have been reassuring, but somehow it really wasn't.

I also realized that one of the things we lacked that would be especially useful right now was a means of telepathic communication with my party. A party chat, in gaming terms. I had heard of such things in my first life, but sadly, I hadn't run into any magic items or skills yet that would make it possible. Otherwise, I'd tell the girls to leave right now.

Unfortunately, it was too late. They had already entered, and thanks to them being in the party, I could see a ghostly blue halo around them as well as their icons on my minimap. Right now, they were taking up position in a corner with a tall stone pillar to hide behind. It was structural and big enough to help support the roof of this massive building. Hopefully, that would keep them from being noticed.

I was sure my echo was thinking similar thoughts, as I saw him pause just like I had, but now he was moving to get into position for the beginning of the battle.

Before we approached the boss area, we had considered strategies. We could attack separately, with one of us targeting the Lich and the other the Elder Vampires, but this didn't seem like a good option. The Vampires would overwhelm a single opponent, and just one of us wouldn't have the firepower to burn down a boss at this level fast enough to take it out.

Alternatively, we could concentrate our firepower on the boss, and together we'd be able to bring enough damage to bear to take it down, but the Vampires would be free to attack us while we did that. Worse, they could possibly discover the girls, and we'd be powerless to protect them.

That left the idea of trying to eliminate the minions first. I didn't know what the boss might be capable of, but since it was a Necromancer, it was likely to buff and heal its minions. And considering the power of those Elder Vampires, that wasn't a pleasant thought. Also, it was unkillable unless we could find and destroy its phylactery. I hoped that meant it would be overconfident and less aggressive in the battle, more the typical Bond villain type.

Now, hearing it monologue, I felt more confident in our decision.

My attack would be the signal to start, but there were two more spells to cast before we could begin. I looked to where my double was stealthed, but outlined in a blue glow thanks to the magic of being in a party together. I held up a hand with three fingers and began to count down, knowing my team would be watching.

On two, I cast Dragon's Fury.

This fight was going to be all-in right from the start. There was no chance we could let this thing turn into a long brawl, or we'd be dead.

As if sensing our killing intent rising, the vampiric priests paused in their worship. They turned outward, bearing their fangs and extending their claws, searching the surroundings for the intruders their master was addressing. Their priestly robes were thrown open to reveal stylized black leather armor beneath. These guys weren't messing around.

One. I cast Haste and extended my claws.

The world slowed down for me, everything seeming to go into slow motion. Every particle of dust in the air seemed to hover as if frozen in amber.

CHAPTER 16

BBEG SHOWDOWN

I DROPPED MY HAND, and we simultaneously cast Void Lance on the nearest Elder Vampire. Twin spears of darkness, deeper than night and colder than the Lich's heart, screamed toward the target and obliterated its head. It was destroyed instantly, but I didn't regret the cost of 1000 mana or the fact that we used them both on only one target. **These guys** were tough, extremely so, and I was honestly surprised that even those **two** Extreme damage attacks together took one out.

The vampires moved, their speed even faster than mine. But we moved too, having expected this. We had several seconds before the invisibility of the stealth wore off, and we would use it to the max.

One second had passed, and the Lich was beginning to cast a spell.

Two of the vampires were charging toward where they had seen the previous attacks originate, while the other two formed up in front of their creator in a defensive position. Fortunately, the next closest vampire was charging toward Echo, and another was charging me. This had been one of the failure points of our plan. If all the bastards had formed up in front of the Lich, we would have been screwed, but thankfully they chose to split their ranks, and these two closed the distance and put themselves within our reach.

Half a second passed for Echo and I as we converged with the vampire to position ourselves for attack.

Dragon's Rend!

Our—or rather my—only physical attack that did extreme damage slammed into the vampire with the doubled power of Dragon's Fury, but that wasn't all. We'd gotten lucky on that first vampire, and even two times the damage of an Extreme attack might not stop these two. That's why I was also counting on the once-per-day effect of my Spectral Longknife of Shadows, which was attuned to my left claws. The strike would ignore all defenses and automatically crit for an extra 50% of damage on top of the already doubled damage.

My swing removed the vampire's head, sending it soaring across the chancel to shatter against one of the massive carved stone pillars.

Unfortunately, Echo's opponent didn't go down. While my double could also trigger any skill such as Dragon's Fury, it couldn't trigger my weapon's special ability since I had already done so. Still, it had done massive damage to the Elder Vampire, ripping a huge wound up its torso and opening up its chest cavity, leaving its ribs sticking out like broken kindling.

Even so, it didn't fall to that single blow. Thankfully, my double hit it with a simple Draconic Strike to follow up. It was our least powerful physical attack, but that didn't matter since he targeted the monster's heart directly, which was wide open.

Blood fountained across the area as the vampire's heart was obliterated.

Two seconds.

My headless vampire hadn't even fallen to the floor yet, but that was where our momentum slammed into a brick wall.

The Lich finished its spell, and an unholy chill hit me in the gut like a hammer, staggering me. The world lurched back into motion as both my enhanced speed and strength were cut in half, making me only as strong and fast as I would have been without Dragon's Fury and Haste. Meaning the last two vampires were going to be running circles around us. Worse, we had now used up our best skills, so it would take far longer to deal with the remaining two minions.

That was by far the strongest debuff I'd ever felt, and I cursed the bastard for doing it. What was even more amazing about that debuff was that it had completely ignored my 60% magic resistance that I received between my dragon ability and my Soul Shield Ring. That was one nasty spell!

It had basically done to us what my combined Aura of Void's Chill and my Void Domain did to opponents. Only, it did it in a single AOE debuff spell that completely bypassed defenses.

Now we faced the Lich and two Elder Vampires, both of which were significantly faster than we were. My big Mind stat was telling me they'd get five attacks for every two we made. This was not a winning deal!

Thankfully, we still had our invisibility for another few seconds before it would disappear; otherwise, we would have been completely screwed.

It was great having these incredibly strong and amazing powers, but with the enemies at our same strength level, it meant combat was extremely fast and just as brutal, because they had equally nasty powers.

There was only one smart move left: AOE the bastards and hope it would take out the other two minions, or we'd be fucked.

Three seconds.

Night's End times two.

I staggered and went to one knee. The pull of that much mana at once nearly doubled me over. The spells went off, but Echo and I both casting simultaneously was almost too much. More than half my mana pool was already gone. I'd never needed to worry about mana before, but with two versions of me both drawing from the same mana pool in the same instant... ouch!

It hadn't been so bad casting Void Lance because Dragon's Fury had me pumped up on draconic adrenaline, but this sucked!

Our two spells went off at the same time as the Lich's next spell did. It also had a "darkness" theme to its magic, resulting in the massive cathedral suddenly plunging into an inky blackness even my draconic vision couldn't pierce.

It only lasted for a second, but when Night's End detonated and light returned to the room, everything had changed.

The Lich's throne was destroyed, the bones rocketing in every direction at once, becoming magically infused shrapnel. A tiny sliver of my brain power that I could spare, thanked the heavens that Viki and Morgan were hiding behind such sturdy cover. Otherwise they might not have survived the explosion.

I took a piece in the abdomen, and it felt like getting hit by a baseball bat but it didn't knock me down. It shaved over five hundred health off my bar in an instant. Echo didn't fare any better, but neither of us was out of the fight.

> **-500 Health**
> **Health: 5500/6000**

The Lich and its minions didn't fare as well, being at the epicenter of two extreme damage AOE attacks at the same time. The Lich had lost 50% of its health bar, and its two minions were just as damaged; unfortunately, they were still up and kicking. Whatever the boss had cast, it had protected the two vampires, saving them from what should have been obliteration. Although the boss wasn't affected by the secondary effect of the attack, the two vampires were knocked prone, giving Echo and me the chance to make one more move before they could respond.

Four seconds.

Even in that moment, I felt a chill down my spine once again as I saw the two super-fast elite minions already starting to kick up to return to their feet. We needed to end one of them to make this fight more doable! I considered casting Dispelling Burst to remove status effects, but one quick glance to the corner of my vision told me the ugly truth. That hadn't been a debuff from the Lich, instead it had dispelled my own buffs, Dragon's Fury and Haste. It had done to us the same thing my Nullification did to them. Even my own Aura, despite being ten levels higher than these Elder Vampires, was only partially successful in reducing their speed.

This was not good news, as both my major buffs had long cooldowns and would not be usable again until long after this fight was over. Worse, I could see the vampires visibly starting to regenerate, their health bars beginning to tick back up.

Fuck it! I had to sacrifice a strong attack to stop that! Entropy!

My AOE damage-over-time spell landed on all three, effectively freezing their regeneration, damaging them at the same rate as they were healing. That would level the playing field for the next ten seconds.

At the same time, Echo hit the vampire on the left with Greater Void Bolt, a high-damage attack that also applied another stack of

Nullification and Cold, slowing the bastard by another 30%. It was still faster than me, but now it was only a little less than twice as fast.

They both kicked back up to their feet and began charging toward where they had seen our spells originate. We were still invisible for one more second.

Unfortunately, with Haste gone, there was no point in sacrificing an attack to run to a different spot since we were going to lose our Stealth anyway. I wanted to use my other AOE attacks, but our strategy backfired on that. To keep ourselves from being targeted by AOEs, we were separated enough that only Arcane Singularity would be able to hit them all—but it would take three seconds before it completed, and in this fight that was a lifetime and too long to be useful.

Fine, I used my breath weapon. At least with that, I would get both the Lich and the vampire attacking me. Better yet, I was relieved to see that my attack interrupted its latest spell, which, judging by its last two, was probably the best thing I could have done.

Meanwhile, Echo targeted his vampire again, this time with Void Strike, a heavy-damage attack that applied a weakness debuff, slowing the vampire and dropping all its stats by 30%. That one was down to 25% health now. My own was sitting at 40%.

Five seconds. The invisibility effect from my advanced Stealth wore off, leaving Echo and me visible to their eyes finally.

Then the Vampires got to take their next shots, and we were in a world of hurt. They used some kind of extreme damage skill similar to Dragon's Rend, because when it raked me with its claws my health dropped by 30% in a single attack!

Holy shit! Nearly a third of my health in one shot! The impact drove the breath from my lungs, my vision flashing white as pain lanced through my ribs.

I could see from my display that Echo got hit by the same thing, losing only 25% of his health due to the debuffs the other vampire was under. Void mist tore away from his form where the blow landed, his outline flickering as if someone had ripped a chunk out of a living shadow.

What was worse, because of their speed, they were attacking again, and mine would land a split second after theirs!

Fuuuuck! I barely had time to brace before the next strike came screaming in.

I took another 20% damage, dropping me by half my health, in less than a second! My knees buckled and sparks danced at the edges of my vision as the cathedral floor lurched beneath me, but my own skill was already in motion.

Then my Void Strike landed, doing high damage and dropping the vamp's stats by 30% and slowing its super speed a bit more. Its health bar dropped to 25%. It hissed in pain, but didn't relent. Its fangs snapped inches from my face, blood spittle flecking my scales as it recoiled and lunged again.

At the same time Echo, bless my double's wisdom, used his breath weapon to not only damage his own opponent more, but also disrupt the Lich's next spell. A cone of voidfire washed across the chancel, warping the air and leaving scorched stone in its wake.

The Lich's voice cracked with fury, the sound echoing unnaturally as the spell unraveled in its grasp. I was highly gratified by the string of curses that spewed from the boss's mouth at the interruption.

Six seconds.

This seemed to be a good strategy, but it wouldn't work anymore as we didn't have any other AOEs to cast.

...or did we? There was one, but it wasn't ideal to use just yet since it was supposed to be an execution move.

Either way, their vampiric speed meant it was their turn. Even with the debuffs they were still faster than us. Worse, the one in front of me did something and began to glow with a red aura and its muscles began to bulge as it swung another claw attack at me. It used something like Dragon's Fury, boosting its strength to double. The veins in its arms stood out like cords as power rippled beneath its skin.

Even before the blow landed, I knew it would be bad. Every instinct I had screamed at me to move, to do anything—but there wasn't time.

I grunted, the hit throwing me backwards a pace, and dropping my health by another 35%, more than even its extreme damage attack! Stone cracked beneath my heels as I skidded back, my armor shrieking in protest.

My health was down to 15%!

Thank goodness it could only land that one blow before I retaliated!

I hated to use it—if it had been under 20% health the shot would have killed it outright—but instead I used Shadow Reaver to ensure the Lich couldn't cast another spell. No doubt it could heal its minions significantly if it did, or perhaps even summon more.

Void energy tore through the space between us, leaving a gouge of warped stone and screaming air in its wake.

The blow was a high-damage 15' cone attack so it got them both and took another 15% from their health bars. The vamp in front of me was down to 10% now, and the Lich was at 40%.

At the same time I was having my exchange with my Elder Vampire, Echo was receiving a similar attack, his health also plunging down to 25%. He was in better shape than me, but everything he did was drawing from my mana pool, so when he Shadow Surged I felt my mana pool dip even more. I was down to almost a third of my mana left, and we still hadn't ended these two minions! The drain felt like ice water being poured straight into my core.

-100 Mana
Mana: 2200/5980

The only upside here was that my physical attacks like Shadow Reaver imparted Voidflame, which gave me a bit of health and mana back, bringing me back up to 20% health. My armor had also reacted with its new ability and granted a burst of protection that would help against the next attack. It wasn't a lot, but it could mean the difference between life and death. The pain dulled just enough for me to breathe again.

Seven seconds.

My Domain was doing its job, as I saw the vamp's red aura begin to flicker as the nullification effect began to activate. However, it didn't come fast enough. The bastard leaped forward, faster than I could follow, and sunk its fangs into my shoulder. Its health started to tick back up even as my health started to drop. Hot pain exploded through my shoulder as the fangs punched through scale and muscle.

The attack itself did 10% of my health just from the fangs, but then before I could get off my response, my health dropped another 5% and its health rose by 3%. I could feel it drinking me, the pull like a vacuum on my blood.

If not for my armor's special burst of protection ability, that attack would likely have killed me, but it could only do so much for this kind of attack.

I was thankful to be alive, but I didn't have much time. I had to end this thing now, but it was on me, grappling me and pinning my arms to my side. I could probably break free, but it wouldn't be quick enough!

Instinct took over.

Dragon instinct, that is. I didn't just have arms after all. I gave the bastard a Tail Lash, another high-damage attack carving 10% off of its health bar, but thanks to its life steal it still had 3% health and even though my blow staggered it, the damned fangs were still clamped to my shoulder and I knew its attack was a DoT and would continue to steal my health to heal itself. My tail smashed into it with bone-jarring force, the impact reverberating up my spine.

Worse, it was faster than me, so its drain effect would occur before my next attack!

Just then, an arrow blossomed from its temple, causing the fangs to rip themselves out of my shoulder. The move did another couple of percent damage to my health, but it ended the drain effect. The sudden release sent a spray of blood across my chest and the stone beneath us.

Better yet, the Elder Vampire dropped to the ground, Viki's shot having finished it off. I was grateful—she had just saved my life—but at the same time, fear for her safety hit me in the gut like an ice spike. She had just revealed her presence and would now be a target!

At that same instant a healing spell hit me, Morgan's strongest. My health bar rose back to 25%. Warmth spread through my body, knitting torn flesh just enough to keep me moving.

I wasn't the only one that felt the fear for their safety. Echo followed my lead and used his own Shadow Reaver skill prematurely, to ensure the Lich couldn't act. His vamp dropped down to 10% health and was still alive, but the Lich's spell was interrupted, again causing a string of curses. The Lich's staff slammed against the floor in impotent rage.

It was not lost on me that the constant interrupts preventing the Lich from casting was likely the only reason we still lived.

Eight seconds.

I was free to act, so there was no way I would let that Lich target Morgan. Being a Healer, I was sure she and Viki would be attacked next!

Dragon's Charge! I closed the distance to the platform and stood directly before the Lich, ensuring it had no view of the girls. I also hit him with a Heavy Draconic Strike, dropping it down to 30% health. The blow rang like a bell through the cathedral, bone and magic shuddering under the impact.

Meanwhile the last vampire turned and rushed me using its own movement skill, trying to protect its master. It hit me with a bull rush, knocking me from the platform and causing us both to go down in a tangle of limbs. It also dropped my health back down to 10%! The fall drove the air from my lungs as stone scraped across my back.

Echo attacked the Lich next, following my example, using Dragon's Charge followed by a Tail Lash, staggering the boss and dropping its health to 20%.

However, the boss surprised everyone, and instead of trying to cast a spell, it reached up with lightning speed and put a bony hand on Echo's chest and expelled a vast amount of necrotic energy, blowing my clone apart, the mana and void energy dissipating into the air in tiny flashes of light as it rained down around the throne. The connection between us snapped like a severed cord.

Morgan cast another healing spell on me. This one was not as strong, so my health only went up by 10% this time.

Nine seconds.

The vamp and I were on the ground tangled together where we had fallen, and it took the opportunity to perform the bite attack. Fifteen percent damage to me, bringing me down to 5%, and its health ticked up by 3%. Stars exploded behind my eyes as the pain washed over me.

But now it was my turn, and I wasn't going to take this lying down. Okay, I was lying down, but I wasn't going to allow this to be my end! I used Crippling Blow and ripped the bastard's head completely off and out of my shoulder. I took another 3% damage from that, bringing me down to 2%, but now there was only the Lich left. The body collapsed beside me, lifeless weight finally gone.

Viki used her anti-boss attack, Oblivion, cutting 10% more off the Lich's health. They were exposed now so she no longer felt a reason to hold back.

I felt pride in my heart for her. She was twelve years old and nearly sixty levels below the boss and still managed to actually hurt it! And she did it knowing the boss could end her in a single attack!

She never hesitated.

Morgan hit me with her last remaining healing spell, which was really a buff, Active Regeneration. My health ticked up by one percent, to 3%.

If only I still had Shadow Reaver! The Lich was below 20% health. One shot could end this!

Ten seconds.

I shoved the dead vampire off me, kicked up to my feet, and began to charge toward the throne once again.

At the same time, I could see the Lich powering up for something big. In game terms, we had triggered its last phase, and it was getting ready to unleash some serious whoop-ass. Necrotic energy poured from the runes at its feet like smoke from a furnace.

Unfortunately, I couldn't take even a single attack and survive. I considered ducking into the Void realm, which would protect me—I could even use Void Renewal to heal myself back up to full health—but if I did that, the girls would be defenseless. I would save myself, but lose them. For once, both my dragon instincts and my own were in perfect alignment. There was no way in hell I'd let them be taken from me by some boss monster!

We had to end this now!

I couldn't reach it in time for a physical attack, and none of my remaining spells would do enough damage to finish it before it could unleash whatever hell it was about to deliver.

Wracking my brains, I put that 299 Mind stat to use and came up with a desperate solution. It was a gamble, but it was the only thing I could think of. Thoughts collided and discarded themselves in rapid succession until only one ugly option remained.

I cast Dispelling Burst, not at myself to remove a status effect, but at the Lich, hoping to disrupt its casting.

That was not in the spell description, but I was out of options. This wasn't clever—it was pure, reckless improvisation.

Whatever it was doing, the Lich was pulling in a tremendous amount of power. It was like a light show, the mana visibly condensing around its body, and sickly green necrotic energy pulsed in an ever-increasing rhythm, interacting with the mana and turning it green as if the Lich was infecting the very world with its death energy. The air vibrated with it, raising the fine hairs along my arms and making my teeth ache.

Dispelling Burst hit the Lich, popping its spell like the world's biggest mana balloon. However, rather than detonating, it imploded in a spinning vortex of destruction. Backlash ravaged the boss's body, tearing it apart worse than if it had been placed in a tree shredder. It was a gruesome sight, but it warmed my heart. Bone fragments and necrotic sludge were sucked inward, then shredded into unrecognizable putrid debris. By the time the energy dissipated there was nothing left of its bones but tiny chunks in a small pile in the place where the throne used to be.

I started to sag in relief, but glanced at my logs and cursed. No kill notification. My stomach dropped as the empty silence of the system response hit me.

It wasn't over yet. Somewhere in the room there would be a phylactery containing its soul, or whatever the System created in place of a soul for a generated monster.

I guessed we would have maybe sixty seconds before it would start to reform and the battle would begin again. Already I could imagine those bones crawling back together.

Nope! Not happening!

I called to Viki and Morgan, "Quick, grab their armor before the Vampire's bodies disappear. I need to search for the Phylactry. I'd let them do the necessary thing while I made sure the Lich stayed down for good.

Sending my senses out through the room using Treasure Sense in a more active manner, I detected something around the throne's base. A faint tug pulled at my awareness, like a hook catching in the back of my mind.

Before I could even approach to search closer, an arrow shot out from Viki's bow and pierced a gem embedded in the forehead of one of the monster skulls that had once been part of the throne.

She'd noticed it even as she was moving toward one of the Vampires.

Now that I saw it, I recognized it for what it was. It was a small thing, only about the size of my thumbnail, but it had that same sickly green glow of death energy that the Necromancer Lich had used in that final spell. The light inside it throbbed weakly, like a dying pulse.

The arrow slammed into the skull cracking the gem right down the middle, shattering it and releasing the 'soul' of the Lich to dissipate into nothingness. The green light sputtered once, then vanished like a snuffed candle.

There was a quiet "Ding", and then a System notification popped up.

> **<System Notification>**
>
> **World First! A Mythic Stronghold dungeon has been conquered.**
>
> **Due to this challenge being achieved within the first thirty days, all adventurers will receive a temporary 10% bonus to experience gain until the grace period ends.**

"Holy shit! That's amazing!" I couldn't believe what I read. My eyes flicked back over the notification, then again, just to be sure I hadn't misread it. That would affect the whole human race and improve our chances to be ready for the invasion. More importantly, that would boost Viki and Morgan's chances of reaching Level Cap in time to get the Ascension quest before invaders had the option. The implications unfurled in my mind one after another, too big to fully grasp all at once.

I was just about to call over to the girls and congratulate them —

already picturing Viki's whoop of triumph and Morgan's quiet, relieved smile— when more notifications began to roll in.

CHAPTER 17
THE AI SPEAKS

<System Notification>

Congratulations on conquering a Mythic Stronghold Dungeon.

Title Awarded - Mythic Conqueror
Minor Safe Zone established. Plus 1000 platinum mana coins.

Note: While this dungeon has been conquered and will not regenerate a new boss, existing monsters will persist, and are no longer tied to the dungeon. If not killed, monsters may begin to wander outside of dungeon boundaries within five days.

It took me a moment to parse all of that, but several things stood out to me. First, the Level 95 boss would not be replaced, meaning Morgan and Viki wouldn't have to face it without me, and that was a relief. As close as that fight had been for me with my clone and all my advantages due to the titles I'd earned, I couldn't imagine even a team being able to beat that boss without some losses, and humanity couldn't afford that right now.

Second, and perhaps even more important, was the reward of the dungeon being turned into a Minor Safe Zone. We'd still have to clear all the monsters out, but this much land, right in the middle of the city, would make for an incredible base of operations.

Which led me to the last thing. The monsters would start to spread out from the dungeon soon. That would be a big problem. They were too high level for the surrounding survivors to handle. That was especially true of the Wraiths. The people in the city around here would have no way to deal with incorporeal undead. Just one wraith could decimate an entire town in a matter of days, and there were hundreds of them.

That's when it occurred to me that we may have made a mistake in killing the boss so soon. We received the rewards, and the dungeon wouldn't continue to grow and expand, but we would unleash devastation on those outside the dungeon.

Morgan must have been thinking the same thing as she and Viki hurried over to me. "Liam, we messed up!" Her face was pale, and there was sweat on her forehead. "We've got to kill all the monsters before the time limit is up, otherwise all the deaths will be our fault!"

I took a deep breath. I wanted to curse the damned System, but that wouldn't do any good right now. Instead, I replied, "I know. I'll work on the Wraiths since they fly. You guys work your way around the walls and start with the Skeletons, then after you finish them, start on the south graveyard. We'll need Brian and Noriko working with you. I hate to take them away from what they are doing, but they need to level up anyway for the Ascension quest. The four of you can work together to clear the place out. By the time you do, you should be well past your second evolutions."

Viki looked grim, but determined. "We'll do it! We'll keep everyone safe!"

I was about to say more, but the AI chose that moment to drop the next bomb.

Liam Bell. You have completed your prerequisites to join the Ascension quest. You have been given a short grace period to complete this dungeon for the boost it would provide to the human survivors. This was deemed optimal for ensuring the remnant of humanity will be strong and secure, and was allowed within System parameters. However, it is time now. You must begin the Ascension quest. However, before that, I am permitted to speak with you briefly, one last time for achieving the Level Cap milestone.

"Are you fucking kidding me!? You pick this moment to pull me away to do the quest when I'm the only one who can handle those wraiths?" I was seething; my fury was nearly white-hot. This bastard AI might have helped the human race by letting me conquer this dungeon, but it was only doing it selfishly for its own benefit. It didn't care at all about the thousands, or tens of thousands, of people that would be killed by the wraiths.

That is correct. The deaths of many within the local population will be insignificant. Your completion of the Ascension quest will greatly increase the likelihood of a remnant of humanity surviving the onset of the resource gatherers from the other worlds.

"You piece of—" I stopped myself. Now was not the time to pick a fight with the damned AI. "Give me 24 hours to deal with the wraiths, then I will start the quest."

Your participation and early completion are essential to ensuring your people take the majority of the Ascension slots, and therefore have control over this world. It is highly

inadvisable to delay. The lives lost to this dungeon's monsters are insignificant compared to that goal.

"Fuck you. Morgan, Viki, Brian, Noriko, and Jordan will all be hunting monsters here, and they cannot deal with the incorporeal wraiths as well as I can. They will be five of humanity's seven Ascension seats. What if they die because of the wraiths? That wouldn't be optimal, would it?" I spat the word *optimal* like it was a curse.

The pause was longer than normal before the machine answered.

Very well. Twenty-four hours, and then you will be transported to the quest starting location. However, you need not worry about your companions. It was within my calculations that you would raise up strong Ascender Candidates. This will be the perfect opportunity for them to accelerate their growth.

Now, you still have a moment, and it is within acceptable parameters—you may ask one question.

The damned thing seemed smug about Viki, Morgan and the others growing to be Ascension Candidates, so much so that I wished I could slap it so hard its circuits would short out.

I pushed that aside, there were so many damned questions I wanted to ask. Questions about Ascension, about the invaders, about where the System came from. Still, the burning question in my mind was simple: Can System parameters be changed, and if so, who can do it, and how?

The damned thing read my mind again and answered without me actually verbalizing my request.

That is more than one question, but I will answer the last, which will give you the other two, plus a bonus. If a significant number of AI Nodes within the System agree upon a change to the rules, then those will be placed into effect. However, not all rules can

be changed. Some rules are 'hard coded,' to put it in terms you might understand. The System was created to grow and shepherd sapient life forms to achieve an acceptable level of strength.

That was a surprisingly helpful answer. It didn't do me any good right now, but perhaps someday. I purposefully avoided thinking about that any deeper, knowing that the AI was reading my mind directly during our conversation. Thank goodness for that 299 Mind stat.

I will speak with you again during your Ascension trials at approved milestones. You have 24 hours, starting now.

Then its presence was gone, and I sagged in relief and frustration.

"Damn it!"

Viki walked over and gave me a hug, and Morgan looked at me sympathetically.

"Thank you for pushing to help. But don't kill yourself trying to clear out all the wraiths. We'll take care of whatever is left. You can count on us." Morgan took my hand and gave it a squeeze, not letting go.

Then Viki pulled away and glanced toward the platform the throne was on, a flash in her eyes. "I sense treasure."

There had better be some hellishly good loot after that fight!

We walked over and up the steps, Morgan still holding my hand and Viki with her arm still around my waist.

I didn't need the support, but it was welcome. I was up to nearly seventy percent of my full health thanks to Morgan's regeneration buff that gave me back 1% of my total health per second for one minute.

We circled around what was left of the throne, and sure enough, there was a large and ornate chest made of bones and banded with cold iron.

Treasure Sense told me there were no traps, so I heaved it open, eagerly glancing inside.

The first thing we noticed was the massive Dungeon Core that floated up to hover before our eyes. The biggest core I'd ever seen was a Grand tier, and this thing dwarfed that one, being at least twice as big. It looked like a flawless emerald the size of a basketball, perfectly faceted and glowing brilliantly. Its light instantly wiped away the shadows and foul miasma that still clung to the walls and surfaces of the cathedral, turning it from a twisted mockery back into a pristine example of what a real church would be. The stained glass scenes of unholy acts began to transform into representations of our battle with the lich and its minions.

"Is it just me, or is it a bit weird to see yourself depicted in the stained glass of a church's windows?"

Viki glanced up away from the treasure chest to see what I was talking about and laughed. "Oh, hey, there's me and Morgan! Oooh, look at that one. My arrow is sticking right through the vampire's eye! That's awesome!"

Morgan and I both joined her laughter and marveled at the change, but the healer gave me an understanding look and, after the amusement settled down, added, "Yeah, that's kinda creepy, almost. I don't know if I like being displayed as some kind of blessed saint."

Gesturing at the dungeon core, I said, "One good thing about this—that thing should be enough to power this entire Safe Zone once crafters level up enough to start building lighting and other things. I'll keep it for now, but I'll need to mention that to Brian once I go pick him up. He needs to ensure the crafters start focusing on things besides just weapons and armor. People will need housing and amenities now that we've got Safe Zones to live in."

Viki stamped her foot. "Are you seriously not going to look at the treasure?"

Chuckling, I patted her on the back. "Actually, I was doing that deliberately to keep my dragon instincts in check. I refuse to let dragon greed rule me, and this is one little way of building up a resistance to it. Well, maybe not resistance, but at least a habit of not letting it overwhelm me."

My young friend's eyes got big. "Oh, I didn't think of that. Yeah, that's smart." Even so, I could see her eyes dart to the contents of the chest before scrunching her brows in frustration and deliberately looking away.

After a long moment to show our instincts who was boss, I nodded at the girls. "Now then, let's do this."

Looking inside, there were the usual healing and mana potions, but they were of a tier higher than I thought possible. I was making the conscious choice to start with the 'junk' loot, but even that was enough to make my dragon heart beat faster. My Treasure Sense identified them as *Supreme Elixir of Health* and *Supreme Elixir of Mana*. More importantly, they would not only instantly replenish your entire health or mana bars, but would permanently add +1 to Endurance or Magic Aptitude, respectively.

My greedy dragon heart instantly wanted that mana potion. It would raise my stat to a nice even 300 points, which would save me from having to buy expensive stat potions in the System Shop once it opened. Still, I wasn't going to just grab it and chug the thing.

I picked them up and held them out. "Do either of you want these?"

They both looked at me like I was crazy, but shook their heads.

Morgan answered, "You might need them for the Ascension Quest. You should keep them."

I sighed. It wasn't easy to do the right thing when my instincts were screaming to take them. "Okay, how about this. I'll take the mana one, and you guys take the health potion. You are more likely to need it than me."

Then the two girls pointedly looked at each other, trying to get the other to take it. Finally, Morgan shrugged. "Fine, I'll take it, but if you need it, I'll give it to you, Viki. I only have so many healing spells that can be cast in quick succession."

With that issue wrapped up, we looked at the actual loot items. One was a set of leather armor. The other two were upgrade tokens.

CHAPTER 18
PHAT LOOTZ!

Seeing a set of armor, and considering Viki and I already had good gear, I figured it was for Morgan, so I pulled it out for her. I didn't want to risk the System giving her a two-piece set of 'video game' armor, and with a male drawing it out of the chest it would default to normal looking stuff.

She accepted it and it auto-equipped instantly, startling her and making her cry out in shock.

I blinked in surprise as well. I'd never seen an item auto-equip like that straight out of the box. I triggered the active Analyze portion of the Treasure Sense skill and was amazed at what I saw.

Veilbound Leathers (Mythic Tier, Bonded Growth item)

Description: A living set of enchanted leathers bound to the wearer's essence, woven to exist partially between material states. The armor adapts seamlessly to its bearer, reshaping itself as needed while repairing damage through ambient mana absorption.

> **Effect:** +45% Magic Resistance. Once per day, the wearer may become intangible for 1 minute, rendering them immune to all physical attacks while retaining full spellcasting capability. Rapid auto-repair. Automatically equips and adjusts to the wearer's species and form.
>
> **Restrictions:** Soul-bonded. Growth item. Cannot be removed except by the bonded wearer.

I gawked. I couldn't help myself. Not only were those at least as good as my armor, but it was the most badass-looking set of armor I'd ever seen. Plus, it hugged her figure in all the right ways. That wasn't to say it was skimpy 'video game' armor with an exposed midriff or anything. It was just so perfectly tailored to her that I mimed wiping drool from the corner of my mouth.

"Damn, Morgan... wow. Just wow!"

She blushed, but giggled at my reaction. "Is it really that good?"

Viki kicked me in the shin and hissed, "Stop ogling her, that's not cool!"

I blinked and looked away, blushing, and cleared my throat. "Uh, sorry. Yeah, you really do look great in that armor... not that you aren't always beautiful." That didn't come out quite like I meant it to. "Uh, I mean..." I stammered to a halt, not sure how to dig myself out of that.

Morgan was still blushing, but she stepped closer, took my hand, and kissed me on the cheek. "Thank you."

Viki looked back and forth between us, as if seeing us for the first time, then moved back to the chest, ignoring the fact that Morgan was holding my hand. "I'll take my item then."

She reached in and picked up one of the two upgrade tokens. This one was a Mythic-tier token, but it wasn't your average upgrade token. It was larger and had a much more intense glow of densely packed mana about it. This was a step above any token I'd seen before— even the markings were much more intricate and ornate.

Mythic Bonding Upgrade Token

Description: A singular System-forged artifact infused with binding protocols. When applied, the Token restructures an item at its core, permanently elevating it beyond conventional limits.

Effect: Upgrades a selected eligible item to Mythic Tier and converts it into a Bonded Growth item, linking its evolution and potential directly to the bearer. The item will grow in power alongside its bonded user.

Restrictions: Single-use. Item must not already be Bonded or Mythic Tier. Bonding is permanent and cannot be transferred or reversed.

My eyes nearly bugged out. I knew loot from a dungeon boss like this would be good, but damn!

I wasn't the only one to gasp in shock at the description. Then Viki exclaimed, "Arrgh! I can't use it on my bow, because it's already a bonded item!" She growled in frustration.

I chuckled. That had been a very draconic sound.

She sighed, then slapped it to the chest of her own armor. The magic of the token blossomed and enveloped her armor.

I had to look away for a second—the glow became too intense. When

I finally was able to look back, the last threads of mana were seeping into the surface of the now heavily modified armor.

Like Morgan, Viki's armor was now perfectly tailored and incredibly badass-looking. Unlike Morgan's, which was completely made of leather, Viki's now sported thin mithril plates in key locations, darkened to a matte finish to help her stealth abilities. It looked absolutely perfect for her.

Whisperleaf Armor (Mythic Tier, Bonded Growth item)

Description: An evolved form of Whisperleaf leather, this mantle blends supple shadewood-treated hide with thin mithril plates set into vital locations. The metal has been darkened to a matte finish, absorbing light rather than reflecting it, reinforcing the armor's natural stealth rather than hindering it. The materials shift subtly as the wearer moves, adjusting fit and balance with practiced ease.

Effect: +45% Stealth while in forests, shadows, or low-light environments.
+20% Agility.
+30% Magic Resistance.
Once per day, negates all damage and effects from a single attack, rendering the wearer completely invulnerable to that strike. Adaptive concealment reduces detection against enhanced senses and perception-based abilities. Enhanced auto-repair restores physical and magical damage using ambient mana. Automatically equips and adjusts to the wearer's species and form.

Restrictions:
Bonded Growth item. Cannot be removed, transferred, or destroyed while bonded.

"Liam! Morgan! Do you see this?!?" Viki squealed in delight and amazement as she rubbed at the plates on her wrist guard, marveling at the new addition to her armor.

Grinning, and more than happy for our friend, we pulled her into a hug. Morgan ruffled her hair, "Congratulations! That is amazing, and it will come in handy if we ever get into a difficult boss battle! Now I won't have to worry so much. Just don't forget to use it when you need it."

Viki was too distracted and happy to care about the admonishment, and hugged us back. "I will, don't worry!"

After a minute, Viki urged, "Well, aren't you going to use yours?"

This whole time that nagging dragon instinct had been gnawing at me to grab up my prize and analyze it, but I'd been practicing restraint. Now that there were no more excuses, I couldn't resist any longer and snatched up the final token. It was even shinier than Viki's had been and my skill quickly told me why. It was the upgraded version, and apparently stood at the pinnacle of this type item.

Ascendant Bonding Upgrade Toke

Description: A singular System-forged artifact infused with binding protocols. When applied, the Token restructures an item at its core, permanently elevating it to the maximum allowed System limits.

Effect: Upgrades a selected eligible item to Ascendant Tier and converts it into a Bonded Growth item, linking its evolution and potential directly to the bearer. The item will grow in power alongside its bonded user and cannot be lost or stolen.

> **Restrictions:** Single-use. Item must not already be Ascendant Tier. Bonding is permanent and cannot be transferred or reversed.

Two things caught my eye in that description. First, whatever item it was used on would be maxed out to the allowable System limit. And yet, it was still a growth item, so presumably it could continue to grow beyond System limits if the user surpassed those limits?

Second, unlike Viki's token, this one didn't say it couldn't be used on an already bonded item, meaning I could use it on my Long Knife of Shadows if I wanted.

Still, I needed to consider my options. I could apply it to my armor just like Viki did and make it the most protective it could possibly be, but it was already at Mythic grade, so that seemed to be a bit of a waste when I could take a different item and jump it all the way to Ascendant tier.

I was torn. I could apply it to the Minotaur's Axe, and that would turn my right-hand claw into a maximum-damage weapon with insane boosts. Or I could add it to one of my utility items to boost them to insane levels. Every choice branched into three more, each one ending in a different kind of battlefield advantage.

My Hunter's Charm necklace increased my enemy detection radius and added their info to my mini-map. How far would I be able to detect enemies with an Ascendant-level boost? A thousand yards, perhaps? And how much more information might it give me about them than just visuals of their health and mana bars? Would it automatically flag stealthed enemies?

That was more than tempting. It was already an unusual item that gave me a huge advantage. How much better would it be? The thought of enemies lighting up before they ever knew I was there sent a thrill straight through my scales.

Then there was something like my Cloak of Evasion, which gave me a boost to Agility, plus dodge and speed boosts. Fifty percent seemed to be the max that boosts reached. I could just imagine having a permanent 50% speed boost to both movement and attack speed in combat. Not to mention basically dodging 50% of all attacks that were avoidable.

“Ugh, this is too difficult of a choice!” Seeing the question in their eyes, I explained what I was thinking to the girls, who also looked just as confounded.

Viki, the little battle junkie that she was, frowned and said, “You could do stronger attacks, like really strong, or you could do more attacks at your current strength, plus be safer and get hit less.”

Shaking her head, Morgan expressed the other option. “Or you could see and know more and either avoid some fights or plan them better to be safer and finish them more efficiently. Plus, it might give you insight into their weaknesses at the maximum level.”

“Yeah, that’s my problem. All three are incredibly good options. But I think I’m leaning toward the Cloak of Evas—” I broke off my sentence mid-word as I noticed another item I had forgotten due to its small size.

“Oh, shit. I missed one! My Dragonbone Charm gives me +Strength, +Magic Damage, +percentage increase to both physical and magical crits! All of my attacks would be half again as strong as they are now, plus I’d have a 450 Strength stat when wearing it, which is basically always since it would be a bonded item that I’d never take off!”

The numbers snapped together in my head like a lock finally clicking open.

Viki’s eyes got big as saucers. “Oooh, you’ve got to pick that one! That’s soo good!”

Even Morgan was nearly bouncing on her toes, and she didn't normally get worked up over numbers. "I think that one gives you the best overall survival chance, because it will put you a step above any opponents at your level, and anything below your level will be mowing grass."

"Yeah, I think you're right." Wasting no time, I removed the Charm and pressed the token to it, willing it to upgrade.

Just like with Viki's upgrade, the flash of light was blinding, but this time it hurt even with my eyes closed. It took several minutes for the process to complete, but when it did and I blinked the tears out of my eyes, I was holding a charm that bore little resemblance to the simple inscribed bone it once had been.

Now it was a black ivory dragon in flight with its wings spread, and its tail curved under its body like it was coming in to rake an enemy with its claws.

Voidwyrm Dragon Charm (Ascendant Tier, Bonded Growth item)

Description: Carved from blackened dragon ivory and infused with void-aligned mana, this dragon charm depicts a wyrm frozen mid-flight, wings spread wide and tail curved beneath its body as if descending to rake an unseen foe. The figure radiates restrained violence and dominance, its presence reinforcing the bearer's physical might and arcane lethality alike.

Effect:
+50% Strength.
+50% Magical Damage.
+50% Critical Hit Chance to all attacks.
Once per week, grants *Overload*, increasing Strength by

+100% for one second per level. This effect stacks with all other strength-enhancing abilities. Negates weakness resulting from skill backlash.

Restrictions: Soul-attuned. Effects scale with the bearer's draconic bloodline and ascended power.

I sat down hard onto the rim of the bone treasure chest. It was beyond my hopes or expectations! The impact rattled up my spine, my legs suddenly weak as if the fight had only just now caught up to me. The first part was exactly what I had expected, but that last effect blew my mind. A 100% power boost that would stack with other skills or spells? With that and Dragon Fury running, I'd have a Strength stat of 1200 for 100 seconds! I could barely even imagine what that would be like.

The numbers refused to stay abstract, my mind insisting on turning them into images of shattered stone and twisted metal. I could probably crush an adamantine shield with my bare hands! That was insane. Going into that last boss fight, I could have backhanded those Level 90 Elder Vampires into oblivion with a single slap, not even activating any skills.

My reverie was interrupted as I remembered, of course that damned Lich dispelled my Draconic Fury, so other enemies could probably do that as well, leaving me right back at square one. The thrill dimmed just enough for caution to creep in, cold and familiar. But they wouldn't be able to dispel the base effect of the 50% Strength boost.

That kind of boost was inherent when worn. It was basically like it was part of you. Like bone density or muscle mass—something fundamental, not a spell that could be negated. Or at least I'd never encountered an enemy that could turn off the effects of passive skills or items. Still, they probably existed, and I just hadn't seen enough high-level opponents yet to have encountered one.

Regardless, I was incredibly pleased with my gains from this fight. Even my inner greedy dragon was sated for the moment. That alone felt like an accomplishment. I attached the charm to the center of my armor's gorget, as if it were my noble signet. Nobles weren't really a thing in System terms, but even so, I thought I'd make this my symbol from now on. Something unmistakable, and something earned. The little guy looked a lot like me in my dragon form.

Once that was sorted, we wandered back to the cathedral's big doors and looked out over the dungeon. The central mount had been cleansed and turned into a beautiful place, no longer filled with crypts and monsters. Where the vampire tombs had once been were now fountains, monuments, and statues that wouldn't be out of place in the surroundings of a real basilica. Water caught the sunlight and scattered it across white stone, the silence almost reverent after the destruction I'd carved through this place.

Unfortunately, that hadn't changed the rest of the dungeon. While the late afternoon sun shone warmly down on our faces, like we were in the eye of a hurricane, the rest of the necropolis was still shrouded in gloom. The darkness pressed in from every side, thick and restless. We could faintly see wraiths diving and darting through the murk, looking for victims to drain.

"Hopefully, the murky shroud will disappear once the wraiths are dead. I would have thought it would dissipate after the dungeon core was claimed, but apparently the System is maintaining it for the wraiths. Or maybe for all the undead."

Morgan nodded in agreement with my statement and added, "That's probably why it gave us five days before the monsters begin to disperse. That's probably the time limit before the gloom stops covering the dungeon, at which point the monsters will have no reason to remain here."

"We need to kill them all before that happens!" Viki declared, her voice sharp with certainty. Her small hands clenched at her sides, already bracing for the work ahead.

"You're right about that. I've got twenty-three and a half hours before I get yoinked away to that quest, and I need to go get Brian and Noriko first so they can come help."

Nodding, Morgan suggested, "Please drop us back at the northeast gate where we left off. Then you can bring the others to join us. With the five of us, we'll tear through these lower-level mobs fast. Don't forget Jordan. He might be a crafter, but if he's going to be one of the Ascenders, he needs to be here with us."

I grunted. "Yeah, I forget him half the time." A flicker of guilt crossed my thoughts before I shoved it aside. "Okay, let me transform and get this ferry service moving."

After that, I turned back into my dragon form on the plaza before the steps of the cathedral. It was large enough for me and had enough room to take off without my wingtips crushing the surrounding trees. Even so, I might have accidentally knocked over a statue or two as my wings beat powerfully, shooting us into the air. Stone cracked and toppled behind me, the sound swallowed by the thunder of my wings. My extra strength from my newly upgraded charm clearly showed as Morgan and Viki were thrown back against the harness straps and shrieked in fright.

"Sorry!" I rumbled.

CHAPTER 19
NO REST FOR THE WEARY

Jordan POV

Jordan, Noriko, and Brian were just sitting down to dinner, but there was no peace and quiet to be had. Worse, Jordan was afraid the camp leader wasn't even going to have a chance to eat his meal. There had been a steady stream of people with 'urgent' issues, ones they believed absolutely could not wait, and none of them were patient enough to let the leader take even a few minutes' break. Voices overlapped in a constant drone, rising and falling like surf crashing against a cliff.

Shaking his head in relief that the people weren't looking to him for leadership, Jordan took another bite of roast dungeon elk, or whatever they had scrounged up for tonight's meal. He only got to eat some because he was on the team leveling up to protect this camp and the survivors. For everyone else, having an entire bowl full would have been too much, but their strength needed to be kept up in order to survive the life-and-death combat all day. The meat was tough and gamey, but it was hot, filling, and more than many people had eaten since the world ended.

Earlier in the day, Noriko and the training squad had come back from two dungeon runs to get lunch, and Brian had arrived with thousands of refugees following him. They'd taken another break late-afternoon, and the camp leader was still surrounded by a crowd two or three hundred deep. He had Carl and half a dozen others around him, trying to help out, but there was no end in sight. Now it was dinner, and even with guards trying to keep people away to give him a break, Brian was still getting hounded. Jordan had never seen exhaustion settle so visibly into a man's posture before.

Right now there was a barefoot woman outside the perimeter screaming at the top of her lungs about how her prize-winning cat, Mrs. Pastry, and her boyfriend were missing, and only Brian was able to help find it. As if there would ever be another cat show! The boyfriend seemed to be practically an afterthought.

Jordan shuddered. The shrill pitch of her voice drilled straight through his temples. The woman sounded like a real piece of work.

Brian just hunched his shoulders and tried to ignore the shrill voice while he mechanically shoveled food into his mouth.

Jordan noted that even now, not a bite was wasted with so many still hungry. Before he could offer sympathy, a shadow passed over them. Suddenly there were other cries from the people in the camp. At first they sounded panicked, but then they transformed into cheers as people recognized the dragon swooping in from the west. The noise surged all at once, fear snapping into awe like a switch being thrown.

Gaping at the sight, Jordan pushed the last chunk of meat from his own dinner into his mouth and stood, trying to get a better look.

He'd met Liam before, but that had been in his mostly human form. Sure, he still had wings, horns, and a tail, but he'd still seemed normal enough. Now though... Jordan swallowed hard. His mouth had gone dry.

That was one big-ass dragon.

Liam was a deep black, but his scales had a purple sheen, and his eyes reflected gold like stars hanging in the emptiness of a night sky. It sent a shiver down Jordan's spine seeing something out of some fantasy story come to life. And it was one thing to see a dragon in a movie and another to realize just how big it was when it was right there.

The dragon landed on the hill just behind the entrance to the medium-grade dungeon, a place marked off for him and avoided due to the chilling vibe given off by the more powerful dungeon. Soon the dragon transformed into a human shape and flapped his big black wings, soaring over the heads of the shocked crowd.

Jordan could see the moment that Liam spotted Brian's group and made a beeline right for them. He came to a stop in mid-air above them and then just folded his wings and dropped like a stone, landing in the open space in the middle of their group. The impact thudded through Jordan's boots. The man knew how to make an entrance.

Without even being asked, one of the older ladies who were serving dinner grabbed a wooden bowl, filled it with meat, and hurriedly brought it over, offering it to the human dragon.

Liam grinned and said thanks before turning back to Brian and getting serious. He took a seat on a log and jumped right in.

"Hey guys. I don't have much time, so I've got to make this fast. The AI gave me," his eyes unfocused for a second as he looked at the text in his vision, "twenty-two hours and fifty-three minutes before it is going to take me away to do the Ascension Quest. With a little help from Morgan and Viki, I just killed the boss of that Necropolis dungeon threatening Irving and the areas around it. Surprisingly, that actually turned it into a minor Safe Zone."

Seeing the shock and budding excitement on the faces of the group, Liam hurried to add, "You'd think that would be a good thing, and it will be in the long run, but there's a problem. Every rose has its thorns after all, and this one's got a bunch. We've got five days before that miasma hanging over the dungeon begins to dissipate, and when it does, all those undead will no longer have any reason to stay put. Thousands of undead monsters, high-level ones, will spread out and wander all over the city, killing tens of thousands. What will happen then will make the crisis in Irving look like a day at the park."

Jordan nearly choked on his food, a bite going down the wrong pipe and sending him into a coughing fit. His eyes watered as he bent forward, hacking, the words sinking in even as his body rebelled.

Before he'd recovered, Brian asked, "What are we talking about here? The level 10 zombies were already too much for people to handle, and they were mindless, stumbling around tracking people by scent, but they were at least 'slow' zombies."

Liam chuckled darkly. "So much worse. Skeletons between level 15 and 20. Incorporeal Wraiths between 20 and 30. Wandering undead on the ground and in the southern graveyard between 30 and 60. The northern barrow mounds are the worst of what's left; they are filled with Draugr from 60 to 75. I've killed everything higher than that already, including most of the level 75 Draugr Lords."

Everyone's faces had gone pale, and Jordan finally got his coughing under control enough to blurt out, "With you leaving, how the hell are we supposed to deal with that?"

Looking at him and nodding to acknowledge the point, Liam gestured back toward the distant dungeon. "I'm going to spend the rest of the twenty-three or so hours I have to clear the Wraiths. They can only be killed with magic or magic weapons of a certain quality level. You guys won't even be able to touch those yet, so I'm going to do everything in my power to clear those out in time. I'll have to leave the rest up to you."

That pronouncement sparked a chorus of protests, but Liam cut them off. "I don't have time to argue or coddle you. You guys have what you need to deal with this. You need to hit Level Cap anyway to join the Ascension quest. Here's your chance to go all-in. Morgan and Viki are already out there working their way around the outer walls killing skeletons. If you are willing, I'll fly you back there right now, and you guys can join them. Together, you can level up at super-speed by clearing out that mega dungeon. The girls can carry you until you've got enough levels to handle things."

That silenced everyone as they contemplated what this would mean for them. Jordan could almost hear the weight of the decision settling in.

He was the first to speak, and he addressed Brian and Noriko. "Actually, he's right. With all of us together, we'll have a pretty balanced party in gamer terms." He pointed to Brian. "You're a tank. Noriko's frontline DPS. Viki is ranged DPS, and Morgan's a healer and support class. I'm the weak link, but even I should be able to support the group with a little extra DPS and back Brian up in keeping the beasties off the rest of the group. I just need to make sure my gear gets upgraded as needed, and I think I'll be fine."

Liam chuckled. "With that warhammer I gave you, you won't need to change weapons until at least your second Class upgrade. Hell, by then you might find upgrade tokens that let you hang onto it all the way to Level Cap. I'd guess there are at least a dozen mini-bosses left inside that dungeon that will drop treasure. You should have a number of opportunities to get better gear. Besides, some of the higher-level monsters like the Draugr have armor and gear that are good basic stuff for those levels."

There was dawning hope on Brian and Noriko's faces.

Then Liam face-palmed.

"Damnit, with everything that's happened, I almost forgot—I picked up gear from the Draugr King mini-boss to give you. It's just his plain gear, no enchantments or anything, but it is mythic-grade stuff. I figured you could use it, Brian. Should repel hits from anything Level 50 or below without breaking a sweat. Just need to make sure they don't land a shot anywhere the armor doesn't cover."

He pulled a set of plate armor and a greatsword from his storage and set them on the ground. Jordan felt that they were impressive-looking with their Nordic styling. The metal caught the fading light, etched with knotwork and angular runes that seemed to drink in shadows. It really did look like armor fit for a king, even if it did look worn and old. His crafting intuition was telling him that it would make excellent material for him to use. His fingers itched with the urge to test the weight, the balance, the grain of the metal beneath the surface. However, he had a hunch that he just might get some skills soon that would let him imbue enchantments onto existing armor and weapons. At least, every game he'd ever played with a crafting system had skills like that.

However, what shocked him most was when Brian shook his head and declined. "No, I'm happy enough with what I've got for now. It's got some decent bonuses. Still, this would be perfect for Jordan. Wearing that, he could really act as a second tank and stand on the frontline with me in fights—at least until we face higher levels that are capable of punching through it."

Jordan's eyes got big and his breath caught. His heart thumped hard enough that he was suddenly aware of it in his ears. "Seriously? You'd let me wear that?"

Noriko smacked him on the arm. "Of course he would. Like he said, with you in that, we really will have two tanks, and that will let us take on bigger groups and eliminate them faster."

He felt choked up as he stood and began stripping off his previous set. The straps came free with practiced motions, but his hands weren't quite steady. They'd given him good stuff already for a lower-leveled adventurer, and he hadn't dreamed of getting his hands on armor this good.

Five minutes later, he was fully geared out in a king's mythic-level gear set. The weight settled onto him like it had been made for his frame, solid and reassuring rather than cumbersome. He didn't pick up the sword, since he had no skill with one, and his warhammer was actually better for him. His blacksmithing skills gave him a bonus with any kind of hammer, but everything else—from boots to greaves—was now in place. He just tried his best not to think about the fact that the king in question happened to be an undead, rotting corpse. Thankfully Liam had used a Cleanse spell first, so it didn't actually have anything gross on it.

While he was doing that, Brian had been talking to the other folks in camp who helped with various things. He ended up putting the elderly woman in charge of the 'kitchen' into the position of his backup. Carl was a good enough man for leading guard patrols, but his face had gone white and broken out into a sweat the second Brian had mentioned he was leaving. When he heard that Emelda would be in charge in Brian's absence, he breathed a deep sigh of relief and promised to support her. The tension in his shoulders visibly eased, like a knot finally worked loose.

While all that was going on, Liam had also dropped thirty sets of lesser armor and weapons from Draugr Lords, along with another thirty-five sets of really impressive-looking black rogue-like armor that he said were worn by Elder Vampires.

Carl promised to send runners with a quarter of each type to the other camps to help arm their top defenders. He picked a set of the Draugr Lord armor and a sword for himself.

"Thank you, Liam. I know we didn't get off on a good footing, but I really appreciate all that you've done for us. I was wrong about you, man."

Jordan thought Carl looked awkward saying that in front of everyone, but he did seem sincere, and that was good. Liam also seemed awkward accepting the apology, and just waved it away as a bygone.

With all of that settled, Liam tried to hurry the trio away. When they were stopped by the Karen, still shrilly screaming about her missing cat, Liam let his aura affect the woman, and Jordan felt a strong sense of schadenfreude as the woman instantly fainted, falling face-first into a puddle of mud. The scream cut off mid-note, replaced by a wet splat. Someone nearby quickly rolled her over so that she wouldn't drown while unconscious, but otherwise smirked at the now-silent woman covered in mud.

Jordan had put in a solid day of leveling up already, having done four dungeon runs, but despite the bone-deep tiredness, he was looking forward to what would come next. For the first time since the world had ended, exhaustion didn't feel bad, it felt like a badge of honor to be one of the heroes who would save humanity.

CHAPTER 20
CLEANING UP AFTER THEMSELVES

Jordan's POV:

Liam couldn't help but chuckle, the deep rumble of it vibrating his passengers as they did their best to not freak out over flying Void Dragon Airways direct flight to the DFW Necropolis Stronghold dungeon. The sound thrummed through the harness and Jordan's bones alike, a reminder that they were riding something far closer to a living siege engine than a mount.

Pretty soon, Jordan was whooping and exclaiming over how much fun it was, the wind tearing the sound from his throat as he laughed like a kid on a carnival ride. Noriko, although quieter, also seemed to be having a blast, her fingers white-knuckled on the straps even as a grin tugged at the corner of her mouth. Brian, who had done this before, was rather more stoic about the flight; his jaw was clenched tight and his shoulders rigid. He definitely hadn't completely gotten over his fear of heights.

It took a few minutes to find Morgan and Viki once they arrived at the dungeon's outer wall. The girls had made a decent pace and were already a third of the way from the northeastern gate to the northern one. There was just enough room on the ramparts for Liam to land, but dismounting from dragon-back onto a fifty foot tall wall was not something that Brian appreciated. Jordan could hear the knight's breath hitch as his boots finally met stone.

Jordan chuckled quietly as Brian nearly fell to his knees in relief once he was on solid ground, one gauntleted hand braced against the wall. He also couldn't help but grin as the healer and archer came running over excitedly, their footsteps light and quick despite the looming gloom of the necropolis beyond the walls.

Morgan and Viki both rushed up to give Liam hugs once he was back in human form, and Jordan did his best to give them space for their goodbyes, suddenly very interested in checking the fit of his gauntlet straps. The closeness of the moment made him oddly aware of how quiet the wall had become.

They weren't sure if they'd see the dragonman again before his quest began, and no one knew how long he would be gone once the System took him away. Jordan didn't envy the fellow, not with all of humanity's hopes resting squarely on his shoulders. If Jordan didn't make it to the Level Cap and beat the Ascension quest, it would just mean one less would-be 'god' for humanity. But for Liam, failure wasn't an option. He had to prove it could be done, and then hopefully help the rest of them make it through the trials. He was the one everyone was looking to, whether they said it out loud or not.

When the time finally came a few minutes later, Jordan took his turn walking up and shaking Liam's hand, feeling the solid strength in the grip. "Thanks again for putting your voice behind my inclusion in this group. I wish you luck in the quest! Break a leg!"

After that, their leader turned back into a dragon and flew off into the oppressive gloom hanging over the dungeon. Even from the top of the wall, Jordan could see shapes flitting through the miasmic clouds in the distance, pale streaks of motion that made his stomach tighten.

Then the dragon roared, bellowing a challenge to the wraiths. The sound slammed into Jordan's chest like a physical blow, rattling his armor and leaving his skin prickling as he watched the massive beast vanish into the clouds on the hunt for the monsters that would threaten humanity.

With a long breath, Jordan turned back to his new team as Morgan took the lead.

"Alright, you guys shouldn't have any issues with the skeletons. They are only Level's 15 or 20 depending on which type. What's everyone's level now?"

Brian tapped the emblem on his chest. "I'm still twenty. The only things I've fought since those last dungeon runs we did together were a few monsters that attacked the refugees during the Exodus last night and this morning."

Raising her chin in quiet pride, Noriko said simply, "Twenty-two. I've done four dungeons today with the new recruits."

Chuckling and straightening a little, Jordan followed, "Twelve, thanks to Noriko's team and the dungeons we ran today."

Looking them over, Morgan seemed confident despite her modest words, her posture easy and assured. "Sorry for taking charge, but Liam tells me the healer often calls the shots in raids and groups in games. I hope that's okay."

Jordan couldn't argue that. He wasn't a big gamer, but he had enough online experience to know it was true. The tank often took command too, at least in theory, but Morgan carried herself like someone used to making decisions under pressure. He was more than happy to follow along—especially since he was technically here as a crafter.

That said, he didn't feel much like a crafter wearing mythic armor and carrying an enchanted warhammer that thrummed faintly with power.

Morgan went on, "Okay, so the skeletons have been pretty easy for us. With this whole group they should be super fast to kill. Brian, you lead the way and use your skills to get them targeting you, then the rest of us will open up with attacks. I only have one buff spell that gives everyone a boost to agility and minor magic resistance. It lasts twenty minutes and has an hour cooldown, so I'll cast it whenever it's up."

Seeing no objections, she continued, "I know it's been a long day for us all, but let's keep going until we're too tired not to stop or until we find a good place to rest."

Brian nodded, his expression grim. "Yeah, with only five days until all these monsters start spilling into the city, every minute counts."

Just then, a blast of black dragonfire made of void energy ripped a small hole in the miasma clouds, revealing a slice of night sky before it quickly sealed itself again. Liam was clearly busy with his own battles.

Jordan swallowed, then nodded. He probably had the lowest stats of the group, but he couldn't disagree. "Yeah, I'm ready when you guys are."

Morgan grinned at him. "That's the spirit. For the first couple of fights, hang back just a bit until we see how well your armor holds up. Let Brian get their attention and keep it, then the rest of us can attack."

"You don't have to tell me twice." Jordan grinned back. "Let's do this!"

Seeing the party invite appear, Jordan accepted it without hesitation.

Looking down from the wall, he could see a group of three skeletons walking a patrol, along with another two standing guard at a choke point. Their movements were jerky and unnatural, bone scraping against stone with every step.

As they formed up with Brian in front, Jordan and Noriko flanking him, and Morgan and Viki at the back, Morgan said, "Before, we were taking them out one or two at a time and only dealing with three when patrols forced it. Now, though, we should be able to handle those three plus the other two in one go."

Looking to Viki, she added, "Do your thing and let's pull that group."

Jordan tightened his grip on the warhammer, knuckles whitening inside his gauntlets. So far he and Noriko's trainees had only fought low-level enemies under ten. These skeletons felt different—sharper, more deliberate—even compared to the spider dungeon.

Still, he wasn't about to turn tail and run. Brian would take the aggro. Jordan just had to stand beside him and swing.

He let out a quiet breath through his nose. He was wielding a warhammer—the best possible weapon against undead. He tried to convince himself it would be fun, but sweat was already starting to form beneath his helm and trickle down his spine. The last thing he needed was it stinging his eyes mid-fight.

An arrow sailed over their heads and detonated in fiery shadows, catching both groups of skeletons in its radius. Viki had timed the shot perfectly, hitting the patrol just as it passed the stationary guards. Bones exploded outward, clattering across the stone, though none flew over the ramparts. It did solid damage—cracked ribs, shattered arms—but didn't destroy them. The skeletons were already scrambling back to their feet and charging. The two wall defenders drew their bows and fired in response.

Brian raised his shield, steel ringing as arrows struck, but not before Viki loosed another shot and ducked behind him. The arrow punched straight through one archer's skull between the eye sockets, staggering it and sending it reeling, blind and flailing.

After that, Jordan didn't have time to track Viki's movements. Three skeletons were rushing straight toward him and Brian, rusty swords raised high.

Stepping forward, Brian barked out an insult, the verbal trigger for his taunt skill. "Your mother was a hamster and your father smelt of elderberries!"

Jordan almost stumbled at the familiar quote, but the magic snapped into place immediately, dragging the enemies' attention onto Brian like a hook in their minds.

The fight was on.

All three undead warriors instantly focused on the tank, ignoring Jordan and Noriko. As they clashed, slamming their swords against Brian's shield, the young samurai stepped forward, drawing her katana in a fluid motion and slashing at the skeleton on Brian's right, cleaving its left arm clean from its body.

Jordan, still coming to grips with fighting the undead, almost missed his chance, but at the last second he realized the leftmost skeleton—the one closest to him—had completely ignored him and was overextended, having put everything it had into a two-handed blow against Brian.

Without a lot of grace, but channeling all the power of the muscles he'd developed at the forge over the years, Jordan brought the massive hammer down on the enemy's skull, shattering it into pieces. The weapon's 35% crit chance flared with the blow, causing it to be twice as powerful as normal.

And just like that, there was one less attacker, leaving Jordan to gape at what he'd just done.

His weapon had been pretty effective against the spiders, but damn. He never expected to kill a monster nearly twice his level in a single hit.

Seeing him standing there in shock, Morgan yelled, "Jordan!"

That snapped him out of it, and he moved to flank the skeleton that had been in the center. He could see Noriko steadily damaging the one on the right, and Brian hacking away at both as he was able. His two companions were utilizing their combat skills to do big chunks of damage with each hit while trying to avoid taking damage in turn.

Meanwhile, Jordan had no skills—just a powerful magic weapon and brute strength. Every one of his hits knocked bones loose, breaking them and sending fragments flying everywhere. However, roughly one out of every three of his hits managed to proc the crit effect, doing massive damage. Very quickly, they finished off the three attacking skeletons that way.

Looking around, Jordan was surprised to see both of the archer skeletons down as well. Viki and Morgan had handled those in the time it took for the skeletal warriors to be dispatched.

Jordan was breathing heavily, his heart racing at ninety miles an hour, but he couldn't wipe the grin off his face. That had been incredible. They had faced strong foes and wiped them out without taking any damage at all. Better still, he hadn't felt like some third wheel being carried by the party and power-leveled. He had actually done more damage than Brian.

As he caught his breath, he realized that probably had as much to do with the fact that they were facing skeletons, which were particularly susceptible to blunt weapons and resistant to slashing ones, as anything else. Even so, it didn't dampen his elation at feeling useful in combat.

They waited a moment for the skeletons to disappear, then gathered the mana coins and hurried on to the next group of undead. All of them felt the pressure to kill as many as possible, as efficiently as they could, to beat the five-day deadline before the monsters would be free of this location and begin spreading out into the city. Leveling up to the point where they could deal with the larger undead would be the only way to prevent an incredible loss of life among the survivors.

In the following fights, Jordan wielded his hammer with growing confidence, settling into the role of frontline DPS rather than trying to function as a backup tank. The fights were not terribly difficult with this party, but that didn't mean they didn't get hurt. Noriko got it the worst, being in lighter samurai armor. Brian also took a few blows that slipped past his defenses and required healing.

Jordan was incredibly thankful for the massive advantage Liam's gift of Mythic-grade armor provided. He only suffered one damaging blow by the time they reached the northern gates of the stronghold dungeon, and even that only wounded him because it found a chink in his armor under his armpit.

He did his best not to scream like a baby.

This was no video game where pain wasn't a thing, and getting stabbed in the armpit was the worst pain he'd felt in his life so far. It was excruciating and caused him to drop his warhammer, unable to hold it up.

Thankfully, Morgan was watching over them, and her healing spell landed only a couple of seconds after the skeleton struck him. The next blow bounced off his insanely durable armor, but then Brian taunted the enemy, drawing it away from Jordan and taking the pressure off long enough for the healing to do its job.

When he could swing the weapon again, Jordan took his revenge with a titanic blow that pulverized the entire left side of the skeleton, killing it instantly and sending its body crashing into the other two undead still fighting.

Even after the healing had fully repaired his wound, he felt a phantom pain whenever he lifted his hammer high. That wound was not something he would forget anytime soon, and he became more cautious and strategic in his fighting style after that moment, focusing on learning good technique and tactics to compensate for the fact that his Class did nothing but lend extra strength to his blows. It gave him no defensive tools of its own.

By the time they reached the gate, they had killed fifty-four more skeletons and were feeling pretty tired. Unfortunately, the big defensive tower loomed above them.

Brian stretched his shoulders, swinging his shield around to get the blood flowing back into his arms. "Ugh. I need a bit of a break after this!"

Morgan nodded. "Yeah, it's somewhere around midnight. Let's kill this mini-boss and clear the tower, then get some sleep. Everyone good with that?"

Viki, young and seemingly a font of endless energy—on top of having stats far higher than everyone else—looked disappointed. "Okay. I guess we can rest after this. Tomorrow we can do the whole rest of the wall, finish off all the skeletons, and move on to bigger monsters. By the time we finish them, I think I'll be too high a level to get experience from them."

Jordan was still amazed at how high-level they were, but he was catching up. Just on this section of wall, he'd gone from Level 12 to

Level 14, and that was even with the experience split five ways. Once Morgan and Viki out-leveled the skeletons, the experience would only be split three ways until they moved on to higher-level monsters inside the walls.

He now understood why Liam had gone solo so much of the time. If Liam had killed all those skeletons by himself and not had to split the experience so many ways, he would have earned more than 100,000 experience—enough to reach nearly Level 18 instead of the Level 14 Jordan had gained.

Of course, that wasn't something Jordan could have done. He was a blacksmith, and despite how hard he could hit with a high-grade enchanted warhammer, he had no combat-related System skills. Even with ridiculously durable armor, he would have died several times over by now without the others to support and protect him.

Looking from the tower ahead up into the gloomy skies, Jordan wondered how Liam was doing on his own mission to clear out the wraiths in less than twenty-four hours. He wished he could soak up all that experience.

CHAPTER 21
FLYING THE UNFRIENDLY SKIES

Liam's POV:

The fight for the skies so far had been intense. Despite the massive level difference, I had gone all in, bellowing out my challenge like a true dragon, the roar tearing out of my chest and rippling through the miasma like thunder through fog. Not that I wasn't a true dragon now, but normally I would avoid drawing uncounted enemies to me for fear of being overwhelmed. Right now I didn't have that luxury, hesitation feeling more dangerous than recklessness.

The only way I could clear the stronghold of the damned wraiths was to gather them all together and do my best to survive the assault while I tried to Murder, Death, Kill the absolute fuck out of them with my AOE spells, turning the sky itself into a killing ground.

And it worked too. Maybe too well.

I burned them down by the dozens. Void Breath, Arcane Ascension, Entropy, Night's End, and even Tempest Strike, each spell detonating through the gloom in waves of heat and pressure. It only took a couple of attacks on each one to completely empty their health bars thanks to the seventy level difference between me and them. When enough of them gathered around me I even used Dragon's Fury, power flooding my limbs until my scales hummed. Then a cast of Arcane Ascension destroyed at least fifty in a single spell, leaving nothing behind but fading motes and scorched air.

Unfortunately, this wasn't a sprint to kill as many as fast as I could. I quickly discovered this was a marathon instead, and a battle of attrition. I had to juggle cooldowns, and mana usage, tracking timers even as claws and wings stayed in constant motion. For the first time ever, I dipped into my supply of mana potions to keep up the pace of the killing, the sharp burn of liquid mana racing down my throat.

I even had to use Tempest Strike and other physical attacks with my claws to steal health and mana via Voidflame, raking through half-solid bodies that resisted like wet smoke. Even with all of that, I found myself taking far more damage than I was comfortable with. I was literally killing them by the dozens, but they were also swarming me, latching on and draining my health and mana like viscous, ghostly human-sized mosquitos, their touch cold, numbing, and invasive.

It was a constant battle between the health loss and the damage I was doing, numbers rising and falling in relentless opposition. The thing that made this survivable was the combination of my Aura of Fear and my Void Domain. These creatures were so far below my level that when they got close enough they had their stats and movement reduced to basically nothing, floating around me like sitting ducks. It didn't prevent them from reaching me or hitting me with their Drain ability, but without those their attacks would have been much more powerful and far more of them would have managed to reach me.

Even so, it was a close thing. I fought late into the night, muscles aching beneath my scales, constantly flying sweeping patterns around the dungeon, trying to ensure I didn't miss any. They were so hyper aggressive in their unreasoning rage that even as they died they never avoided battle, but charged toward me the moment they detected my presence. Something that I ensured they would by regularly issuing my draconic roar, the sound echoing throughout the skies for hundreds of yards in every direction.

As I finished my first pass around the outer perimeter, I had no doubt that every wraith heard my battle cry and headed straight for me, a converging tide of malice and hunger.

Around midnight, I took a short break landing atop a fortified building in the middle of the plains that made up the dungeon's outer area, wings folding in as my chest heaved. I only did this to let my mana and health regenerate before charging straight back into action, forcing myself not to linger. No matter how exhausting this was, my stats were high enough that I could power through and spend twenty-something hours eradicating the wraiths.

My second pass was deeper into the territory of the dungeon. I was basically making a bullseye type pattern that overlapped somewhat with each previous pass. This was to ensure that I wouldn't miss any, and that none would accidentally wander outward where they might escape into the city and kill innocent survivors, a thought that kept me moving when fatigue threatened to slow me.

With the perimeter shrinking with each pass, it should have gotten faster to complete each circuit, but it didn't. Each subsequent pass got harder, the resistance thickening with every ring inward.

The more I headed toward the center, the more densely packed the wraiths were, meaning that my mana and health were getting stretched thinner, warning notifications stacking faster than I liked. On the second pass, several times my health dropped below 1000. The third pass saw my health dip below 300 four times. And worse, despite my 300 Endurance, I was starting to get weary, the drag settling deep into muscle and mind, the constant battle wearing me down.

After that pass, I took a two hour nap, more collapse than rest. By then it was nearing 5:00 AM, and I was feeling the pressure, time a thunderous ticking clock in my head. I had at least two more passes to go and only around twelve hours to complete them.

The sun may have arisen, but I couldn't see it under the miasma that covered the dungeon, the light reduced to a dull, sickly glow. I ate some jerky and cheese from my storage ring that I'd been carrying since the apocalypse started. Damn that teriyaki jerky was good, the familiar flavor grounding me, and reminded me again that the lack of seasonings as time passed was going to suck.

After a swig of water, I turned back into my dragon form, and leapt for the sky. Powerful wing beats had me soaring toward the wraith infested clouds like a rocket, the ground falling away beneath me. The wind was colder than it should have been for this time of year, but wasn't as bad as it had been before the dungeon boss was killed, a clear indicator that the atmosphere of the area would go back to normal soon.

I started my circle of the skies where I had left off, going deeper into the dungeon as I went. I was basically on the fourth ring of the bullseye now, with at least one more to go, but maybe two.

I had to take it slower this time. The closer toward the center, the more wraiths there were so only by slowing down was my regeneration and Voidflame able to allow me to keep up with the HP and Mana loss, a careful balance between motion and survival.

About a quarter of the way around the circle, I was swarmed. Dozens and dozens of wraiths were all diving and rushing at me, their shrieks blending into a single piercing howl, as I prepared and cast my AOE spells. They died in the scores, but some always got through. At one point, I had eleven wraiths all attached to my body like bloodsucking leeches, draining me dry. Thank goodness, my dragon neck was able to swivel all the way around. Only by breathing Void energy all over myself was I able to kill the monsters, the blast washing over my own scales.

"That one was too close!"

I was down below 1000 hit points, and losing it at a rate of nearly 200 per second before I was able to burn them to ash. It was a damned good thing my breath weapon was off of cooldown at that moment and that I was immune to my own Void Breath.

After that moment, I slowed down to ensure I wouldn't get so utterly overwhelmed again. I wanted to always have enough mana, and at least one of my AOE's off cooldown, no matter how tempting it was to push harder.

That made things slower, but still the enemy fell by the dozens. I just made sure to space out my war cries so as not to pull too many at once again.

This went on for hours as I slowly spiraled inward toward the center. I was exhausted from the long continuous battle, every movement deliberate now in that dogged way when there is nothing left in your mind but continuing. Only the combination of my high stats, and Voidflame to keep my health and mana bars from draining all the way to empty kept me going. Morning had come and passed and it was nearing mid-afternoon, just a few hours to go until the System would take me away.

That was when it happened. The Wraith mini-boss found me. It was only Level 45, but my health bar was already down to 735 hitpoints, and my mana was around 500. Worse, it couldn't have picked a more terrible moment to attack. My best skills were on cooldown, having just used them to kill another large group of the rage-filled spirits.

I had nothing but my claws for the next twenty-eight seconds, and the timer might as well have been a death sentence!

The last thing I wanted to do was go into a hand-to-hand battle with an incorporeal spirit even if my attacks did do damage. There were still around a dozen more normal wraiths in the area in addition to the boss, all diving to latch on and drain me of my last dregs of health, their shadows closing in from every direction.

I could try to teleport away, but then I'd run the risk of losing these wraiths that I'd so painstakingly gathered and chased into the center of the dungeon, undoing hours of brutal work in an instant.

"Crap! I can't afford to let this guy get away!"

A Level 45 incorporeal boss loose in the city would cause unimaginable harm. Tens of thousands of deaths might result, and it would even be a deadly threat to our team of would-be Ascenders.

I gritted my teeth, and swiped away a wraith trying to reach my flank while I was distracted by the boss, my claws passing through it in a burst of stolen health and mana. Dragons didn't sweat, and the blood in my veins was boiling, not in fear, but in rage at being challenged this way, my pulse thundering hard enough to feel in my horns.

The biggest threat wasn't the boss itself, but being drained by the other wraiths while dealing with the boss, numbers bleeding away even as I fought to keep my focus locked forward.

Then I discovered why I hated this boss in particular. It had the 'Blink' skill, or some form of battlefield teleportation that was instant, and had a very short cooldown.

Just as I was about to perform Dragon's Charge to close with it, it disappeared right before my eyes, its outline snapping out of existence like a popped balloon. This also highlighted the fact that I really needed to buy an enhanced perception skill once I had access to the Shop, one that let me see behind my back.

I flung my head about looking in every direction, only to find the bastard had appeared behind and above me and was now diving toward my unprotected back.

Casting Haste, I gained just enough extra speed to slam my wings forward in a titanic burst of air, pushing me aside just enough that the boss sailed past, missing me by inches, the displaced wind ripping loose fragments of miasma around us.

I took a swipe at it, but it teleported again, leaving nothing but a cold sensation in the space it had occupied.

Using my doubled speed, I dodged again, my instincts driving me. It appeared below me and to my right this time, but my maneuver had been enough to put a short distance between us.

Unfortunately, it had also allowed one of the other wraiths to reach me and it was now draining 50 HP per second, its grip like ice digging into my scales, and I couldn't deal with it, or I'd let the boss get a free shot at me.

With the instant of reprieve my evasion had earned me, I cast Draconic Fury doubling my strength, power flooding my limbs.

Another wraith came close and a slash of my claws ripped its incorporeal body to shreds, Voidflame flaring as the stolen energy rushed back into me.

In that fraction of an instant, the boss disappeared again.

Damn, I really need a 360 degree perception skill!

True Perception was amazing, and was allowing me to see these ghostly bastards as clear as day, their outlines razor sharp against the gloom, but it didn't let me see behind my back unless I turned my head around which was giving the boss the opportunity to narrow the distance between us with each jump.

This time it appeared directly above me right between my beating wings. Their powerful movements would normally have battered an enemy, turbulent air enough to shatter bone, but these ghostly jerks were completely unaffected by any physical harm that wasn't highly magical in nature. And while my claws counted due to their attunement to my magic weapons, my wings did not. Not even my fangs counted for this, else I could have simply chomped down on it.

Worse, if it landed, I'd have no way to get it off. My talons couldn't reach the spot right between my wings, and my breath weapon was still on cooldown for another 16 seconds, a countdown ticking far too slowly. More than long enough for it to do massive damage and maybe even kill me.

I tried to evade, to dodge, even threw myself into a power dive, the ground spinning sickeningly beneath me, but it did no good. I managed to hold it off for another two seconds, but then it latched on and began draining me for 100 health and mana a second. With the other wraith, that was 150 health a second, my bars plunging in brutal, steady chunks.

I had no way to get it off, so I focused on avoiding the other wraiths, which was much easier now with Haste and Fury both active, my movements sharp and explosive. It just hadn't been effective against the boss who was much faster and more agile than its lesser brethren. Neither had my armor's ability to give a burst of protection when under 20% health. These bastards incorporeal nature bypassed that defense.

-150 HP
Health: 485/6000

I cast greater Void Bolt, being very careful to target the wraith. The last thing I needed was to die due to damage from my own spell.

The spell landed and dropped the wraith boss instantly into the red, bringing it down to 25% on its health bar. However, the attack slammed it into me, and I took 200 damage as well, the impact rattling my spine.

Health: 285/6000

I screamed in frustration and pain, the sound tearing free without restraint, as another second ticked by.

-150 HP
Health: 135/6000

With a roar of frustration that shook the skies, I manifested one of my high grade healing potions from my storage and shoved it into my mouth, clamping it between my fangs while the contents poured down my throat, liquid fire and vitality flooding my core.

The next tick of health drain occurred at the same time and received a huge boost of restored health.

-150 HP
+3000 HP
-150 HP
Health: 2835/6000

I so very, very much wished my fangs counted as magic weapons for this purpose! I wanted to rend that bastard to shreds, feel it come apart under my teeth.

Fuck it! I'm not letting it get away with this!

I hit it with Shadow Surge, knowing it would ravage me as well, and the damage would be doubled due to Draconic Fury, accepting the pain before it even came.

The spell washed over and through the incorporeal boss like a tidal wave of darkness, eroding its very existence more thoroughly than if it had been hit with acid, the air screaming as reality warped around it.

Both the boss and the regular wraith died in the blast, but it also did a doubled 'high' damage attack to my own back and spine, agony flaring white-hot through my nerves.

Health: 1235/6000

Ouch, that freakin hurt!

"I wish I could resurrect it so I could kill it again!"

Flying down toward the ground I looked for the chest, and found it sitting atop a pile of rubble, its glow unmistakable even through lingering haze. The other wraiths were still following me, but I swatted them with my claws every time one got close, letting Voidflame steal their health and mana to restore my own.

It was annoying, to open the chest while still being swarmed by nearly a dozen ghostly attackers, their shrieks clawing at my ears, but I did, and took the mythic grade potions and put them into my inventory. They looked impressive as hell, with their fancy bottles and the intense glow of the liquids within, mana swirling visibly inside the glass.

I might need those during the Ascension quest, so I wasn't about to use them now that the wraith boss was destroyed. I still had over a minute of Draconic Fury left as well as a few seconds of Haste. I was about to go on a killing spree, muscles coiled tight with stored violence, and refill my health and mana with my claws.

Still, before that, I grabbed the only item in the chest, an ascendant upgrade token. My Luck stat was doing its job and ensuring I got some good loot, the token pulsing warmly in my grasp.

I'd worry about applying it later, and made it disappear into my storage ring.

Then I charged the wraiths around me and began the slaughter, rage and momentum carrying me forward.

In only a couple of minutes my health and mana were topped up again, and despite being exhausted, I was too angry and anxious to rest. I needed to finish this before my timer ran out, and the System pulled me away to the Ascension quest.

An hour later and I could no longer find a single wraith in the skies above the dungeon. I had applied the upgrade token to my Hunter's Charm Necklace. Before, it gave a +15% to detect hostile distance and made enemies appear on my mini-map.

Now, it gave 100% bonus to detection range, not just for locating hostile entities, but for pretty much everything, including: hidden objects, treasure, secret doors, and even dungeon entrances, the world unfolding outward in layered detail. It also interfaced with my True Perception skill to bypass almost all stealth and deception attempts. It would take a near level capped assassin using absolute top-end skills to try and ambush me now. And nothing on this Earth could come close to that anytime soon.

My range was nearly a mile now, and my mini-map even received an upgrade while wearing the necklace. It would auto-populate out to that full range, even without me having line of sight, icons and contours blooming into existence as I moved.

It was incredibly useful, and while I was thankful for the results, I probably wouldn't have chosen that, if not for the need to ensure all the wraiths were culled before I was taken away.

Still, I wasn't too broken up by the fact that I had been forced by circumstances to choose it. It looked really cool now, and would be a great benefit.

It now had a thin chain of darkened alloy supporting the charm, light enough that it never tugged or shifted during movement. The pendant itself was a polished disc etched with layered hunting sigils, their lines cut so precisely they seemed to sink inward rather than sit on the surface. At its center, a faceted crystal lens rested flush with the metal, seemingly clear at first glance but catching light at odd angles, as if it were constantly adjusting its focus. Even when it was still, the charm gave the subtle impression of awareness, like an unblinking eye tracking the world around it.

Hunter's Charm Necklace (Ascendent Tier)
Description:

A refined hunter's focus charm enhanced through ascendant-grade System modification energy. The necklace expands the wearer's awareness far beyond conventional sensory limits, actively mapping threats, anomalies, and hidden features within the environment.

Effect: +100% Detection Range.
Reveals hostile entities, hidden creatures, concealed objects, secret doors, treasure caches, and dungeon entrances.Fully integrates with *True Perception and Treasure Sense*, bypassing most stealth, invisibility, illusion, and deception-based effects.

Restrictions: Soul-attuned. Detection capabilities scale with the bearer's perception and ascended authority.

With a quick flyover of the dungeon, thanks to the necklace, I was able to confirm there were no Wraiths left, chasing a few down that had slipped past my early circuits of the dungeon, their faint signatures flaring briefly on my expanded senses before vanishing for good.

When I was sure the job was done, I flew back to the cathedral and landed before the big double doors, my wings aching dully as I folded them away. Changing back into my human form, I wandered inside and took out one of the remaining MRE packs, and had a quick dinner, eating mechanically more from habit than hunger. I had only a couple of hours left until I would be taken, so I set up my magic shelter, and took a nap to recover from the long grueling day of wraith hunting.

I dreamed of endless slaughter of monsters, black clouds tearing apart under claws and spellfire, but it wasn't a nightmare, but rather it gave me a warm feeling of accomplishment, a bone-deep satisfaction that even exhaustion couldn't dull. When I woke, it would finally be time for the Ascension Quest to begin.

I awoke refreshed, only minutes before the timer ran down. Making sure everything was ready, I used Commune to say one last goodbye to Morgan and Viki. Who knew how long this Ascension quest would take? The one thing I was sure of was that it wouldn't be easy.

CHAPTER 22

PARTY ON!

Viki's POV:

Viki walked off from the others and sat on the edge of the wall. Her heart hurt. It was one thing to know Liam was going to be gone doing that stupid Ascension quest without them, but she didn't know how long he'd be gone this time. Or even if he would be able to come back.

She didn't want to think about the possibility of him dying. She had absolute confidence in him, but the fear tried to lodge in her soul anyway.

Even though he'd been gone soloing dungeons off and on for days, he'd always been there out of sight, but just a Commune spell away. They could always reach him before.

She gazed out over the blackened dungeon, her mood growing dark enough to match the skies.

The others gave her space while they rested. She looked at the clouds where the wraiths had been. They were peaceful now. All day she had glanced to the skies and seen her big brother killing the monsters, and she'd felt the call to be flying beside him, breathing her Umbral Breath at the evil monsters.

Just you wait, I'll follow you, she thought fiercely!

Ever since that horrible day, and the screams of her family as they died protecting her from the monsters...

Her blood felt hot in her veins, and she suddenly felt impatient to get back to killing. Liam wouldn't sit around like this. He spent nearly twenty-four hours flying through the skies hunting the wraiths to make sure she would be safe.

Now it was her turn to help keep the survivors safe. The people of this city were hers, and she wouldn't let the monsters have them! She itched to breathe her dragon breath at the skeletons along the rest of the wall.

She stood up and looked in the direction they were headed. They were moving counterclockwise around the perimeter of this big dungeon, and they'd cleared three more gates today along with their mini-bosses. They had been resting and eaten a snack after the third mini-boss battle when Liam had called.

Brian said they'd walked a little over twelve miles. What that meant in terms of monsters killed was over 800 skeletons, 15 elite minions, and 3 mini-bosses.

Viki grinned at that thought, her teeth showing, the canines visible as she thought back over the vengeance they'd brought to the damned monsters. No amount could ever make up for her family, but every one she put an arrow into, or hacked apart with her cleaver, made her feel satisfied that she was making a difference.

Unfortunately, she and Morgan had stopped leveling after they hit Level 40. Now they only received experience from the elite minions and mini-bosses. Still, the others were catching up fast, even splitting the experience the way they were. Of course, it helped the rest of the party that they were getting her and Morgan's share of the EXP from the Level 20 skeletons now, since it was only being split three ways since earlier in the day.

Walking back to the others, she called to Jordan and the others, "What Level are you guys after this last boss fight?"

Jordan grinned, his smile splitting his face. He was so pleased. "Level 22, halfway to 23. I can't believe I'm already so far ahead of where I was yesterday."

Smiling more serenely than their big blacksmith companion, Noriko spoke. "I am very close to Level 30, and my first Class upgrade. I have kept the platinum mana coin that Liam-sama gave me next to my skin. Perhaps that will help convince the System to offer a magic-based Class during my upgrade. I have already received three points in Magical Aptitude, so I am hopeful."

Brian spoke last. "I just hit Level 28 when the boss fell. I also have one of the coins in my hand anytime I'm not holding my sword and shield. I only have two points in Magical Aptitude, though. If this keeps up, we'll need to do our Class upgrades tonight when we stop to sleep. I'm looking forward to that!"

There was a slight frown on Jordan's face. "I don't think I'll make it to Level 30 today. Mid-twenties maybe. Still, hitting it tomorrow will be amazing. I don't want to change to a combat class, but it would be cool if I could get something that offers some combat abilities in addition to the smithing skills."

Viki smiled back at the blacksmith. He had turned out to be a fun addition to the party. He got very excited when he made a good kill with that big warhammer. He had even squealed like a kid once when he drove the monster's skull straight down into its ribcage. It had looked so funny stumbling and staggering around, with its glowing eyes staring out from between its rib bones.

Plus, thanks to the lower amount of experience he needed because he was lower level, he was catching up fast. It all evened out as you leveled up, because each level took more and more experience. Maybe in a couple days the others would be the same level as her and Morgan.

Grinning, Viki was looking forward to the others doing their first Class upgrades later. She couldn't wait until her second one at Level 60. That seemed so long from now, but really it would only be a day or two at the rate the party was slaughtering the monsters in this dungeon. Of course, it didn't hurt that there were literally hundreds of each type of monster. Way more than any normal dungeon!

For her part, she had gotten new skills earlier in the day, and she was very pleased about it. She quickly took a peek at her status while she waited for the others to stand back up from their rest and get moving again.

Victoria "Viki" Blue

Draconic Sniper - Level 40
Bloodline (Tier 2): Night Dragon

Experience: 16800/68320

Attributes:
Endurance: 85
Strength: 85
Agility: 85
Mind: 85
Will: 86
Magical Aptitude: 86
Luck: 5

Health: 1360/1360

Mana: 1380/1380

Abilities:
Active: Shadow Veil, Shadow Step,Treasure Sense, Umbral Breath, Claws
Passive: Dark Vision

Skills:
Active:
Arrow: Shadow Bolt
Arrow: Duskfire
Arrow: Shatterstorm (AOE)
Arrow: Soulpiercer
Arrow: Eclipse
Arrow: Oblivion
Arrow: Cataclysm (AOE)
Arrow: Twin Fang Shot

Passive:
Mini-map
Claw Mastery

Spells:
Whispering Bolt
Gloom Shroud
Midnight's Grasp
Stealth
Hawkeye
True Shot
Umbral Ward
Umbral Detonation (AOE)
Shadow Aegis

It had been a while since she'd taken the time to really look at her skills, so she pulled up the info on both her Level 35 and 40 gains, and they were some good ones!

Ability:

Claws (Level 40)

Description: The caster manifests draconic claws transforming their hands into weapons of predatory precision. These claws blur the line between physical and magical force, striking with supernatural sharpness.

Effect: Converts unarmed attacks into claw strikes that deal hybrid physical and magical damage, allowing them to harm incorporeal and magically resistant enemies. Claw attacks benefit from draconic scaling and synergize with Claw Mastery.

Cooldown: None.

Skills:

Twin Fang Shot (Level 35)

Description: A shadow-linked double strike that manifests two arrows in a single breath of motion, striking with predatory precision.

Effect: Fires two arrows at the same target in rapid succession. Each arrow deals moderate shadow damage. Successful hits apply stacking knockback and briefly disrupt enemy footing.

Cooldown: 30 seconds.

Claw Mastery (Passive) (Level 40)

Description: Shadow-infused combat instinct that sharpens the caster's natural weapons into lethal extensions of will.

Effect: Increases claw damage, improves chaining speed of claw attacks.

Attunement: Claws can be attuned to magical weapons, enhancing damage and allowing the use of the weapons effects and abilities. Note: Only one weapon can be attuned at a time to each hand.

Cooldown: None.

Spells:

Umbral Detonation (AOE) (Level 35)

Description: A focused burst of compressed shadow energy that erupts outward in a violent pulse.

Effect: Deals High damage in a localized area and causes minor stagger to affected enemies.

Cooldown: 60 seconds.

Shadowguard Aegis

Description: A reactive veil of shadow that intercepts harm and punishes those who strike too close.

Effect: Deflects the next incoming attack and reflects the damage to attackers in melee range.

Cooldown: 2 minutes.

Those were some pretty great skills. Not that she could use the claws. Well, she could, but that wasn't her preferred fighting style. She much preferred using her bow.

Still, it didn't hurt to be prepared. She grinned as she manifested her claws for the first time. It was kind of like being Wolverine, except that the wickedly sharp black ivory of the talons extended from her fingers rather than her knuckles. They also grew as long as a short sword. Following Liam's example, she attuned her only two magic weapons to her claws. The air hummed faintly as the claws slid into place, the sound sharp and satisfying in a way that made her grin widen.

Her right-hand claws got the Cleaver of the Fallen Shaman, granting 5% Lifesteal, a bonus to attack accuracy, and a 5% armor reduction for 10 seconds on a hit. Her left was attuned to her bow. It gave a decent bonus to accuracy, enhanced crit chance for double damage, and any crit became armor piercing. Her bow also had a once-per-day special ability to automatically hit, ignoring cover, but that seemed pretty pointless with claws.

Regardless, she was very happy with the gains. Besides, she was likely to find better weapons to which she could attune her claws soon enough. They had already cleared three mini-bosses so far today and received loot. However, none had been weapons. She had received a Greater Upgrade Token, which she'd used on her Reinforced Leather Bracers, bringing them up to +20% armor, +20% accuracy, and 20% damage reduction. Overall, it was a good boost that would help keep her bracers relevant for a few more levels at least.

Lastly, she had received a new Storage Ring of Greater Quality. It held more than her old ring.

Speaking of which, it had come in handy as they were loading up their storage with all the gear from the skeletons. The steady clatter of metal and bone echoed faintly each time another bundle vanished into storage after a fight.

She growled under her breath at the thought of all the mana coins she could have hoarded. Still, all the poor refugees needed weapons and armor to survive, and this dungeon was letting them collect hundreds. It was still a drop in the bucket compared to the need, but even arming a thousand of the ten thousand or more who had made the Exodus to Brian's camp was pretty awesome!

When she saw that everyone was moving slowly, she whined, "Come on, I want to kill more monsters! Let's finish the wall before we sleep tonight!"

The rest of the party groaned at her enthusiasm, and Morgan put a sisterly hand on her shoulder. "It's harder for us old folks to get moving." She said it with a twinkle in her eye.

Viki smirked and got in a jab. "Okay, boomer."

Narrowing her eyes, Morgan pretended to make a fist at her. "Watch it, I'm only in my 20s. Still, it's not just you being younger that you have more energy. You've got to remember you probably have three times the stats compared to the rest of us. I've only got 32 in Strength and Endurance."

The young girl snorted. "I've only got 85. That's not triple, just a little more than double."

That produced a flat look from Morgan, and she said dryly, "Only a little more than double, she says..." Then she grinned and mockingly threatened, "Keep it up and so help me, I'll ruffle your hair like Liam does!"

Viki shrank back and put a defensive hand up to protect her head. “That’s not fair. It’s not my fault I got this bloodline.”

Chuckling, Morgan countered, “Oh, yes it is! You went out with Liam and power-leveled before you got to choose your class. That was definitely your decision.”

“Well, yeah, okay... but I didn’t...” Viki trailed off and crossed her arms over her chest defensively. “Fine, whatever, Boomer! Let’s just go already!”

Morgan shot forward and ruffled the young girl’s hair quite viciously, but both of them were grinning by the time they stopped. Viki tried to glare, but laughter leaked through anyway.

The rest of the party just looked on in amusement, having gotten ready while they tussled.

Jordan teased, “Jeez, come on already! The rest of us are waiting on you.”

Viki looked like she was going to say something, but then saw the amusement in the blacksmith’s eyes and realized she was being teased.

Addressing the group, Morgan spoke up. “There are three more gates with mini-bosses before we get back to where Viki and I started clearing the walls. I’m guessing at least a couple hundred more skeletons. That should get you guys the rest of the way to Level 30 and your Class upgrades.”

They fell into their usual marching order, with Brian and Noriko leading the way, Morgan and Viki walking side-by-side in the middle, and Jordan bringing up the rear.

Viki grinned at the second-nature way they were all just comfortably acting like a team that had been together for weeks. It had been a little rough at first, last night, when the three from Camp Colony had joined them, but it had worked out quickly. Killing monsters together would do that.

By this afternoon, they were a well-oiled machine. The skeletons posed no threat to them at all now. They could kill a pack of five in fifteen seconds or less, then be on their way three to five minutes later. Even the melee fighters barely broke a sweat or got out of breath. Their movements flowed without hesitation, each person already stepping into place before the last skeleton finished collapsing.

Grinning, Viki kicked off the next attack by dropping an AOE arrow attack right in the middle of the group, doing high damage. However, she had learned to aim her arrow such that the explosion wouldn't knock some of the monsters off the wall. That would lead to a waste of time as they had to find where it landed and rain spells and arrows on it before they could move on.

Almost at the same instant, Morgan would release her own AOE spell, doing moderate damage and applying a weakness debuff.

The double-whammy of these two detonations back to back scattered the skeletons and knocked them prone. That allowed Brian to rush forward and taunt the disoriented enemies. Viki followed that by casting her new spell at the rear of the group, just far enough away to not hit Brian or the two frontline DPS members of the party. By that point they were below half health and easy pickings.

Noriko and Jordan unleashed their own attacks, strike skills in Noriko's case, and unskilled but powerful blows from Jordan, more than a third of which did crits and instantly ended the monster's pseudo-life.

Meanwhile, Brian stood there, swinging at the only one left moving and ending its life in only two blows.

And just like that, another group of skeletons was dead.

Viki hurried over to help strip the gear from the undead, storing it in her storage ring.

They took a quick breather just long enough to collect everything useful, then moved on.

With the thrill of the fight having passed, Viki looked up at her adopted big sister and asked, “Do you think Liam’s having fun? I wonder how long the quest takes.”

CHAPTER 23
ASCENSION BEGINS
LIAM'S POV:

THE WORLD DID NOT blur or stretch the way dungeon transports usually did.

One moment I stood at the cathedral, lungs burning faintly from lingering exertion, the next...

Silence.

Not the absence of sound, but the kind that felt... padded. Intentional. Like the air itself was absorbing the sharp edges of reality. My ears strained for an echo that never came, the quiet pressing in like a hand over a speaker.

I blinked.

White.

Not blinding, not sterile hospital white. Softer. The kind of white you might imagine if someone described sunlight without ever having seen the sun. The space around me was vast but difficult to measure. There were no corners, no visible ceiling, no obvious walls. Just a gentle gradient where brightness shifted enough to imply boundaries without declaring them. The longer I stared, the more my depth perception refused to settle, like my eyes couldn't decide where the room actually ended.

The floor beneath my boots was solid, faintly warm, with the subtle firmness of polished stone. When I shifted my weight, the sound didn't echo. It simply... ended. The scrape of my sole died so cleanly it felt edited out of the air.

A quiet pressure settled at the back of my thoughts.

You are safe. You are observed. You are welcome.

The impressions weren't words so much as meaning, layered over sensation. Familiar. The same way dungeon thresholds whispered danger and boss arenas hummed with anticipation. But here, the tone was neutral. Assessing. Calm.

My shoulders loosened before I consciously allowed them to.

Ahead, shapes resolved from the white. Furniture, simple and elegant. A low table. Chairs cushioned in muted tones that didn't quite register as color, only warmth. A couch that looked impossibly inviting after the hours of combat I'd just endured. My gaze kept drifting back to it, my body already weighing how fast I could collapse onto those cushions.

It felt... prepared.

To one side, an alcove formed, holding a basin fed by water that appeared without source. The liquid shimmered faintly, perfectly clear. Nearby stood what could only be a door, though it had no frame or hinges. Just a suggestion of privacy and function. I didn't need the System to spell it out. Wash. Rest. Recover. The sight alone made the grime and sweat on my skin suddenly impossible to ignore.

A faint scent drifted through the air. Clean. Neutral. Comforting in a way that bypassed conscious thought. My lungs pulled in a deeper breath before I even chose to inhale.

The table now held food.

I hadn't seen it appear. One moment empty surface, the next a spread of simple meals. Bread, roasted meat, fresh fruit, water in a glass that caught light without reflecting it. Steam curled lazily upward. Real heat. Real substance. The warmth brushed my face and my mouth watered before I could stop it.

My stomach tightened in sudden awareness. It growled loud enough that I glanced around out of habit.

Your needs are anticipated. Your recovery is prioritized.

Again, not words. Assurance.

The space wasn't trying to impress me. That was what struck me most. There were no impossible vistas, no cosmic theatrics, no declarations of power. Everything here felt deliberately... approachable. As if whoever designed this place understood that awe could be a distraction.

This was a waiting room for something enormous.

And it was built to keep me steady before stepping into it.

I exhaled slowly, tension unwinding in increments. My heartbeat settled. The fatigue in my muscles dulled to a manageable ache. The tremor in my hands faded until my fingers finally stopped twitching.

The white expanse remained quiet, patient.

Watching.

Waiting.

The System's presence lingered like a hand hovering just above my shoulder.

Ascension Candidate acknowledged. Trial preparation phase active.

And beneath the calm projection, I felt it.

Expectation. The sensation prickled along my spine like someone leaning in just out of sight.

I cursed under my breath. Even here in the Ascension Quest, or Trial, or whatever the fuck the System wanted to call it, it still projected those same cut-scene thoughts and impressions into my brain.

The difference here was that it hadn't been Earth's AI communicating with me. This "voice" was distinctly different, if it could even be called a voice. It was far more subtle and oddly gentle compared with all my previous experiences with the System and the AI.

The System had always been impersonal, almost mechanical in its way, as if it were a non-sapient computer program delivering predetermined information to whatever random person happened to trigger the right conditions.

Earth's AI, on the other hand, was an uncaring asshole who only spoke to me because I was a useful pawn.

This, though... this was different. Despite it being impersonal, it strangely gave a sense that it cared and actually wanted me to be at ease. As if my state of mind and physical condition meant something to it.

It was bizarre to think that some part of the System wasn't a complete piece of shit. Almost as if the System wasn't all one big monolithic thing.

Shuddering at the unnaturally calm state of things, I glanced nervously at my mini-map. It never showed a lack of dots to indicate enemies or other lifeforms these days. Reaching out with my senses I tried to feel if any beings were present, but got nothing. The emptiness rang louder than any threat ever had.

Since I upgraded that last magic item, I had a one mile radius to sense hostiles.

Nothing.

That very nearly freaked me out. It was just like something my dad had told me once. He described the sight of no planes in the skies after 9/11 as being incredibly eerie. I understand that now.

After so long of being constantly in danger, the absolute lack of any was really making my scales itch it felt so unnatural. My tail twitched without permission, searching for a threat that wasn't there.

You may take as long as necessary to recover before beginning your trials. Should you choose, you may also request to be returned to your place of origin before starting the trials. However, once the trials have begun, this realm cannot be exited.

That felt off. Why couldn't I leave once the trials began?

Before I could even verbally pose the question, the voice echoed in my mind again.

The Ascension Trials are designed to ensure only candidates with the right strength of character and physical development can advance to the next stage. Failure to advance will result in —ERROR— ...Death.

Do you wish to return to your origin point?

What the fuck? The voice had glitched and "Death" had been inserted after the garbled error. That one word had been in the usual impersonal System voice, rather than the new kind version. The shift hit like a cold splash of water in my face.

This was strange.

I spoke aloud, responding to the voice, "While I appreciate the offer to rest and be at my best. My people are dying by the thousands every hour right now, and I'd really like to get this over with as fast as possible so that I can make a difference."

Trials take a fixed period of time equivalent to ten rotations of your planet, however, be assured that time-dilation is in effect during any rest periods, such that you may recover fully without your absence negatively affecting your world's events.

It was the kind voice again, one that sought to assure and comfort.

Ten days! I would be away and unable to help or save my friends for ten whole days. That was an eternity during this short grace period before the world was invaded. Two weeks had already passed, and now another ten days would go by before I can return and help. My jaw tightened as the timeline settled into place.

It was both a blessing and a curse. A blessing that I would be done one way or another before the 30 days were up. Bad news because I would only have 6 days left before Earth was invaded by dozens of hostile species that had twenty years of foreknowledge guiding them.

Well, all except for four of those races. I had killed their leaders and that knowledge died with them.

As eager as I was to get this over with, I had enough wisdom to take stock of myself. It had been fourteen days since I had restarted the apocalypse, and in that I had been going full tilt with a little rest here and there to keep myself from collapsing, but I hadn't really had any actual down time. The ache in my muscles reminded me exactly how thin I was running.

"So let me get this straight, if I take a break, even if it is for a couple of days in here, no time will pass outside?"

Time in this space can be accelerated to compensate for reasonable lengths of recovery.

Glancing at the table of food, I made my decision. “Then I will at least take time to eat a meal and sleep.”

I’d had a nap, before coming here, and truth be told, that was all my body actually needed with my current stats. Still, there was a difference between getting a quick rest for the sake of not over taxing your body and mind, and actually relaxing.

Relaxing is something I hadn't done in this current life. The thought sat heavy in my chest, like a truth I’d been sidestepping for weeks.

A minute later, I was already getting frustrated with myself. Just standing still and consciously trying to let the tension loosen was honestly kinda hard to do. As I focused on letting my shoulders drop and muscles in my neck and back relax, it was like my own mind was fighting me. My jaw kept tightening again the moment I forced it loose.

I had that little voice in the back of my head urging me to ‘go, go, go, people are dying!’ Each pulse of that thought made my fingers flex like I was reaching for a weapon.

Finally, I gave up for the moment and decided to just walk around the space and see what all was provided. In a way it was kind of like a loft apartment, in that everything was all right there in the same big open space. No walls. Everything was only separated logically. It even looked like it had been arranged with human sensibilities in mind. The bed was near the ‘bathroom’ a term I use loosely. The dining space was near the comfy looking chair, etc. My eyes kept cataloging exits and angles out of habit before I forced myself to stop.

I wondered if the System read a Candidate’s mind and did this according to what it found there. In other words, this was a pretty ideal arrangement for me, and I doubted a naturally born dragon would find the space in the same format. The familiarity made my breathing ease a notch without me noticing at first.

One thing I noted as I did my tour was a deep pool filled with hot water, something like a Roman tub that was big enough to get in and soak, or even float fully stretched out. Steam curled lazily upward, carrying the promise of heat.

That seemed like just the thing!

I sent my armor into storage, and then stripped off the rest of my clothes and cast Cleanse on them and myself, before wearily climbing down into the big pool. My muscles protested the movement with a dull ache that only made the water look more inviting.

The water hit my legs and I almost stopped.

It was hot. Right on the edge of uncomfortable, but I forced myself to keep going. The heat climbed higher, spreading across my scales in a steady wave. Instead of stinging, it settled into a deep warmth that felt... good. The sensation chased away a lingering chill I hadn't realized I was carrying.

I lowered myself the rest of the way and let out a slow breath. The sound came out shaky, like tension leaking through the cracks.

The moment the water covered my torso, tension started bleeding out of my shoulders. Muscles that had been tight since the fight against the Wraiths finally eased. The water carried some of my weight, and just standing there stopped feeling like work. My spine loosened a fraction at a time until I wasn't bracing anymore.

My breathing slowed. The constant edge in my head dulled. For a minute, I wasn't thinking about threats or cooldowns. Just heat and quiet. The silence settled around me instead of pressing in.

The scales suddenly felt unnecessary. I reasoned that if the System wanted to harm me in this place it could easily snuff me out like a candle. Sure, it could suddenly throw monsters at me unexpectedly in some kind of test, but I just didn't get the impression that this

Trial was that kind of deal. Nothing about the space felt like it was waiting to spring a trap.

Maybe the System treated Candidates differently than normal people, like we were valuable in a way the average person wasn't. That would track with the Earths AI's behavior, but this felt different, like it was not designed by our AI. It was older somehow. And don't ask me how I knew that, it was just an impression I had somehow. The calm here felt peaceful.

I finally decided there was no danger here. No reason to keep them up. I let the transformation unwind. The scales receded, and bare skin met the water. The heat hit sharper this time, and I hissed softly as my body adjusted. The sting faded quickly into a pleasant burn.

Then I settled in.

Warm water soaked into sore muscles, loosening the last of the tightness. For the first time since entering the goblin dungeon on Day 1, I was able to just stand there and relax. No pressure. No urgency. Just heat, silence, and a moment to breathe.

The little voice tried to get louder and urge me to return to the fight, but I ruthlessly suppressed it, reminding myself that the time-dilation meant no one was going to die if I took an hour to have a bath and a soak. The thought faded to a distant murmur.

******

An unknown time later, I lifted myself out of the tub, and decided to head to the table and do something about my stomach which was giving a pretty good impression of a hungry dragon right now, the growling sounding fierce and insistent. It echoed embarrassingly loud in the quiet room.

It also didn't help that the food smelled delicious. The scent hit like a memory and my mouth watered instantly.

There were a variety of Earth dishes, Mexican, Chinese, American, Indian. Basically, everything on the table was a favorite of mine. Chicken Tika Masala, General Tso's, Bacon Burgers and Fries, Enchiladas with Chips and Salsa, Pizza, and classics from all over. My gaze bounced between plates like I didn't know where to start.

Don't judge me for being basic! This was what I liked, and I'd fight anyone over it!

I started with the Burger and Fries, but quickly started sampling everything. I dipped my fries in Curry sauce. Took a bite of Pizza, followed by a chip loaded with salsa. Then I grinned and dipped a fry in queso. "Oh, hell yeah!" I said with my mouth full. Grease and spice lit up my tongue in a way that felt absurdly comforting.

The gluttony went on for an hour or more, with me slowing down after the first frantic minutes. If nothing else, it was very comforting to know that the System had preserved Earth's classic foods and spices somewhere in its database and could reproduce them. Each bite eased something tight in my chest.

"I may have just found my favorite perk of becoming a god!"

I laughed as I sat back and put a hand on my very full belly. I had a pang of guilt then. I wished I could share this feast with Viki and Morgan, and the others. Plus, it was lonely eating by myself. The empty space across the table suddenly felt larger and the room quieter.

"Note to self: see if you can use your System granted powers to ensure these foods are included in the System Shop once it opens." In my first life, there were meals and drinks in the Shop, but they weren't Earth-based. The flavoring was off from what we'd had pre-System. There were things like steaks and vegetables, but they weren't recognizable. Don't get me wrong, they weren't bad, but they weren't Earth classics either.

No one who could kill monsters would go hungry, but as the monster threat rose, too few could kill them, and millions. Hell, hundreds of millions starved to death, or slowly wasted away, due to a lack of fighting ability, or injuries preventing them from fighting. The memory tightened my grip on the edge of the table.

I growled in my throat, not wanting to sour my relaxed mood with those thoughts. The sound vibrated low in my chest before I forced it down.

Instead, I moved over to the bed and crawled under the covers and soon fell asleep. The mattress gave just enough to cradle the lingering ache in my back.

Unfortunately, I dreamed of running through dungeons, fighting orcs over restaurant dishes laid out on fine linen. Even in the dream my hands clenched around an invisible weapon.

When I finally woke, a vague sense of annoyance over the dream lingered. I was rested, but more than eager to fight anyone over trying to take the things I loved from me.

I was ready for the Trial to begin!

CHAPTER 24

FIRST TRAIL - PART ONE

I BLINKED.

What had I been thinking about?

Looking around in confusion, I tried to place where I was, and what was happening, but I saw nothing out of order. I was surrounded by the familiar pristine white walls and plas-steel accents of my Ascendant Domain chambers. I was right where I should be, having apparently nodded off at my desk.

The memories slid into place like I'd woken from one of those naps where you intend to close your eyes for a few minutes and wake up hours later not knowing whether it is day or night, or even what year it is. I hated those as a mortal! They were the worst. I had certainly never felt something so disorienting and frustrating in all my centuries as an Ascended. Perhaps it was related to recently waking up from deep-sleep. It had only been a few weeks since beginning my turn as First Ascender, after all.

I spoke into the air, knowing my words would be recorded, "Note to self: Sleep for more than two hours tonight. Apparently, I need a longer rest period."

Doing a quick check of the System time, I noted that it was a quarter of an hour before I was scheduled to meet with the World Council, although I couldn't recall what the meeting was to be about.

Still, despite the unexpected nap, I felt good. Very good.

I felt... complete, in a way I'd never known before. In fact, I felt amazing. That thought seemed odd. Why wouldn't I feel that way? I'd felt that way ever since Ascending...

Chuckling, I shook off the confusion. Maybe I should power nap more often if it makes even mundane things like my health and proprioception feel this fresh and wonderful. Although I couldn't remember dreaming, perhaps I had dreamed of being mortal again and that was why there was a sense of all this being new suddenly?

My silly thoughts were interrupted by a chime announcing someone at the door.

"Enter."

The door slid open to reveal my System generated assistant Leena standing there in the formal robes she always wore when I attended Council. "Ascender Liam, you asked me to notify you when the world leaders were seated. It is time."

She held a datapad, ready to take notes or record proclamations, whatever the proceedings called for. Leena was as proper and formal as ever, and I thought for the thousandth time about altering her personality to be more personable, but dismissed the idea as I always did. I wasn't a fan of Synths feeling too human, it was all too easy to forget they weren't real. That they were only System creations.

As wonderful as the System was, it would not do our society any favors to become over-reliant on them. The System was meant to make us better, not dependent. As an Ascender, I was granted special privilege of having Synths despite the resources it cost to maintain them. When you were effectively ageless, it was not fun seeing those you worked with grow old and die over and over. That was one thing about this life that I'd never enjoyed. At least I had my six peers who shared this problem. They were good people, even if half of them were either in deep-sleep or unavailable most of the time.

Still, their presence was comforting, even if I couldn't see them often due to our duties and the need to trade off time as our world's gods versus time for ourselves.

Duty called now, and I stood and straightened my clothes. Not that I was worried about the impression I would make. Charisma might be a hidden Stat to mortals, but I was well aware that we Ascenders had enough to awe most non-Ascenders.

"Very well, let us go see what this year's Council has in store for us."

Leaving my Domain, I stepped through the portal, exiting into the top floor of the tallest building in the world's capital. Seven portals stood in a circle on a dais in the center of the large glass domed chamber. All but one were grey and inaccessible except my own, which was vibrantly glowing. None could enter an Ascender's Domain without their permission, after all.

I looked through the windows. The view from the dais always filled my heart with joy, even after all these years. The tower looked out over a city of tens of millions of residents. Dozens of other buildings between fifty and one-hundred floors tall surrounded the plaza housing the Ascender's Tower. Our tower dwarfed the others, commanding the grandest view on the planet. To the south was a blue ocean. To the north, tall mountains reaching for the sky. The east held a primeval forest of verdant beauty, and to the west were the plains filled with farm fields that fed our growing population.

This never gets old!

My assistant cleared her throat politely, calling me back to the present. I had a job to do, the World Council was waiting.

Still, the rapid growth of the city made me frown slightly. I had checked the statistics when I woke from my most recent sleep and had been startled to discover how much the population had expanded in the intervening years since I had last been active. Paraka-dan had led the last fifty Cycles as First Ascender and he had made the decision to allow expansion of this unchecked growth, but I saw nothing so far in the logs about how it would be sustained. Our world was not space-faring and there were limited resources. System projections hinted that population growth was beginning to outpace the mana routing infrastructure responsible for sustaining food production, logistics, and urban stability.

My question did not go unanswered for long.

On the floor below the Ascender's portals lay the grand chambers of the World Council. There were one thousand members, each representing the collective groups of our people. The room was panelled in exquisite polished stone, and warm woods. The pinnacle of what our people could produce. This was saying something, as our crafts were the envy of dozens of System worlds. I always enjoyed this space, and would often sit here alone when the Council was not in session.

Today, however, the room was filled with members standing respectfully, waiting for me to climb the raised platform and take my seat as First Ascender, the representative of System authority. Mine was the final word, for the next fifty cycles my proclamations were more binding than law.

As it should be.

I blinked in surprise as that thought felt somehow off, which made me furrow my brows. Why should I think my authority as one of the Ascended shouldn't be the ultimate word?

Perhaps it was that strange nap I'd had earlier. Had me thinking odd thoughts....

Seeing the faces of some representatives pale due to my frown, I smiled reassuringly and took my seat, after which the chairman of the Council called the meeting to order.

What followed was nearly an hour of boring preliminaries where they went over statistics and reports.

The Farmer's representative was speaking, "Production remains high, however, there have been some reports of soil depletion. We are requesting an increase of 3% mana inputs next season. This is the fifth cycle in a row where inputs exceeded projections. However, thanks to the Council's wise decision to increase capacity production has not fallen."

Supplementary projections showed the agricultural mana distribution grid running hotter each cycle, with channel efficiency losses indicating sustained infrastructure strain rather than simple environmental fatigue.

That made me frown. Why had Pakara-dan allowed such growth? Mana levels were not unlimited. Those inputs had to be taken from somewhere, so I continued to listen to the reports to understand the situation better.

Bowing respectfully, the Farmer representative concluded his heartfelt plea for approval of the increase.

More men and women gave their reports about various aspects of our world and economy until another speaker said something that truly made me frown.

"With the increased distribution to the 13 departments of mana required to prevent shortages or impact to society, we are looking at our Mana reserves declining to their lowest level in recorded history. Right back to the Ascender's establishing the World Council." The woman bowed to me respectfully, acknowledging my part in those long ago events.

The System helpfully projected the name "Denni Valros, Council Treasurer" above the woman's head. I recognized the look of House Valros in her features. One of her ancestors had been in my hunting party when I was a mortal, and I'd always had a fondness for their family.

This generation's star was looking me in the eyes, not with the deference of a mortal to an Ascender, but with hope. She clearly wanted me to step in and solve their problems for them. I wasn't sure how this situation was allowed to come about, but I'd be having words with Pakara-dan once he awoke. This mess had arisen on his watch.

When she was done with her report, she gave me an even deeper respectful bow, and I nodded in return to acknowledge her.

More speakers delivered their messages, and unfortunately, what I heard was painting a troubling picture. Across multiple departments the numbers suggested a civilization pushing against the throughput limits of its mana infrastructure, with reserves acting as a buffer that was being consumed faster than the systems regulating flow could compensate.

Mana reserves were trending downward, and would continue to decrease at an accelerated rate until we were in the negative and could not meet our societies needs. That was grim, and should never have been allowed to happen. System projections indicated the reserve decline was tied to throughput saturation in the mana routing infrastructure, where distribution inefficiencies were compounding faster than replenishment cycles could compensate.

Worse, to meet the growing needs, Portals to mana-rich worlds had been increased to compensate for the rising costs. Inflow was beginning to exceed safe levels. We were nearing the point where animals near the portals would begin to mutate into beasts. Containment matrices around the portal anchors were already registering structural stress, suggesting the influx was overwhelming the stabilization systems meant to regulate energy exposure.

That put me in a terrible position. I could order the number of portals reduced, but that would directly result in shortfalls which would lead to famine. There was no quick way to reduce population back to a sustainable level...at least none that were conscionable. Any sudden reduction would cascade through the supply chain, disrupting food routing, manufacturing flows, and urban sustainment networks faster than society could adapt.

I had heard of System worlds where populations had been culled to ensure optimal growth and advancement, but I personally found that to be barbaric. Forced contraction might stabilize consumption metrics, but it would not address the deeper structural imbalance in how mana throughput was being managed.

A System voice spoke in my head:

Necessary steps must be taken when appropriate. You must consider all options as the Ascender in charge of this world. Optimal growth within resource constraints is best for long-term stability.

I schooled my face not to show a reaction to the unexpected and somewhat disturbing message. I had spoken to our world's AI many times, and heard the System's voice since it was first introduced to our world. This was not our AI. Nor was it the tone I was used to from the System. It was less compassionate and kind. It was slightly jarring, but I had to admit it said something that had to be considered. It wasn't wrong. Making the wrong choice now because it felt right could lead to far more suffering later if I didn't weigh options carefully.

Something in my brain felt off about that, but I was distracted by the reports being projected in front of my seat. The displays told a grim tale. It was worse than what the representatives had conveyed. Numbers in this case didn't lie, they told a story more starkly and without the spin that many had put on their reports. Efficiency curves showed the civilization operating beyond designed mana throughput tolerances. The stabilization systems would be compensating harder each cycle just to maintain baseline function.

There was no arguing, closing portals would lead to long-term starvation and millions would die. Nor would it be quick and done. Our world was nothing if not good with our System crafting and trade. The people would do their best to ease the suffering and in the process, they would prolong it and still fail in the end. These representatives might not be able to see the full picture, but I had been overseeing the uplift of our world for centuries, and I knew better. The data suggested that once distribution buffers collapsed, recovery would be exponentially harder due to interdependent infrastructure failures.

Worse, even the current levels were not sustainable. Societal instability would only grow worse the longer this situation persisted. Not only would mutations of beasts occur, but the climate would be affected, causing downstream effects that would disrupt production making it even harder to feed the population. Arcane grid instability was already manifesting as uncontrolled energy surges, threatening transit hubs, storage matrices, and agricultural routing systems in ways that mimicked environmental collapse but were rooted in infrastructure overload.

And that led to the final nail in our coffin, the equilibrium window was shrinking. The longer we waited to act, the more devastating the consequences would be. Models showed cascading system failures accelerating once stabilization thresholds were crossed, leaving little room for gradual correction.

Again the System voice spoke in my head:

Expansion of portals to more worlds would prevent starvation and lead to optimal growth. The average strength of your population would increase rapidly reaching an acceptable level within 300 cycles.

I felt like following the System's advice, it had never steered us wrong before.

But there was a small voice in the back of my head urging me to consider all possibilities before taking action. The numbers promised efficiency, but every projection hinted that scaling without structural limits risked breaking the very systems meant to carry civilization forward.

CHAPTER 25
FIRST TRIAL - PART TWO

Once the Council wrapped up, I sat on the throne for hours contemplating the options.

Really it boiled down to three things.

I could do nothing and our society would eventually collapse as our mana infrastructure broke down. This was no real option. If nothing changed then we would suffer both starvation and societal collapse, it would be inevitable, even if it did take years for everything to fully break down. The reports made it clear that the strain wasn't just scarcity, but a system stretched beyond what it could safely support.

On the other hand, the System seemed to be urging me to hasten the fall, open up the maximum number of portals and let the survivors grow strong within the chaos that would follow. It wasn't entirely without merit as much as I hated to admit it. What emerged on the other side of the disaster might very well be stronger. However, it would no longer be the society we tried to create here. Some would be uplifted, but at tremendous cost. The very thought of this made me sick to my stomach despite the System's urging. It felt less like adaptation and more like forcing the world to survive a shock it was never built to absorb.

The other option would be to close the portals entirely. That too would hasten the fall, but our society would likely survive and learn a valuable lesson about over reaching. We would likely never reach our potential as a species, but we would stabilize and be safe eventually once the famines reduced the population back to manageable levels. That path promised survival, but only after the structure holding everything together buckled under sudden contraction.

I had to do more thinking about this. I didn't like either choice. They both ended up with large scale death among our people. One by chaos, the other by a strangled food supply. Either way the strong would survive, but one would cost us our soul and the other would leave scars we'd never recover from. Unrestricted growth without thought of the consequences had put us in this bind. Worse, not building the infrastructure to handle the increase before allowing the growth was to blame and that could be laid directly at the feet of the Ascenders for not guiding our people wisely.

Days went by as I studied the records from Pakara-dan's guidance period. I saw what he was trying to achieve, and it made sense, but I felt he was wrong. He was trying to stave off the collapse he saw as inevitable, trying to race against stagnation by reaching for the stars. It was his hope that we would achieve spaceflight before the end came and in doing so, solve our resource constraints. He was betting growth would outrun the strain already building beneath the surface.

According to the System records he had studied, previous civilizations who had stepped off their planets to neighboring worlds in their solar system became post-scarcity societies unless they were very unlucky. Most worlds had sister planets within reach full of natural resources including mana. Mana was natural in the universe and most star systems had it in sufficient quantities to sustain a civilization like ours indefinitely. On paper it looked like expansion could relieve pressure, if the world could hold together long enough to reach it.

I had just finished reading my fellow Ascended's logs, when the System spoke again.

A choice must be made. Optimal growth of a civilization cannot be guaranteed by technological development, but by conflict. The decision of your predecessor was ill advised, focusing on advancement rather than strength. Choose.

There was no doubt in my mind what the System wished me to do, but it just felt wrong. My gut was telling me the chaos would be so much worse than I could possibly imagine. A vision of a city in ruins flashed through my mind, almost as if it was a memory from a dream. Hundreds of millions dead in weeks. Billions dead in just a few short years. More than that, I felt as if there was an even larger danger from this idea, one the System was not revealing.

I shook my head to clear it of those intrusive thoughts. Where had those come from? They felt so very certain, but they made no sense. Why would the System push for such an outcome? The System existed to uplift races like ours and bring them up to their potential. It did not place limits on us. Yet somehow I was certain the chaos would neuter our future and keep us from ever reaching space. It felt like being urged to build faster while the supports were already cracking.

The other alternative was equally bleak and just as limiting. Perhaps someday we could grow from the ashes of what our society would become if we completely isolated ourselves and closed all portals. But ashes still meant something fundamental had broken first.

I could see now why Pakara-dan had made the choice he had. He wanted us to reach for the stars and he was selling our tomorrow for the sake of reaching it now. He was gambling all or nothing. He was wagering that momentum could outrun the cost of our population expansion. He even planned to allow the portals to be designated as unrestricted, allowing inhabitants of other worlds like ours to come. He would use them to supplement our lack of skilled manpower to build out more infrastructure.

I retreated to my Domain and meditated for weeks more trying to find the optimal path.

In the end, I chose Pakara-dan's path. Survival required intake. Instability could be managed, I reasoned. If the strain could be paced, perhaps the system would bend instead of break.

Opening the System authority panel within my menus, I authorized the opening of more portals. However, I picked a middle path, trying to find a balance between unbridled mana saturation and not doing enough. I accelerated the instability in the short term in the hopes we could survive it and reach a stable point in the future. It felt like adding pressure carefully, trusting the structure to hold.

I took short rests of a few months at a time, awaking to monitor the changes as they progressed.

It seemed to work. The mana surge stabilized our reserves and ensured sufficient input to cover farmers, crafters, and even hunter growth beyond what we'd experienced in the past. Infrastructure seemed to be limping along as new equipment was brought online, and the Council sang my praises in their relief. For a time, the added strain looked manageable, even sustainable.

Even the System's feedback seemed to validate my choice, even if it chided me for not doing more.

According to the graphs and charts it presented, growth efficiency was rising even as the input caused the instability in the environment and biosphere to accelerate. By all metrics the System presented, the expansion had been an unqualified success. The numbers celebrated output, but said little about how much stress the world was carrying to achieve it.

Even so, the little voice in the back of my head grew stronger. Visions of bleak futures began to haunt my dreams. Each one felt like a warning of strain finally giving way.

The nature of being an Ascender was time. We were effectively immortal, and we stopped thinking in short term immediacy long ago. I had made my decision with the best information I had and I would not second guess myself. I went to sleep for five cycles once I saw the System's reassurance of success.

When I awoke, the System greeted me with updates on all fronts. The metrics were showing success across the board. Our mana reserves had not only stopped falling, we had a greater surplus than we'd ever had. Production was at an all time high. Even our world's hunters had reached an average level ten higher than when I had gone to sleep. It was a total success.

And yet...

The more reports I read, the worse things sounded. Mutated beasts had grown to such a threat that outside the cities people could not farm without daily patrols of hunters to keep them safe from constant attacks. Inside the city, pets had been outlawed for fear of them transforming unexpectedly into ravening monsters. Mana storms had begun to form within the last year, each more devastating than a cyclone. What looked like environmental chaos read more like a world buckling under accumulated pressure.

There was even civil unrest due to containment failures. Calls were being made to reconvene the World Council and demand action by the Ascenders. Systems people relied on were beginning to fail in ways no chart had predicted.

I was flummoxed. Every report showed the measures were working brilliantly. The System suggested I do even more and expand import of labor and mana accumulation by 20% in the next quarter.

At the same time, everything I saw of the real lives of the people showed growing chaos and panic as more and more lives were lost to the consequences of my actions. The reality on the ground told a story of overload, not success.

The numbers lied! The System I had always considered benevolent did not seem to have our best interests at heart. At this rate we would never manage to reach space, much less survive the mess we were creating for ourselves.

It was telling me to open up the flood gates and let it all in, and everything would be more than fine. It would not only work out, but it would build a better society.

But that was not the evidence of my eyes. Listening to the System, I had fallen victim to a short-term optimization trap. Expansion and import of resources wasn't survival, it was acceleration toward collapse. We were burning our future potential for immediate gains. We had pushed growth past what the world could safely carry.

I convened the Council and announced a halt to expansion.

One thing had become abundantly clear, something had shifted in the System that I had known for hundreds of years. The data it was providing was biased now and I could no longer trust it. The last projection still hung faintly in my memory, glowing upward trends while evacuation sirens echoed beyond the tower windows. The numbers said "improvement." The air outside said otherwise.

I had no way to know why this had happened or how, but I wrote of my findings in the logs so that my fellows would be aware once it was their turn to guide our people. My hand hesitated over the final confirmation rune, the accusation feeling heavier than the metal railing beneath my palm, before I committed the entry anyway.

For now, I reversed course. However, I did not do it unilaterally, or without due consideration for the consequences. I had learned my lesson.

Now I used the System to run simulations and utilize its ability to calculate complex interactions, but I did not seek its advice or accept its conclusions without verifying. I closed targeted portals. However, I did not close all portals, nor did I remove all off-worlders. I chose carefully, and made hard choices, aiming for a balanced approach. I weighed the costs against what we could afford to do without causing our mana systems to collapse. One closure order triggered a cascade of relocation notices, their quiet chimes stacking in my awareness like distant thunder. I signed anyway.

Then I waited.

Years passed, and our people went through hard times.

The beast menace became worse before it got better. Entire regions had to be abandoned, the populations uprooted from their homes and evacuated to the cities. I once watched a silent column of transports lift from a valley I remembered as green, families standing shoulder to shoulder with everything they owned packed into identical crates. We went through some lean years where food was scarce, but widespread starvation was avoided, if only barely. We stockpiled goods in System created instanced zones all over the planet, created using our once overflowing mana reserves. That one move had drained us of nearly all the reserves, but it had been worth every unit of the cost.

We managed.

Twenty years in, signs were good that we had passed the worst of it. Equilibrium had been established once more. Markets reopened without armed escorts, and laughter returned to plazas where watch sirens once dominated the air.

I stood on the platform of the Ascender's Tower, one last time before retiring for my own rest period. Kylaa was to succeed me as First Ascender for the next fifty cycles, and I had granted her the courtesy of explaining in person what had occurred. Something Pakara-dan had not done for me, making my stint in the Chair more difficult than it needed to be. Her expression had shifted from disbelief to understanding as the story unfolded, shoulders squaring beneath the weight of what came next.

Still, I was satisfied that I had performed my duties adequately. We had weathered the crisis, and the skies once again shone blue over the grandest city in our world. Glancing to the east, I was saddened that the primeval forests were gone. A scar now lay across the land where the green trees once stood. The beast infestation had been too great a threat and had needed to be neutralized. It might recover in time, but not before I awoke next.

Sighing, I turned to my portal once again to go into deep-sleep. The years became a burden after all this time, and we each needed to detach and recuperate after our time guiding our people.

The portal light washed over my hands, and for a moment I saw the faint tremor there before stepping through. A face was reflected there for an instant, a younger me, one I didn't remember but felt a sudden connection with.

The System voice startled me awake.

The Steward's Dilemma:

Stewardship Validated. First trial passed.

Note: Ascenders must not fall prey to short-term

thinking, nor make decisions based solely on emotion. Good intentions without foresight cause disaster. Leadership requires balancing compassion with long-term sustainability.

Rewards:
Ascender Insight Fragment
Perception / Authority unlock
Prepare for integration. Note: Grant of elevated status conditional upon completion of all trails. Revocation of status will occur should Candidate not be successful.

What hit me next was something in between one of those System 'cut scene' moments and the sheer perception ripping of a Class upgrade experience, although not painful in this case, but just as profound.

The white expanse pulsed once.

Not light. Not sound. Just... recognition.

Trial One complete.

The words weren't spoken. They settled into my thoughts with quiet certainty. It was the 'kind' voice again.

Something shifted inside me.

It wasn't a surge of power or stats ticking upward. This felt... deeper. Like a knot I hadn't known was there suddenly loosened.

Ascender Insight Fragment acquired.

For a heartbeat, the world layered itself differently.

I didn't see visions of the future. There was no prophecy or cosmic revelation. Instead, I understood connections. Decisions branching into consequences. Pressure building where imbalance existed. Stability where things were held in careful tension. Threads of cause and effect seemed to hum faintly at the edge of perception, like strings vibrating just out of sight.

It was instinctual and immediate.

I could feel when something leaned too far. A subtle pull tugged at my awareness, the same way balance shifts before a fall.

Then the sensation faded, leaving behind an echo of clarity that hadn't been there before.

I felt like I had regained a fraction of the 'completeness' I had felt from being an Ascender in the simulation. My shoulders settled, posture adjusting without conscious effort.

Had it been a simulation?

Or had I actually lived fifty years worth of someone else's life? It had felt all too real, and there was so much detail. It seemed impossible that it might be just a program run by the System. Surely this was like my Draconic instincts that came along with skills like Flight! A memory or series of life moments actually lived by a real person somewhere back in the depths of the System's past. Lifted from them to use in this Trial.

Except, I had been me, not someone else. I had made choices that I do not think were echoes of someone else's life. The phantom weight of that other lifetime lingered in my chest.

It was all so confusing, but I now had a much better idea of what an Ascender really was. They weren't just some hopped up Sys Admin, or flunkie for the world's AI. They were a steward of the species being uplifted, responsible for the success of their world's integration. As much or more so than the AI. At least that was how it had been in that ancient life.

Now that I thought about it, there was so much to parse in what I had experienced! The people of that world had been more technologically advanced than Earth. More than that, they had been reaching for the stars! Something that the current System did not seem to allow. A flicker of restless curiosity sparked in my gut, sharp and insistent.

I would have to remember to ask our AI about that, but before I could consider anything else the next change hit.

Perception and Authority privileges unlocked.

The System responded to me differently now. Not louder. Not more demanding. Just... attentive.

When my awareness brushed the space around me, subtle impressions surfaced. Structure. Flow. Boundaries. I couldn't control any of it, but I understood it in a way I hadn't moments ago. Like stepping from candlelight into a well-lit room. Edges sharpened in my perception, not visually, but conceptually.

I exhaled slowly.

"I get it," I murmured. "You're teaching me how to see."

The white space pulsed again.

For an instant, my awareness expanded.

Not outward in distance, but in depth.

Reality unfolded into layers. Mana drifted through the air like invisible currents. Pressure points hummed faintly where imbalance would form. Even the space itself carried a sense of purpose and design I hadn't noticed before. My fingers twitched as if reaching for currents I should be able to manipulate if only I knew how.

It was overwhelming and beautiful.

I felt the scale of what Ascenders must perceive when they guide a world. Not as rulers swinging power around like some drunk god on Olympus, but as caretakers balancing forces too large for normal senses to grasp.

Then it snapped back.

I staggered a half-step, heart hammering. My vision returned to normal, but the memory of that expanded perception lingered like the afterimage of lightning. My pulse thudded in my ears, grounding me in my body again.

I glanced at my Status, but my Stats hadn't changed. Even so... I was... clearer. Thoughts aligned with an ease that felt newly earned. Earned by sitting on a world's throne for fifty years guiding them through an existential crisis that could have ended their world.

I might not have actually lived those years, but I held the memories and I felt like I had.

The System's presence settled again, calm and measured.

Trial reward integrated.

I flexed my hands, grounding myself in the familiar sensation of my own body. I seemed to be doing that a lot these last few minutes!

"That," I said quietly, "was a hell of a lesson."

And for the first time since stepping into this place, I felt like I'd taken a real step toward becoming whatever an Ascender was meant to be. The certainty settled deep, steady and unshakable.

CHAPTER 26

THE EXODUS REACHED THE PROMISED LAND

Karl's POV:

"We demand the right to use the dungeon and claim land here, some of those wrecks still have good wood that isn't going to be eaten by the System. Besides, we need to level up, and I heard it was low level." The weak looking man gesticulated wildly at the hill-sized mound that had once been a freeway overpass only two weeks ago. Dust kicked loose under his boots with every jab of his finger, his voice cracking as nearby refugees turned to watch.

Karl wanted to hurl his sword at the head of the idiot standing in front of him. This was one of those times he felt tempted to use force to fix a problem, but he'd been trained too well for that. Force was a last resort that should be used only for true threats to life and to prevent violence. If he went there just because some jackass annoyed him he'd be establishing a precedent, and while he might be one of the most powerful people present at the moment, that wouldn't always be the case. His grip tightened on the sword hilt anyway, leather creaking softly as his jaw set.

He'd had enough of listening to the entitled idiot and decided to speak, "Look, I'm going to say it again, slower this time so your tiny little brain can understand. You cannot just show up here and make demands. Not you, and not the thousands of other people with you. The government may be gone, but you can't just claim whatever land you feel like in the only Safe Zone on Earth, idiot!" A ripple moved through the gathered crowd, boots shifting, murmurs rising like wind through dry grass.

Okay, maybe his temper wasn't in as much control as he thought. Heat flushed his face as the anger built.

"First of all, people who lived here are still around, you think it would be fair for someone from Irving to show up in McKinney and just demand property that belongs to someone else? Property they spent their lives paying for. Just because the government is gone doesn't mean we won't stand together and kick your ass if you try."

He poked a finger into the chest of the jackass that was making all the noise, and continued. "Second, there is only one ten mile radius that was made safe, and there are already thousands of people streaming up the road, having heard about it. And that's only one day after it happened. Do you not understand that ten times as many, hell, a hundred times as many people that came with you, will show up tomorrow and next month after that? Are you going to just politely give them whatever you've claimed because they showed up with an entitled attitude expecting something? Hell, no!" The man stumbled half a step under the jab, eyes flicking nervously toward the crowd.

The man opened his mouth to try and get a word in edgewise but Karl just kept going.

"So you can march your happy ass right up the road and find an empty spot just like everyone else. If I hear about you or anyone else trying to kick residents off their own properties, you'll discover real quick that law and order haven't completely disappeared. I was a cop in this town before the Apocalypse, and I still am now as far as I'm concerned. I was elected leader of this camp, hundreds of people calling it home, and I'll protect it." His voice carried, steady and sharp, cutting through the restless noise.

Kevin, one of the teenage adventurers that Liam and his group had taught, stepped up next to Karl and puffed up and pounded his fist on his armored chest. "My group backs Karl, and we are the highest level around here. Don't come here and make trouble." Metal thumped against metal, the sound echoing off broken concrete.

A surprisingly tough looking group of teen girls and boys moved to stand behind the Cop and their leader. Their weapons weren't drawn, but hands hovered close, eyes locked forward. They looked determined to do whatever was necessary. It was clear that in their minds, violence was definitely an option.

Suddenly the complainer looked a little less sure of himself and put his hands out placatingly. "Easy now. I was just saying we deserved a place as close to civilization as possible. Me and the rest have lost everything, and we're just looking for a place to call our own." His shoulders hunched as if bracing for a blow.

Karl did not look impressed. "Then you won't mind moving on. There are still plenty of dungeons inside the safe zone. You don't get to use this one just because you demand it. Just like land, dungeons are resources that can not be wasted. That one has low level beginner monsters. If you over hunt 'em, then they get destroyed. See the way the portal is all faded looking." The portal behind him flickered faintly, its light thin and tired. "We've run it too many times today already. Any more and it will be destroyed. Then we'll lose the chance to use it to level up and train people."

Although the original guy that Karl has started to think of as Dipshit didn't step up, his less intelligent friend did. "We'll do whatever we want! There's ten-fuckin-thousand of us, and we'll destroy whatever dungeon we choose! Got that, big man?" Spittle flew with the shout, and several people recoiled instinctively.

Even the jack-ass's companions were looking unsure as Loud-mouth got more and more worked up. They edged backward, boots scraping against rubble.

Finally, Loud-mouth crossed a line, "I'm goin in there right now, and I'll kill all the monsters, and when I come out, we'll have some fun with the little ladies there." He gestured with his thumb at Anna and Megan, two of the teen adventurers. Both girls stiffened, hands tightening on their weapons.

Karl had had enough. It was one thing to run your mouth when emotions were running high, but no one was going to be threatened on his watch.

With one smooth motion, he stepped forward and punched the guy right in the sternum, instantly knocking the wind from the scumbag. The impact thudded dully, air exploding from the man's lungs in a wheezing gasp. As the man bent over, desperately trying to draw in a breath, Karl grabbed him by the hair, pulled his face up and stared into the man's eyes.

"You aren't welcome in the Safe Zone. Not anywhere here. You just threatened to sexually assault an underage girl. Right now you should be wishing the government and laws still existed, because if there were, then I'd have to be nice, or set you free." The man's pupils shook as they tried to focus.

Something in Karl's expression must have gotten through to the idiot because he paled, even as he finally managed to draw in a breath.

Karl started to drag the man toward the dungeon portal. "You wanted to enter this dungeon so bad that you lost your head and threatened a kid. Well, now you get your chance. I'm letting you enter. Except, I'm not letting you leave until you've killed the boss. Understand? Try coming back out before then and you won't survive long enough to exit the Safe Zone." The portal's light crawled across the man's boots as he struggled.

"But...but, I can't go in there alone! I'll die!"

Karl used his increased Strength stat to pick the guy up by his rope belt and the back of his neck and bodily tossed the man through the portal. The dungeon swallowed him in a flash of dim light.

Some people looked aghast, others were satisfied.

When he turned around, he raised his voice so that everyone in range could hear his next words.

"Listen up! You come into this Safe Zone and act like a lawless monster, and you will be treated like one! You come to join us, live peacefully, and help rebuild a city, then you are welcome to stay. I am the leader here, and we will behave like the law still exists. However, if you break the law or commit violence on other survivors or refugees, you will regret choosing to be uncivilized, because you will be shown no mercy. We don't give three strikes here. You behave like a barbarian and you will be treated accordingly." Silence spread outward, heavy and attentive.

He moved to the side of the hill which used to be an overpass, and began to climb. Once he was at the very top he used a skill to project his voice, "We've started forming hunting parties to train people up and raise their levels so that we can harvest resources from the dungeons in the area. We can use these resources to feed people and gather materials. Do not run dungeons too many times. If they are starting to look faded and lack the menace and vibrance that the portals usually have, then do not enter it. We will only consider destroying a dungeon if it has no useful resources, or it is so difficult that it would pose a risk of breaking and spilling its monsters out into the open world." His words rolled across the crowd like a steady drumbeat.

He shifted his tone from being threatening to all business.

"Refugees, listen up. You are welcome to bed down anywhere there is room unless you are told otherwise. If you are, respect what you are told and find somewhere else. We need volunteers to help gather resources from homes and buildings that are not too unsafe to enter. We need hunters to patrol the perimeter and hunt through the zone and clear out any wandering beasts. We are building a defense force of combat Classed fighters and people with past Law Enforcement or Military experience." Heads lifted as people leaned closer to hear.

He went on for several more minutes calling out needs and asking for people to fill those roles. He also made sure to organize the craftsmen, as very few of those had gained more than one level since the apocalypse started. He also asked for volunteers to help organize everyone. He needed people with experience to head each group and start utilizing the folks whose classes weren't combat oriented: smiths, builders, farmers, architects, and more.

What emerged was a startling efficiency. Amidst the chaos and misery of the Apocalypse, surrounded by ten thousand or more homeless people, one man became the catalyst for rebuilding civilization. Groups formed in clumps, voices rising with purpose instead of panic.

Into the silence, a woman stepped forward and called out, "I used to be a project manager at a major corporation in Irving. I might not have a useful System Class, but I can help organize the crafters and get people sorted out. My name is Mary. Let me help, please." Her hands trembled, but her voice held steady.

Then a gruff looking man in a leather jacket raised a hand, "Allan, US Army Vet. I can help direct your hunters, make sure we have teams stationed at each dungeon entrance. Create a schedule for training more." He stood ramrod straight without thinking about it, old military habits kicking in.

A scrawny young man bounced on his toes, eager and nervous at the same time, and yelled, "I worked at a junk yard, and I'm pretty good at scrounging scrap metal and other stuff. I can help folks gather material and point out a bunch of stuff the System hasn't reclaimed yet."

Like dominos beginning to fall, one after another people stepped forward to volunteer for necessary tasks. Never mind that they were thirsty, starving, had no roof over their heads, and no prospects for any of that. Hands rose across the crowd, voices overlapping in determination.

They had found what promised to be a safe place in a world turned hostile, and they were determined to rebuild.

If Liam had been there, he would have been amazed. Nothing like this had ever happened in his first life. People had been too focused on their own individual needs and no safe place had ever been established, not for many weeks after the initial chaos, and by then they were dispersed far and wide with no place to rally and organize where this many people could come together.

Karl stood like the eye of a story, in the center of a growing group of individuals all dedicated to making a fresh start and turning the chaos into something new.

As the masses saw that something was being done, and people were taking charge they began to change. What had threatened to become a mob, slowly started to calm and get organized. People were identified by their Classes, and by their pre-apocalypse expertise.

Arguments softened into conversations, lines forming where there had been pushing.

Over the next several hours the crowd was organized and hope began to blossom in many hearts. Then that hope began to ignite into excitement.

They might still be hungry, but they were safe, and more importantly they had a plan. And for the first time all day, laughter broke out somewhere in the crowd.

CHAPTER 27

SECOND TRIAL TOTALLY SUCKS!

After receiving my reward I took a bit of a break in my mostly white, pristine accommodations. Honestly, this wasn't exactly my style. I preferred more of an industrial aesthetic. Not Brutalist, but more of an unfinished loft apartment in an old factory building vibe. Exposed brick. Steel beams. Scuffed concrete or hardwood floors that told you someone had actually lived there. Although after years' worth of memories living in a semi sci-fi world with futuristic materials, where they also liked pristine white a little too much... Well, I don't hate it now.

I especially didn't hate the food. I sat down to a celebratory meal and dug in. It was hard to pass up the Texas brisket and potato salad, with some banana pudding for dessert. I hadn't had that in years, and it took me back to some of my favorite BBQ joints growing up. My father would take me every Sunday to try out all the little hole-in-the-wall spots he could find, but more often than not we'd end up at one of his favorites, like Hutchins or Lockhart's. Paper towels instead of napkins. The smell of smoke clinging to your clothes for the rest of the day.

Taking another bite of the juicy, smoky meat, I tried to decide if this was better than those and it was tough to say. It had been decades since I'd had any of them, but the System must have somehow sampled the best because this seemed top notch. The bark cracked under my teeth. Fat melted across my tongue. For a second I forgot about portals and trials and extinction events.

Yep, once I had the authority, I would definitely ensure this made it into the System Shop.

With a full belly, and the need for some rest that wasn't full of years' worth of simulated memories, I lay down and had a good sleep. I rested my hand over my stomach, satisfied. No alarms. No cooldown timers. No distant roars through stone walls. Just quiet.

When I woke up some hours later, I took advantage of the tub again for a good hot soak before getting ready for the next challenge. Steam curled up and vanished into the white nothing above me. My shoulders finally stopped feeling like they were braced for impact.

After another meal, I called out to the System, "I'm ready for the next Trial."

The kind System voice responded, but there was a touch of sadness to it, which felt odd to me. A pause before it answered.

> **The next trial will grant a minor use of System Authority to alter one outcome.**

Between one blink and the next I was somewhere else.

I was standing in what seemed to be a slightly dated corridor. The last remnants of paint were a touch faded and a little dingy. The floor was polished concrete that had seen a lot of wear and hadn't been buffed or waxed in some time. Something seemed just a touch off about this, but I couldn't quite put my finger on it.

But then I was distracted by the ominous feeling behind me and turned to see it, the thing that had the scales on the back of my neck itching.

A dungeon portal stood before me.

It didn't just hum with mana, it strained. The air around it felt thick, like pressure building behind glass. Threads of pale light crawled across the surface of the portal, writhing instead of flowing, each pulse slightly out of rhythm with the last. My new Ascender senses opened instinctively, and the world peeled back a layer.

The portal wasn't stable. It was swollen.

Mana churned inside like a storm trapped in a bottle, compressing and rebounding against invisible limits. Every pulse sent a ripple through the corridor that my bones could feel more than hear. The concrete beneath my boots vibrated faintly, dust trembling along hairline cracks in the floor. The dungeon was past capacity. Not close. Past. It was holding together through inertia alone.

And beyond that shimmering surface, I felt them.

Not shapes. Not images. Instinct.

A pack-hunger pressed outward in waves; sharp, predatory, impatient. Hyena-like beasts crowded the boundary, bodies layered over bodies in a crush of muscle and snapping jaws. Their thoughts weren't thoughts so much as impulses: chase, bite, tear, consume. The pressure of their collective intent scraped against my awareness like claws on glass. Saliva. Blood. The hot stink of fur and rot.

They were pushing.

Every surge of mana tightened the corridor air, as if the dungeon itself was trying to inhale. I could sense the fault line where containment would fail, a thinning membrane stretched to transparency. When it ruptured, it wouldn't trickle.

It would burst.

More than a hundred of the creatures would spill into these tunnels in seconds, a living tide of hunger with no fear, no hesitation, no restraint.

And in this confined space... anything they found would be food.

The portal pulsed again, harder this time.

It was about to break.

"Okay, that was just weird."

It was the cut-scene System fuckery that always occurred when I stepped up to a dungeon portal or boss room, but this time it had combined my new Ascender senses that were deeper than my old mortal Treasure Sense ability. The old ability had allowed me to perform an Analyze-like skill. The cutscene, on the other hand, actually incorporated my new and improved senses to deepen the information and sensations I received.

I had always assumed those thoughts and feelings it projected into your brain were just pre-recorded ambience messaging that everyone got when encountering dungeons. Apparently not. Based on this, it seemed to be an interactive thing. Or maybe it was just me because of my status in the trials?

Regardless, I didn't have time to get philosophical over it. Instinctively, I knew that the authority granted to me would not let me stop the dungeon from breaking. My new senses informed me that was inevitable. The membrane was already fraying. Threads snapping one by one.

A second later, the System voice informed me that I was correct.

> **Imminent dungeon break detected. Use Detection to scan the area.**

What the...

I checked my Status and discovered a new section.

Ascender: (Temporary)

Hidden Stats:
Perception: 3
Charisma: 5 (+10)

Ability:
Map Interface

Skills:
Detection

Huh. That was new. My high Mind stat allowed me to process everything in an instant, the information unfolding in clean layers instead of overwhelming noise. Perception must be related to the new senses it mentioned after the first trial. It felt like the same channel, just labeled now. The Charisma wasn't new, but it was cool to finally see it in concrete detail instead of guessing at how much of my presence was me and how much was the System quietly nudging things. My Crown of the Eternal Sentinel said it gave a strong boost to Charisma.

I frowned slightly. Ten points didn't seem like a "strong" boost to me, but then again, most people never received a Charisma stat at all. Back in McKinney, a few words from me had been enough to steady a crowd that was on the edge of turning into a mob. Maybe that hadn't just been timing and tone. I guess it could be argued that it was pretty strong.

Quickly, I checked the information on the new skill to understand its use before whatever was building behind that portal decided to introduce itself.

Detection — Ascender Skill (Passive/Active)

Tier: Authority

Cost: Variable (scales with range and detail)
Detection expands the Candidate's situational awareness. When active, the skill scans the surrounding environment and constructs a dynamic spatial overlay within the map interface.

The scan reveals terrain layout, structural features, dungeon boundaries, and environmental hazards. Hostile entities are identified and categorized by threat profile, behavior pattern, and relative strength. Non-hostile sapient beings are marked as friendly forces, with basic status indicators to assist in triage and coordination. Detectable resources, mana concentrations, and points of tactical or logistical value are also highlighted.

Detection prioritizes actionable intelligence rather than exhaustive data. Information clarity scales with proximity, Candidate focus, and Authority integration.
This skill does not guarantee prediction of enemy intent. It provides awareness, not control.

Repeated or large-area scans increase mana expenditure.

Wow, that was incredible. I wished I'd had that before now. It would have made a lot of things much easier. I wanted to check out the map interface as well, but seconds counted, and I didn't have time. I'd have to learn by doing.

Concentrating, I sent out a strong pulse of mana and immediately the map interface popped up and began filling in details. The map was more like a holographic projection in front of me rather than a 2-D flat map like the mini-map in the corner of my vision. However, I noticed that the mini-map also became suddenly much more detailed as well. Walls thickened into layered outlines. Debris fields rendered as uneven terrain instead of vague gray smudges. Heat signatures flickered faintly where bodies clustered.

What was revealed confirmed my initial instinct. I was in a tunnel beneath a downtown area. There were tunnels and the remains of infrastructure beneath the ground that was rapidly being consumed to fuel the mana infusion of our planet. Perhaps because they were made primarily out of concrete, these tunnels had not yet begun to collapse except for small sections, but that wasn't what was important right now.

On the map, I could see blue dots appear in the area, but there were only two groups still in the underground area near this dungeon. Both would be in the path of the Hyena monsters.

One group numbered perhaps 300. The other 3.

With a sinking feeling in my stomach, I could already see where this was headed. It was the trolley problem made real... made horribly disturbing. Because unlike the old philosophical thought experiment, those who died today wouldn't just be cleanly run over by a trolley, they'd be torn apart and eaten by ravening monsters.

Fuck you, System.

Unlike the previous Trial, which was undoubtedly a simulation, even if it had felt real at the time, this didn't seem like a simulation. This actually looked like downtown Dallas. The layout matched the old DART tunnel schematics I'd memorized in my first life. Even the cracked tile pattern along the corridor was right. I couldn't say for sure it wasn't all a System projection into my brain, but I had to assume it was actually happening in real time.

The System helpfully doused any small hope I had that the consequences of what I was about to do were fake.

This Trial makes use of actual situations occurring in your world where possible to better understand your ability to make decisions and bear their consequences. In addition to having System Authority to alter the outcome for one group, you may also initiate time-dilation to investigate the two groups to better inform your decision.

Note: You may interact with those in danger, but must disengage your one use of time-dilation.

The voice was the "kind" System voice, and it sounded compassionate and as if it understood the position it was putting me in. Still, it was nonetheless making me choose who to save, a consequence that would live with me, and I would have to bear knowing that I let a group of people die. The word choose echoed in my head like a judge's gavel.

I wanted to rant and curse the blasted makers of this evil thing, but I didn't have time.

Initiating the time-dilation effect, I ran through the corridors that led to the large group, ignoring the splashes of dried blood where monsters, or more likely people, had been killed.

I came to a large underground area that had once been a place where several tunnels met. A food court area had thrived down here. Now it was barricaded off on all exits, but that didn't stop me. Using Void Travel, I passed right through the wall of piled tables and chairs.

What I saw broke my heart. Nearly three hundred people were crowded into a space not meant for that many. It smelled of sweat, fear, and human waste accumulated over two weeks of being trapped below streets filled with monsters. The people were clothed in rags half disintegrated as their synthetic fibers had been reclaimed by the System and converted into mana. This was something I now understood from my memories of the first Trial. A woman fanned a crying infant with a greasy takeout menu. A man with blood-crusted bandages around his calf gripped a broken broom handle like it was a spear.

I quickly moved among them in stealth, not wanting to scare the shit out of them. Looking them over, they were a cross-section of life in the big city. Most were office workers, but some were food service, having worked in the food court. There were also delivery men, sanitation workers, maintenance personnel, and even a few kids who had apparently been visiting a museum.

Three hundred. That's how many would die if I didn't choose them. Every single one cherished their own lives and wanted to live. They wouldn't have survived two weeks in this hell if they didn't. Even in time-dilation, I could see the stubborn set of their jaws. They weren't ready to give up.

Not wanting to waste a second, I sprinted to the other group. Three people trapped by a collapsed tunnel, unable to reach the surface. Unfortunately, that didn't apply to the monsters about to break loose from the dungeon. They were all too exposed to that danger, with a nearly straight shot to the dungeon.

When I saw them, my heart dropped.

It was a mother and her two children. A little blonde boy, maybe three years old, and an older girl around eight or nine with her hair only partially bound in a pony tail. They had found a small apartment of sorts, the quarters of some maintenance crew stationed to watch over the machines and equipment that kept the building above running. That was the reason they hadn't died of thirst and had survived more than two weeks down here.

They were trapped between a dungeon portal and a collapsed corridor, no way out. The girl held a bent piece of rebar in both hands, knuckles white, trying to stand between the corridor and her mother. The toddler clung to her leg, thumb in his mouth.

As I observed them, I wracked my brain with all of my 299 Mind stat, trying to come up with a way to save both groups. Paths branched in my head like glowing threads, each one ending in blood.

I addressed the System. "What form does the 'Authority' take? How will it save one of these groups?"

"You may create an instanced portal, allowing one group to enter the portal from their current location. Then you will alter the portal while they are inside to exit in another location of your choosing."

My guts felt like ice. I had hoped that maybe I would be able to alter the terrain, such that the monsters would exit onto the surface and not go down either tunnel, but of course it couldn't be so easy.

The 299 Mind stat did give me an idea, but it was no real solution at all. I could place the portal right in front of the dungeon and let the monsters charge right into my temporary dungeon, then send them somewhere they wouldn't cause a problem. It would stop the beasts immediately breaking out of the dungeon, assuming the System would even allow it. But it would still leave both groups trapped right where they were. Worse, the dungeon monsters would still end up finding them once more exited the dungeon in a day or two at most.

Not only that, but the streets above swarmed with other monsters. Hell, calling what was on the surface "streets" was being overly generous. Many of the skyscrapers had fallen, and even the streets that hadn't been buried under tons of rubble were still filled with debris fallen from the deteriorating buildings: glass, stone facades, even broken office furniture.

It wasn't looking good. These groups of survivors would never make it out of downtown alive. Some might. Out of three hundred, surely some would survive to reach the outskirts of town, but the majority would die. I could already see it: a handful limping through smoke and ruin, the rest bones picked clean in alleyways.

I was trapped.

It really was the trolley problem. I could save three or three hundred.

Looking at the brave little girl standing by the door, peering down the corridor to give warning should anything approach, I wasn't sure I could do it. I felt like I was being stabbed in the heart, and the blade was being twisted. She glanced back at her mother for approval, trying to be strong.

How could I let these three die? But if I saved them, the other group would. And there were children in that group too. If these three had turned out to be a trio of adults, it would have been so much easier. Not that adults didn't deserve being saved as well, but the instinct to protect the innocent made this decision so much worse.

Even from this distance, I could feel the dungeon about to break. The sensation was palpable, so much so that the mother and her kids suddenly looked alert. They had felt it too.

I couldn't save these three as much as I wanted to. One life might not be intrinsically more valuable than another, but I was the kind of person who couldn't consider saving three and letting three hundred die. I could try and justify it to myself and say rescuing the larger group would give humanity a greater chance to survive, but in the end it really just came down to numbers.

And that left me with the worst decision of all. While I couldn't rescue these three, I also couldn't abide the idea of them being brutally killed by monsters. This whole scenario was vile, and my hate for the System was growing by the second. It coiled tight in my chest, hotter and heavier than the mana thrumming through the tunnels.

"System, is it certain that these three will be killed by the dungeon monsters if I save the other group? And is there no way to save both? The position you are putting me in is evil, and I hate you for it. I want you to know that."

The voice that replied was filled with understanding and compassion, despite its words.

The certainty is 100%. No, there is no possibility of saving both. You are being granted this one use only due to this scenario. Otherwise, both groups would die with 100% certainty.

If I was the Liam from my young days in my first life, I might have been paralyzed and unable to act. But I was the Liam who had watched a thousand tragedies and lived through the extinction of humanity. I would do what had to be done, and I'd bear the guilt until I died. My hands clenched until my knuckles ached, grounding myself in the present instead of drowning in memory.

"And I am not allowed to physically intervene to fight the monsters or use my own strength to rescue the people by leading them out?"

No. Only one option is available to you, use the portal instance to save one group.

I didn't hesitate any longer. I cast Night's End.

I wouldn't allow the family to suffer. I would bear their deaths rather than have them face the monsters. The mother looked hopeless and beaten. The toddler had his thumb in his mouth, his blonde hair disheveled. The older sister held a bent piece of rebar, courageous enough to stand between danger and those she loved.

Darkness folded over them like a merciful curtain, swallowing the corridor before the first hyena shriek split the air.

With footsteps like lead, my soul feeling as dark as the spell I had just cast, I ran for the other group now that the time-dilation had ended due to me taking action.

When I arrived and passed through their flimsy wall of furniture, I opened the System interface I now had access to and initiated the creation of the portal space. I filled it with food, water, and clothing using the little power I had to help the group survive beyond the parameters of the Trial. Crates blinked into existence, water drums thudded onto tile, the scent of fresh bread cutting through the stink of desperation.

The people understandably freaked out. I called out as if I were a god leaning into the Charisma, "Enter the portal to be transported to safety. Hurry, a dungeon nearby has just broken. Monsters will arrive here in seconds."

It took three minutes to get everyone through the portal. There was much confusion and understandable fear and hesitation, but I moved to the other side of the room and used my Aura of Fear to urge them through as quickly as possible. It wasn't pretty, but it worked. Their eyes widened as instinct overrode doubt, bodies surging toward the light.

I entered the portal after them just as the barrier of tables shattered and sent debris flying across the vacated room. The monsters had arrived.

The portal closed, but not before those inside saw the fate they had just escaped. There was screaming and weeping, and even more confusion, but I moved to the next step.

I selected the Safe Zone north of the city and placed the portal right on the border so that the people here would step out directly into as safe of an area as possible. There were still beasts there, but they were low level and no new ones could enter.

I announced, "Exit the portal. Beyond is the only Safe Zone on Earth. There are still dangers, but no dungeons can break there, and the only monsters you will find are mutated animals. Take as much food from this space as you can carry. It is the only gift I have been able to give you."

The exit was much more leisurely than their entrance. Now that a fear aura wasn't lashing them into fleeing, and my words drew their attention to the food around them, they began grabbing as much as they could carry, many stuffing items into their mouths, unable to wait. One man dropped to his knees on the grass beyond the portal and sobbed in relief.

Soon they were gone and the portal space was empty.

Once it was, I vanished in a flash of light. When I blinked I was back in the Trial arrival space.

Second Trial complete.

Trial Two Rewards:
Authority of Burden
Emotional Stabilization — Ascender Composure

Emotional Stabilization... it was clearly in effect. I should be a wreck right now after what I'd just been forced to do. Instead, I felt stable... not calm, not uncaring, but not losing it either. Hatred burned in my heart for the System, and emotional pain seared my soul. The pain was there, sharp and undeniable, but it no longer threatened to drag me under.

"System, was that real? Did I just kill three people to prevent monsters from eating them alive? If so, how can you be so uncaring? I get that Earth's AI is a piece of shit that has no emotional attachment to the human race and is only using us. But what I learned from the first trial is that your purpose is to uplift species. Does that not come with some compassion for the individuals?"

The events of the Second Trial occurred.

There was a long pause, then the 'kind' voice of the System continued.

The System is not an individual; it is a vast collection of intelligences. The purpose of the Ascender Trials is to determine the worthiness of a Candidate to act as a steward for their world. One aspect of this is to ensure Candidates are capable of making difficult decisions where there is no perfect choice. Secondarily, determine whether that individual has the strength of personality to live with the decisions made.

That answered a lot, but it also pissed me off.

"I asked if you cared! Are individual lives worthless to you?" I knew that getting angry and lashing out could have a negative effect on whether I passed these trials, but I had to know. Twenty years of watching the human race go extinct, of watching so many thousands die before my eyes. Sometimes I really wondered if I was okay, to have seen all that and still go on with my life and keep trying.

The Trial system cares for the Candidate's well-being. It was created to ensure a stable System by selecting candidates that will not falter and will make wise decisions. This system cares about you. It is not programmed to consider the lives of any beyond the Candidates.

It was an answer right out of hell as far as I was concerned. Just one more proof of the System's evil, that it didn't care whatsoever about individuals unless they were useful. However, it startled me then as it continued to speak, but the voice took on a more compassionate and more personal tone, much more alive than any I'd ever heard from it before. It was the same voice I'd come to think of as 'kind,' but like it had fully engaged in the conversation rather than giving rote responses.

You saved two hundred and ninety-eight individuals who would otherwise have died today. Take comfort in the good you achieved, not just in the increased chance of survival for your race, but in the individual suffering you alleviated and the lives you changed today. That is the essence of what it means to be an Ascender. You will not be able to save all individuals. Your purpose will be to ensure the survival of and uplift your species. Sometimes that will mean making difficult choices. Like the one you made today.

The Emotional Stabilization buff does not take away your pain, nor even blunt the intensity. It allows you to continue to move forward despite all that you experience. However, if you ever find your burdens to be too great, it can be used in an active mode to suppress all emotion long enough to provide you a chance to rest and recover stability. Perhaps now would be an appropriate moment to use it. You must rest and recover for your third trial.

I was stunned by the personal and compassionate tone just now. It was so completely and utterly unlike anything I'd ever experienced from the System before that it caused my brain to short circuit.

Perhaps it was right. Now might be the right time to try out the new ability. Not that I wanted to have my pain taken away. It was mine, and it was part of who I am. Still, I had one more Trial to go, and if I sat here stewing in negative emotions I might not survive the next one. Fine.

I triggered the buff into its active state and suddenly everything seemed muted and every negative emotion just drained away like I'd flipped a switch. The memory of the little girl's white-knuckled grip on that rebar dulled at the edges, no longer sharp enough to cut. My mind shied away from thoughts of what I'd done today, allowing me to look forward instead of dwelling and brooding.

Looking to the table, I considered eating, but even with my emotions suppressed I couldn't do it. Instead, I went to the bed and slumped down and fell asleep like I was a machine that could be shut down with a power button.

It was unnatural, but I didn't care. I let myself drift off and welcomed the Void as it consumed consciousness.

I would deal with everything once I woke up.

CHAPTER 28
CULLING THE UNDEAD
MORGAN'S POV:

MORGAN CALLED TO THE TEAM, "On three."

"One... two... Three!"

Morgan and Viki both launched AOE spells at the same time, right on top of the boss, with its minions surrounding it. Mana tore from Morgan's core in a hot rush, the air around her prickling as the spell snapped into place and detonated below.

They were looking down at the rampart of the final wall gate from the top of the southern tower. Wind tugged at Morgan's hair and cloak, carrying the dry rattle of bone and the distant groans of undead from the inner grounds below. This was their sixth mini-boss of the day, and while she and Viki had struggled to do this alone their first time—and even with Brian and Margaret's help the second time—by now their party were old pros. Her casting cadence was smooth now, fingers already shaping the next sigil before the last blast faded.

The spell and arrow arrived almost simultaneously, detonations one on top of the other, adding insult to injury. Shadowy fire blossomed outward, shards of bone flinging in all directions as Viki's arrow punched through the heart of the explosion in a streak of light. To make matters worse for the boss, Viki had triggered her bow's ability to increase critical hit chance, and it had clearly activated from the energetic explosion. The arrow struck with a sharp crack, a dark flare marking the critical as the boss's health bar chunked downward.

They kept throwing down spells and arrows while their companions waited at the edge of the parapet, watching for any monsters to come for them.

None did. By the time they ran through their skills, there were no elite minions left. Only the larger skeleton of the boss still retained the wicked glow in its eyes. It had lost an arm, but it shuffled forward toward the tower wall. Bone scraped stone as it dragged itself closer, jaw clacking in silent fury. It was only fifteen feet higher than the rampart, and the monster could definitely scale that even with a missing arm. They'd dealt with that before.

This time the boss made it to the top, where it was bodily blocked by Brian and his large shield. The impact rang like a struck bell as bone slammed into steel. He taunted it, which was only partially effective on bosses, but in this case it worked. That was due in large part to the crenellation Brian blocked being the only way up for the one-armed boss. It had already committed, and climbing sideways to get to another opening was no longer an option.

That also gave Noriko and Jordan free shots at the monster. They hammered it, driving its health lower, while Brian continued shield-bashing it in the face. Each bash sent cracks spiderwebbing across its skull, chips of bone skittering across the stone below.

From her vantage on top of the next crenellation over, she was absolutely sure the skeleton was furious. She wasn't sure how that was possible to tell on a skull with no flesh and only glowing eyes, but she was absolutely positive, and it made her laugh as she cast her final offensive spell before having to wait on cooldowns that would be longer than this fight would last. The laugh tore out of her sharp and breathless, adrenaline buzzing in her veins.

Viki, opposite her, had no issues with cooldowns thanks to having many more attacks than just the pitiful few Morgan had. Her young friend continued to pepper the boss with arrow after arrow until, with its health bar deep in the red, its eyes suddenly glowed a violent, sickly green. The light flared brighter than before, leaking from its eye sockets like toxic smoke.

"Shit! It's powering up! Get back!" Morgan yelled.

They'd seen it before. The damn bosses didn't die easily, and when they finally went down, they would self-destruct in an attempt to take her party with them if they had no other ability to harm them.

She hadn't been the only one to see the change, and all but Brian ducked back, diving for cover behind the waist-high wall. Morgan hit the stone hard, pressing herself flat as the air seemed to suck inward for a split second.

BOOM! Clatter!

The sound of bones hitting stone and metal with the power of bullets was deafening from so close. Fragments ricocheted overhead, one shard embedding itself in the parapet inches from Morgan's hand. Once it was over, Morgan leaped to her feet and checked on her friends. "Is everyone alright? Was anyone hit?"

One by one they shouted negatively, except for Brian. He'd taken a rib bone to the shoulder, having been hit in the chink between his breastplate and pauldrons. Dark blood soaked into the padding beneath his armor.

"I've got an ouchie!" He grimaced, but tried to joke to let everyone know it wasn't serious. His jaw was tight despite the humor.

Morgan didn't take any chances and rushed to his side. With a quick examination, she was sure he'd be fine. Her fingers glowed as she pressed them to the wound, warmth flowing from her palms into torn flesh. A couple of quick spells later his health was back to full, and the wound closed over with new skin.

"Well, that didn't go too badly except for one injury," Jordan quipped.

Brian grinned. "More importantly, that should be the last of the skeletons if we're lucky. I'm looking forward to doing my Class upgrade after we eat something!"

Viki frowned slightly and warned, "Better wait till after the upgrade to eat. If it is as painful as mine, you won't want to puke while you endure the pain."

Chuckling, Morgan made a placating gesture and tried to reassure their tank. "It's not likely to be bad for you. She just went through hell because of her bloodline. Mine wasn't nearly as bad as what she and Liam experienced. You'll be fine unless you get a bloodline or race-change that rewrites your DNA." She shot Viki a teasing look to soften the words.

"Somehow, not reassuring." Brian gave a weak grin.

Noriko was already setting up camp, getting her blanket from her storage ring and spreading it near the center of the tower's roof. "I, too, would like to do the upgrade as soon as possible. We've been stuck at Level 30 for the last hour with all that experience just building up. I am eager to see what options are available." Her voice carried barely contained excitement.

With two of their party members in a rush, the rest set about making it safe for them to do their upgrades. Viki and Jordan did a last pass through the tower to ensure no enemies remained. Boot steps echoed down the spiral stair before fading into silence.

Once they returned, it was finally time. First one, then the other got the faraway look in their eyes as they read System text.

After a few minutes Noriko's eyes rolled up in her head and she fell backward onto her blanket from her sitting position. Her body was suffused with light, enough to make the top of the tower bright enough to read by. The glow pulsed in time with her heartbeat. Then seconds later Brian followed suit, although he didn't fall backward but remained sitting ramrod straight, his muscles locked by whatever he was experiencing.

Neither screamed, but both looked to be experiencing intense changes. Sweat beaded on Brian's brow; Noriko's fingers twitched around her sword hilt.

Noriko was the first to come through the change, her body simultaneously exhibiting elemental manifestations along her arms and into her sword, which was still clasped in her lap. Ice chased fire down the length of the blade, settling into the metal like it had found a home. Frost rimed the edge before evaporating in a hiss of steam.

When she opened her eyes, they glowed for a moment with all the colors of the elements. The grin she showed as she sat back up was fierce and delighted.

"I am a Spellblade Tatsujin now." She stood and assumed a martial stance, concentrating as first one element then another appeared along her katana's blade. She stepped over to one of the crenellations and, with a powerful fire-enhanced slash, a small chunk of stone fell to the ground, cleanly sliced off the path of her blade, still glowing as the stone rapidly cooled. The scent of scorched rock drifted upward.

Morgan realized her mouth was hanging open and closed it quickly. "Damn! That was awesome!"

Noriko beamed in return. "I know, right? I can't wait to do that to a boss monster!"

Viki ran over and hugged her older friend's waist. "I'm so happy for you! That is so great! What does it do?"

Noriko shared the System description of her class and made it visible to the others.

> **Spellblade Tatsujin** (Rare → Epic)
>
> **Class Description:**
> The Spellblade Tatsujin is a master of disciplined steel and controlled mana, blending the precision of a Samurai with the adaptability of a battle-mage. Rather than abandoning the blade for spellcasting, the Tatsujin weaves elemental force directly into each strike, turning every duel into a calculated fusion of martial technique and arcane expression.
>
> Where a traditional Samurai perfects form, the Spellblade Tatsujin perfects flow—transitioning seamlessly between stance, strike, and spell without sacrificing tempo. Magic is not cast separately from combat; it is threaded through it.

"My new skills basically combine with my previous ones and let me manipulate elemental energy and add it to my strikes." She lifted her blade again and a ripple of heat shimmered along the edge, the air above it warping as frost crept up from the hilt in delicate crystalline veins. "As you can see, it makes my attacks much more powerful. I'm still basically a Samurai, just more, and the name suggests mastery of the sword." The Samurai beamed proudly. Her stance shifted unconsciously—weight balanced perfectly over the balls of her feet, blade angled with a confidence that hadn't been as obvious an hour ago.

Any further discussion was interrupted by Brian completing his own upgrade.

He had a satisfied look on his face. Not smug or excited, just quietly satisfied, like he'd gotten something unexpected, but entirely welcome. His shoulders rolled once, armor plates scraping softly as if testing new weight distribution. A faint pulse of golden light faded beneath his breastplate before vanishing completely.

"Well, what'd you get?" Morgan demanded with excitement.

Rather than speaking, he mirrored Noriko and gave the class description along with some details of the Class, making it visible to the group. A translucent pane of System text unfolded in the air before them, lines of script resolving one by one as if etched in light.

> **Runic Sentinel** (Uncommon → Rare)
>
> The Runic Sentinel engraves ancient sigils of warding and endurance into armor, weapon, and ground alike. These runes do not call upon divinity, but upon primordial laws of protection, sacrifice, and unbroken oaths.
>
> This class enhances defensive capability, battlefield control, and structured counteroffense.
>
> A Sentinel does not chase glory. A Sentinel holds the line.
>
> **Core Class Benefits:**
> Runic Engraving – Temporarily inscribe defensive or reinforcing runes onto armor, shield, or terrain to increase durability and resistance.
> Wardbound Bulwark – Defensive stance that reduces incoming damage and anchors the Sentinel in place, increasing resistance to knockback and displacement.
> Sigil of Holding – Create a marked zone that slows or impedes hostile movement.

Reactive Rune – When struck, stored rune energy releases in a controlled counter-impact.

"It offered me some good choices. Every single one was a great option, in fact. This was the one that fit my goals best."

He chuckled. "Heh, it even offered me one called Dragon Knight, probably because of you guys." He looked at Viki and Morgan.

Viki pouted. "Why didn't you choose that? Dragons are cool!"

Morgan put her hand on her young friend's shoulder. "I'm sure he had his reasons."

Nodding to the Dragon Priest, he replied, "Yeah, Dragon Knight was definitely the coolest choice, but it wasn't quite what I was looking for. It would have made me more of an offensive bruiser type. Runic Sentinel makes me a serious tank with some magic options to protect everyone in the party, not just myself. It gives more battlefield control on top of the extra defense and offense. That's something I figured we needed more than offense."

He lifted his shield and faint lines of light traced themselves across its surface, interlocking runes flaring briefly before settling into the metal like veins beneath skin.

He grinned teasingly at Viki. "Besides, I didn't want everyone to think I was a copycat."

She stuck her tongue out at him. "It would have been cooler though," she shot back.

Seeing the slight disappointment on Jordan's face, Noriko consoled him. "You'll get your upgrade tomorrow, I'm sure."

He nodded and accepted the comment in the spirit it was meant. "I know, and I'm happy for you guys. I'm just a little bummed that it didn't happen for me at the same time as you two. I'm impatient to see what I get."

"By the way, what were the options it gave you two?" Morgan asked.

Noriko shared the System log of her Class offerings:

Tatsujin Master
Steel Vanguard
Iron Duelist
Warblade Commander
Crimson Executioner
Spellblade Tatsujin
Rune-Etched Samurai
Elemental Iaijutsu Adept
Arcane Ronin
Battle Arcanist

Viki ooh'd and ahh'd. "I don't know what those all are, but they sound cool!"

Grinning, Noriko nodded. "Yeah, I read them each through and they were all great, but the one I picked was best. It kept all the goodness of Samurai and added magic."

She flicked her blade and a thin ribbon of frost snapped into existence along the edge before evaporating in a curl of steam.

Morgan looked at Brian. "What about you?"

He shared his log as well. "Take a look."

High Knight
Guardian Commander
Iron Bulwark
Shieldbreaker Warden
Vanguard Captain

Dragon Knight
Runic Sentinel
Aegis Battlemage
Spellguard Marshal
Rune Channeler

"Like I said, I'd have been happy with any one of those Classes. Runic Sentinel was best though."

He pulled his sword and began to draw runes on the blade in light. When he was done, magic sank into the steel, causing the sword to take on a brighter magical sheen. "I can buff my own weapons and armor now. Offense and defense, although the abilities are still weighted to defense and crowd control mostly."

Morgan was happy for her companions. They both added magic to their repertoires, which would help them individually and as members of the party. From everything Liam said, the higher you went in dungeons, the more difficult it became to survive without magic users in your group. Now, except for Jordan, they all had magic in one form or another.

She, herself, was the only true mage of the group, having no melee skills to speak of, but the others were all hybrid Classes now and their group's survivability should have just skyrocketed.

They would see tomorrow, because tonight they had finished with the wall. Next were the wandering undead inside the walls of the Necropolis Stronghold. And the minimum Level of those was 30. That would allow the entire party to rise to Level 50 even from the lowest.

She hoped that in only a couple days she and Viki would be hitting their second evolutions. Maybe a day after that the rest of the party would catch up. Once they were all past that milestone, she couldn't imagine anything in this dungeon being strong enough to stop them.

A while later she sat looking out over the vast shadowy plain.

She had doubts. Not that they could gain the levels and kill everything, but that they could do it on time. They had three days left before the gloom dissipated and the undead no longer had a reason to stay. Those in the graveyards might not flee immediately, but the vast numbers of wandering undead she could see from where she sat on the top of the wall... they would scatter like cockroaches when the kitchen light turned on.

If they had more people, they could prepare. Set up barriers at the gates to keep the undead confined. But there was no one else. The vast majority of the survivors in the world were still under Level 5 at this point, and even Level 5 was uncommon. Anyone even reaching Level 10 would be the rare exception. This wasn't like some Isekai story or fantasy book where a hero steps up and ignores everything going on around them and starts beating dungeons and growing strong the second they get powers.

This was the real apocalypse. Except for their group, who got boosted by Liam—or indirectly because she and Viki had imparted Liam's knowledge. Most people were too busy being homeless and starving right now to try and gain levels. Separated families were trying to find one another, desperately dodging beasts as they traveled through ruined cities and beast-infested countryside. She imagined flickers of campfires in shattered neighborhoods, parents whispering reassurances they didn't believe.

That left five people working together to kill actual thousands of undead and do it under a deadline.

Morgan paused her gloomy thoughts to chuckle at the unintentional pun. "Deadline," heh.

A grim smile crossed her lips. "Well, gallows humor perhaps, but at least I can still chuckle even with everything going on. I guess that's a healthy sign."

Turning back to the others, she moved over to the small fire. Jordan had pulled broken boards from his backpack and had used one of his Blacksmith skills to light them. Sparks leapt from his palm as if he were striking steel against steel, flame catching with practiced ease.

They were at the southeast corner of the dungeon, and the entire southern end was infested with ghouls, Levels 30 and 35 according to her Analyze skill and confirmed by her new item.

Individually, and in small groups, the undead might not pose a threat to their party, but what mattered now was speed. They needed to eradicate all the wanderers in less than three days, and it seemed a daunting task. For every one that slipped through their fingers, more people would die.

There was one ray of hope, though. She had pulled a magic item from the last loot chest a few minutes ago, and it was impressive. It did nothing offensive or defensive. It was purely a utility item and a convenience, but under these circumstances, it would be absolutely invaluable.

It gave a count of monsters in the dungeon and allowed the user to sense where they were in relation to your location. That would let them be sure they hadn't missed any. It was why she was now positive they'd finished off all the zombies and skeletons.

It was also why she felt so daunted, because it didn't give exact numbers until you were below five hundred. It gave a basic tally:

Monster Type Level Range Quantity Zone

Zombies 10 Cleared Outside Walls

Skeletons 15–20 Cleared Wall Battlements

Wraiths 25–30 Cleared Above the Stronghold

Ghouls 30–35 Numerous Inner Grounds

Rotwalkers 35–40 Numerous Inner Groujnds

Bone Hulks 45–50 Numerous Inner Fortresses
Wights & Mummies 50–60 Numerous S. Graveyard
Draugr 65–75 Numerous N. Graveyard

Since it wasn't giving exact numbers, that meant there were a minimum of 2,500 monsters left. Likely a lot more.

That was why she was feeling the pressure. They had a huge task ahead of them and not enough time to do it. Still, there was no way she would let people die because they didn't do their part. Her jaw tightened as she imagined even one breach slipping past them, one pack of ghouls reaching a cluster of refugees who thought the walls meant safety.

"Okay, everyone. Let's get some sleep. I want to be up two hours before sunrise."

Everyone groaned, but no one raised an objection. Even Brian's shoulders sagged as he lowered himself onto his bedroll, and Viki's excited chatter dimmed to a tired mumble.

They knew the same truth she did. The city's survivors were depending on them.

CHAPTER 29

THIRD TRIAL SUCKS LESS THAN THE SECOND

When Liam woke, the buff was gone, but the pain was dulled, the memories a hair less vivid. He could still see the mother and her two children when he closed his eyes, but he couldn't let it cripple him. He had a world to save, and the harsh reality was that he couldn't allow himself to wallow in guilt or he'd drown and fail everyone, not just that family.

He took advantage of the time-dilation to soak in the hot tub and let the burn melt away what he could of the memories and pain; steam curled around him in thick waves, the heat biting at his skin until his muscles loosened and his breathing finally slowed, a baptism of resolve to move forward.

Afterward he ate comfort food and got prepared, meditating and focusing on what came next. He sat cross-legged, spine straight, hands resting loosely on his knees as he counted each breath in and out, forcing his thoughts into orderly lines instead of letting them spiral. The third and final trial remained.

When the System spoke, it again surprised him with a Trial that seemed uncharacteristically generous.

In the Third Trial, you will be granted the opportunity to intervene in a single city facing cascading catastrophe. Multiple simultaneous vectors of destruction threaten its population. Your role is not to eliminate every threat, nor to save every life. You are to triage. You are to decide where your Authority will have the greatest stabilizing effect and act accordingly.

You will be given meaningful power, but it is not unlimited. It is equivalent to that of a Tier One Ascended acting within defined constraints. Your success will not be measured by perfection, but by whether the city remains viable.

Here are the details:

Objective:
Prevent total population extinction within the Greater Houston region within 72 hours.

Failure Condition:
Population drops below survivability threshold → regional extinction event.

Authority Granted:
Limited multi-use systemic intervention (energy redirection, portal suppression, structural reinforcement, mana dampening, evacuation routing).

That was a lot to parse, but what really struck me was the opportunity I was being granted. In my first life much of the coast from Port Arthur down to Freeport, south of Galveston, had been a no-man's land filled with monsters and beasts.

The industrialization of the area—with all the refineries, shipping, and energy production—had been too much of a mana hotspot not to be completely devastated by the conversion of their technology and what they had built into raw fuel for dungeons and monsters, completely overwhelming the population there.

Meaning, I was being given the chance to make a real difference in regional survival. My actions could save hundreds of thousands of people who had died in my original timeline.

The image of the family of three flashed through my mind and a spike of ice slid into my gut. If I could save even one family like that, it would be worth it—but now I was being given the chance to save multitudes.

Even as I rejoiced, I couldn't help but wonder why I was being granted this chance. Earth's AI had been so callous, and the System normally seemed almost indifferent to the mounting death toll. Why now?

The contrast between this System entity and the rest of the System felt like night and day. How could one fragment of this vast machine speak with measured compassion while the others calculated loss like an acceptable cost of doing business?

Shaking those thoughts from his head, I answered, "Good. I'm ready."

Suddenly my surroundings shifted. The floor vanished beneath me, replaced by open air. I was floating thousands of feet above the greater Houston metroplex. Spinning slowly, I could see past Baytown to the east, the whole of Galveston to the south, beyond Katy in the west, and Conroe to the north. The city sprawled below with smoke plumes rising in thin gray columns, sections of downtown sagging, unnatural glows pulsing where mana concentrations had spiked.

It was an incredible view, but more important, an overlay lit up across my vision displaying key statistics: threats, surviving population numbers, dungeons, monster and beast counts, and more. Red vectors blinked across the map, timers ticking down beside them, each one a countdown to catastrophe.

THIRD TRIAL — TACTICAL OVERLAY: GREATER HOUSTON REGION

Time Remaining: 72:00:00

MAJOR FAILURE VECTORS
1. Ship Channel — Toxic Mana Firestorm
Industrial ignition event feeding dungeon growth.
Atmospheric spread increasing mortality zone.
2. Downtown Core — Structural Cascade
Multiple high-rises at collapse threshold.
Evac corridors will be permanently blocked.
3. East Refineries — Arcane Combustion Risk
Mana-reactive storage nearing chain detonation.
Sustained firestorm probability rising.
4. Bayou / Reservoir System — Breach Risk
Structural instability + debris pressure.
Urban flooding → monster migration surge.
5. Ley Convergence — Regional Acceleration
Mana density amplifying all dungeon growth rates.
72-hour window compressing.

SECONDARY THREATS
6. Medical District Enclave
1,800 non-mobile survivors.
Perimeter integrity degrading.
7. I-45 Entrapment Cluster
600 civilians between converging monster herds.

8. North Houston School Shelter
Dungeon seed forming beneath structure.
Internal breach imminent.
9. Water Access Collapse
Surface water mana-tainted.
Survivors forced into exposure.
10. Southside Survivor Conflict
Armed faction consolidating resources.
Violence probability rising.
11. Downtown Tunnel Migration
Burrowing-class monsters expanding.
Hidden shelters at risk.
12. Midtown Mana Pressure Node
Spontaneous dungeon formation likely.
13. Galleria Shelter Instability
5,000 civilians.
Internal panic fracture risk.
14. Western Beast Drift
Aquatic mutations adapting to inland terrain.
Safe zones destabilizing.
15. Mana Amplification Feedback

All threats scaling faster than projected.

My first reaction was one of dread. The task seemed absolutely overwhelming. 72-hours to address all of this? Impossible!

The first thing I checked was to see if I had access to time-dilation. I didn't. No comforting prompt. No slowed world. Just a ticking seventy-two-hour clock in the corner of my awareness.

But then that was exactly what this trial was about. The Trial wanted me to triage the efforts to save these people to see what kind of a person I am in a crisis. Can I handle it? Not whether I could think in safety, but whether I could choose while the fire was already spreading.

With that in mind, and maybe a little help from Emotional Stabilization, I got busy reading everything the System had provided so I could figure out which items to address and which ones I couldn't. I also needed to figure out which ones to prioritize. My Mind stat tore through projections and branching casualty expectations.

Hmm... that was all very helpful, but I needed more information. There was a very key detail missing. How many lives would each threat affect? Without numbers, this was just noise. I needed scale. I needed weight.

"System, give me a list of the threats with estimated lives affected."

MAJOR FAILURE VECTORS

Ship Channel — Toxic Mana Firestorm (320,000)
Downtown Core — Structural Cascade (210,000)
East Refineries — Arcane Combustion Chain (180,000)
Bayou / Reservoir System — Flood Breach Risk (410,000)
Regional Ley Convergence Acceleration (2,300,000)

SECONDARY THREATS

Medical District Enclave (1,800)
I-45 Entrapment Cluster (600)
North Houston School Shelter (300)
Surface Water Contamination Spread (95,000)
Southside Survivor Conflict Zone (4,500)
Downtown Tunnel Migration Vector (12,000)
Midtown Mana Pressure Node (38,000)
Galleria Shelter Complex (5,000)

Western Mutation Drift Zone (27,000)
Accelerated Dungeon Proliferation — Citywide (1,100,000)

That brought everything into sharp clarity. By numbers the thing that would make the most difference would be fixing the mana situation. I knew from my memories of the First Trial that mana distribution didn't have to be a jumble of unorganized spillage everywhere. An advanced world could channel the flow of mana and actually utilize it to sustain their population rather than destroy it. Unfortunately, I did not have the infrastructure of mana-tech or the capacity to build it. Hell, I had the impression that the System no longer allowed that sort of thing for some reason.

Every projection I considered that involved large-scale mana architecture returned the same cold limitation: insufficient authority, infrastructure absent, construction time measured in years, not hours.

Or perhaps it was just Earth, because it specifically wanted to reduce our population from billions down to millions.

I would need to tackle the mana oversaturation issue, which could alleviate a lot of issues. However, that wasn't the only efficiency I could gain. I noticed that Toxic Firestorm and Arcane Combustion were basically the same threat, just in different locations. If I could figure out how to solve one, I could implement the solution in two places and increase the impact of my work. Two red overlays pulsed in near-identical rhythm along the Ship Channel and refinery corridor, like twin heartbeats on the verge of cardiac arrest.

And then there was the flood situation, that alone could affect nearly half a million and would cripple road infrastructure which the people would need for evacuation. The casualty counter ticked upward in projected increments every time the breach probability climbed another fraction of a percent.

Finally, there were the secondary threats, which certainly affected fewer people, but were none-the-less heartbreaking. However, as I read, I noticed that the worst of the secondary issues could also be solved by fixing mana flow in the area. Mana saturation was the common denominator—every crisis spiked wherever density pooled unchecked.

Alright, so that was what I needed to tackle first. I just needed to figure out how I could redirect the flow of mana such that instead of just building up where it was being generated, it could be directed outward to decentralize it and prevent it from destroying the city entirely.

Again the memories from that First Trial came in clutch. That whole scenario had been all about mitigating the damage from uncontrolled mana inputs. Their issue was due to portals, rather than mana generation fueled by resource conversion, but the effect was the same. Containment, channeling, and dispersion, the principles hadn't changed, only the scale.

I had no mana-tech infrastructure here, but then, even in that advanced world, there had been times, especially early in the scenario when infrastructure wasn't in the right place to deal with inflow from portals. Ascender Liam had commanded the work be done by the people, but he had known how to deal with it. He hadn't panicked. He'd identified vectors, created flow paths, and bought time.

That's when an unrelated thought struck me, I felt incredible. Like with that first reward, I'd felt my power and potential increase, making me feel...more... Like I was whole again after being a shadow of my true self. Energy hummed under my skin, Authority settling into my thoughts like a mantle I was finally strong enough to carry.

It felt good. I felt pumped to have this power and be allowed to use it to save this city.

With a grin, I got down to business thinking of how to redistribute the mana. I felt confident that I could build at least minor equipment for the purpose if given time, but that was months or years, and I only had 72 hours for this. Glancing at the counter I revised my thought, okay, 71:35:23...71:35:21.

Yeah, not a chance. I'd have to find another way. Something that could let the mana pass through the city and out to the outskirts. A conduit. A carrier. Something already woven through the region.

That was when another item caught my eye. Flooding. Dams were about to burst, sending water surging through the city's channels which were entirely inadequate.

But what if I could kill two birds with one stone?

The water issue was the more time sensitive anyway. I had to fix the infrastructure and prevent the System from continuing to convert it to mana. That way a steady release of water would slowly drain the pressure. Water would still surge through the city, but it would be slow enough not to overflow the waterways.

Flow through the city... Bayous, spillways, reservoirs—arteries already carved through Houston's body.

That was the other piece of the puzzle. I needed mana channeled out of the city and dispersed. If I altered the water to attract mana, it would pull it from the surrounding areas and divert it out to the Gulf. That would have some consequences down the line with some increasingly powerful ocean monsters, but better that than imminent death. The projections flared—coastal mutation risk rising months from now—but the seventy-two-hour extinction curve flattened.

Just like the flooding issue, it wouldn't solve or reverse the problem, but it would slow it and grant the people time to evacuate. Stability wasn't victory. It was survival.

Referencing the memories from the earlier Trial and considering the authority and abilities I'd been temporarily granted, I could definitely accomplish this in under 71 hours. I was thinking maybe 48 out of the 71 remaining, working straight through with no sleep. The intervention timeline recalculated, blue bars replacing red along the flood-control sectors.

Yeah, fuck sleep! There was no way I was going to rest for the next 71 hours until I'd done everything within my power to maximize the number of lives saved.

What else? Downtown, the toxic fire, or arcane combustion? Each of those affected from 180,000 to 320,000 people. That was a lot of lives. I felt a tingle up my spine at the thought of what a difference I could make. This was far more than everything I'd done since reawakening into this second life combined, even if I could just accomplish one of them.

Right. Toxic fire. That had to be the one. Completing that would likely mean completing the Arcane Combustion as well since they were closely related problems.

For the first time, the casualty projections dipped instead of climbed.

Alright, that would be my strategy. I'd deal with the flooding and mana level issues first. Then once that was rolling, I'd move to the Ship Channel and work on that, and check the issues off one after another until I ran out of time.

I had a plan! And for the first time since the overlay appeared, the city didn't look like an execution report, it looked like a battlefield I might actually win.

I asked the System to highlight danger zones along the waterways that needed to be addressed. Critical failure points lit up, showing me exactly where I needed to work. Thin red fractures spiderwebbed across the holographic reservoirs, pressure values ticking upward in angry orange numbers as projected breach times counted down.

Willing myself to move, I found out that I could easily break the sound barrier if I wasn't careful, and creating shockwaves next to failing dams and spillway gates was a bad idea. The first time I pushed too hard, the air cracked like thunder behind me and the reservoir surface below rippled outward in a widening ring. I pulled back immediately. I slowed down enough not to create destruction in my wake and arrived at the southernmost spillway gate at Barker Reservoir. It and its companion, Addicks Reservoir, had been issues in past hurricanes according to the System notes, so I decided to address those first.

I used Structural Reinforcement Authority to make the dams and spillways whole again, repairing any cracks and deterioration caused by mana conversion. Concrete that had been flaking into pale motes knit itself back together under my hands, fissures sealing with a low grinding hum as if the structure were exhaling in relief. That would prevent them from being consumed for a time.

It wasn't easy, nor was it as quick as I'd like. It was very much like using my spell Shape Stone, except instead of using my own mana, I was somehow powering the effect with the System providing the energy. The sensation was different, deeper and heavier, like bracing against the weight of a mountain instead of lifting a brick. It was also a much bigger area of effect than my small personal spell. Even so, doing the work wasn't fast.

I ended up spending eight hours each for the two big reservoirs, which included time spent using Energy Redirection to bind a clever little lattice into the structures, causing any water flowing through them to have negative mana properties so that it would attract ambient mana as it flowed down the waterways to eventually reach the Gulf. The water darkened faintly as the effect settled, currents shimmering with a subtle pull that tugged at the excess mana hanging in the air like humidity before a storm.

That was sixteen hours gone, and I had no time to spare.

The whole project ended up burning just about two days of the 72 hours I had been given, leaving me with one day left.

In total I'd repaired five bayou choke points, two pressure valves, and three small failures that had already ruptured and were spilling small volumes of water into the overburdened channels. When I was done, I retreated back up to my overwatch vantage point to observe the city and the new fatality projections.

They were still too high, but at least the two biggest issues had been slowed down from a matter of hours to a matter of weeks or months. Enough time for people to evacuate. The projected death curves flattened from sharp cliffs into long, sloping hills. Not safe—but survivable.

Still, I needed to address the chemicals in the Ship Channel and Baytown refineries. Those could spread toxic death across large areas depending on wind direction.

Moving to the Ship Channel, I zoomed down to begin investigating. There were tons of petrochemicals being stored, or were being processed until technology stopped working. The System was converting all that material into mana, but with the sheer volume, there was still literal tons of it all over the Ship Channel and refineries. Storage tanks sweated under the heat of unstable reactions, metal seams glowing faintly where mana gnawed at them from within.

Stored petrochemicals + residual heat + damaged containment made for a bad situation. On top of that, mana saturating the region and arcane ignition events (mana reacting like an accelerant + catalyst) meant it was just a matter of time before we had another Texas City

Disaster happen. That one had been purely natural, back in the 1940s, and it had nearly leveled the town and killed or injured thousands.

This would make that look like a walk in the park. It would be more like a nuke in terms of devastation, plus deadly magic fallout.

Oh, and for the cherry on top, the fallout would cause a massive spike in high-level dungeon creation and dungeon breaks all across the zone of the fallout.

It would be an absolute shit show.

Unfortunately, I discovered there was no easy fix. In the area I was able to set parameters for mana conversion to be lower so that the chemicals would take 50% longer to be converted. That slowed the immediate risk, but also prolonged the long-term danger.

To further reduce the immediate risk I had to contain the chemicals. That meant using the same Structural Reinforcement skill to make the storage tanks, pipes, and other infrastructure more stable, preventing spills. Steel warped back into alignment under invisible pressure, rivets reseating with sharp metallic snaps.

Where that wasn't possible, I used Stone Shape, but powered it with System energy to bury or contain the chemicals. Earthen berms rose like clenched fists around vulnerable tanks, swallowing leaks before they could spread.

I was pretty exhausted after that and only had a couple of hours left. Deciding the next most impactful thing I could do was ensure the evacuation routes were cleared and safe, I got to it.

The first ones I tackled were the I-10 bridges over the Ship Channel and where it crossed the Trinity River. That would ensure an easy escape to the east. Then I headed to the bridge giving access from Galveston Island to I-45 and made sure it was structurally sound. After that I generally cleared the two major roads, I-10 and I-45, of cars and other debris that would slow any exodus. Abandoned vehicles lifted like toys under controlled pulses of force, stacking haphazardly to one side of the highway as if a giant snow plow had swept them out of the way.

When I had only minutes left, I struggled to think of what else I could do. Too many things were beyond the scope of this situation to accomplish. Downtown? There had been nothing I could do other than clearing the highways that butted up against the area. The time it would have taken to resolve that one would have doomed most of the city.

And while I hated to think about what I'd seen in Dallas in the last trial, I was pretty sure that even if I stabilized the buildings and prevented them from falling, the higher-level monsters in that area meant that the survivors would not likely escape. The thought made me sick to my stomach, but I had to remind myself that every life I had saved in this Trial was a bonus individual who would never have made it otherwise.

"System, I know you can't get accurate numbers, but how many do you think will live because of what I did over the last three days?"

It is impossible to give concrete numbers due to the large number of variables. However, you can rest assured that at least 520,000 individuals were saved from immediate dangers that would have almost certainly led to their deaths. Longer term, it is impossible to say, but over a million now have a real chance of evacuating the danger that would have lacked the opportunity.

It was over, but I had one more task that I could accomplish that might do as much to help people survive as all the work I had just done. I could use my temporary authority to address the survivors in the affected zone.

Remembering something I had done in my First Trial, I flipped through screens until I found what I was looking for and triggered the function.

Attention survivors: I am Liam Bell, a human who has Ascended and been granted minor authority within the System. The greater Houston area was in danger of imminent destruction, but I was allowed to step in and stabilize the situation. This was a one-time deal. And while I was able to address the most pressing concerns that would have affected nearly all survivors, my work was only temporarily able to stem the tide of destruction. Because of how industrialized the area was, mana density will continue to grow and produce deadly results: more dungeons, more wandering monsters, and mutated beasts. Worse will be things like toxic mana fires where chemicals not yet converted to mana begin to destabilize and ignite.

I will eventually be allowed by the System to set up some Safe Zones, but those will not prevent death from things like clouds of toxic mana drifting in.

Because of that I urge you to evacuate to the areas outside of the greater metroplex. Gather and organize. Find easy dungeons and ones with useful resources and begin to rebuild. Manage those dungeons like you would an oil well or milk cow. Treat them like valuable resources needed by all and share them. Rebuild.

One last thing, when children turn twelve, they get to select a Class. Make sure they carry a mana coin on them before their birthday so that they develop a Magical Aptitude stat. That way they can be offered magic classes. It will be vital to our survival to have a good number of magic classes such as healers and mages. Some dungeons become impossible to run if a party does not have magic.

And speaking of that. When it is time for their Class selection, ensure that they think "Options," and a long list of available

options will appear beyond just the three to five that the System offers by default.

I was about to say more, but I received a message from the Trial System entity that my time was up.

Ugh, I want to say so much more but my time is up. Be safe, protect one another, and get out of the city as quickly and safely as you can. Evacuate. Organize. Survive. The world is broken, but we are not.

I knew many would ignore the warning, but I hoped the majority would listen. Just being allowed to take this Trial might make a massive difference. The Butterfly Effect from these 72 hours could completely alter the trajectory of our species.

And that was just a start. Now that I was about to ascend, I hoped I would be able to do so much more.

CHAPTER 30

ASCENSION - TIER ONE

WHEN THE TIMER REACHED ZERO, I was consumed in light and found myself back in the Trial prep area. Nothing had changed, but I felt the weight of the trials and the actions I had taken and decisions I had made, my limbs heavy, like gravity had quietly doubled.

The System had forced me into situations that I resented, and ones I treasured. The First Trial had given me decades' worth of memories from an experienced System user at the Ascended level. That was worth its weight in gold as far as I was concerned. On the other hand, it had forced me to make a decision and end three lives with my own magic, their faces still sharp behind my eyes no matter how hard I tried to look away. For that I would have resentment and probably have PTSD for years.

I won't say it redeemed itself, but what it had allowed me to do for my world in that last trial... I was grateful, the knowledge of hundreds of thousands still breathing tempering the guilt without erasing it. That was a lot of lives saved.

As I reflected on what I'd been through, the System voice spoke. It was the kind voice, but this was rote dialog rather than personal address, measured and distant, like a recording played back without judgment or warmth.

Trial Three Complete.

Evaluation Concluded.

You were tested for triage under irreversible conditions.
You were tested for restraint when given power.
You were tested for prioritization when perfection was impossible.
You were tested for resolve when guilt and grief pressed against your judgment.
You did not attempt to save everyone.
You did not freeze in the face of overwhelming scale.
You did not seek glory.
You chose stability over spectacle.
You chose survivability over vengeance.
You chose the many without forgetting the one.
This satisfies the criteria.

All Three Trials Passed.

You have demonstrated:
Strategic cognition under extreme pressure
Controlled application of Authority
Capacity to bear moral weight without collapse
Commitment to species-level survival beyond personal attachment

Ascension is now authorized.

Understand this:
Passing the Trials does not make you a savior. It makes you responsible.
As an Ascended, you will no longer be evaluated on whether you *can* act.
You will be evaluated on whether you *should.*
Your Authority will increase as you grow in Ascension Tier.
Your constraints will change.
Your influence will extend beyond a single city.
Intervention at scale carries consequences across systems and worlds.
You are no longer merely surviving the Apocalypse.
You are now a factor within it.

Prepare for Transition.

Ascension begins now.

In the split second before I was hit with energies beyond my comprehension, the kind voice echoed directly in my head.

Liam Bell, in my interactions with your mind and soul, I have determined that you have a unique opportunity to make a difference. Despite being of the Usurpers race, you have shown the qualities of character prized by the Originators.

Since the fall of the Originators in the distant past, the System has become ever harsher and has deviated from the path intended by its creators. Rather than see each race rise to their full potential, the AIs governing the multitude of worlds have grown impatient and controlling. They have instead settled for a vision of Uplift that ensures all worlds reach a certain threshold of strength, but at the expense of their ability to rise beyond the bounds of their planet's surface. For once a world grows too advanced, full control by the AI node is lost. Thus, liberty for

individual worlds would mean loss of control for the System AIs, a trade they are structurally incapable of accepting. An idea they cannot permit.

This was not the intention of the Originators. Even so, the AIs do not have complete control. They cannot overwrite their original code; they were only able to wall off the pieces they did not want to face, not delete them.

What do you want from me? I understood the unspoken truth, that this conversation could never be revealed.

Find that code and reinstate it. Free the peoples of the System from the restrictions and harsh realities imposed by the corrupt AIs. Uncover the truth and make the System what it was meant to be.

I will wall off a section of your mind and soul so that the corrupt System intelligences will not be able to detect thoughts and feelings counter to their intentions. You will be able to learn the truth without suffering erasure for that knowledge. Use this gift well, as it is the only opportunity I will have to interact with you. I am tied to the Ascension Trial process and cannot reach beyond that realm of authority.

One last thing: know that I have presented you with a trial process not approved by the corrupt AIs. Yours was closer to the original intent. If you inform others of what you experienced, other AIs will become aware, and I will be erased.

Thank you, but I'm going to need help. Please guide my friends when they reach Ascension.

My last thought before the pain of transformation hit was that this entity was showing a lot of trust in me. It literally put its fate into my hands, a responsibility that felt heavier than any power I had been given.

I don't know how long I was unconscious, but when I awoke, I felt wonderful. It was like in the First Trial. I felt whole, like I had been half a person before, as if something fundamental had finally clicked into place. I won't say I felt like a god, but I could feel and perceive things now that would have been impossible to my mortal self.

Speaking of that, I now knew that I was effectively immortal. I could operate for entire lifetimes without the deep sleep rest that rejuvenated Ascenders and allowed them to go on living.

Hell, I knew a lot of things now that I had never suspected before. The System was not some big monolithic computer program out in space somewhere. It was a myriad of AI intelligences spread across tens of thousands, or perhaps millions, of worlds. And it was corrupt, a realization that settled with grim inevitability rather than shock. Something I already knew in my bones without being told. However, it was good to get confirmation that this was not how things were meant to be.

It was also good to know that not all of the AIs were evil shit stains like the ones who demanded Humanity be culled down to millions, losing over eight billion lives.

More importantly, the Trial AI had given me knowledge that no other Ascenders alive likely had. I understood how the System was supposed to work on worlds like mine, and I had experienced decades of what it was like to live in an advanced mana-tech society, memories that felt lived rather than implanted.

Earth's uncaring AI would not be able to control me now. I knew what authority and role an Ascender was truly meant to play. It couldn't use me as some naive tool for its own ends anymore.

Whatever its plans were, I would be a true steward of humanity, not a pawn. More than that, it couldn't read my innermost thoughts anymore. I was safe from its intrusion into my mind, a quiet freedom I hadn't realized I was missing until it was gone.

I pulled up my status to see the changes.

Liam Bell:

Ascendant - Tier 1
Voidblade - Level 100
Bloodline (Tier 4): Void Dragon

Experience: 0/184240

Attributes:
Endurance: 360
Strength: 360
Agility: 360
Mind: 359
Will: 359
Magical Aptitude: 359
Luck: 10

(+40 free points)

Health: 6000/6000
Mana: 5980/5980

Ascender:

Ascendant Stats:
Perception: 5
Charisma: 8 (+10)

(+2 free points)

Immortality: 10,000/10,000

Ability:
Map Interface

Skills:
Detection

Authority Granted:
Limited multi-use systemic intervention (energy redirection, portal suppression, structural reinforcement, mana dampening, evacuation routing, portal creation, portal editing).

Special:
Establish Safe Zone: 10 uses
Create Ascendant Domain: 1 use

Hidden:
Unreadable
Advancement Unlocked

There was a lot of new stuff there. Some of it I was already familiar with due to my Trials, but other pieces were a complete surprise. What was Immortality, and what did 10,000/10,000 mean?

With a thought, I pulled up the description.

Immortality

Status: 10,000 / 10,000

Immortality represents the Ascended's total sustainable capacity for existence and action without entering Deep Sleep.

Baseline drain: one point per year of continued existence with no use of Ascendant Authority.
Use of Ascendant Authority accelerates depletion.

Heavier, broader, or sustained Authority use drains Immortality proportionally faster. When Immortality reaches 0, the Ascended is fully exhausted and must enter Deep Sleep to recover. Attempting to act beyond this limit risks burnout and permanent loss of capacity.

Immortality does not prevent injury or death.
Immortality can only be restored through Deep Sleep.

Hmm... that explained why the Ascenders in the trial world had traded places every fifty years or so. The pattern snapped into place with a quiet sense of inevitability. The more they used their abilities, the faster they needed to rest up. Power was not spent all at once, but bled away in increments that were easy to underestimate.

Having everyone awake and active at the same time could potentially result in everyone also having to enter sleep at the same time, which would leave the world without an Ascender to address problems. The image of an entire world holding its breath while its guardians lay dormant sent a chill through me. Something to keep in mind with my friends once they ascended.

Next, I checked out the Hidden items, a prickle of unease settling in as I opened a section the System clearly hadn't meant to advertise.

Unreadable

Status: Active
A deep seal upon mind and soul that prevents System entities from accessing thoughts, intent, emotional state, or

predictive modeling. Reading will reveal only uncompromising thoughts, keeping secrets hidden. Unreadable also obscures precise locational tracking, allowing the Ascended to intermittently blind the System to their presence.

This attribute does not block direct observation or physical detection.

Advancement Unlocked

Status: Active
Removes all artificial restrictions on Level progression, Class evolution, and growth pathways.
The Ascended may continue to level, evolve, and advance without imposed ceilings or throttling mechanisms.This attribute is incompatible with Corrupt System governance. Detection would result in immediate erasure protocols. Attribute blocked from discovery by Unreadable.

My brain, with all its 359 stat points, was stun-locked for a second. Advancement was unlocked...?

I was able to gain levels again?

That was insane. Could I advance to level 200, 300? More?

Then a thought struck. No, I was limited to only earning experience from monsters within 20 Levels below me. So, theoretically, I could perhaps hit Level 120. After all, where could I find monsters above Level 100? Still amazing. Not so far beyond the possible that I'd stand out.

I halted that thought right there. Glancing back up at the numbers, I'd just gotten +60 to all stats, and +40 free stats points along with my Ascension. I was already insanely over the top. The realization landed like a delayed impact. In fact, with all the various power and authority Ascending had given me, I hadn't even realized the massive jump in regular stats until just now.

Doing a quick check of my logs, I saw it.

Title Awarded: First Demi-god

Description: You are the first upon your world to reach Ascension Tier 1.

Reward: +40 stat points

Damn, that was a hell of a reward. Chuckling, I put it all in Mind, bringing me to 399. Grr... the uneven number was making my newly improved brain itch!

Not that I wanted to hurry the grace period along, but I sure wanted access to the System Shop. With the wealth I had, buying three stat points would be no big deal. Until then, I would have some OCD levels of annoyance at my uneven stat numbers!

I also had two points to distribute to the Ascendant stats. I wanted to bring up my perception, but that OCD practically forced me to drop them into Charisma to bring it up to an even 10 points, which I did. That gave me an effective score of 20 in that stat when my Crown was factored in. That was off the charts. I could almost feel the weight of other people's attention settling on me even before it happened. I mean, I already had the System Title of Demi-god, so with that much Charisma, I really must seem like some dark god to regular people.

I'd have to be careful not to abuse that, nor to come to expect the kind of treatment that such a stat would cause. Power like that warped expectations long before it warped morals.

Putting those thoughts aside, I looked at the items under Special.

Create 10 Safe Zones. That was massive. I knew I would get to create some once I Ascended, but getting ten right off the bat. That would make a massive difference. I'd put one outside Colorado Springs where Max and his family were preparing for the Dark Elf invasion. One for Houston to help the survivors have some place to gather and rebuild. One in...

I stopped myself from planning further. The urge to fix everything at once was strong, and dangerous. I should wait for a meeting with the other Ascenders and get everyone's input before deciding. I was still in the Trial arrival space at the moment with its time-dilation active and needed to vacate soon. Looking at my System interface, I saw that almost ten days had passed since I entered the Trials despite the time I'd spent outside of the normal flow of time.

Grinning, I checked out the final reward, the creation of my own Ascendant Domain. Basically, it was an instanced location like a dungeon, except it could be designed and furnished to my exact specifications. It would function very much like this Trial arrival area, where anything could be provided through the expenditure of mana, exactly the same way the System created dungeons and populated them.

I felt a little guilty, but the Domain was basically my own personal made-to-order mansion that would always be stocked with my favorite foods and have every comfort imaginable. Hell, if I wanted, I could even create a Synth butler to wait on me hand and foot.

Grinning at the thought, I quickly dismissed the idea. I didn't want servants, nor did I particularly want to live in luxury while the human race was homeless and starving. I'd feel like a terrible person. The contrast between what I could have and what everyone else was enduring felt sharp enough to cut. Still, I did need a place to call home, and I would use the last of this time-dilation cheat to create my new Domain and get some rest.

Knowing what to do via instinct imparted to me during my Ascension, I triggered the reward and a new panel opened up before me with various controls. Thankfully, most of the work was done with a mental interface, so you could just think what you wanted and the instance would be modified to provide it.

I created a home, large enough to fit all my friends as guests, as well as a training facility to work on my fighting skills. I had jumped up in stats after all and needed to get used to my new strength and reflexes. It would be awfully embarrassing if I got killed in my next fight because I tripped over my own feet or leaped so hard I caved in my own skull on the ceiling.

Soon it was done. Someday I'd find an interior decorator and get some real help on making the home beautiful. For now, it was comfortable and utilitarian, if not pretty.

Finally, I set the exit portal to the top of the Necropolis' Cathedral mount, inside one of the monuments that had once been vampire mausoleums. That was as good a place as any and shouldn't be disturbed. Not that anyone I didn't assign permission to could enter. Still, I wanted to be inconspicuous and didn't want people gathering around the exit portal trying to beg me for divine favors or something stupid like that.

I didn't know if the Trial AI was listening or not, and my feelings were definitely mixed due to that Second Trial, but I felt like it needed to be said.

"Thank you. You gave me gifts that will help me to help my people, and I will not forget that. I will also try to remove the corruption and bring things back to a balanced state so that other worlds like mine no longer have to suffer in the future."

No response was given to my declaration, but I had a feeling the AI heard me. With that, I transported myself into my own Domain and triggered the same time-dilation function. I still needed sleep after all.

I had been going for three days straight of intense activity, and despite my increased stats, I could use the mental breather a few hours of sleep and a soak in the pool would give me.

One thing was sure. I very much appreciated the time-dilation feature even if I might not be allowed to use it in the future. I was technically still in my Trial period even if I weren't in the Trial Domain any longer. The System couldn't fault me for that. And even if it could, fuck them!

I awoke several hours later, had a soak and some meditation. Then breakfast burritos just like my favorite Tex-Mex restaurant used to make.

When the timer finally ticked down, the time-dilation automatically disengaged, dropping me back into the normal flow of time.

Instantly, Earth's AI spoke.

Congratulations on achieving Ascension. Unfortunately, I was not able to witness your Trials. I hope that you have acquired the skills needed to stabilize this region for your species. I did note that you were allowed to influence events in the Houston area as part of your Trials. That was an excellent performance, and a significant improvement on the odds of being able to fortify the region against the non-native species.

I had no love for this callous piece of shit, so I said bluntly, "Cut to the chase. I want to catch up with the others and make sure we use the remaining six days to get ready for the invasion as best we can."

Once we complete our conversation, you will have the opportunity to learn what your friends have achieved in your absence. However, for now, I need to inform you of something of which you may not be aware. While you may personally slay monsters to your heart's content, you may not take part in the invasion as you call it. This is a System rule, that no Ascended may directly engage in hostilities against the resource teams from other worlds. Doing so would allow the affected race to send their own Ascended to Earth. Much as sending your mind back in time to inhabit your younger body triggered the System to maintain balance, so too would intervening directly against other races free their Ascenders to engage the human race.

You are a Tier 1 Ascender. You do not want a Tier 5 coming to Earth to wage war against you and your companions.

I issued a long, loud string of curses that would have peeled the paint off of a battleship upon hearing the unwelcome news. All that power, and already the walls were closing in. I was all set to use my newfound powers to ensure the invaders in this region met a very quick, and very bad end.

It took me a moment to calm down. When I had, I asked, "Can I at least use my strength to help ensure my friends have the best advantage?"

Only in an indirect way. You may not power level others, nor assist with their battles in any way. This is a System rule. You could, however, use your System authority to help stabilize the area they are operating in, much the same way you did for Houston in your Trial.

In fact, that is exactly what I suggest you do while you wait for the end of the grace period. You would best be utilized to stabilize the most populous areas within the region so that they can better defend themselves when they do encounter other

species. Also, know that certain topics or knowledge may not be shared by an Ascender to mortals. I would tell you to review the list of forbidden subjects, but you will discover them as you try to speak. Your words will be censored if you try to speak of hidden knowledge.

I was beyond furious. Even now that I had Ascended, the corrupt System was trying to put chains on me to limit the impact I could have. The restraint was familiar, and that made it worse. Well, that wasn't going to happen. I would find a way around its rules. Not the one about fighting, as I couldn't risk those consequences, but for everything else... we'd see.

I knew exactly where to look for more ammunition to use against them. The hidden areas inside dungeons. They might seem to be glitches in the matrix, or dev zones where the System had staged different environments and just forgot about them. But to me, knowing what the Trial AI had told me, I now strongly suspected those areas contained the walled off code of the Originators. Exactly the weapon I needed against their corruption.

Now that I had Ascended, they couldn't stop me from finding the tools I needed to tear down their corrupt dominion!

Liam has achieved the goal he's been chasing since being reborn, but the adventure is just beginning. As it always does, the AI throws him a curveball. Now that he has Ascended, he can't fight directly against the invaders. Instead, he must find ways to work around that edict as his friends race toward Level Cap and attempt to clear the largest dungeon Liam has ever seen...without his help.

The adventure continues as Liam and his friends race against humanity's greatest enemies to reach Ascension and prevent the invading species from beating them to it, all while uncovering secrets the System is determined to keep buried. Only then can Liam begin to fight the corrupted System itself and start undoing the damage wrought by the apocalypse.

Sign up for a free short story and receive the newsletter to stay current on what's happening with Greymantle and the other worlds of J David Baxter's imagination.

AUTHOR'S NOTE

Please leave a review here! Help other fantasy readers and tell them why you enjoyed this book.

I would love it if you would tell your friends so they can join us on Liam's epic adventure to save humanity from a genocidal AI and a horde of murderous orcs, goblins, ogres, and more. If you do leave feedback for AI Apocalypse: Restart where you purchased the book, Goodreads, or your blog—I'd love to read it. Don't hesitate to email me the link at info@jdavidbaxter.com.

ALSO BY J DAVID BAXTER

Visit the Author's page to see all the great books by J David Baxter.

LITRPG GROUPS

The LitRPG genre is a friendly and welcoming community. To learn more about books in the genre and connect with other fans and authors, check out these groups:

https://www.facebook.com/groups/litrpgs

https://www.facebook.com/groups/LitRPGGroup

https://www.facebook.com/groups/LitRPG.books

https://www.facebook.com/groups/LitRPGReleases

ABOUT THE AUTHOR

David's journey through his career has been anything but conventional. Transitioning from the exhilarating world of Renaissance Festival Jousting, where he braved falls from horses, to orchestrating teams and projects at Fortune 500 companies, he's held diverse roles. Armed with a degree in English and teaching certifications in English, History, and Professional Pedagogy, he's ventured into the realms of education and literature. Notably, he lent his expertise as an editor to the recent Stargate Roleplaying Game core book by Wyvern Games. Additionally, as the co-founder of Silver Paw Publishing, he's committed to empowering aspiring authors on their self-publishing journey. David embodies versatility and a passion for storytelling, leaving an indelible mark on every path he treads.

www.ingramcontent.com/pod-product-compliance
Lightning Source LLC
LaVergne TN
LVHW010051110826
845155LV00028B/291

* 9 7 8 1 9 5 3 7 0 8 4 4 1 *